Lion Rising

DIANA DERICCI

Published By Purple Sword Publications, LLC
ISBN 9798409202682
Edited by Traci Markou
Cover Art Layout by Traci Markou
Cover Art Image Copyright Dan Skinner

Prophecy of the Valda-Cree

Cull the darkness, share the light.
Arise, brave soul, foretold to fight.
Upon that soul, lay the mane,
Of lion's blood coursing in man's vein.
Hear the roar of pack and pride.
Honor the strong, the fearsome, the wise.
Come the day the heart of darkness be slain.
By truth's side, justice shall forever reign.

Cast of Characters

Jayce Morrow: Valda-Cree exiled generation, Lion, King

Valda-Cree: The original skin shifter lion pride blessed by the goddess Ahdrer to rule all of Kielbos

Rune (Runybathaczar): Elf Mage, Fifth circle, Fire, First Counsel to Jayce

Iba: Raven, Rune's familiar

Raquel: Human neighbor, *sabra* berserker

Helen: Human neighbor, *sabra* berserker

Master Theil: Elf, Elder Mage, Eighth circle, Water and energy, Rune's mentor

Carden: Elf Mage, Master Theil's twin brother, standing advisor to the Alendaren throne

Brin: Elf Mage, Senior acolyte, Fifth circle, Wind, Keep Master

Leodinn (Leodothanbar): Elf Mage, Fifth circle, Water, Rune's keep backup

Rox: Peregrine Falcon, Leodinn's familiar

Grayson (Iragrayz'sthan): Elf Mage, Fourth circle, Earth, Keep Liaison

Duran (Akithaduraninx): Elf Mage, Fourth circle, Fire, Keep Liaison

Ulcieh (Ulciehdi'orian): Elf Mage, Fifth circle, Water, Engagement Advisor

Terne Vorverrian: Mercenary, group leader

Blood Spawn Army: Bad guys. A *lot* of bad guys

Mogalls: Fire breathing lizards in gnarly scales with a nasty temper

Cedri Arin: Skin Shifter, Tiger. Kygo's brother, Tanglewood clan

Royce: Skin Shifter, Snow Leopard, Tanglewood clan

Bankor: Villager

Gegli: Villager

Lori: Cook

Sophie: Lori's daughter

Kirn: Kitchen helper

Javi: Keep steward

Harmony Morrow: Jayce's adoptive mother, King Bail's nurse

Nolen Morrow: Jayce's adoptive father, Harmony's mate

Natugenus: Mage who enchanted Raquel's axe

Gods and Goddesses

Ahdrer: Goddess of nature and animals, blessed the lion spirit to the Valda-Cree line as her chosen rulers of Kielbos and all lands
Volin: God of lightning
Rinattoah: The highest god still recognized and revered, Ahdrer's sire

The World of Kielbos

Kielbos: Planet, two times the size of Earth
Grand Continent: The standing center of Kielbos, encompassing Rinattoah, Caduthien, and others
Trajanleh: The burning village depicted in Rune's visions when he is called to Earth to find Jayce
Sevenwood: Area of the continent where Windmere and the Windwise temple are
Caduthien: Lands encompassing the crowned center, capital city of Rinattoah and others
Rinattoah: Capital city name before Alendaren coup, in the age before the usurping of the throne
Windmere: Seaside cliffs, home of the Windwise temple
Windwise Temple: Training temple for mage schooling
Lehflande Temple: Earth acolyte temple
Alendaren: Current king's castle by name and ruling family being controlled by Carden
Sucábul: Another region far south of Caduthien

Prologue

Rune studied the pre-dawn horizon with an accepting stance. His visions had brought him to this place, to this location deep in Sucábul, to this time, for a reason. Billowing mounds of gray smoke clouds erratically rose to scatter in the lightening morning skies overhead, the blackened waves laden with the bitter stench of dry grasses, well-weathered wood, and more he didn't want to dissect. It was far enough in the distance that the screams of destruction couldn't reach him, but that same distance didn't deter his watchful stare as he followed the snaking movement of the smoke. Across miles of fields and low rolling hills lay the village's remains, in its death throes, unable to reach them in time to offer aid. He wasn't there to stop the destruction, sadly. Their demise was the harbinger sign he'd been waiting for. That this was where he needed to be, that this was the moment he'd been preparing for. The prophecy had been set in motion centuries ago when the royal line had been destroyed from within, murdering the crowned king, placing the current Alendaren ruling family on the throne as undisputed ruler, claiming all of Kielbos as their spoils. A spiraling descent of evil and destruction that currently pulled at his soul and called his name to join in the fight and do what was needed to correct a centuries old wrong. Because as his visions directed him, his next steps were to find the one his world needed to balance the prophecy. Good versus evil.

The evil had been released from its cage and now had a full striding lead against them, a scourge spilling ever so slowly northward. They were at a disadvantage, and he honestly didn't know to what extent. He squared his shoulders, aware going forward from this point, nothing was going to be easy. Years in the making to bring him here to this very location. Being brave and sure was never easy when destiny came knocking.

The Alendaren family had fully usurped the Valda-Cree lineage and in doing so, tipped the scales in a direction destined to destroy their world if he didn't find the will and strength to take the next steps. Rising sunlight broke through the smoke like spikes of gold slicing through the heaviness, but it didn't fill him with hope or anticipation of a new dawn. Dread lay heavy against his heart. He truly had no idea if his ability to accept the coming hours and days was going to be enough.

The known beat of broad wings sliced the air seconds before granite hard claws delicately grasped his padded shoulder. The raven's weight stilled, adjusting easily to her perch. "Hello, Iba." He offered a bit of dried meat from his pouch to be plucked from between his fingers. The raven gulped it down then nuzzled into his temple. "I know, heart. Our time has come. Did you find him?" A quiet raw caw was his answer. "Good. Stay close. The world we are about to enter is not our own. We must be quick to bring him back."

The bird's wings rustled, black feathers tickling over his chin. A hint of chastising sarcasm in avian speak. He smiled at the raven's tone. "Yes, I'm aware." He'd sent the raven into the air two nights before as he'd neared this destined spot, and Iba had succeeded in her mission. She'd located the one they sought. Images sent to him during her scouting would guide him now to create the spell that would allow him to walk from his world to the next. Animals could travel at will between planes through the eternal gateways. Man, and others of their ilk, needed a slightly more deliberate manner of travel between worlds and only those with the knowledge and training would dare. The last thing any mage would want was to start a time paradox in their own world. For this reason, he had been waiting in the one spot he'd envisioned in his dreams when he'd first seen the fires blaze miles away after sending Iba on her mission. Consistency was always key, even if the interpretation of the vision was questionable.

The burst of images that scrolled through his mind from Iba's were sparse. She was a bird after all and their brains were skewed to survival, not reconnaissance. Iba, however, was multitalented. Their connection spanned more years than he could count, and understanding between them was as fluid as a running stream.

The view of the man they were seeking was clear enough. Dark hair, leaning toward rich sable or even mink brown. A fairly tall and solid build from the bird's eye view, likely as tall as himself. Strong shoulders, in apparent good health. He had an aura that seemed to confirm he was who Rune sought. Someone bred with confidence, raised with strength of will. Only time would tell if he was true Valda-Cree. Only a strong man's will could harness the soul of the lion, the king of beasts, and survive. Sharing, because taming was never going to happen. Not even for the king of the Valda-Cree.

Their future, their people, needed that bright light of hope that this male represented right now. After watching the destruction of his lands for decades, the worst was yet to come, but it was time to bring home the one he sought. He knew walking forward to find him, he was accepting his life would be permanently attached to this stranger's. He didn't see it as a sacrifice. The moment the visions began, he knew he was being chosen, directed. He had been given his chance to walk away, and it had long since passed. If this one man was the hope, the savior Kielbos needed, then he would see him through his trials, support him through his days. When he stepped forward, his future ceased being his own. He accepted and embraced all it meant.

Watching the first rings of the sun's bright rays crest the horizon, illuminating the sky to chase through the morning gray darkness, he flipped his cowl over his head, pushing his ponytail down his back, to call his staff into his palm. "Ready?"

Iba settled securely to his shoulder. He murmured words under his breath, using his free hand to create symbols in the air with different forms of his fist and fingers, until a golden door stood before him. There was nothing to see through the portal, only the glow of the outline that blinded the walker to the other side. He'd traveled through his visions to view the other side frequently enough to know where he was going to appear with the help of Iba's scouting. However, he'd never been where he'd dreamed, a place that so loudly called from the unknown.

"Goddess guide us," he murmured as he took a step through.

Chapter 1

Jayce wiggled onto the bench with his plate loaded with pepperoni pizza, hip bumping Helen over at the table. The little pizza joint catty-corner to their apartment complex was packed for an early Saturday evening. Young college kids from campus mostly, stacked in the booths like stuffed toys on a shelf, lap to lap, shoulder to shoulder. Music played from the corner speakers, the top hits channel. He barely heard it. He wasn't there for the music. The pizza was hot, fresh, and cheap. Which was really all that mattered to a kid on a tight scholarship budget.

"So you going to Joni's tonight?" Raquel asked from the other side of the table. A plate with crusts on it sat before her. She never did eat the crusts.

Jayce chomped through the still tongue-burning cheese, huffing to cool the roof of his mouth. Helen and Raquel were roommates two doors down from him, meeting up with him a couple times a month to get him out of his apartment and his nose out of his books. They'd moved in about two weeks after he did and formed fast friendships once he discovered they were attending the same school. When Raquel found out he liked Dungeons and Dragons, she'd dragged him by his belt loops to one of their weekend games. The last one had been a complete blast, but he couldn't sacrifice every weekend when he had major grades to complete and turn in.

One more semester and his bachelor's degree was his. But people-ing, breathing fresh air every now and then was supposed to be good for his health. Or so the professionals said.

He wiped his greasy fingers on paper napkins before saying, "She running a dungeon?"

"Yeah, said she had a whole new campaign mapped out." Her eyes glistened with the hope of adventure. "I'm totally doing it. New characters, new battles. I'm in. I'm so tired of studying, I'll even be the medic orc if I need to."

Jayce snorted. Raquel was a petite blonde with wicked cat-eye makeup and a bright blue streak in her hair that brought out her blue eyes. There was no way she'd play an orc, of any kind. She was a vicious ranger type who loved slaughtering her foes. He'd seen her strategize to do exactly that. Small and petite packaging with absolutely zero chill and nil mercy.

He wiped his mouth with the least damaged part of his napkin. "I don't know if I can, to be honest. I have a project due and it's been kicking my ass."

Helen looked up from her phone where she'd likely been texting her boyfriend. "You mean Professor Stahl's PowerPoint, right?"

He sagged on the bench. "Yeah."

Helen nodded. "I had that project last semester with him. He's got a hardon with failing people for that damn presentation."

"Did you get a passing grade?"

"Barely." She made a moue with her glossed lips. The beads in her thickly braided hair tinkled like glass pipes in a gentle breeze when she moved.

That didn't make Jayce feel any better about what he'd already accomplished on the assignment. He pushed the wave of hair off his forehead that had fallen forward. Someone laughed obnoxiously loud two tables over, slapping the tabletop like they were hitting the Family Feud buzzer. He frowned when he glanced that way.

Then blinked.

Then blinked again.

But the guy was gone.

Okay that was weird. "Hey, Helen, did you see someone just now, standing over there by the wall?"

She glanced up, searching around them. "Someone you know?"

Jayce breathed slowly, knowing he'd seen *someone*, wondering why he saw the guy but now couldn't. Was he a ghost? He was in a shadow, but the room was lit bright. And was he wearing a...cape?

"No. No, I don't think so." He waved a hand, palming his pizza. He took a bite, chewing carefully around the hot spots, glancing

6

furtively toward the area where he'd seen the shadow, *and* the guy who'd been in the middle of said shadow. He swallowed. "It was nothing." *Probably a play of the lights. Or hunger. Or both.* Hell, it could be sleep deprivation for all he knew. He'd been busting his ass on his assignments to finish this semester. *So close.* He knew he still had work to do, but finishing his degree was going to be such a relief.

She bumped a shoulder with him, going back to reading her phone. "So, I think Rocco just broke up with me." She bit her lip and handed her phone to Raquel. She glanced over the screen, scrolling up, then reading again. Raquel's eyes grew soft and sympathetic.

"Aw, damn. I'm sorry, Boo."

Helen sighed. Taking the phone back, she mumbled a quiet, "It's alright," then louder, "I wasn't going to take him home to meet the fam, y'know. He was so not that kind of guy. Loser, and now he's dumping me. I hope his curlies and bits dry up and fall off. I can do better than him with my eyes closed."

Jayce winced. "Ouch."

Helen giggled. "Not *your* curlies. Besides, we know you like the Tab B kind of lovin'."

Jayce snorted, carefully covering his mouth with his last napkin. "Uh, thanks, I think."

Raquel laughed. "Any time."

An unexpected rush of wind over his head made him duck with a yelp.

"Whoa! What was that?" Helen barked, hopping to the other end of the bench as if avoiding all the parts of a flailing Jayce.

"Did you see it?" he demanded, whipping around to see what was thrown at him.

Big, slightly confused, brown eyes gaped at him. "See *what?*"

"Whatever was just thrown at my head? I felt it in my hair."

Helen stared at him in dumbfounded silence. Raquel searched around the table. "There was nothing thrown, bud." She looked him up and down, then tipped her head. "You feeling okay?"

Looking down to his pizza, the last two bites suddenly didn't seem so appealing. Something was off, either with him or... Yeah. Something was definitely off. "Yeah. I think I've got too much on my mind right now." He dropped his wadded napkin to the plate. "I'm gonna toss this and bug. You two okay to get home?"

Raquel beamed. "Yeah, we'll be fine. I have my pepper spray."

"Never leave home without it," all three said at the same time, then laughed like loons. "Okay, okay." He ran his hand through his hair, unable to fully avoid staring at the spot on the wall where he swore he saw a shadow and a guy in a cape. A dark red cape.

It was his imagination, or something of the sort. He didn't really believe in ghosts, though he knew to some degree they were likely. He hadn't met one, so he still checked that under the unconfirmed and questionable column.

"Okay, if you need anything, call me and I'll come walk you guys back."

"Thanks." Raquel smiled for him. "Probably heading to Joni's for the night."

"No worries." He stood from the table. "Have a good time." Palming his plate, he made his way to the front, dumping his trash and sliding the plastic plate on to the partially full busser tray against the wall. He blinked when he opened the door, gazing into really bright, and right in his eyes, sunlight.

Walking through the door to the sidewalk, a sudden sensation chilled his neck and he hurried outside.

Must've got hit by the AC. He glanced over his shoulder as the door was closing but couldn't see anything to say otherwise. No one was behind him. But there was a sense of *something,* right out of reach. Something unseen. A fresh shiver slid over his skin and he spun to put some space between him and whatever was giving him the heebie-jeebies.

Stuffing his fingers into his jeans pockets, he ambled home, his mind wandering. Late day sunlight was warm on his skin. He would've loved to go to Joni's with the girls, but unfortunately, the PowerPoint waiting for him had to be a priority. His grades were counting on him. Scholarship requirements. As much as he hated it, there would be another weekend where he could stay up all night eating snacks, talking shit, and harassing marauders for their gold and weapons.

He was walking up the stairs to his floor when he felt it again. A gossamer brush against his flesh. A wave of goosebumps marched up his arm, and he rubbed bare skin to kill the chill of his nerves.

Twisting a smidge on his neck, he hunted behind him, but found no one. *This is so damned freaky.* He fisted his keys out of his pocket, ready in case. Nothing happened on the way to his own door. The hallway was empty. But somehow, he knew something was there. Something was following him.

His hand trembled a little when he finally managed to bullseye his door lock. Unlocking the door, he swept it inward. Everything looked the same, but he couldn't shake the uneasiness that he wasn't alone. Every nerve under his skin was screaming at him that something or someone was there. He could *feel* them.

He stomped into the apartment and slammed the door. "Show yourself!" he barked.

A shimmer swam before his eyes across the room and then as solid as he, stood the guy he'd seen in the red cape.

"Oh, fuck," he gasped. His legs gave out on him and he dropped to the floor. His heart leaped into hyperdrive. Embarrassing as hell, but at least he didn't faint. He didn't think he fainted. But he was definitely not standing. "That's never worked," he croaked.

The stranger tilted on his neck. "I'm surprised. You're quite gifted for one so young."

Jayce swallowed. "W—what?" *What...gifted?* The guy was giving him a concerned stare, where he was looking down at Jayce.

"You sensed me in the dining room. You knew I was there. That's rare for one of your age, untrained."

"Who are you?"

"My name is Rune."

He flipped back his cowl and Jayce all but gasped. He was beautiful, beyond beautiful. Pale, almost white blond hair lay thick and pulled taut in a ponytail at his nape. Wide almond eyes that formed a downward tip at their corners. Eyes that were... They had to be contacts. They weren't normal. Jayce blinked and drew a breath. Not important. "Okay, *Rune.* Who are you? Why are you here? And how the hell did you sneak up on me like that?"

Rune steadied his staff, and when he released it, it stayed standing upright in place. Jayce's eyes goggled as Rune took a step away from him. When he twisted his head, he got his third shock.

"Are your ears..." He slapped a hand over his mouth. *Shut up. Shut up. Shut up.* It was all too much to believe, but... No it had to be fake. Someone was playing a prank on him. Had to be.

Rune arched a fine eyebrow, but didn't rebuke him when nothing else followed. "As for who I am, I'm Rune, Mage of the Fifth Circle, Master of nature and fire." He bowed low. "It's a pleasure to make your acquaintance."

Jayce's mouth popped open on repeat, unable to form words. What the hell? This guy was good at whatever he thought he was LARPing. Jayce never took his eyes off the person in his apartment. He had a few ways to protect himself, though it was usually him scaring off guys from the girls down the hall and he never thought he'd be doing it against a cosplayer nutjob. "Did Joni send you? She really must need people to join her game if she's hiring RPG characters to be part of her campaign."

Rune offered an elegant hand, he guessed to help him up off the floor. Where he legit still sat. "I apologize. I do not know a Joni."

Jayce clasped his hand and was eased back to his feet. The flare of power that rocketed up his arm at the contact had him gasping again and leaping backward. "Holy fuck," he murmured. He shook his hand out. He thought he could see the electrical zaps in the air surrounding them after touching his hand.

For the first time, Rune looked uneasy. "How old are you?"

"Twenty-two. Why? How old are you?" he shot back.

"One hundred and forty-two."

This time when Jayce fell to the floor, it *was* a faint.

Chapter 2

Rune grimaced. "I guess I shouldn't have admitted that, huh, Iba?" He *tsked* at the man out cold on the floor. Iba was perched on the back of the long seat by the single window in the room. He waved a hand and her cloaking dissolved. She extended her wings with a ruffle. "I agree. I don't like using it either to hide us, but at least only he could sense us." His lips pinched. "But I don't know yet if that ability is a good thing, or not."

Gathering the young man's slack frame under his legs, he eased his could-be new friend's body onto the long seat. Once he was stretched out and appeared to be comfortable, he looked around the abode. A caw had him open the pouch he carried without looking. "Yes, heart." He tossed her the strip of meat, which she caught out of the air easily. "Go ahead and rest."

Iba shook herself, then launched to circle the room, looking for a higher perch. She settled on a tall shelf filled with books. Once she was taken care of, his focus returned to his charge.

How did someone like this young man slip through the celestial monitoring? All mages who had any ability were sent for training, regardless if elf or human. He chewed on his lip in thought. Yet, they weren't on Kielbos. Was that how he'd remained undetected? Was the fact that he wasn't from Kielbos, or Caduthien, why Rune had been sent to locate this man? He wasn't from their world so how could he have been sensed? How could an outsider have any effect on the prophecy? That question troubled him greatly. Rune had watched him for several hours, daring to close the distance between them through the day. By the time his target joined his friends at the eatery, Rune lingered only feet away, able to hear as well as see.

While this one's physical strength was common for one his age, his magical signature was unlike anyone else's he'd come near that day, bright and pulsating with life, even as it was muted because of this plane of existence. How strong would he become when he finally took this man home?

The king of the Valda-Cree had to be exceptional. He wondered over the discoveries. Was this man going to be enough to fulfill the prophecy? With his hands gathered behind his back, Rune paced quietly across the room, flicking glances toward the sleeping man.

Watching him rest, he had to admit he had strong features that were softened to be approachable by a button tipped nose. The wave of dark hair he'd caught him playing with through the hours of the day was swept back now with him resting, revealing smooth skin and thick lashes as dark as his hair. A firm jaw barely shadowed with growth. A single hoop earring in one of his ears appeared to be the only jewelry he wore. An interesting male he'd been seeking.

Nearing his resting form, he stretched hands outward, palm down and sought this man's magic. The fierce flare he found was true and deep. He released it instantly.

"Valda-Cree," he gasped in an awed whisper. Stepping back, he blinked. Then it was true. He didn't know how. It had been centuries since the Valda-Cree line had been killed off completely. Yet, somehow, this was the man he sought. Oddly at that, as young as he was given the demise of his forefathers. But that youth meant he could learn. Could be enlightened. Molded and trained. And become undoubtedly stronger, because the king of the Valda-Cree was a man of will and conscience, strength and magic that could rule a world.

Seeking Iba, he found her with her head bowed in sleep. He supposed he should do the same. They had a long journey ahead and he didn't know how long his new charge would be asleep.

Clearing the distance to the door, he immediately invoked a protection spell, something he should have done as soon as he was indoors, but had gone with his gut to make contact first. Then he sank to the floor, crossing his legs and resting his palms on his thighs. Evening his breathing, he allowed his heart to calm and his mind to relax. To go blank. The meditative state wasn't a true sleep but it would be enough to get them home safely.

By the time he heard the first stirrings across the room, darkness had filled the room and the windows showcased a night sky. Iba was awake and watchful. Her eyes were his, but his own curiosity had his drifting open to peer across the gap.

The young man sat on the long cushioned bench, bent over his knees, scrubbing his eyes. Rune didn't move or speak, observing. It seemed the man he'd been watching had forgotten about his presence, as it took a moment before he whipped his head up, hunting through the room. Then he jumped to his feet, his gaze zeroing in on Rune.

"You're real?" His voice quivered.

Rune allowed a small snigger but hid it swiftly. "That I am." He unfurled his legs to stand. "Though you have no reason to fear me."

"Riiiight. Why are you here?" It struck Rune as odd that he didn't really fear him, but was demanding *why*. What was this man thinking in the face of nearly unlimited power? Was he thinking strategically? Or planning an escape? The brunet folded his arms over his chest and took a scant step away. The room wasn't large enough to actually allow him to run. It was minimally filled with furniture and a table, but he didn't know it to name it. It wasn't important in any case. "I don't believe in ghosts or any of that shit. I don't know what you are, or who you are, but I know you're only playing with my mind right now. So what do you want?"

"First, may I suggest a real introduction. Your name?" He opened his palm and called his staff to him from where he had left it suspended a few inches inside the doorway.

The guy tilted his head, blinking slowly, following the staff's movements as though he was merely becoming aware of it. "You... I didn't imagine any of that? You really are magic? Are you really an elf?"

"Yes." Jayce shook his head in disbelief. Rune frowned. He still didn't have a name. "I need your name."

He glared. "Why? Where did you come from?"

Rune didn't move. He knew he had the best advantage directly in front of the door. There was no escape and no way anyone could sneak up on them. "Do you know who your parents were?" he countered.

He froze on the spot. "No. I was adopted."

Another piece of the puzzle, but it would fit soon enough. "Have you ever sensed something more in a person, like you did with me? Felt someone unseen?"

Jayce shook his head. "I don't know. I don't think so." Curled arms tightened around his middle. "But that doesn't explain who or what *you* are." A furrowed arrow formed on his brow.

"I'm not deceiving you. I am Rune, and as of this morning, I am your guide and your guard."

"This morning?" He tried to take a step further but found himself blocked by the leather seat.

"I've been with you all day."

Jayce gaped, trembling while clearly trying to hide his shock with the way he stiffly stood. "No. You need to leave. I don't know what drugs you're on, but I have homework to finish. I can't go to Joni's, so you can tell her I'm not—"

Rune waved a hand and his voice fell quiet. A hand wrapped around his throat as shock paled his features, yet not a sound was formed. "I apologize for the strong arming. I need your name to keep you safe. I have found you by the goddess's will. I will not be the only one searching for you now that the prophecy is in play."

Apparently either taking away his voice or the mention of the prophecy had an effect on his disbelief meter. Rune wished he knew which it had been. He didn't know how this young man could know about the prophecy though and his reaction was worrisome. There was no doubt he was scaring the young man and he needed him to trust him at least enough to follow him to Trajanleh.

There was a rapid knock at the door. "Jayce! Hey, open up!"

"Who is that?" he whispered harshly, reversing the silencing spell.

He gulped air. "It's Raquel. She is my friend, a neighbor."

He flipped his cowl up and summoned Iba to his shoulder to fade into his cloaking spell. "Open the door. Let her and her sister in."

He moved away from the door and waited for *Jayce* to do as he ordered. The name held no power for him now. It had to be given willingly and freely, but it was just as well. He didn't want the young man's obedience unwilfully given. He wasn't there to control him.

"They're not sisters," he bit out, but neared the door to unlock it. For their sake, Rune left the protection spell in place, regardless.

"Hey, guys. You okay? Someone give you shit coming home?"

14

He stepped back and frowned when neither attempted to cross the threshold, both standing on the other side of the entry. The blonde's hands were clenching at her side. Her blue eyes flicked from corner to corner of the room.

"Come on in." He stepped back. "Everything okay?"

The one he called Raquel cleared her throat. "Uh, yeah. We're okay. Thought we heard something."

"Weren't you going to Joni's?"

Helen piped up. "We changed our minds. You sure you're okay?"

Jayce laughed and Rune could easily hear the tension in the sound. "Thought I was the one who protected you two."

Raquel smiled tightly. "Yeah, well. Neighbors look out for each other, right?"

"Always."

Helen pulled on Raquel's arm, forcing them to take a step away. "Well, we're headed home then. Have a good one."

"Sure. See you guys tomorrow." He waited until they went into their own apartment then shut the door. "See? Nothing but my friends."

Rune hissed with growing impatience. "Your friends are *sabra*. We need to go."

"What?"

He growled. "They are warriors." Rune didn't have time for anyone else's interference or to try to make explanations. It was enough that they were there, and apparently unknown to Jayce. Which meant Jayce didn't know anything about who he was, as he suspected when he'd first spoken.

"Look, *Rune* with the phony elf ears," he argued. He waved absently in the door's direction. "Those are my friends."

Rune started the spell for the portal. "They are not who you think they are. You are not safe here. We need to go."

"Why should I?" Jayce demanded, reaching for the door handle. "I don't know a fucking thing about you."

Rune heard the slam of the door down the hall. They were running out of time. "They're coming. We need to go! I can explain it once we're safe."

"But they won't hurt me...*eeep!*" He leaped clear of the door when a heavy blade sliced into the wood down the middle with a loud cracking boom.

Rune eyed the axe blade carefully. It was scrolled with protections. There was no way to negate the blade's magic without getting his hands on it, and that wasn't possible. Escaping was their only option. He grabbed for Jayce. Staring directly into his wide eyes, he stressed, "I know you don't know me, and can't trust me, but trust when I say they are not here as your friends. They are a warrior race, berserkers. They were hired to watch you."

Jayce's troubled gaze jerked to the doorway, where the screech of splintering wood warned them the blade was being wrenched free. Not a sound came from the other side. Until the next whack at the door made it splinter with a gaping hole in the wood.

And as much as he clearly doubted Rune, locking gazes with the blonde who now had red glowing eyes, created a far better argument than any he could conceivably give. She snarled and hefted the axe again and this time, Jayce wasn't standing there to watch it fall.

Chapter 3

Jayce jumped through the glowing whatever Rune had created in his living room. Then started to run, following closely behind the red cape until they were some distance from wherever they'd popped out. Panting for breath, he leaned with a palm against a tree when they finally stopped. His chest hurt and his heart was pounding too rapidly to hear over it.

"Iba, fly!"

A rush of feathers blew past him, and he ducked his head. He was beginning to think whatever that was enjoyed the fly-bys that were too close to his head.

He flipped, resting with his back against the tree. Rune stood still, his eyes closed.

"Shouldn't we keep moving, or something?" he grunted.

He raised a hand, gesturing for patience. "Iba is ensuring the door was not used to follow us. I was able to drop the spell before your *friends* reached it."

Jayce ran a hand over his face, ignoring his snarled sarcasm. And when he blinked, he shook his head. "Where are we?" he asked a moment later, kind of in awe, and kind of a lot concerned. Nothing looked familiar. Nothing but wilderness and trees as far as the eye could see. And if he had to guess, without a city in the way, it was quite far.

Rune opened his eyes and faced him. "We are in Trajanleh."

Jayce's knees started to feel weak. Bark bit at his shoulders but he ignored it. Standing on his own at the moment wasn't happening. *Good, solid tree.* He wanted to pat it for being there for him. "Trajanleh? I don't know where that is."

"There is no reason you should. It is not on your plane, your world."

"My world?" he whispered. Tipping high on his neck, he followed the trunks upward as high as he could. Tall trees that looked like some kind of coniferous species spread wide limbs overhead. "These look like pine trees, but they're too tall."

"Did you think your planet had the sum total of life's possibilities?" Jayce eyed him warily as he neared while dropping the cowl from his head. Reaching underneath his cape he withdrew a canteen. "Here, have a few sips. We have a long way to travel yet."

Jayce backed away. "I am not touching anything until you do some explaining. Who *are* you? Why did you come find me? Why am I here?"

Rune studied him then put the canteen away. "Very well. But may we at least walk while I speak?"

"I don't guess telling me where we are going will do me much good." He bit his cheek but couldn't help the petulant tone in his words. Wasn't sure he cared enough to hide it completely. Not after what he'd experienced.

Rune shook his head. "Unfortunately, no. But I will tell you what I know."

Jayce huffed but fell into step with Rune. "Fine." The shade was cool and he regretted only having a T-shirt, but at least he was wearing his sneakers and jeans for this impromptu trek through the woods.

Rune was silent for several minutes as he studied the bark of a couple trees, splaying his hand to them as he fell silent. Jayce simply thought he was weird.

"This way," he said after a moment. He motioned with a hand deeper into the shadows.

Jayce kept his focus on where he was walking, since he had no idea where he was, or where he was going, or where he'd started from. Everything but the next step was irrelevant.

"As I said, my name is Rune. For the last two years, I've been receiving visions that had slowly drawn me to a location near a village. It was burning when I arrived. My place at that time wasn't to stop the destruction, but to witness the start of the clock of the prophecy."

"You mentioned a prophecy before. What prophecy?"

Rune's rich voice was melodious when he recited it.

"Cull the darkness, share the light.
"Arise brave soul foretold to fight.
"Upon that soul, lay the mane,
"Of lion's blood coursing in man's vein.
"Hear the roar of pack and pride.
"Honor the strong, the fearsome, the wise.
"Come the day the heart of darkness be slain.
"By truth's side, justice shall forever reign. "

Jayce pushed a low hanging branch out of his way. "Sounds…vague. What does that mean?"

Rune glanced at him. "Interpretation has varied over the centuries. The prophecy was written over a millennia ago."

Jayce huffed. "Okay. What do *you* think it means? Since you're the one who accosted me in my apartment and proceeded to drag me into Train-la-lee."

Rune snorted, shaking his head. "It is Trajanleh, but we'll only be here to cross it." When he didn't continue, Jayce nudged the back of his shoulder with a 'Well?' type jab. He sighed. "As for what I believe it means, we are being challenged by evil forces and are being tasked to push them back. The next king will be of man's heritage." He seemed to hesitate over the explanation, as though seeking the best words, maybe. Jayce couldn't say. He didn't know Rune from a stick on the ground. And those ears… *Holy hell, a god damn elf.* He listened when Rune continued though. "He will stand with a powerful army when his time comes, and he will live to provide a just legacy."

Jayce quietly chewed on all of that. "So one vague quest, add a clueless person and off we go." He chuckled derisively. "Yeah, I can see *exactly* where I fit into all of that."

"More will be explained, but I was tasked to be your guide and guard." He walked evenly with his staff in one hand, his other hand relaxed at his side. One foot in front of the other, as though walking without a compass, or without any maps or view of wherever the hell they were was an easy way of traveling through a shady forest.

Fuck, are there wild animals?

He did his best to hide his shiver. Surreptitiously, he inched a bit closer to Rune's side. If he noticed, he didn't say anything about Jayce's apparent nervousness. "I guess mentioning it now that I'm a

19

city boy, that my biggest adventure was one weekend of camping next to a converted lake, wouldn't make a difference, would it?"

"You are young enough to learn," he answered cryptically.

"Says the man who's over a hundred years old, or so you say."

Rune merely smirked.

"Okay, so there's a prophecy and somehow I'm your guy. Who are we looking for to be king?"

Rune glanced upward, maybe looking for the sun. Like Jayce could possibly know. "I don't know for sure," he replied cryptically.

"What's my part in it? Why do you need me to find him? Especially to pull me from where I was to here?"

"You are Valda-Cree. Why do you think your friends were hired to watch over you?"

Jayce made a raspberry sound. "Please. Raquel is five feet of candy fluff. She'd be blown away by a hard breeze."

"Interesting. I thought she was the one wielding the axe."

Jayce narrowed his eyes at his caustic answer, but didn't say anything to refute him. Because, yeah, she had been. "Fine. So there *might* be some truth in what you're saying."

"In a lot of it," he jibed. "But as for what I need you for, that is not my stake in this. I am your guide and your guard. The visions have told me this. Beyond that, what will come, will come."

Jayce shivered again. "That makes me feel, oh so much better."

"Really? Great!" Rune smiled broadly, his step taking on a little more pep.

Jayce harrumphed, his eyeroll unseen by his…whatever this guy was. "Okay, what is Valda-Cree? And why am I one of them?"

Rune looked away, disconcerted for the first time. "My master will be able to explain that better than I."

Jayce glared at him askance. Evasion 101. So much to unpack in that one sentence. "Master? Like servitude? Are you a slave sent to abduct the poor human?"

Rune actually barked a laugh all while following some trail that only he seemed to be able to see, because if Jayce closed his eyes and spun three times, he would be so lost. All the trees looked the same. Like so very much the same.

"No. My master is Master Theil and he is my instructor and mentor. Has been since I was a lad. He is an elder Mage of the Eighth circle."

"And I'm guessing older than dirt."

Rune stopped and poked his chest, echoed by a low growl. "Don't be insulting. He is a wise man who has seen many things in his time."

Jayce hopped backward from the fierce sharpness of that single digit. "Okay, sorry. Feeling very out of my element here."

Rune dropped his hand and nodded once. "Fine. Let's keep walking."

Jayce bit his lip and stared ahead. But that didn't last long. It was still boring. Tree trunks galore. And scared. Even though he wasn't about to admit that to his *guide*. "So, what can you tell me about the Valda-Cree?"

"Their bloodline was believed extinct."

Jayce's feet froze to the loam and debris beneath. "Okay, hold up, right there. Extinct? Yet you're saying I'm one of them." Seriously? He was human. *Hu-man.* In the dictionary.

Rune avoided looking at him when Jayce tried to meet his eyes. Oh, yeah, nothing like a little guilt to add to the drama. He waited until Rune broke. He uttered, "I verified your magic signature while you slept."

"You did something to me while I was passed out on my couch?" A fist formed at his side. "That's cold, man." Heat gathered in his chest. Too much to take in. What else was he going to say? Reveal? Or accidentally let slip that Jayce wasn't supposed to know?

"I never touched you," he snapped out, exasperated. "Any being of magic has a signature. If you knew how to do it, you could sense mine, but you've had no training."

"Show me what you did." He crossed his arms. He wasn't moving another step until Rune showed him exactly what he did to *sense* this signature.

Rune sighed with undisguised impatience. "Fine. Stand still." He lifted his hands, and a moment later, he felt a light tingle reverberating through his chest. "There."

He couldn't stop the drop of his jaw as he gaped at Rune. That was it? He still had massive doubts and didn't trust him as far as he could throw him, but seriously? *That* was it? And *that* proved he was this missing bloodline? Jayce leaned to a hip, staring him in his eyes. Well, trying to. They still freaked him out a little. Because now he knew they *weren't* contacts. "And you still think I'm this missing link of Valda-Cree?"

"I'm positive," he drawled. "I don't make mistakes." He spun on a heel and started walking again.

"Okay, moving on then." Keeping a pace behind and to his shoulder so he could still hear, he asked, "You didn't exactly explain what the Valda-Cree are?"

"It is said they were skin shifters."

Jayce swallowed, his feet slowing to another stop. "What?" he whispered.

Rune frowned. "Please keep moving. We are not in a safe place yet. Your friends are trying to find a way to follow us, and if they were watching you on your plane, then I am not the only one aware of you, or seeking you."

Jayce tossed his hands. "Then tell me why I should trust you?" he demanded.

Rune turned and walked into his personal space, crowding him. His face was so close he could trace the odd composition of each eye easily. They were a lake water blue, but so much brighter, shimmery, as though they had harnessed the energy of a lightning bolt. A shiver danced over his skin. It wasn't fair that this one man, this *elf*—Really? An elf?—was so damn beautiful. Beautiful with smooth skin and lips that… *Gah!* He could *not* be attracted to him. Not like that, this! And that irked him as much as anything. He couldn't be attracted to the man who'd abducted him, could he? They were roughly the same height making it seem so perfect for a kiss. He itched to take a step back, but held his ground. "Because while they might have been friendly with you, they were still hired. And I know *I* do not want to kill you. I can't say the same for them or their employer."

Jayce gulped. "This is all really happening, then, isn't it? You're really magic, a mage, and you have a bird familiar and we're nowhere near my apartment and I'm really in some crazy place I've never heard of and—"

Jayce flinched when Rune lightly touched his arm, his tumbling words jerking to a stop instantly. "I'm sorry. I will keep you safe. We are entwined now that we are together. I don't know what will come, but I know, given time you will understand."

"Rune." He tucked his chin. "Am I ever going home?" He hadn't sounded this forlorn since he was a child, and he hated it. He loved his parents. Even though he knew he was adopted, they'd *chosen* him. That made him special in his eyes and in theirs. Chosen was equally as special as natural born, because then the child knew they were wanted. So many times he'd heard of those who were up for adoption because while they'd been born, they weren't *wanted*. It mattered to him that he was chosen. His heart pounded as he waited for Rune to tell him what he was desperate to hear. He'd been ripped from his home, his life. His parents. The sob burned in his throat daring to break free. Only a fierce will kept it from happening.

The evenness of Rune's face never changed. A squeeze to his arm and he turned to start walking again. His silence was answer enough.

Snugging his arms against his chest, he focused on the ground and trailed behind the elf's straight back, no longer wanting to hear more.

Chapter 4

Rune was thankful for the silence, but regretted hurting Jayce. It was out of his hands. He hoped Master Theil would be able to provide some guidance now that he'd found Jayce. The man's demeanor was subdued because he was processing, but he knew once he had a grasp, he was going to come out fighting. Exactly like he had every step of the way since they'd met in his living quarters. The sun shifted ever so slowly as they trekked through the woods. Iba was keeping a watch overhead and as of yet, the berserkers had not found a gate or portal to bring them through. It was a small relief. They needed more distance between them before the *sabra* caught their trail.

He didn't know who would have hired the warriors, and had less of an idea who was already aware of Jayce's existence. But clearly someone was. There was no way to know for how long though and that left him on edge.

"Rune?"

"Yes?"

"Can we stop soon? I'm not sure if you're aware of this, but our worlds don't line up time-wise. My body thinks I should be in bed, not traipsing through some forest of unknown."

Rune dipped his head. "I apologize. We should be nearing a village with a tavern soon. We can stop. We both need rest and you need clothes that will allow you to blend in better."

"Unless they take Mastercard, I think I'm out of luck," he quipped with a snarked bite of bitterness.

"I can make the arrangements." He sought Jayce over his shoulder. "It's likely best if you stay out of sight, regardless. You're too conspicuous in your current garments."

"Fine. So long as we can stop soon." His stomach grumbled, but Rune pretended he didn't hear it. He knew Jayce was stretched to his breaking point. He'd been sullen and quiet for well over an hour. Somehow, he doubted this brooding silence was his normal state.

The scents of damp ground, sunbaked bark, and the surge of life began to thin and he slowed his pace. "Stay close," he murmured.

A wafted breeze brought the natural tang of a stable. If they had horses for sale, he'd consider it his lucky due and be happy for it. He doubted his new charge knew one thing about a horse, but he was going to get a rushed instructional, because if there were two to be had, they would be leaving on horseback.

He circled through the trees, studying the buildings. The stable was close, but it was the tavern and the homes nearby that he was cautious of. The fewer people who saw him, the safer they'd be in not being able to pinpoint his presence there. Also looking like he belonged made it easier for people to overlook him, to not see him but not remember him even if they did.

"Stay here. I won't be long, but you need clothing and I'm going to see if I can procure us some horses."

"So we're not stopping here?" Jayce leaned tiredly against a tree with a shoulder. It seemed the adrenaline and shock were wearing off, leaving him exhausted.

"Soon, but no. I will bring us both back food." He closed his eyes and sent requests to Iba. "Iba will be nearby even if you don't see her. I can put a protection spell around you but you cannot leave this spot."

"Fine." He sank to the ground and folded his legs up, wrapping his arms around them. "I'll be a quiet little captive."

Rune frowned, but he didn't have time to argue over his pithy remark.

"And I've never ridden a horse in my life, just so you know." There was a spark of challenge in his eyes.

Backing up, he stamped the ground with his staff and created a circle surrounding his charge. How he was supposed to be this man's guide and guard eluded him, but he was going to try. He would do his best regardless of what he thought of Rune at the moment. He was more than capable of protecting him.

Guiding him was yet to be seen.

He unwound the canteen and handed it over. "Drink some water. I won't be long."

Jayce clutched the leather strap and set it by his side. "Don't forget I'm here, okay? You're the only person I know."

Rune lowered to his haunches. The forlorn heartache beginning to overtake Jayce's gaze made the elf ache for him, but there wasn't anything to be done now. They were on Kielbos and they weren't returning any time soon. "I know we didn't have the most auspicious introduction, but I've sworn myself to your protection when I accepted the visions as my calling. I may be more familiar in my own lands, but that is the only advantage I have to you."

Jayce nodded, a small smile breaking over his mouth. "I know. We're figuring this out together, right?"

"That we are." He stood and shook out his robes. "Rest while you can. If you see or hear anything, speak to Iba. I will know."

He glanced upward through the branches. "Me and the bird, huh?"

Rune grinned mischievously. "Be careful calling her a mere bird. She is a bit sensitive, being a raven and intelligent for that fact."

He peered upward again. "Sorry, Iba!" A quiet caw followed. Jayce blinked with surprise. "You better go. I'm about to fall asleep and you should use that time." He uncorked the canteen and drew a few swallows.

Speaking under his breath, he raised the barrier that would blur the area Jayce was hiding within to anyone laxly searching. "Like I said, don't move."

"Not going anywhere," he mumbled.

All right, Iba. I'll be back quickly. Stay alert.

Gliding through the trees, he found a more common track, not wanting to come out directly in a line to where Jayce rested. With his cowl up, he dipped his head and softened his stride to a more casual approach as he studied his surroundings. A few people moved between the huts. A blacksmith and his helper moved a barrel of ore on the outskirts. The stench of hot iron was easier to discern now that he was in the open, among the village. Curious stares came his way, but he never changed his pace and no one called out to him.

It wasn't long before he reached the tavern's door. Seeking outward with his senses to his immediate surroundings, there was no magic that he could taste or feel. He pulled his in to keep close, skin level. He didn't want to be refused for being a magic user. It wasn't uncommon to be mistrusted.

Walking inside, the stored heat of the afternoon flowed over him. No one really paid him any mind as he strode through the room. Sitting at a table away from the cold fireplace with his back to a wall, he settled his staff near, no more important than a walking stick if anyone were to question.

"Aye, traveler. What's to yer likin'?"

He smiled warmly at the matron who approached. Without looking directly at her, he attempted to appear meek. A boy only doing his master's bidding. "I need two meat plates if you please, a man's change of garments, my height but a little more muscled, with boots, and if you know of two horses for sale, my master is tired of walking on his old bones."

She laughed, her grease smudged cheeks appling brightly. "Meat and wares be easy. I'll ask the stable master if there be any horses."

"Something gentle. I know it's a hard request, but my master is ailing and the easier our journey…" he murmured quietly keeping his gaze pointedly down while plying for a little compassion with a dipped shoulder.

"You have gold to pay?" And there was the bartering firmness he was expecting.

"Enough for what I asked, but not more. I was sent with my instructions and not much else."

She laughed again. "Ain't that always the way? They be sendin' their lackeys to do their duty. Molly will fix you up. Let me check out the stable to see if we have any takers."

Keeping his gaze lowered, he nodded with subdued piousness. "I am in your debt for the effort."

She swept away after, the trailing scents of grease and burnt charcoal lingering on her leather skirt going with her, likely from manning the pits if not doing all the cooking. If she was Molly or if there someone else he would need to speak with, he hoped they had horses. They needed to get to the temple so he could speak to Master Theil.

The last thing he wanted to do after the day they'd already spent was be the one to explain to Jayce his destiny. He knew it wasn't being fair to him to look at him now and expect to see the king in him. He wasn't ready. Jayce didn't have an inkling.

A tankard of ale appeared before him and he graciously dipped his head, bringing it close to sip heartily. It wasn't his favorite drink, but it filled the need and made it easier to fit in with the locals.

A moment later, a plate piled high with ribs and potatoes thunked onto the table. The smells enveloped him. It had been some time since he'd had a full meal himself. He started eating, waiting for news of his other requests. He cleared the plate in record time. He didn't want to leave Jayce alone for too long. It wasn't long before a tied off papered package appeared, followed by a cheesecloth knotted together that smelled a lot like the ribs and roasted potatoes he'd devoured moments ago.

"Thank you, very much, for your hospitality." Carefully extracting the coins from one of his pouches for the shopkeeper, he set them in her hand. "And the horses?"

She jiggled the coins before slipping them into a blousy pocket. "Go 'round back to the stable. Ask for Elim. He says he has two if the price is right."

It was more than he expected for them to actually have two. Hopefully they weren't expecting a king's payment in coin.

After some negotiation, he led the two horses out of the village with Jayce's food and clothing tied to one of the saddles. The older horse would be good for Jayce. Hopefully he picked riding up quickly.

Releasing a bubble of energy, he waited for any hits of someone poking where they didn't belong. When the bubble reached the edge of his ability he pulled it back, keeping a steady pace. Good. No one was suspicious of the young lad doing his master's bidding.

About a quarter mile from the village, he turned into the trees, meandering with no real seeming intent. Confident he wasn't being followed, he neared where he'd left Jayce. And good to his word, he was asleep on the ground, his arm beneath his head as a pillow.

Looking at him now, Rune could admit he was very handsome. A strong face, a very nice body. He couldn't help but wonder if the chest outlined by the thin shirt he wore was actually that defined. The clothing he wore revealed far more than he had witnessed before. Taut thighs, long legs wrapped in a deep blue fabric. Broad shoulders. His raised hand hesitated, not wanting to disturb the sleep he'd obviously been needing. It was getting late, but he'd rather leave under the cover of darkness.

Dropping back on his calves, he let him sleep. They could do what they needed to continue their journey when he woke Jayce.

Chapter 5

Jayce rolled over and yelped. Jerking up, blinking, he rubbed his eyes, then brushed his hand over his back, swiping for the jabbing sensation. His fingers found it.

He stared confused at the twig he pulled from his back. How did a twig get into his mattress? He tossed it and looked around.

And immediately closed his eyes again with his head sagging to his chest. There was no mattress and he wasn't at home.

Weak moonlight glowed through gaps between the tree branches creating a canopy of cover where he currently rested. It was dark beneath the trees' boughs, amplifying an eerie quiet that he'd never known living in the city.

"You're awake," a known, and completely unwelcome, voice offered.

"So it would seem."

"I have food."

Jayce grimaced, dusting his hands off as he straightened where he sat. His stomach grumbled loudly at the thought of food. He leaned against the tree at his back, to reach for the white cloth in front of his face. "So I guess, there's no chance of a microwave?"

Rune ignored him.

Jayce unknotted the top and unfolded the fabric in his lap. Meat of some kind and possibly boiled potatoes. He sniffed. It didn't smell deadly. His stomach seemed to approve.

"Eat what you can. I have clothing for you to change into, then we need to leave."

He bit into the blackened rib, the taste dry, but edible. It wasn't the worst thing he'd ever consumed, but it wasn't a burger dripping in fatty juice by any means either. There wasn't any point in fighting the inevitable. He did need to eat. And Rune had been kind enough to make sure he didn't starve.

"Thank you," he murmured, wiping the back of his hand over his lips. "For getting me this."

Rune sank to the ground nearby, his raven on his shoulder. He fed her little bits of meat from his fingertips. Up close she was larger than he had envisioned. "She's lovely," he offered.

Iba tilted her head, shaking her tail feathers a little.

"She says thank you."

Surprise widened his eyes a little. "Does she actually talk to you?"

"Not like us, like this, but in a way, yes." Another piece was plucked neatly into her beak.

Watching the way he cared for her wasn't what he was expecting. The raven nuzzled against his head. And for some reason, he suddenly wanted to be able to do the same thing. To feel the weight of hair between his fingers, or to learn the smoothness of skin curving down his neck. It made no sense to Jayce. This wanting to burrow his nose into the thick pale hair tied against his head, or even better to see it loose and flowing down his back confused him.

He lowered his gaze and focused on his food, calming the sudden interest parts of his body were showing in the elf. There was no way the reaction made sense. This guy had all but dragged him from his apartment, marched him across some world he didn't know two shits about, all while still managing to not tell him *why*. Something about a stupid prophecy that Jayce didn't have any knowledge of, as if those were an everyday thing. Prophecies. Abduction. Dumb.

So instead he ignored the inexplicable interest his dick was showing in the tall and beautiful elf and ate his caveman food.

"Once you are finished, I have garments for you to change into. It will make you less notable."

"What will I do with what I'm wearing?"

Rune avoided looking at him. "They will need to be destroyed. You must appear assimilated, or those who are also seeking you will be able to find you by tracking your unusual appearance."

"Destroyed?" he yelped. "But if we can hide them, why destroy them?"

Rune sighed and Iba launched with a lazy spread of her wings. He scooted around to sit closer to Jayce on the ground. "You asked me if you would be going home before."

Jayce waited, almost holding his breath.

"Destiny has a path for you to travel. I know this isn't your world, and you know nothing of it, but this is your destiny. Every vision I have had for the last two years has been bringing me closer to you." A hand fluttered in the air, like he wanted to connect them, but didn't know how. Or was thinking better of it. "I also know I am asking a lot, for you to trust me. All I know is we are in this together. In time, it will make more sense, but you have to trust me to get you there. The first place we need to go is the Windwise temple, to speak with Master Theil. I will guide you and I *will* protect you."

"Protect me from what?" he demanded. He balled up the cloth his meal had been in and all but threw it away. "I wouldn't need protection if you'd left me alone."

"Berserkers, for one. And their employer. And we don't know if that's true, that you would have been able to continue living your life in ignorant bliss." He glanced into his lap, his fingers knotted together as he deliberated his next words. "Jayce, someone hid you on your Earth. *Sabra* warriors do not simply appear, whether they behave as your friends or not. They are not of your world. Was it your birth family? I can't tell you that. Was it to protect you? Again, it's a guess. Was hiding you meant to keep you away from here entirely? Or was it meant to protect you? Do you see all the possibilities now and why being sent to find you has to have a meaning? And if someone wants to stop you, you are untrained, have no connection with your shifter heart. You are utterly vulnerable." He drew a slow breath. "So do you want to try to find those answers, keep yourself safe? Or do you want to go back to your abode where the door has been destroyed to see if your friends, as you insist on calling them, can finish the job now that they know your time has come?"

Jayce dropped his head into upturned palms with a heart-wrenching groan. "Why me? I'm a college student. I was one damn semester from my teaching degree. And my parents? What are they going to think? If I vanish, it will destroy them. I don't know anything about anything happening to me. And do you have any idea how hard it is to *even* imagine I'm some almost extinct race of..." He blurted, sweeping his arms wide. "Of shapeshifter. Do you have any idea how ludicrous that sounds?"

"Which is why we need to speak to Master Theil. There is more, and he has a better understanding of the prophecy and of what we can't see. But we must leave if we are going to do that." The firm yet almost soft skin of his fingers on Jayce's chin were a shock. "Are you ready to face that challenge, Jayce? Are you ready to live?"

He sucked a breath, blinking to bury the pressure behind his eyes. "It's really all gone then? This is it? I will never see home again?"

"I can't swear to you that it will be never," he answered gently. A thumb stroked beneath an eye, capturing a tear that escaped against his will. "But believe me when I say if there is a chance I will find a way to make it happen for you. Your choice of will was taken from you when you were chosen for your part in the prophecy. However unfair that is, it is happening. I will do what I can to ensure you have choices going forward."

Jayce sniffed, squishing his eyes to stop the buildup of tears. He could fight, demand he be taken home, but Rune had a point. If Raquel and Helen were only there to keep tabs on him…because holy mother, her eyes. He'd never forget their red glow through the demolished door or the size of the axe she'd been throwing around like a fishing rod, like it weighed next to nothing. But if anyone else *now* knew, then the first place they'd look for him was his apartment. The risks were too great. "Fine. Where are the clothes you have?"

Rune rose to his feet, gathering another wrapped bundle from the back of one of the horses. "These should fit you."

Jayce stood and grasped the paper. It crinkled faintly in his fingers, seeming louder due to the calm of night. "Okay." He untied the knots of string and unfolded the paper, revealing a bland pair of fawn brown trousers with a simple white peasant shirt. There was a satchel with a pouch and a belt. Lastly at the bottom was a pair of boots. Those might be a problem but he'd see.

He changed his shirt first, tossing the T-shirt he wore over a low branch. Centering the shirt over his abdomen, the ties at the front were loose at his throat, and it was surprisingly comfortable, even across his shoulders. "No underwear?" he asked taking out the trousers and giving them a shake.

"I don't know what that is," Rune admitted.

Jayce rolled his eyes. "Sorry, I'm keeping them." He shot out a hand when Rune started to argue. "They go under. No one is going to see them, and it's unsanitary to wear clothes like that."

Rune frowned but didn't fight him. At least it proved he was willing to bend. Though how anyone didn't know about underwear... He turned his back to work with the pants. The trousers had a draw string placket and two button waist, and molded to his thighs above the knee, curving down his calves. His sneaker socks would have to do with the high-calf boots. He wasn't going to ask if there was a style of those here, he felt he already knew the answer. The boot leather slid up his legs, over the trouser cuffs, as he stomped his feet into them. They were a little tight, but they were pure leather, so they would eventually mold to his feet. With his trousers up, he tucked in his shirt to button his pants, and then ran his hands down everything. None of it was like anything he'd ever worn in the past and he knew it would take some getting used to, but at the moment, he had to trust Rune's judgement.

Placing his wallet with his jeans, he turned to face Rune. "Well, do I pass inspection?"

Rune stood still, swallowing once. "You—You pass inspection, very well." Iba cawed overhead and Rune startled. He blinked and drew a slow breath. "Yes, well, let me put your things in one of the travel bags for now. I don't want to draw attention here."

Jayce handed it all over, his fingers lingering over his wallet. There wasn't much in there. His bank card, a few twenties, his IDs, pictures of his parents. It almost tore at his heart how little actually tied him back to his college kid life. It all seemed so insignificant when compared to the prosperity and future of an entire people, or world.

Rune took them kindly, folded each piece and packed them into one of the saddle bags. Then he walked to the pitched cheesecloth to shake out the rib bones and folded that as well. Studying the ground where they'd been resting, he nodded, satisfied with whatever he was looking for. Jayce had no idea.

"We need to walk the horses to a better mounting location."

Jayce didn't repeat anything about his lack of horse riding skills. He guessed at this point, he had a lot to learn regardless. What his part would be in everything being one of the many.

Chapter 6

Rune kept an eye on Jayce, his grip on the saddle horn steady and no longer clenching. The relaxed gait they'd kept through the nighttime hours helped ease him into the horse's plodding pace. They would stop again before reaching the Windwise temple, but the coming day was going to be hard on Jayce. And they really couldn't go much faster until he learned proper horsemanship.

Iba, guard our rear.

She swept low overhead, cawing to circle in the direction they'd come from, riding the air currents with ease. The sun was on its rise over the horizon to their right, and they were making decent progress.

"How far is it to your master's temple?"

"We'll be there tomorrow. There is another village on the way. We will stop and rest for a full night."

There were a few minutes of silence, then "Tell me what your visions have warned you of. How do you know they mean anything about me?"

Rune rocked his heels in the stirrups, stretching his calf muscles. Flashes of the visions he'd received played through his memory. "I had dreamed not quite exact images of you in my visions. I knew the person I sought wasn't light of hair, dark of skin, or exceedingly tall or short. So there were factors I could discount immediately."

"So average?"

"If you insist. But I don't believe you're average."

The sight of him biting at his lip in contemplation made Rune wish he could bite it as well, then soothe it with caring kisses. It wasn't normal in his recent memory to harbor cravings for another, and it left him unbalanced around this young man, a man who was more a duty than a friend as of yet. A mage's study was his only mistress. Though it had been nigh impossible to turn away when Jayce started changing in the trees last night. First his shirt to reveal a chest that Rune had most definitely wanted to caress with his hands, and if it were allowed, his tongue. It was as defined as he'd first expected and better than he'd imagined. Changing into the pants had been a lesson in agony. With the undergarment he'd worn forming to his frame like a second skin, he'd nearly swallowed his own tongue to halt the plaintive whimpers hiding in his throat. He'd never seen another who had stolen his breath as well as his ability to think so easily. The views had been permanently pressed into his mind's vision. Never to be forgotten. Gratefully, those stolen peeks were hours ago and he'd since been able to put his mind to more necessary matters. Such as making sure Jayce maintained his balance in the saddle.

Morning sunlight warmed skin and he dropped the cowl covering his head to his shoulders. A deep inhale of the morning, the heaviness of dew and the waking world, was an elixir his soul craved. One of his strengths had formed with his bond with nature, the natural world and living things. This time was one of his most favorite. When the world was waking and it was fresh from a night's rest. Every plant, tree, and animal's presence sang to him, drifting over his nerves to invigorate him. Since he was a boy, he'd loved the rise of the sun, the gradual spread of light and life. For Rune, there was no better peace.

"I have to tell you, this might be normal for you, but I've never met an elf."

Rune smiled, glad Jayce had relaxed enough to initiate talking. Interest meant learning, and curiosity, and he could work with those. Jayce had been tense after mounting the saddle but in the hours since seemed to find the comfortable rhythm in the animal's gait. "I gathered that when you were so easily stunned when I appeared before you."

"Well, actually your eyes caught my attention first."

"Oh?" Rune twisted to peer at Jayce a little easier. Jayce was flipping the reins back and forth in his hand, letting the tips brush his legs as he did so. Rune found it endearing that he was playing with them like a child. Granted, horseback riding may be duller than Jayce had expected, but he wasn't complaining, either. Not yet. Rune knew there would be a lot of complaining once he was out of the saddle and his muscles tried to remember how to work properly.

"I've never seen that color of blue before, and I swear the iris looks like lightning is piercing them. Silver streaks."

Rune's mouth opened, taken by surprise that Jayce had such a complimentary thing to say about any part of him after what he'd already put him through. "I—I thank you."

"You said earlier I was untrained. Untrained how?"

"I believe you have some of your ancestor's magic in your veins."

Jayce snorted, then shook his head. "Like I'm this Valda-Cree that you keep mentioning?"

"Yes."

He lifted his head enough to meet Rune's gaze, and in the rising sunlight, there was a golden aura in Jayce's own eyes, a bright honey brown that he hadn't noticed in all the hours before. While the derision was clear, this was something else entirely that caught his attention. "What color are your eyes?" he asked curiously, yet doing his best to sound casual. He was almost positive their brighter color was a new aspect, and more proof that Jayce was exactly who he was supposed to be. He simply didn't know what would have triggered the new color's appearance around the iris that way. Another question for Master Theil.

"A plain brown. Goes with the hair and the rest of me. Average height. Average in looks. Average enough intelligence to get into college, but nothing extraordinary." Rune didn't know what those things were but he had a feeling he was only average in the life he'd led to keep him hidden, safe, and secure. Time would tell if his real purpose brought out the extraordinary in him. "Like I said, I'm the average person of your visions. Which is why I'm really not convinced I'm who you think I am. There's nothing special about me. I'm young, not brave or full of ideas to help you find and battle this evil you say has been freed in your lands. I've never even been in a fist fight, and that seems pretty relevant to right now."

"Even the bravest of men can feel fear," he mused. "All the bravest men and women start in the same place of the unknown."

"Didn't say I was scared," he snapped. Neither horse twitched an ear at his outburst.

"You didn't have to," he observed. "I would be in your place, and to some degree, for even as powerful as I am, I'm scared of what I can't control."

Jayce was silent for a moment. Rune noted the only noise between them was the clop-clop of their mounts' steps it was so quiet. He purposely scanned the distance but couldn't see anything out of the ordinary. He couldn't let his attention falter because they were seemingly alone. They weren't following the common roads, giving them slightly better cover, but it was also going to take them longer to get to the temple.

The cart path they traveled was narrow and empty, with a sweeping dry grassland prairie to the left and one of the low reaching mountain ranges in the distance on the right. Snow was visible at the topmost peaks, glinting brightly in the morning rays. The *sabra* were still out there, even if he'd managed to cut them off from using the same escape he and Jayce had used. Rune frowned. The largest problem they presented was making him question who else knew of Jayce's existence. Were they protecting him from something on his plane, or were they there to stop anyone *else* from finding him? Like Rune? There was no way to know. Sticking around to ask had been his last wish.

At best, they had a day's lead on the *sabra*. By now, he had to assume they would be in Trajanleh. Rune and Jayce needed to reach the temple in Windmere. It perched at the top of cliffs overlooking a turbulent sea. Which had always made sense to Rune as Master Theil's strengths and power were derived from water and energy. And both could be found in great quantities when living near a rocky shoreline beset by frequent lightning storms and a supposed dormant volcano. It had benefited his early training to have a water mage nearby when the youngling he'd been had fought with the control of his own abilities.

"Do you have any weapons?" Jayce asked.

"I carry a short blade, but nothing more. Mages aren't masters of metals, we are more masters of the elements and energies. And a lot of spell work," he added drily. "We will take time at the temple." He sighed. "I haven't had a vision past that point, and I haven't slept since I found you."

Jayce jerked a little on the reins of his animal and she stopped easily. Rune was glad he remembered what he'd taught him at the beginning of their journey to not hurt or startle the animal.

"You mean you haven't slept in what, two days?"

"Almost two days. It is why we will be stopping at the next village. Once I'm sure we've put a distance between us and the *sabra*, we will rest. I am not near my limit but I will be if we don't stop tonight. I will not risk your safety and ignore what we both need. You will be equally as exhausted, and I'm sorry to say, sore, by this evening as well. We will need to stop."

"Now that you mention it." He shifted on the saddle, groaning. "Oh, yeah, that's going to hurt."

He tapped the side of his mount with a heel. "Let's get moving again. Iba says we are still clear in the distance, but I don't want to take any chances by lingering."

Jayce sighed and nudged his mount alongside Rune's.

Rune was able to convince Jayce to attempt a trot and an easy lope a few times, but didn't want to strain either him or their horses, but any extra distance they could put into the journey was to their benefit.

The sun was high when they made a brief stop.

Jayce moaned pitifully when he slid from the saddle to his feet. He leaned against the animal's side, braced by an arm.

"Let's walk a little. It will help your legs and refresh the horses."

"I don't think I can. Damn, this is not like riding a bicycle."

Rune blinked twice. The things his charge said.

"What if I tell you there will be a hot bath at the end when we stop?"

Jayce looked skeptical. "Like a real, hot water bath? Not ground, not leaves and sticks?"

Rune chuckled, patting his horse's muscled neck. "Yes, a real hot water bath. I'll make sure of it."

"Fine," he grumped.

They walked for a while, eating the dried jerky and nuts Rune carried out of habit. Iba needed snacks too, but she could fend for herself while she was in the air. Midafternoon, they were back in the saddle. With a sigh of relief, he spotted the first hazy signs of chimney smoke in the distance. He lifted an arm and pointed. "We're going there. We have crossed into Sevenwood."

"Are these different countries?"

"Merely different lands. They all fall under one kingdom, Caduthien." Before Jayce could further question that line of thought, he added, "Do you think you can pick up the pace? The quicker we are there, the sooner you will be able to rest."

Jayce rolled his shoulders and shifted in the saddle. "I'll see what I can do."

"Keep your balance. You've done well."

"Trying," he muttered.

Chapter 7

Jayce was in agony. His legs felt like mushy noodles as he slid from the saddle one more time to land on feet that may or may not have been attached. He'd lost feeling above his ankles. His legs, calves, his ass. He *hurt*. Muscles he didn't know he had were screaming at him. Even his hands ached from clenching the saddle and gripping the reins like a lifeline. Glaring at Rune didn't help when he all but ignored Jayce's misery. How the elf could sit in a saddle for what had to be over twelve hours, from before dawn to now stupefied him. It felt like leather bonded steel was attached to his ass and for all he knew, was still there.

"I'm never getting up there again," he protested.

Rune chuckled kindly. "Tomorrow will be soon enough."

"No. Never."

He patted a shoulder as though humoring a child. With their horses boarded for the night and their saddlebags over their shoulders, they wound their way from the stable where the horses would be cared for toward the inn-slash-tavern Rune had promised him existed.

Though whatever hopes he had of creature comforts went up in smoke as they neared the building. Rough timbers, stacked and packed with some kind of mud or clay in between, weather worn and cracked, were topped by a shingled roof that looked like sliced stone flats that sloped to allow for runoff and possible slow melt. If it snowed here. Not a thought he wanted to consider at the moment. He had no idea where he was, or if it compared to his world. He didn't even know if they had seasons like he knew. The single window on the side of the building appeared to be covered by a leather sheet. He wasn't going to get close enough to find out for sure. There was smoke coming from two different chimneys, so there was life inside. Not that he had high hopes it would look anything like what he could recognize. "This? This is where we're going?"

Rune didn't reply, leading him to a large open room in the very front of the building. "Sit down, please," he offered quietly, once they reached a bench seat, sitting side by side with their backs to the wall. "Let me do the talking."

Jayce huffed, too tired to really argue, but far too sore to stalk off. Even with a sore ass, sitting still won out.

A serving woman approached gripping tankards in one hand and a stack of dishes in her other. "Aye, good eve to ya. What will you be askin'?"

"Evening. We need two meat plates with a cold apple ale, if you have one."

"We do, we do. Cold ale we have plenty. We have pork tonight for the meat plates we turn," she informed them, happily. How odd. Was this normal? It made so very little sense to Jayce. Was Rune ordering food, or discussing how to pit roast a pig?

Rune nodded, keeping his face averted. Jayce hadn't thought much of it, but recalled he'd turned his hood up when they neared the stables, before anyone would be able to see his head. "Would there be an inn, or rooms for the night?" he asked.

"There be rooms. Go south and look for the house with the lantern on the door. They have rooms to rent."

"I thank you kindly for your hospitality."

"Fine gents you be. Let me get your dinners."

Jayce had watched and listened to the exchange. She seemed bubbly and eager to help them. "So I guess the first thing that would tip someone off is that I have a different accent and way of speech," he said after she'd left them to themselves.

"You do. You would come across as very cultured to most, if they tried to guess, like from one of the royal houses. And we're trying to keep you from being noticeable. Someone speaking like you do, would definitely make a memory."

"Not like the red cape hides you, right?"

Rune grimaced. "I'm not alone in wearing them for protection, and it is more common."

He had to concede that point. "You really think someone is after me?"

"I have to assume so. I've been waiting for my opportunity to find you. Who is to say I'm the only one?"

Jayce tapped the scored and scarred plank of the table they'd chosen. The dim room had six long tables total with scattered men sitting around them, eating and drinking. Torches were mounted in wall sconces, their flickering flames and trailing tails of smoke had left years if not decades of soot scars on the walls. It was primitive and so unlike anything he could have imagined. The only woman he'd seen had been the...

Server? Wench? He honestly didn't know. So maybe Rune was right this time. The minute he opened his mouth, he would stick out like a sore thumb. "Will you tell me more tonight? About why you think you were sent for me? I'm trying to wrap my head around this, but it's so hard. I feel like I've been thrust into a Lord of the Rings movie, and never got the script.'"

Rune drew a slow breath. "That is why we're going to the temple. What I know is my assumption from my own experiences to interpret the visions I've received." He tipped close, keeping their voices low. "Am I in the right because of my interpretation of the visions? Or am I in the wrong, and only creating the paradox that is needed for our entire world to be destroyed? It is that simple and that difficult to be certain."

Jayce studied the blue eyes before him, trying to gauge his words. It caught him off guard that there was a true hesitation in his expression, a level of thoughtful deliberation he wouldn't have expected. This man, elf, whatever, was really only following what he believed was right as far as he knew it. Instead of making Jayce doubt Rune's perceptions by arguing that his was the only right way to proceed, and dictating his choices were the only options they possessed, it actually helped Jayce to grasp that maybe everything to this point was what it was supposed to be because Rune wasn't any more confident than he was.

Rune had kept him safe, had fed him, had even consoled him as he struggled to process the ongoing drama that his life had become.

"Then I want to thank you. If for nothing else, then for ensuring I stay alive, and as you said, well-guarded." He wasn't a hundred percent convinced that Rune was who he should be trusting, but until he was shown differently, then he would stay.

Diana DeRicci

Rune's long, kind fingers ghosted over his thigh briefly. A touch that conveyed so much more than his words. Jayce felt their tenderness and their allure all at once. Then they were gone. The breath caught in his chest, but it was one of those things he instinctively knew better than to address now. If Rune wasn't sure of exposing his eyes or ears without caution, then saying what he was feeling when Rune touched him was definitely not going to happen. There was no way to know if that truth would even be welcome.

The rest of the meal was spent in quiet, though he was aware Rune was staying attentive to those who came and went as they ate their fill.

Jayce sipped some of the apple ale, and licked his lips, enjoying the sweetness as it slid down his throat. It tasted like apple cider with something tangy added to it, and though he couldn't taste the alcohol in it, he didn't doubt that one tankard would be more than sufficient.

"If you're finished, let's go talk to the room owner and see if we can get some sleep."

"And a hot bath," he whispered.

Rune smiled kindly, but kept it low key. "Yes, I did promise, didn't I?"

A little movement was helping him stretch his muscles, but by the time Rune was done bartering for the room, because of course there was only one available, he was weaving on his feet from bone-weary exhaustion. The little sleep he'd managed the night before had only been a reprieve for two days of hard traveling and high adrenaline rushes. If he didn't get some decent sleep soon, he was going to be sleepwalking.

Rune motioned with his chin to get Jayce to follow, and staying close, they traipsed down a narrow hallway to a second door. Rune used the key and then said a few words before he opened the door. The door swept open with a slight creak, but the sign of poorly kept hinges was actually good in his mind. If the door wasn't silent, less chance of someone sneaking in on them during the night.

The room was mostly filled with something he assumed was supposed to represent a bed, but so long as it wasn't a bed of nails, he was going to fall into it and not wake up for at least eight, maybe twelve hours. With the sun lowering to dusk, that seemed wholly possible.

46

The rest of the room revealed bare walls of stacked split wood, and a single table. Nothing with drawers, and no floor coverings. He'd never seen anything so barren or…medieval in his life.

Rune shut the door and immediately went to the window to pull away a hanging leather flap, letting the late day breeze blow in. Iba appeared a few minutes later to perch on the sill.

"Hello, heart." She spread her wings and hopped into the room, before settling on the wrought iron headboard as a perch, then proceeded to comb through her feathers. "I requested a bath, but it will take them some time to bring it." He leaned his staff in a corner, hanging his held bag over a hook on the wall.

Jayce dropped his saddle bag to the corner of the bed. It was mostly empty, but when Rune said to bring it, he did. He figured no reason to give anyone a chance to snoop, or to stick out more than he would than anyone else traveling who *would* bring their bags with them. He blinked slowly as what he'd said finally registered. "They…bring…the bath?" He was feeling so very sluggish.

Rune tipped his head in confusion. "Yes, the tub. It will need to be filled with water. I really expect you to be uncomfortable in the morning if you don't."

Jayce sagged to the bed. He couldn't tell what it was stuffed with but it sure wasn't a mattress. He splayed a hand next to his hip and pushed into the material, feeling the give and debating how hard it would be to fall over right there. "I'm exhausted. The apple ale has me so relaxed already. I don't know if I'll be awake to wait for them to do it."

He sat beside Jayce on the bed, studying him with concern. "If you're sure? I did promise."

Jayce nodded, his eyelids drooping as he tried to focus on Rune. *No more apple ale.* He felt warm and tingly, from his tummy to his shoulders. "I'm sure."

"Get ready to sleep, then. I'll be right back." He stood and spoke to the Raven. "Iba, watch until I return."

He turned and with a quick step, left the room. Jayce sagged and toed off his boots with a few grunts. They hit the floor with dull thuds that for some reason had him giggling. "Oh, Iba. I'm in trouble. I think I'm drunk." He twisted on the bedding and crawled up to the lump that he assumed was supposed to be a pillow. It felt like he'd landed right.

He couldn't open his eyes to make sure. Hoping he was on the bed was the last thought he had.

❧

Rune returned to the shared room after cancelling the hot bath request. If Jayce could hold out to the temple, then he would surprise him with the thermal-pressure hot springs running beneath it. He'd done so well, and after the initial shock had worn off, had been trying to work with Rune. His young charge had proven to be very adaptable and level-headed. Once inside their shared room, he warded the door and locked it. Dropping the cloak he wore to the end of the bed, he toed off his boots and stretched out beside Jayce. The poor man was snoring hard.

An image of a slurring Jayce appeared in his mind, and he shook his head while watching him briefly. "Drunk, huh? Never had apple ale." He flexed, easing the soreness in his body. The last two days hadn't been easy on either of them, even if he was better at hiding it. Some rest was what they both needed. Especially if Jayce was feeling the ale enough to believe himself drunk. Exhaustion wasn't helping that.

He closed his eyes and quickly found his own rest.

Chapter 8

Jayce was in pain yet Rune couldn't look away, couldn't break the moment to stop it, either. They were in the temple, of that he was certain. Carvings and runes that he'd known all of his life were contrasted by the large fire pit and the precisely distanced torches with their flames flickering along the wall. The temple was dark with nighttime everywhere but in there. He tried to study the moment the dream vision had gifted him with, the same way he had for the last two years. But…Jayce was in pain. He didn't understand that, couldn't look away. If the dream was trying to tell him something, he couldn't see beyond Jayce's pain to decipher it. Master Theil wouldn't hurt Jayce. He was the only other person who knew any part of Rune's visions. His stomach clenched as he waited for the dream to show him more.

The three stood gathered in the large altar room of the temple, Jayce's arms outstretched by an invisible force, his legs braced wide, as he screamed. Corded muscles pulled and stretched through his arms and bare chest. It only briefly occurred to Rune's awareness that Jayce stood utterly naked, but he couldn't take any delight in the view before him. Not like this. *A sheen of sweat made him glisten as he strained against the pain. A golden glow surrounded him. Pulsed. It would brighten then fade, like a living presence intent on devouring him. The screams grew, echoing back off marble walls and ceiling as they deepened, changed.*

"Master, please make it stop. He didn't ask for this." Rune's discomfort was not easy to contain, but he dared not order his master. He hated the way his voice pleaded. He didn't know when it had happened, but he liked this young, sarcastic, handsome human. His heart pounded as Jayce suffered. Knowing that he was standing by

and doing nothing while Jayce's agony tore through him was more than he could take. He'd trusted Rune and he'd brought him to the temple for help, for more information. Not for this. Yet he raised no hand to stop his master or the coming moments. So what did all of this mean? Why was it being allowed? What was Jayce's part in this?

Rune knew the way of visions. They were to show him possibilities, but not the whys or hows, but it still did something to his mind and aching heart to know that Jayce could be made to suffer like he was witnessing. Had he been the one to bring Jayce's pain? How did they get to this point? Had he betrayed Jayce? Again, questions that could not be answered by the vision.

Then Jayce's eyes opened and they zeroed in on Rune. They burned like the firelight, fierce and unforgiving. Golden and bright. A glow that reflected more than the light of the flames between them. A shiver traveled along his back until the hair on his nape felt charged.

In that moment, he felt like prey.

Jayce's throat convulsed then he dropped his head back and roared to the heavens.

Rune lurched awake on his side, blinking to clear the pictures in his sleep-blurred view. The echo of dream-Jayce's screams faded. Dim light was beginning to fill the room. The first hint of morning, but the in-between when shadows still existed. Reaching mentally for Iba, he found her flying above the trees, enjoying the growing dawn while keeping a lookout. The night cooled air brushed over her feathers as she soared and dipped with the roaming breezes and drafts. He loved when she flew, and he could feel the pureness of the moment through her. *Thank you, heart. You take good care of me.*

She preened sending affection while her eyes scanned the ground. Then felt her attention grow focused as she straightened her flight.

He couldn't see how far out she was, but in the distance there was a group of riders moving at a steady clip. He recognized the blonde from the door attack. She wore different garments, more leathers, but there was no mistaking her petite stature. And she wasn't alone. The *sabra* had gathered reinforcements.

Time wasn't on their side. They needed to wake and get moving.

That was when he realized Jayce had curled around him in his sleep, nestled against his spine like a living blanket. They'd fallen

50

asleep above any coverings so he'd probably done so seeking warmth. Regardless of how or why, Rune hated to make him move. It had been a decade if not two since he'd last had a lover of any note. To a mage, training and growing knowledge was the only priority.

His attraction for the brunet was unlike any he could recall. None that had made a mark in his memory could be found with Jayce's strong arms wrapped around his chest. Hot breath ruffled through his hair. And when he shifted his weight, the hard press of Jayce's morning arousal was apparent. He stifled his groan before it could slip between his lips.

Why you? Why now? Not that it mattered. Jayce wasn't blaming him yet for the way his world was about to change. He would. And with that blame, he'd grow to hate and resent Rune. With all of that still pressing on them, there was no time to assuage their waking bodies. They couldn't do anything about either of their morning conditions with hell descending on them.

He lifted Jayce's arm carefully and slipped from the bed. Stomping into his boots quietly, he clasped his cloak around his neck and palmed his staff. Before opening the door, he murmured a blurring spell over Jayce's sleeping form. Then outside, a protection spell on the door.

He would take care of his morning needs and get the horses ready for travel.

Maybe Jayce wouldn't hate him too badly for making him ride again today if he returned bearing food and drink.

ࡠ⸎

"Jayce," a voice whispered close by. Jayce moaned pitifully. "You need to wake. It's time to leave."

He mumbled. Drew a breath. And then he smelled it. Hot. Dark. "Oh, god, please say that's coffee."

"It's coffee," Rune deadpanned.

Jayce huffed a laugh then opened his eyes. The sun was barely rising. There was still a gray tinge to everything. "Already?" He was not embarrassed that it was nearly a whimper, not in the least. It was far too early. He tried to burrow deeper into the bedding.

Rune offered the steaming mug in an attempt to lure him into wakefulness. "We must. The trackers have found our trail."

Jayce relented and sat, then grasped the mug, preparing for the bitterness. Even as good as it smelled, he tried to ready his tongue for the coffee he doubted was going to be coffee like he knew it.

He drew a sip. Smacked his lips. Then drew another. His taste buds weren't screaming in bitter agony. He pried open an eyelid to stare up at the blond beside him. "You put sugar in it?"

"It seemed like something you would prefer," he offered, looking away with a small shrug.

"That was thoughtful," Jayce remarked. "Thank you." He drank half in a large swallow. The heat felt good hitting his stomach. He clutched the mug close, trying to make his brain lock into a usable gear. The coffee was helping, however, Rune's next words made waking up far less pleasant.

"We do need to go. We have maybe half a day's lead on them as they're also riding. I have food we can eat while we're moving."

"Fine." He gulped down the rest of the coffee to put the mug aside, not bothering to voice his complaints. He knew on this ground, he'd lose and arguing would only cost them time. Jayce stood to his socked feet, wincing as his thighs screamed and his knees tried to buckle. "Oh, shit." He stumbled when his legs threatened to give out completely, but Rune caught him with an arm wrapped around his chest. Jayce gulped. He was so close. God, why did he have to be so beautiful? Jayce thought he could drown in his eyes alone. He really wanted to hate this man for tearing him away from his life, and thrusting him into this crazy quest prophecy bullshit.

Except he really hadn't done anything to make Jayce hate him, well, barring the abduction part. He hadn't hurt Jayce, had kept him safe, kept him protected. And he was helping to keep him standing on mutinous legs waving the white flag after the previous day's abuse.

He had no idea why the flair of need was so strong, or why he was responding to this one man when what he really wanted–what he *needed*–was to wake up on his couch after falling asleep from working on his PowerPoint assignment all night.

Worse, he was so attracted to him, he wanted to eat him by the spoonful, licking every inch of his strong body.

Except with the world he was now in, he didn't know if there was such a thing as gay, if men loved men. If love was used as a weapon like it was on Earth against those who were not a societal norm. He needed to wait and see, and keep himself alert.

"Steady," Rune offered kindly, sympathy filling his bright blue eyes when he stepped away, seemingly assured Jayce wasn't going to fall on his ass.

Jayce stiffly sat and started to pull on his boots, glad his private thoughts could not be so readily known. They had other details that needed their immediate focus. He needed to relieve himself before he got too much further. His bladder was informing him it was a very important focus at the moment.

"How far is the temple?" He pushed into the heel of his boot before trying to stand again. He'd been warned his body was going to rebel after being in the saddle all day. He felt it would be unnecessary to stress exactly how underemphasized that warning had been.

"We'll be there before sundown if we leave now."

Standing once more, he danced on his toes, rocking back and forth on his heels to warm up his thighs and calves. "Okay. Not saying I won't complain, but let's go."

Rune gathered his bag and staff, and Jayce threw his own over a shoulder. Rune whispered words at the door then quietly undid the lock. The door still creaked but as the building was starting to show signs of life elsewhere it seemed louder in the quiet hallway.

He followed Rune outside, weaving past buildings until they reached the stable. Their horses were saddled and tied to posts not appearing any more enthused than he felt to be starting the day so early. Rune neared, gripping Jayce's horse's bridle. "Up. I'll give you a boost."

Jayce grimaced as he lifted his leg to the stirrup. "This does get easier, right?" he griped.

"And there's the first complaint of the day." Rune winked when Jayce pursed his lips.

"I haven't even started," he warned.

Rune dipped his head in answer. "Challenge accepted."

Jayce bit his lip to not smile. In some ways, it was so easy with Rune, like a comforting friendship that stretched years. It didn't make a lot of sense, but he put it to the anomaly of what his life had become. Then he was heaving himself up and got a hand on his ass to help him get centered. "You sure you didn't do that to grope me?" he asked, staring down from above.

Rune's attempt to appear playfully affronted made him laugh through his groan as he settled. "Even as magnificent an ass as it is, that ass must still be on the horse before I'll look at it again."

Jayce winced. "Oh, *ouch.*"

Rune snickered before striding to his own animal and hefting into the saddle. "Ready?"

"If I must be."

Rune tapped his mount with a booted heel and led them in a direction only he knew. Jayce's followed without a lot of convincing. He grimaced as he settled against leather.

They rode in companionable silence as they filled their bellies with the warm rolls and sausages Rune grabbed them for their breakfast. Jayce had to admit, while the food was definitely more organic, there was something savory in the simplicity of its homemade style that made it taste better than he would expect.

Iba made an appearance but only long enough to get a snack and take off again. He envied her that freedom, but then again she went where she wanted. Apparently, Jayce had a prophecy to fulfill.

Chapter 9

Rune studied the shadows' movements on the ground, gauging how long they'd been traveling. Stands of trees were interspersed with gaping views of the openness surrounding them. Sunlight shining down on them made the day seem so peaceful when he knew it was anything but. Iba had been keeping tabs on the *sabra* and their trackers. They were gaining on their two horses. Because of Jayce's inexperience, they hadn't been able to travel as speedily as the pack of *sabra*. Unfortunately, they had to increase their speed regardless of his inability if they didn't want to have to fight their pursuers. Six on one was more than he wanted to face alone.

"We need to put some distance. The *sabra* have reached the tavern."

Jayce groaned, clutching the saddle. "Okay." He raised his knees to stretch sore thighs. "I'll do what I can but I'm dying here."

"Not yet you're not," Rune offered.

"Says the man who's been on a horse before," Jayce retorted.

He tapped his mount into a light jog knowing Jayce was doing his best, and refusing to waste energy on a verbal battle. They rode in tense silence, but the pressure of their pursuers was biting at his nerves. He knew they were gaining.

And he feared they weren't going to outdistance them.

The ground leveled considerably as they traveled toward the coast where the Windwise temple stood. He searched the horizon for any sign that they were close to the cliffs, but as of yet, there was still open ground before them.

He heard Iba's cries in his mind. She was warning him. He swallowed. They were closing in.

"Hang on tightly, and whatever you do, do not let go of the saddle," he ordered. Then he pressed the horses into a gallop. Jayce yelped as his own mount leaped into a run to not be left behind, but a quick glance showed him holding on. He'd fisted a thick hunk of the animal's mane, leaning close. The dust would alert those following but it was a risk he had to take. They had to reach the temple. They would be protected there.

"Rune! I'm slipping!"

Rune quickly slowed his animal and aligned with Jayce's. "I have you." He caught him by a shoulder and slotted him back into the saddle. "Don't let your feet slip out of the stirrups."

"I can't. My legs are shot." He was panting, sweat on his brow and dust clinging to him. "I can't hold on anymore."

"Give me your reins." He folded them over his hand. He glared into the distance behind them. He could almost feel their pursuers breathing down his neck. "Now, both hands on the pommel. Grip with your thighs. They're gaining on us. We have to run."

"Are you sure you're not trying to kill me first?"

Rune grimaced. "No. But I don't want to watch you die, either."

"Fine," he grunted. He curled his hands firmly around the saddle. "Let's go."

Rune started the horses with an easy lope to be able to lead Jayce's, moving them into a steady gallop.

Determination and speed wasn't going to be enough. Iba was cawing at him. He didn't bother to look over his shoulder. It wasn't long after that he heard Jayce's cries His burgeoning fear was loud and clear.

"Shit! I can see them."

"Stay low in your saddle," he shouted over a shoulder in warning.

A war cry filled the air.

"Shitshitshit. Rune!"

"Hang on!" he ground out. *Please, hang on.* Then, *Iba, distract them! Slow them down! Aim for the leader!*

A moment later, there were shouts from behind them as Iba dive-bombed their group.

He hunted the surrounding berms for anything he could manipulate to slow them down more. Ahead on the left were several trees close enough to the path to be of use. Staring at the bases, he spoke to their roots, commanding them to his will. With a grinding, groaning, rending rumble, he forced them through packed soil to shoot across the road as their pursuers flew past them. Like whipcords, they unfurled and snapped, spearing one of the horses. The closest screamed as it reared on hind legs, trying to avoid the snake-like strikes of the brutal roots. Its ungainly attempt to evade forced it into colliding into the closest rider's mount next to it with a sickening crunch as hooves connected with bone, two going down in a heap with their riders. The crash of horses and hooves slowed them all down but not enough. Four would be a little easier to fight alone. He couldn't look behind him to see what else was going on.

The following bloodcurdling war cry was too close. He hissed under his breath. He ducked, hugging his horse's neck, urging it into a frantic gallop.

The next thing he knew, his horse was collapsing forward, her front legs buckling and he went flying through the air.

"Rune!" Jayce screamed.

Still clutching the reins to Jayce's mount, he flung them free but not before Jayce's horse whipped a bone-jarring swerve, throwing Jayce from the saddle into the grasses as it rolled over its saddle. Rune heard the loud snap of a leg breaking followed by the terrified scream from Jayce's mount. He shuddered, lamenting the animal's loud cries of pain.

Jayce disappeared out of Rune's view and he scoured the immediate area, searching for any sign of him. Arrows rained around him making him stay low. "Jayce!" *Iba! The archer!*

A groan from yards away told him he was alive. For the moment.

Rune immediately started spelling fireballs, throwing them in quick succession at the remaining charging *sabra* as he stumbled to his feet. The bow and arrow attacker was the next to go down, aided by Iba as she sought eyes and exposed flesh. She was the other *sabra* from the attack at Jayce's domicile. He recognized the blonde sprinting on foot in Jayce's direction with her axe at the ready.

His first fireball curved wide in front of her, sinking to disappear against the sparse coastal grass. It didn't slow her down one whit. He cursed under his breath, and he refreshed the fireball spell. Iba was working on distracting the others, giving him a chance. Rune had to stop the blonde. He feared what she would do to Jayce when she reached him with that red, feral berserker light in her eyes. Lurching forward, he kept up the assault of fireballs. She was closer than he was, reaching Jayce before he could.

"Damn you, Jayce! Why did you have to go with him?" The axe whipped over her head, spinning savagely before whistling through the air as it slammed downward. It struck plain dirt. Jayce had rolled out of its deadly path at the last second.

Her focused attention on slaughtering Jayce left her defenseless as a fireball struck her back. A direct attack was going to be his only option. She wasn't going to be deterred from her goal. She screamed, dropping the axe on her next upswing. The stench of burning hair, skin, and leather filled the winds. Even as flames licked at her, she refused to go down. Snarls and curses fell from her lips. Berserker energy was almost unstoppable.

Trampled grasses rustled and grunts followed as Jayce crawled away from her.

"Grab her axe!" Rune yelled over the noise of the remaining two evading Iba and his fireballs. They were trying to rush Jayce but well-timed fireballs were making them stagger and balk, torn between killing Jayce or attacking Rune to stop him. Rune was closing the gap to get better aimed shots as they all converged on the lone man. Smoke was filling the air as dry grass smoldered from the fireballs and falling flames of his hits.

Jayce lurched to his knees, clawing at the haft of the axe and yanking it out of her reach. "What the fuck, Raquel!" He scrambled out of her range while she absently slapped at the flames on her body, reaching him her only goal. "Why are you trying to kill me?"

"Because you can't succeed."

It was so flatly said that Jayce stood there agog. "By killing me?" he screamed, panting harshly. "Succeed at what? I don't understand!"

Rune saw the exact moment Jayce realized he was facing a life threatening foe. Burned on almost every inch of visible skin, her leather crisped to remnants that hanged ablaze without stopping the flames, she closed the gap between them intent on her goal as though she wasn't burning alive where she stood. He palmed the axe and hauled it above his shoulder in a white-knuckled grip.

"The Valda-Cree must die!" With her leathers scorched into raw skin, blood dripping from burn wounds that had split down to the bone, she snarled as she launched through the air. Rune saw it the same time

Jayce must have. The glint of polished steel in her hand. Another fireball engulfed her in a flaming blast. He immediately threw more at the last two berserkers, trying to circle around Jayce. Their screams wailed through the air. They fell to the ground, their rage no longer providing energy.

Raquel never once looked in their direction as she lunged for Jayce.

Jayce swung the axe wildly. It landed with a bone-splintering thud, cleaving into her middle.

Raquel staggered while blood spurted from the gaping wound in her side. The blade made a sucking sound when he yanked it free, ready on his shoulder for another swing.

"You were my friend," he spat.

Her slender body folded to the ground. Blood began to pool around her as the berserker energy in her red gaze faded. He panted, waiting for several seconds, his body stiff with white-knuckled fingers clutched around the axe's wood handle. The silence that dropped around them after the screams and sounds of battle felt pervasive.

"Oh, god." Jayce fell to his knees like a string was cut, the axe barely supported by limp fingers. "Why?"

Rune stumbled and crashed to the ground next to him. "Are you hurt?" He didn't have to look to know she was dead. He didn't want to look. He knew how much damage the fireballs had done.

Jayce swallowed thickly but shook his head. He was scratched up, and there was a bruise on his forehead but otherwise he looked whole. "Didn't break anything when my horse went down."

Rune studied the fight area. All six were dead, somehow. And they'd survived. "We need to go."

"She... I killed her. She was my friend." The axe head thudded to the ground.

Jayce was swaying where he sat, trying not to look in the berserker's direction while not really focusing on anything. "Why?" His eyes were pleading with Rune. *Why him? Why now? Why did he have to kill his friend?* He knew those and more were truly being asked, and he didn't have a single answer, not yet. "What did she mean? What was she saying about me succeeding? At what?" He choked as he gasped, the overwhelming stench making them both breathe in slow gulps. "I killed her."

Jayce was going to go into shock if he didn't get him moving. He eyed the axe. With a squeeze to his shoulder, he said, "I don't know yet. Not all of it. And not enough that we can delay here. The scavengers will come. We need to move on. We need to get you where it's safe." It put Jayce's focus on something other than the woman at his feet and his own part in her death. Rune needed him safe. This was only the beginning. He nodded toward the axe at his side. "Bring it. The spells inscrolled on it may be able to tell us who hired her and her kin." Reaching shaky legs, he offered Jayce a hand to stand. "Let's find one of their horses. We can double up and get to the temple."

Rune stumbled to his downed mount and yanked the arrow out of its hide to toss into the dirt. The way the poor beast was gasping told him a lung had been punctured. Whether by the arrow or by the fall, he didn't know. "Sorry, lovely." He put a hand to its chest and stopped its heart to end its suffering. "I'm so sorry."

Looking up, he found Jayce squatting next to the horse he'd been riding, tears falling silently. Rune ripped his saddlebags free and managed to reach his feet until he shakily sank down with Jayce. "I'm sorry. They both tried so hard for us."

"I know a broken leg is the end for a horse, but I can't leave her in pain."

"Untie your bags. I'll make sure she doesn't feel it anymore." He forced his words to be even. No reason to enlighten Jayce that magic wasn't always meant to be a good thing. Taking a life, even an animal's to end its suffering, was no small choice or to be made lightly.

Jayce blinked, big golden-brown eyes awash in sorrow. His mouth opened, but then he pinched his jaw tight and shook his head. Rune didn't have time or words to explain. Jayce shot to his feet and stalked to the saddle, his back to Rune.

Rune did the only thing he could for the animal.

Once they had gathered their belongings, they hunted for any of the remaining horses and found one not too far from the road, grazing. Tying their bags down, Rune hefted himself tiredly into the saddle, then after sliding a foot out of the left stirrup, he offered a hand. "Up behind me. We'll be there soon."

Jayce didn't utter a single complaint when he wrapped his arms around Rune's middle and clung like he was his only lifeline.

What scared Rune, was he feared he might be. If the screamed words of the blonde were any clue, then he wasn't wrong. Someone had enough foresight to keep eyes on Jayce. He simply didn't know if the *sabra* were a recent addition to his life, or how long they, or anyone, had been following Jayce on a world that knew nothing of him or of Kielbos. He'd heard her screams, the shrill charges against Jayce. Who else knew? Where were they? And how much danger was Jayce in now that he'd been brought to Kielbos?

Rune kept the horse at a steady gallop, intent on reaching Windwise. Jayce had fallen silent and that worried him. His grip remained strong with his chest pressed into Rune's back, but his silence felt wrong.

Finally, there was a change in the air. A hint of sea breeze. Relief was hard to hide. "We're almost there."

Jayce's head pressed into his spine, but there were no words. He accepted that he'd heard. The day was growing late, but there were still a couple hours of sunlight. Rune knew they were both done with traveling. He was ready for a hot bath and a full meal.

And then, on the horizon, he saw the first wall to the temple. He nudged the horse in that direction, veering off the path to cut through the low coastal grasses. Gradually, Windwise came into clearer view. Its tall spires and towers offset by the large altar dome of the main chambers. All white stone, it reflected late day sunlight to glow a brilliant yellow and orange hue that could only be seen a few weeks of the year by the sun's descent and the planet's turn.

This was one of those days. Even as many times as he'd witnessed it, its beauty still caught his breath. Rune eased the horse's pace and landed a hand on Jayce's knee and squeezed to bring his attention forward. "That's the temple. We're almost there."

He nodded, his hands gripping tightly against his midsection that he'd heard, a heavy exhale rocking his body. Rune frowned. Still not a word.

The horse's hooves clattered over the growing stone and rock bed of the ground until he was pulling up on the reins to slow their gallop. Three bodies exited the main doorway. He immediately sighed with relief.

The person standing on the steps in the middle was Master Theil.

He and Jayce were safe.

Chapter 10

Jayce hurt. There was no other way to describe it. His body was screaming at him because of the long hours horseback riding and then taking the projectile nosedive off the back of his horse that left him shaken and breathless. He felt like one huge bruise. At least nothing had been broken. But that thought only brought more anguishing pain. His horse. He'd heard the snap of bone when it went down. And the scream. That sound was going to haunt him for a very long time. He'd never meant to hurt anything, or anyone. And now he'd hurt a horse.

And killed Raquel.

He squished his eyes tight, pushing the memory of the ugly blade sinking into her side far away. He'd known her for three years. He hadn't seen Helen, but had a gut feeling she had been one of the riders the horses had taken down when Rune had done whatever he'd done to the trees that made the horses scream and fall all over each other. He hadn't been able to look, keeping close to his mount's neck and fighting like hell to stay in the saddle at the breakneck speeds they were racing.

Being ripped from his saddle was a blur when Rune went down. Then he'd been looking up at a red-eyed, enraged Raquel and only for the sake of self-preservation had he been able to roll out of the way of that dropping axe.

He didn't understand what was happening. None of this was making sense. All he wanted to do was go home, back to the life he knew. His mediocre life at college, where there was no excitement of being attacked by axe-wielding maniacs. Where fireballs didn't exist. Where ravens couldn't communicate.

He felt the horse's gait slow and eased the clutched grip he held on Rune, trying to peer over his shoulder to take it all in now that they were closer. Rune had pointed out the temple but he'd barely looked. Coming closer to it, it took his breath away, at least enough to distract his tumbling thoughts.

Beautiful white brick that could have been polished limestone reflected a brilliant glowing aura of gold, oranges, and reds. The peaks towered over him, and he had to crane his neck to see the very tips.

He looked around when the horse finally stopped in what looked to be some kind of courtyard and was surprised to see two young men rush up with arms outstretched.

"They'll help you down," Rune offered quietly, circling a wrist to get his attention.

Jayce flexed his fingers, relinquishing the tense grip keeping him pinned to Rune's spine. Rolling his shoulders, he let out a breath. Then braced his hands on the horse's rump to swing a leg over.

The ground felt weird under his feet when they touched dirt. Trying to stand, he almost went down right there, unable to hold his own weight. His legs didn't want to work right. When he felt kind hands on his elbows and waist, he was grateful they were there when his knees threatened to buckle.

"Come inside," one said gently. Rune was sliding down next to him from the horse.

"I'm going to take care of the horse. I'll be right with you," Rune stated, patting its neck with a hand on the bridle.

Jayce was slowly feeling steadier standing, though his limbs still felt shaky after he dismounted, vibrating with the percussive rhythm from the long ride. He locked gazes with Rune. Silently, he pleaded *don't leave me*. Rune gave him an easy smile, his eyes saying he wouldn't be long. God, he hoped he was reading him right. After everything he'd been through, he didn't want to be handed off like a baton.

Gingerly walking with the two at his sides guiding him toward the stairs, he groaned when he had to put his weight on each climbing step. Yeah, those pains and sore muscles were coming to roost now.

"Thank you, Brin, Ritter. Welcome to the Temple Windwise." The man speaking stood tall and proud in a lord of the manor type of way, an inch or two taller than Jayce. He was obviously the one in charge here. His sapphire blue robes hung from solid shoulders to his ankles. Long, black hair swept down his back with thick stripes of silver from his temples. He bowed his head in greeting. It was less of a surprise now that he was also an elf. "It is a pleasure to make your acquaintance. I am Master Theil."

Jayce thanked the two at his elbows for their help when they made sure he could stand on his own before leaving him, then said, "It's nice to meet you too though I'm not thrilled with being here. I don't understand what's been happening."

Master Theil motioned with a hand to join him at his side. "I imagine you have a lot of questions. But first, you have had a rough journey, or so it would seem, since Rune found you." A flicked gaze at the center of his forehead seemed to confirm why he'd had a headache for most of the afternoon. He must've whacked his head when he jettisoned from his horse. "A meal and some rest first, yes?"

"I would like that." His stomach growled loudly, in case he had any ideas of arguing.

Master Theil chuckled. "Come. We'll share a meal and then one of the younglings will show you to a room."

Jayce took in the interior of the temple once they crossed solid wood doors standing wide open. The ceiling was high above his head, carved and painted with frescoes depicting what looked like battles and signs of the seasons with moons and suns. Elegant pillars were spaced at intervals with a few doorways on either side beyond the pillars. Veering to the right, they soon entered an antechamber with wide windows that overlooked the sea in the distance, beyond the edge of the cliffs where seabirds swooped and called. It was impossible to ignore the full beauty and he found himself stopping to look.

"That is a stunning sight."

Master Theil paused as well, his hands cupped behind his back. "I've spent many hours watching the force of the seas. To some it is never changing, a vast chasm of water and nothing else, and to others, all it does is change, with tides and life, a challenge to be bested. I find it peaceful considering the ways the seas can change, harness so much energy and life." He drew a breath and exhaled evenly. "Today, the seas are calm, forgiving."

"And when they are stormy?"

"Equally as harsh a master as any on this earth. Nature is not one to be trifled with."

"Do all mages share a natural energy through nature?"

"Most. Some have a different source, but those of our kind, of Rune's kin, we are more tightly wound through nature and the energies that nature and the earth grant us. I can't speak for the other races. Many don't share the same beliefs as the elven societies, but that is a discussion for another time. Come, the meal should be ready for you both." His voice didn't reveal a lot but Jayce was positive there was more he wasn't willing to say. All energies had a natural positive and negative counterbalance. Were there bad mages too? Bad magic? And how much of that affected what was happening to him? When he had a chance, and when he wasn't about to crumple from sheer exhaustion he would have to ask Rune.

He followed to the end of the hall, his gaze occasionally being pulled to the sun's rays being split by the rolling waves as they crashed off the cliffs further away. Jayce had never been so close to a sea or an ocean. It was beauty and danger, and he felt its pull in his bones.

The doors at the other end of the hall were split wide in invitation as they approached. He spotted Rune already waiting in the room near the set table. As slow as he'd been shuffling, he wasn't that surprised, and was grateful the elf elder wasn't hammering at him for his inability to walk normal at the moment. Surviving the fall he'd taken and the fight with minimal injuries and no broken bones was a win as far as he was concerned. He shook his head when the memories started. He couldn't focus on that, not yet. His mind was scattered, and he simply didn't have the energy for that deep of thought.

Rune bowed low at the waist as they approached. "Master Theil."

Master Theil dipped his head in answer. "Good journey's return to you, young Rune. I see you were successful."

He met Jayce's gaze with a slight grin playing over his lips. "A journey not without its challenges."

Three chairs slid unaided from beneath the far table's end where three plates waited. "Please, let us eat, and I will answer what I can, to give you both a night's rest."

"I thank you, Master Theil." Rune waited for Master Theil to sit at the head of the table then sat himself, with Jayce sitting on the third waiting seat opposite. He squeaked—him, not the chair—when it moved on its own to settle against the table.

Another young elf came up to his shoulder with a water bowl. He peered questioningly at Rune, and watched as someone did the same on the other side at Rune's shoulder. As soon as Rune dipped his hands in the bowl and rubbed them with the water, Jayce twisted to do the same. He blanched when he realized how dirty and bloody his hands, and his clothes, were. He staunchly hadn't thought of the fight with Raquel and what had happened, even with evidence of it being cleared from his skin to enjoy his meal. He hadn't wanted to. Right now wasn't the right moment either. He then wiped his hands on a waiting cloth. *It's just washing our hands.* Easy enough. He could ignore the color of the water for now.

Dishes were brought out and soon they were saying little as he fed his belly. There was some type of fish, a meatball in a flavorful mushroom and wine gravy, and root vegetables seasoned with salt and spices. Watching Rune from beneath his lashes, he mimicked him as he used the bread rolls instead of utensils to eat his meal. Jayce supposed the common fork and knife weren't all that common here. He had yet to see any, anywhere.

Soon the dishes were all but licked clean. Wine was offered, as well as a warmed cider. He chose the cider after making sure it wasn't the apple ale he'd already learned made him drunk.

Rune chuckled at the memory, catching his questioning stare when he gripped the mug. "No, only pressed apples heated through with spices."

Jayce cautiously drew a sip of the heated drink, then sighed. *Yum.* Tension almost evaporated from various muscles as he finally allowed himself a moment to breathe.

"I understand you have questions," Master Theil offered once their plates were taken away, enjoying a glass of wine as well, even though he had only nibbled at a plate of cheeses and crackers.

Jayce did have questions. So many, but where to start?

"I guess. I'm still processing that I'm even here, and *why* I'm here. I know it's only been three days, but it already feels like so much longer. The question that I can't seem to get an answer to is why am I here at all? I know of the prophecy now, but what is my part of that? Rune says I'm Valda-Cree, which I can't see. I'm not magic, and I know I'm not some kind of shapeshifter or whatever he called it." He huffed a breath. "I'm just me."

Rune sat across from him, his hands cupped around his own cider cup. "There are parts of the prophecy that no one can truly agree on."

"Not arguing that. I said it sounded vague in the beginning. It still does." Jayce hunched over a little.

"Only time will tell," Master Theil offered. "The question that really must be asked is, when your options are presented, will you embrace them, or spurn them?"

Jayce shook his head. "I really don't know. I never in a million years imagined I'd be fighting one of my closest friends to the death."

Master Theil's eyebrow rose a smidgen.

"He was being guarded on the other side by *sabra*. They followed us through and caught up with us on the outskirts of Windmere." He looked into his mug. "It wasn't an easy battle."

Master Theil's long fingers thrummed lightly on the stone table. "*Sabra*? Really?"

"What made them so special?"

"*Sabra* are berserkers but are trained in the art of adaptation. They do not look like killers, and can be at your throat before you suspect them. They are trained in the ways of war and know of many ways to kill a person."

"But they were girls I knew for years." Jayce couldn't believe it. He'd played D&D with them, talked about homework, walked from the apartments, and even from the diner with them because they said they didn't feel safe.

"Not all women are nice," Master Theil pointed out. "Some will slit your throat for money alone."

Jayce swallowed slowly, the memory of the axe and all the blood making him push his cider away, unable to stomach any right then. "So they only pretended to be friends to stay close." He wasn't into girls, but knowing his friendship wasn't worth its own weight hurt. That they'd been hired to do those things with him as a job. Betrayal burned.

"The fact is, they won't be the only ones looking for you. Whoever set them to watch you, already knows about you, or has suspicions," Rune offered, though by his tone he was trying to at least be kind with the warning.

Jayce pushed out a breath. "So, what does that mean?"

"There's only one thing we can do," Rune offered. "To keep you safe, we must follow through. The visions told me I had to bring you to Windmere. That it was you and you alone that held the key to the future of the Valda-Cree."

"You keep saying that, and that I'm Valda-Cree. Are there any others? Why am I the only one you're trying to find?" *And what makes it so important to you?* But he bit his tongue on that one. He didn't trust Rune's motives one hundred percent, trusting Master Theil even less. He did trust Rune to keep him alive. But that particular trust was about as far as he could go.

Master Theil spoke. "The others went into hiding centuries ago. The Valda-Cree lineage was broken when the king died a horrible death, a betrayal of one of his most trusted advisors."

Rune was listening as well. "I didn't know that."

"I was there," Master Theil offered solemnly. "The kingdoms collapsed. Caduthien fell. Chaos ensued for months until the council played their hand and picked their new ruler, someone they could control. The powers that supported the true royal line of the Valda-Cree were given an ultimatum. Join the new rulers or be put to death. Many of us fled. Those who were too weak, were murdered. Some tried to fight, but if they survived, they vanished."

"So the new rulers? Who are they?"

Master Theil gazed unseeing at his own mug, then raised his head after coming to a decision. "I believe you've already come to the conclusion from the little we've spoken that all magic has a good and an evil counterpart."

Jayce nodded, raptly listening.

"I truly don't know much about who is currently on the throne, as I've avoided all direct contact with the royals since the murder of King Bail. The usurper ruling line has a corrupt magic at their disposal and that magic has only grown over the centuries. In the time since the passing of the king's lineage, that corruption has grown more and more out of balance with the natural order of things."

"That's why the visions are saying the evil was now. It's always been here, but it's grown too far out of balance and is leading to destruction." Rune played with his own mug as he thought over this new information.

Jayce filled his lungs and exhaled slowly. "And they're now stronger than whoever else is still in charge."

"Yes. I believe the reigning king has become a puppet to this insidious magic. As for who that is…" Master Theil's shoulders sagged with defeat. "The king's advisor is my twin brother, Carden."

Chapter 11

Rune sank back, fighting to keep the shock of Master Theil's revelation off his face and sincerely doubting he was successful. "Your brother?"

"We have not spoken since the time of King Bail, but I know he lives and I know from friendly eyes surrounding the palace that the current king hasn't been seen in a fortnight. Carden is acting in his stead."

"Is the current ruler a human?" Rune needed more information. From the tense tilt of Jayce's shoulders, he could tell he was also listening avidly.

"Yes. A simple man from what I can gather, born and raised in the castle as was his father."

"So Carden has had unfettered control over the shaping of the throne for generations."

"Yes." Master Theil frowned, not happy with having to share that. "But he cannot proclaim himself as king with any validity as the crown will not respond to a mage's magic. It never has."

"Respond? What does that mean?" Rune's confusion matched Jayce's. How did he know none of this?

"The Valda-Cree crown holds a deep magic, justice and peace. It only ever awakens when a ruler with the blood of the Valda-Cree claims it. It's a way to proclaim a true ruler of the royal blood."

"A litmus test," Jayce muttered. Rune didn't bother to have him explain. He deciphered the intent.

"A test, yes," Master Theil confirmed. "In all the centuries the crown has been with the current linage, the crown's power has been dormant. I would be willing to say that most people of our time have forgotten its true power. Truthfully, it's been so long since there has been talk of it, or speculation to its power, it may not even exist any longer. I truly don't know. It hasn't been a thought to me. The one thing I do know about it is only the Valda-Cree with their own balanced magic of nature, animal, and spirit can bring it back to life, can keep the balance across our lands with so many different breeds and layers of magic."

Jayce gulped. "Wait. Say that again? The balance part."

Master Theil turned his unique piercing stare toward Jayce. "There must be balance. Mages have the ability to call on magic and earth's bounty for their strengths. Others can share an animal spirit, which gives them the benefit of spirit and man to be able to skin shift. Only the Valda-Cree share all three: nature, magic, and beast. They are harmony. That is what makes them the royal line."

"The power of three," Jayce whispered.

"Yes."

He dropped his head into upturned palms, massaging his temples. He barked a laugh. "It's not possible." He was whispering under his breath while rocking his head in disbelief.

"What's not possible?" Rune asked.

"Me! It's not me. It can't be." His shocked cry whittled down to a defiant whisper quickly. "It can't be."

"We don't know if it is you," Rune hedged. "All I know is you carry the blood, and I can sense your magic." He'd never told anyone of his interpretations of his own visions, not even Master Theil. There was too great a chance he was wrong, or that an unknown power or influence would impact Jayce's endeavors. The future had to be borne by him and him alone. Thus why he'd claimed his station was guide and guard only.

"But I'm not a shapeshifter."

"It's skin shifter," Master Theil corrected. "You don't lose your humanity, you become one being, as though the beast which claims you has wrapped you into its body."

Jayce snorted roughly. "Yeah, hate to break it to you, but in my time, that's a fantasy, and it's the same thing. I can't become, or share, an animal's anything."

Master Theil's fingers tapped restlessly again. "We shall see." He seemed to come to a decision as he said, "But that is enough for tonight. You both need to wash and rest from your day. Rune?"

"Yes, Master Theil?"

"You are to continue with the visions as you've seen. I will be in meditation but please find me later if you have need of me."

The chairs slid from the table, catching Jayce off guard, and he jerked on his seat with a quiet yelp when their chairs pushed away from the table with nary a whisper of sound. Rune hid his smile. Master Theil was a master, but he was also a bit of a prankster. And yes, his seafoam green eyes were twinkling as he departed from the table. Another way to show Master Theil's inclusion of a wary Jayce.

Rune waited for Master Theil to leave the room before rounding the table. "I can show you to a room, but after, I have a surprise for you."

Jayce groaned with a spark of petulance. "Nothing that's going to require me killing anyone, right?"

"I promise, no killing required."

"Then I'm all yours."

Surprisingly, Rune's stomach fluttered a little at the words, knowing they were flippant and not intended the way his heart heard them. He needed to push that desire far away. Desire and need were not part of the visions, regardless of his body's insistence. He walked with a steady pace, unwilling to study the feeling as he led Jayce through the halls. They went down a flight of steps and he opened another heavy door, grabbing a torch on his way. "The bedchambers are down here, cooled by the cliffs, sea tides, and winds. There will be a fresh change of clothing for you to wear. Once you are changed, I will be waiting in the hall. I have something I want to show you that will make you feel better."

Jayce waited for him to open the oak door then sighed in resignation. "No bed, huh?" The torchlight illuminated several feet of space. It was exactly the same as every other room in the temple. The same room style as every acolyte who'd ever stood within this building's walls for training.

"It is a pallet and it is freshly stuffed. Clean garments are on the stand with sandals beneath." He waited for Jayce to enter then followed, lighting the fat candle on the table. "Once you are changed, leave your current clothes to be cleaned and join me outside in the hall." He started playing with the pouch at his waist then dropped his hand to his side, pushing his fretting far away. He really wanted Jayce to like his next surprise, but wasn't sure he would, given how distracted by worry and exhaustion he appeared to be.

Jayce ran a hand through his hair. He must not have hidden his disappointment as well as he'd hoped, because he offered, "Sorry. I'm... I didn't mean anything by it. I'm not used to this. I'm tired and I'm sore. So much is different. Everything I know is non-existent here."

Rune put a hand, a mere ghost of a touch to his forearm. "I know. You've been put through a lot and it's because of me. Let me do something for you. Please."

"Okay. I'll be out in a minute."

Rune nodded and escaped to the hall to wait. He didn't want to think of Jayce stripping out of his road-weary clothing to nothing, but then, once he had, he couldn't stop the images of toned skin from appearing in his mind. Thankfully for his sanity, it only took a few minutes for Jayce to appear in his doorway. "I'm ready."

"Good. Follow me." He led them down another stairwell from the acolyte sleeping hall, going ever deeper into a carved darkness.

Jayce kept pace, not saying anything until they reached the chamber of pools. He froze right inside the entrance, his mouth agape. "This is amazing."

Several pools gave off steam with a fairly strong scent of sulfur. The walls glittered from the torchlight, both mineral and humidity refracting the bouncing flames to create an underworld of glistening beauty.

Rune pointed to pools several yards away. "Those pools are for bathing. They cycle constantly and stay fresh. Those are for soaking, which is actually why I brought you."

"You remembered." Jayce was beaming. Goddess, he liked that smile on him. Rune nodded. He hadn't seen that particular smile often, but he would do whatever he could to see it more. He turned away first, hoping Jayce didn't notice his reactions where his trousers were showing the tightening of his approval.

"I did. Go to the bathing pools first." He lit several of the cold torches and candles surrounding them on the walls as well as more freestanding poles until there was warm light all around them to brighten the chamber.

Jayce stooped down and ran fingers through the water. "It's heated! How?"

"Thermal vents in the cliffs. It's partly why there is so much turbulence to this sea. There are histories and stories of a long dormant volcano below us."

Jayce straightened with his held shirt hem in his hand. "There is?"

"So the books say." Once he was satisfied with the lighting, he tugged off his boots and let them drop. His cloak and garments fell into a muddled heap at his feet. He needed fresh clothing as well. Everything was either covered in blood, dirt, or grass from his fall from his horse.

It wasn't until he was ready to strip his britches that he realized Jayce had stopped moving. Glancing upward, he locked eyes with a brown and golden gaze that burned as bright as any flame in the room.

His cheeks grew warm as he stayed frozen under that compelling stare. He hoped Jayce blamed the room's humidity on the sight of his suddenly heating face. A blink released him and a slow exhale seemed to help center the other man. But it was torture watching Jayce strip to skin to move to dip his toes into the pool. Stretches of beautifully smooth skin gleamed in the wavering light as he lowered with a groan into the warm water.

"Oh, oh," he breathed, his face a gasp of ecstasy and relief. A hiss followed. "Oh, this feels so good." He dunked himself under.

Rune bit his lip. The sounds this man made. Finally equally naked, he moved to one of the many pockets of worn away rock in the wall and grabbed bathing soap and two drying cloths. Setting those within reach, he lowered himself into the same pool as Jayce.

He hissed as well, feeling the heat invade his sore body like a fully heated blanket wrapping around him. "This is to get clean, the hotter water will feel even better." He sank to his armpits, letting his eyes flutter closed. He'd missed these pools.

"Your hair." Jayce started to reach for it, but paused midair. "Can I... Would you let me wash it?"

Rune could barely breathe now that they were so close again. Something about this man drew him, compelled him with a ferocity he'd never encountered. And he didn't know how to not let it happen. He wasn't strong enough to keep him away. It didn't help that every vision he'd ever had inferred that Rune was going to be a major part of this man's future. To whatever that degree would be. But for right now, this moment was theirs and theirs alone.

Slowly, he nodded his head.

A light hand on his shoulder encouraged him to face away and careful hands removed the leather tie that kept it all pulled back.

"So beautiful," Jayce whispered as he combed through the length with gentle fingers. There was a tug on the strands and Rune slowly lowered until his shoulders were submerged. Then Jayce dipped his head with a tenderness that made him shiver. Strong fingers massaged his scalp, and he closed his eyes in bliss. The light rub moved from his temples to his crown all the way to his nape, working the soap through the length thoroughly. "I've never seen blond hair this pale, not without it being treated. It's almost silver when it's wet."

"Treated?" Rune mused.

"My mother is a hairdresser. I've seen hair of every color under the sun." His fingers paused for a heartbeat in their massage. "That's how I know how to do this. I helped for a few summers in her salon earning extra money for books and stuff when I was starting college." There was a hitched breath, then a sigh. "I never got to say goodbye. Do they even know I'm gone?"

Rune's heart clenched for the forlorn sound of his voice. "I really don't know. Time moves differently between planes."

"So there are different realities, not just mine, not just yours?" Rune hummed in agreement. Jayce's fingers had taken up their massage again, turning him into a puddle of goo in the swirling water. "Do you know by how much? Or which one is faster?"

"I do not. Traveling between worlds is dangerous."

"Because of the time paradox?"

Rune moaned when he hit a particularly tight spot on the back of his neck with a thumb. "Yes." It didn't occur to Rune to wonder how Jayce understood the intricacies of time, or the fated luck and goodwill behind the mark of the three. To the mages, it was common knowledge with different levels of importance depending on their magical study. Right then, it was hard to think at all.

Jayce's fingers stilled. "If... If I am supposed to be some kind of key to your world, can I please find a way to tell them? To tell them goodbye?"

Rune's heart ached. He didn't remember his birth family. He'd been sent to train and had never seen them again. He couldn't do that to Jayce. He'd lived an entire life before Rune had found him and jerked him in to this world. A wave of guilt made his mouth taste bitter and he swallowed, fighting the tightness in his throat. Why did Jayce's happiness affect him so deeply? So many strands were tying them irrevocably together, tighter and tighter. He should be able to keep a distance from his charge. He should be able to treat him like any other mage in training. While the temple and the acolytes were his brethren, Jayce didn't fit that mold. Whatever his future was meant to be, he would not be the one to take away his family. He wasn't that cruel, to anyone.

"I will do my best."

Jayce wrapped his arms around him from behind for a quick hug. "Thank you." He cleared his throat when he released him. "Dunk backward." His voice was firm again, his fingers methodical. Rune did, knowing the closeness they'd found in those brief moments was now over.

But it had seeded something powerful within his chest, and he guarded that feeling like a zealot now that it glowed warmly.

Chapter 12

Jayce laid stretched flat on his pallet, his hands gathered behind his head. A light blanket covered him to his waist with something that he supposed was to resemble a pillow under his head. His body was less sore, his muscles more relaxed after the time spent in the heated pools, yet he couldn't sleep. He supposed everything was finally hitting him. Staring at the carved rock of the room wasn't exactly helping. None of it looked even remotely like his own place.

He'd been abducted, for lack of a better word, by a mage.

Brought to a land he never could have imagined beyond fantasy and fiction.

And was somehow supposed to be the key to finding whoever the true king was.

He snorted under his breath. "Yeah, right," he muttered derisively. Him. He wasn't special, regardless of what Rune thought he'd found.

He stared at the ceiling, watching the lazy flicker of the single candle against the stone's unevenness. Did his parents know he was gone? Had anyone found his apartment door broken down? Did someone tell the police? Was he a missing person now? He didn't think his professors would notice. They had large classes to concern themselves over. One missing body wasn't going to cause any kind of blip on their radars. He frowned when he realized there really weren't that many people who would notice he was gone. At least he didn't have any pets.

Nothing was familiar to him in Windmere, or Kielbos, or whatever this crazy land was called. It was as though he'd been tossed into a J. R. R. Tolkien tome with a George R. Martin backdrop wondering when the next scene would start. Because as of yet, he hadn't seen a script, or thankfully, any dragons. He coughed when he giggled. *Dragons.*

He hoped not. It was bad enough he had to deal with magic-wielding mages.

And apparently some kind of shapeshifter.

Yeah, there is no way.

They couldn't possibly mean him, did they? Rune had shown him he had *some* kind of magic. He'd felt it when he'd done his little finger wiggle in the woods. But what did that mean? *Was* he magic? Or was it a case of mistaken identity? What if Rune was utterly, and completely wrong? There really wasn't anything special about him. Not that Rune was convinced of that. For him, there were no doubts. Jayce didn't get it.

He slipped a hand from behind his head and stared at his palm. It didn't look like anything special. And how had he lived twenty-two years and known nothing about his bloodline? About magic? How was he supposed to know about this Valda-Cree stuff if he was living on a plane, in a time, where Dungeons and Dragons was as close as anyone got to believing in magic? He knew there were illusionists, several talented ones who used their physical bodies in ways that he couldn't. And the wiccans and pagans who practiced the old ways, with natural herbs and such. But he wasn't like them. He was just...Jayce. Jayce without a family now.

A burst of homesickness struck him as he let his thoughts wander over the last three days. He'd been in such a state of constant action since yesterday morning that demanding Rune take him home again hadn't popped up. So thinking about magic, doing magic, hadn't been anywhere near the front of his thoughts.

Then there had been Raquel.

His hand fell to his hip. He swallowed the slight rush of bile that surged from his stomach at the memory of the axe, the swing. And the memory of her pain-marred face as she went down. A steadying breath helped to ease the growing tension to a more normal calm. But he'd never in his life seen anyone like her, act like her.

Or try to kill him like her. Granted, *no one* had ever tried to kill him before, either.

"Why must the Valda-Cree die?" he murmured to the silence. *Does that mean I am really part of this race? Part of some lost bloodline? Or was she mistaken? On drugs?*

He shook his head even as he mulled it over. It wasn't merely not likely, it was utterly fantastical. He was from his world, his time. Not this one.

But... Why would anyone be watching him? And how long? Were there others? And if there were, where were they? If Rune closed the doorway they'd jumped through in his apartment, how did she follow them? The unbidden questions weighed heavily on his thoughts. There were so many unanswered probabilities.

Deliberating over the what-ifs was going to drive him crazy. Bringing the lit candlestick closer, he blew out the wick. Then he turned over to a shoulder and closed his eyes, willing sleep to take him. It took a while in such a strange place but eventually, sleep and long days caught up with him and his frame went slack.

A light tapping on his door roused him. The room was abyss dark without having any way to relight the candle.

"Master Jayce, Master Thiel has asked that I wake you." The door muffled the quietly spoken words.

He hefted himself to an elbow. "Uh, okay."

"May I enter?"

He rubbed over his eyes trying to focus in the darkness, then said, "Sure. Come in."

Torchlight made him blink until his eyes adjusted when the door swept open before him. The young man bowed low. "I am Brin. We met yesterday at your arrival. I have fresh garments." He relit the candle beside the pallet with the torch he carried then placed the wrapped bundle of clothing on the lone stand in the room. "Master Thiel has asked me to invite you to the morning meal. I'll wait in the hall for you." Then he backed up and quietly pulled the door closed.

Jayce rolled over and stretched. Another day to try to get answers, or go home. And find a way to take a leak. Priorities.

Do these people know what a toothbrush is? His mind was still in the twenty-first century even if his body was somewhere else entirely. *Hmm. Would this be considered pre Henry the Eighth?* He swallowed his chuckles and finished dressing aware Brin was waiting for him.

Once he was dressed, he joined Brin in the hallway. They wound from the hall of rooms to the stairwell that took them to the wide hall with the doors, then through there to the entrance of the dining room.

There were a few more people than Master Theil and Rune this morning, and there was a chair waiting for him opposite Rune once more. The night before, candles had been lit along the walls as the setting sun was filling the room with shadows. This morning it was fully lit and bright through the ceiling high windows with morning sunlight that made the room so much larger. He swallowed, hoping he was only imagining all the eyes following him, and that he wasn't really feeling their weight as he neared his chair.

"Morning," he offered, taking his place.

"Good morning," Master Theil replied. "I'm glad you could join us. After the meal, I would like to speak to you and Rune once more."

Jayce quickly sought Rune's gaze but found nothing there. Not even curiosity. If anything, he looked tired. "Sure. I think it's time."

Rune's unblinking gaze dropped and he exhaled, then seemed to stiffen his frame to sit straight. Jayce didn't know what to make of his reactions. Was he nervous? Angry? Resigned?

It wasn't uncomfortable but it was odd not speaking at all until everyone had finished.

"Younglings, you're dismissed this morning to your studies. Use your time wisely." The dozen or so who'd eaten with them, including Brin, stood and bowed then filed out of the dining room. The dishes were quietly and efficiently picked up by young boys in a type of uniform of cloth britches and belted shirts longer than the one Jayce had been given.

"Please close the doors," Master Theil requested, and as the last servant went through, he pulled the heavy doors shut behind him.

"Is it always that quiet?"

"Only during the breakfast hour. They are to reflect on their dreams and focus on their pending day. Focusing on the past is a good measure, but reaching for the future keeps their ambitions motivated." Master Theil sipped on his tea, settling it back on the table without a sound. "That and it would be rude to focus so much on our guest that they and you were unable to eat."

"Well, I'm here, and I do have questions."

Master Theil tucked his hands into the billowy ends of his sleeves, his attention calm. "Please, do ask," he encouraged.

Jayce rocked forward on his chair and leaned over his own cupped elbows. "I'm here for a reason, because I'm Valda-Cree." A flicked gaze roamed from Master Theil to Rune who finally nodded. "That means that I'm something more than human."

"Correct," Master Theil remarked. "We need to reveal the level of the inherited Valda-Cree heritage, and what magic you have."

Jayce swallowed. "How do you do that?"

"Well." Rune, if it were possible, blanched. "We need to awaken your magic. I believe it's already begun."

"It has? How?"

Rune's gaze lowered, avoiding him. "Remember when I asked you what color your eyes were?"

Jayce thought back. "I think so, after the first night here."

From somewhere near his waist below the table height, Rune pulled a small mirror from the folds of his clothing. "Please look."

Jayce reached, hesitating briefly before grabbing it in his palm.

"Magic manifests itself in unique ways to the user. Mages are almost always blessed with a telling eye." Master Theil watched with rapt patience, not forcing him to move any faster. Now that he mentioned it, Master Theil did have an unusual color of green. But who was he to say what was natural when apparently he'd stumbled into a world of different races and species of human-like people.

Jayce gripped the mirror in front of his face, almost scared to lift it to peer in to its reflection. "And you're saying I have some kind of magic."

Rune nodded. "Please, look." Then he dropped his gaze again. Jayce would almost say he was behaving as though he were guilty of something, but what, he couldn't say.

Jayce slowly tilted the small looking glass upward and in turn, tipped down to meet his reflection. A gasp was impossible to stop. "My eyes," he choked, his fingers poking below one. "They're golden. They were brown, a plain dirt brown." But staring back at him was his face, and that was most definitely his eyeball, but it was *not* brown. Not any longer. It was a dark, golden honey.

"They are the color of a large cat," Rune whispered, like that meant something.

Jayce sucked a deep, deep breath. Okay. So he *was* something, the question was what. "So, what do I need to do?" He placed the mirror face down for now. Staring at his own eyes that weren't what he'd known for twenty-two years was unsettling.

"You need to unlock your magic," said Master Theil. "You will need to be instructed, and if Rune's visions are correct, you will have to focus, as time is not on your side."

"And if I don't want to continue? Will my eyes go brown again if I go home? If I don't want to be a martyr or someone's special project in this world?"

Distress flashed across Rune's blue gaze, but his voice was even when he answered. "Your eyes will not revert, however, what has happened here will cease in your plane. Your magic will not continue to manifest, exactly as it hadn't presented itself before your journey to Kielbos, through the lands into Windmere. Your plane does not have the influences needed or the training. Your life would continue as it had."

"But if I stay, I can make a difference?"

"We all can make a difference," Master Theil offered sagely. "Whether your differences happen to make a large enough impact to matter to you is ego."

Jayce hid his wince. Yeah, he supposed he deserved that. Damn it! He was so far out of his element. "So if I look at what is in front of me as a possibility of a lot of small differences or even one really large change that could be a good improvement, the depth of that impact shouldn't matter, only that it is done."

"Wise words."

"Exactly."

Jayce sighed. He knew he could make a difference at home, but would it really matter in the grand scheme of things? There were literally millions of college students every year, everywhere. At least some of them would become teachers, the same as he was studying for but what if he had the chance to do something even more profound? If he were at home and had been presented with a carte blanche invitation to take this kind of a chance, he would've jumped at it. If he'd been *asked*. If he was there or here, his impacts would still be of note, but here was an opportunity to maybe become more than he'd originally believed had been the sum of his life at home. It was the unknown factors that were tugging at him. Intrepid and all that. The question was: Could he do it? Was he strong enough, brave enough, to take on the challenge the last few days had painted for him? Because this was going to be huge, whatever it was he was supposed to do.

He tapped his fingers on the back of the mirror, then cautiously lifted it up to investigate the eyes staring back at him one more time.

"I have to admit, with it laid out like this, it's very intriguing to think of the possibilities. Am I a Valda-Cree mage? Am I a skin shifter who will lead? Am I connected to an animal at all? Or am I going to be the one to sacrifice myself to be the catalyst to bring about the next stage?" That particular question didn't fill him with happy expectations, but he had to believe that he wouldn't have been found to go through all of this to simply die on a pike somewhere. At least, he hoped.

Rune's lips twitched, but it was the sparkle in his eyes that told him he was saying the right things, and that Rune may have more answers than he was willing to reveal himself right then.

"It is your choice if you wish to continue. Rune's visions were to find you and bring you here. I wish we had more information, but without knowing your ability, we can't postulate the next stage of your journey."

Jayce met the icy blue gaze across the table and caught the almost imperceptible shake of his head. So there was more, but he was playing it close to his chest. Okay, he could wait it out to see what Rune knew. But he had something he had to take care of first. It was mandatory.

"The first stage of your training will commence if you decide to stay." With a shallow dip of his head, he moved his chair away. "I will leave you to consider your choices. But I must warn you to not delay more than you need."

Jayce stood, and Rune copied them. He turned to the elder mage and bowed at the waist, mimicking what he'd seen the other acolytes do. "I thank you for your wisdom."

Then he and Rune were left alone.

Once Master Theil was out of the room and earshot, he turned to Rune and rounded the table to stand in front of him. "Take me home."

Chapter 13

Rune stifled the pained gasp. "Take you…" He almost cried out with the no on the end of his tongue, but the touch of Jayce's hand cut him off. His next words allowed him to think again, easing the race of his heart as his worst fears soared then were clipped short.

Jayce's hand was warm on his jaw. Tender. It completely derailed his growing dread and fear. "I need to tell my mother I may not be around for a while. I'm trusting you, Rune. If anything ever goes awry with this, you must go to my world and tell them. Don't leave them worrying about me into their graves."

"That is a trust I will gladly keep for you," he murmured, relief making him press into the palm holding him.

He couldn't seem to help himself around Jayce. The more time they spent together, the more his body turned into some kind of magnet that he couldn't escape. Since last evening spent in the pools together, he'd been meditating, trying to recenter himself. But every time he thought he was balanced, his world tilted and he immediately started looking for or thinking of Jayce.

The man his visions had said he was going to guide and guard. And they seemed to be fully correct. In such a short amount of time, he'd become almost a sole source of need and comfort in Rune's mind. What made it worse was he didn't know if he wanted to stop it, or race toward the unknown. He didn't understand the pull, or how he was supposed to treat it. Or if Jayce felt it also.

Because he suspected he was only going to become more enraptured by this man the more he grew to know him. A young soul who had proven to be brave, resilient, adaptable, strong, and wise in ways that he had no reason to believe Jayce would or could know. Yet he'd shown the real man beneath. This man before him seemed to be who his visions said he'd needed to find.

What's more, he would protect someone he had feelings for with his life.

Rune's challenge was letting Jayce come to terms with his destiny on his own, as well as keeping those secrets. He couldn't be more of an influence than his visions had revealed.

"When did you want to go?"

"Now." Jayce stroked his cheek then dropped his hand. "Apparently I have training to start."

Rune smirked. "You don't do anything by halves, do you?"

"Not really. I had already considered my options last night and wasn't too surprised by this morning's conversation. I will always want to know more, and the truth, but I'm not going to run simply because it's not my typical state of normal."

"You are a remarkable man, Jayce Morrow."

Jayce's cheeks warmed with a telling pink. "So what do we need to do?"

"Do you want to see your home first?"

Jayce scratched his jaw. "Yeah. I need to see if there's anything there I can do. Maybe give my mom my laptop and stuff to keep. And find my phone. She's probably been going nuts trying to find me."

"We'll have to go in under a blurring spell. We don't know what we're walking into."

Jayce nodded. "Your rules."

"Follow me." Rune led them from the dining hall, out of the temple. "It's best to do portals where others cannot stumble across them." He sent a message to Iba of what he was planning and got a cautionary flex back from her. He grinned. Always his watcher.

"Do you need your staff, or Iba?"

"Yes, and no." Rune waved a hand and his staff materialized in his grip. "She's hunting this morning. This land is her home and well known. She will be safe. And if I have need of her, she can come to us through an eternal doorway."

"What is that?"

They walked together over familiar broad stones, following the slope of the cliffs until the temple was some distance behind them. "Animals can travel from land to land."

Jayce stopped suddenly. "Oh my god. You mean stories like the sasquatch and yeti and dragons are real? They can use those gateways? They are from other worlds?"

"If they are seen in your world but not true to your world, yes. They have found the eternal doorways and for lack of a better word, visit. It's not their home, but they can use the doorways. It's usually a place of natural power, like a crossed ley line."

"Like a fairy ley line?"

"I suppose." He paused, tipping his head back and feeling the sun on his face. "This spot will work." He faced Jayce. "You must stay close. The protection spells do not stretch over a great distance. I am the source, and including you in the protection."

"Got it, no running away."

Rune shook his head. That sounded more like the joking, sarcastic Jayce he'd first met. At least now he also sounded more relaxed. A few spoken words and he felt the blanketing sensation as the blurring spell coated them. He didn't know how long they would need in Jayce's world, but he could hold it for several hours if necessary, even with sharing it over the two of them.

Rune waved his hand in an intricate pattern and the bright glow of the portal began to shimmer in the air. He felt Jayce inch closer.

"That is absolutely amazing. Can all mages do that?"

"No. And only Master Theil and two others of the elder council know I can."

"So, no bragging you can flip doorways."

Rune coughed to his surprised gurgle of laughter. Jayce was always taking him by surprise. "What is a safe place to come out?"

"Behind the apartment building. There's a delivery alley for the businesses on the block. No one should see the portal and even if they did, they'd think it was a glare from a car or something."

Rune nodded and focused. "Ready?"

Jayce's head jerked.

He led them through with Jayce only a half pace behind him.

89

༚

Jayce blinked, bright morning sunlight fading to softening dusk in a heartbeat. He didn't think he'd ever get used to that. Rune motioned for him to take the lead. Cautiously, he cleared the corner of the building to reach the doorway in the front.

"Huh. That wasn't there three days ago." He pointed to a security panel on the door facing wall.

"Let me see if I can get through it." Rune placed a hand on the buttons and stilled. The click of the door was sharp as it dislodged.

Jayce yanked the door open and started climbing the steps to the second floor. The lights looked the same, but everything else felt *wrong*. He shivered when he stepped onto the landing. He rocked his head, not speaking. Rune followed his lead.

He approached the door that *had been* his apartment, but blinked. The door had been replaced, and painted a dark blue, in fact all of the doors had been repainted. The incongruity of what he expected deepened. His door should have been shredded but it was as though it had stood for months, maybe longer. There was no damage anywhere.

There was a new brass number screwed into the wood now, too.

"This is my apartment, but it's not possible that this is all repaired already." He drew a breath. "Stand to the side. I've got a bad feeling about this."

Rune swiveled and leaned against the wall. Praying he wouldn't be visible under Rune's spell, he knocked.

And held his breath.

A moment passed before the door was opened by a young man. He looked right through Jayce, then down the hall in the both directions. "Odd. Thought I heard…" he murmured with a Boston accent. Jayce was able to see beyond him and had to lock his knees in place as shock made his legs weak.

Nothing in the viewable area of the room was his. The furniture was modern and sleek, and there was a child's school backpack leaning against the leg of a table. The carpet was different, as was the color on the walls. Nothing that he'd known remained.

"Daddy, who is it?"

"No one, love. Probably someone else's door."

This wasn't his apartment. And hadn't been for some time. He waited for the door to close before stumbling backward into the opposite wall. He ran a hand down his face. "Rune." His voice cracked noticeably.

Immediately strong arms gripped him, holding him steady and holding him upright.

"What does it mean?"

"I didn't conceive so much time would have transpired in the three days you'd been with me."

"My parents." Anguish coated his words. "I have to know."

"I can't create a portal to an area unless I know something about it."

"We can't walk. It's too far." His voice was thick, fighting back the heat of tears. The part of him that was still the little boy was terrified. He didn't want to face what he feared was coming. He couldn't conceive of not having his parents in his life. They'd always been there. And now they weren't.

Jayce's steps were considerably slower, reversing their way out of the building. Though he dreaded he already knew what he was going to find. No matter how much he tried to convince himself otherwise, his heart was in his throat, his chest tight with apprehension.

They were a block from the apartment building when Jayce spotted his bus stop where he'd usually catch the bus to campus. "We'll hop the bus. It's the best way. No one can see us, right?"

Rune shook his head. "Only each other as we're in the spell."

"Fine." He gave Rune a pointedly challenging stare. "This will be an adventure for you."

They waited for the next bus and hopped on with the loading riders. Rune's discomfort was obvious as he blanched with the first lurching movement, but he sat in a seat with little complaint. Then it was a matter of waiting for a stop close enough to shorten the distance they'd have to walk. They slipped off the bus with none being wiser.

The walk from the bus stop took a little over an hour crossing through parks and over streets. It wasn't like he could call up an Uber. His phone had been in his apartment. An apartment that no longer existed. Fading daylight turned to early evening. There wasn't any way to learn the current date either. No billboards or anything that would stick out while on the bus. The world surrounding him looked the same, though like the apartment building, it *felt* wrong, different. Little things that he couldn't pinpoint, or explain what had changed.

What surprised him was about ten minutes away from his mother's house, Rune wrapped his hand around his fingers. Shoring his strengths, he offered silent support. He squeezed once. Neither said a word.

Two houses away, he simply stopped in his tracks on the opposite sidewalk facing the line of steps and doors that should have looked familiar, welcoming. But so much had changed, more noticeably than anywhere else. "We don't have to go any further." He felt dead inside, his shoulders slumping.

"Are you sure?"

He nodded, his throat tight. Streetlights illuminated the block now that the sun had set completely. His gaze was locked on the townhouse they'd lived in since he was adopted. The memory of the banner over the doorway would always be with him. But… There was no way the paint had been refreshed in three days. His father wasn't capable of that kind of maintenance. It was partly why they'd lived in the townhome. He wasn't a handyman kind of guy. He was a professor, which was why Jayce had wanted to be a teacher. He loved his parents, had wanted them to be proud of him.

He could have lived with them while he attended college, but he wanted the freedom of being closer to the campus, of being independent. Had he known how his life was going to be ripped to shreds he would have never left.

Then as if to break his heart a little more, the doorway opened and a woman he didn't recognize came out, talking to a standard poodle on a leash. He didn't have to hear her voice. She didn't belong in that house. She used a key to lock the door. The door to his home, his parents' home.

They were gone. His soul shattered and he bowed his head swallowing hard against the burn of tears. Why him? Why did he have to sacrifice everything? His future? His family? All he knew and loved was gone. There was no way to tell how much time had passed. Cars looked the same. The trees looked the same. He blinked rapidly as the woman and her dog walked down the street, utterly unaware of them standing there.

His chest ached. His entire world had vanished in the three days he'd been in Windmere. He whirled and snarled at Rune. "You!" He yanked his hand free of Rune's hold and poked Rune's chest. "You took me away. I've been gone three *days!*"

"I warned you, there is a danger to going between worlds."

"So what happens when we go back now? How much time is going to be displaced on that side?" he demanded.

"I don't know. It isn't relative or exact."

He stomped away a few feet, his hands gripping his hair, tugging until all there was was pain. "What aren't you telling me?" he demanded. "You came looking for me. You know why when I don't." He pointed at his eyes. "This happened! I've lost my life, my parents. I don't even know if any of my friends are still alive!" he stressed, nearly shouting. "You didn't want me to ask in front of Master Theil. I'm demanding you tell me now. What is going on?"

He evaded, looking away, down the street. "My visions are not guaranteed. They are only possible."

"And yet, you found me." He thumped his chest with a flat hand. He should have demanded this sooner, so much sooner before his life became a page in history. And now, none of it could be reversed or replaced. He was at Rune's mercy. Bitterness and anger made his blood heat as he fought the pain. Before he did something he would regret even more. "What aren't you telling me? Or I'm not going back."

He crossed his arms and braced his legs as though he rode on a ship in a cross wind. He wasn't budging another fucking inch unless Rune told him the truth.

Chapter 14

Rune's hands were tied. As a seer, he wasn't supposed to reveal the keys of someone's destiny. He was only supposed to guide Jayce. Train him, give him direction, and protect him as his own visions had made abundantly clear. Yet there was no lie in the fact that it was because of Rune's visions that his entire life as he had known it had been destroyed.

There had to be balance and he needed Jayce's trust to continue on the path they'd been given. The debate was swift. There was only one way to proceed. He would accept the consequences for his own decisions. *Guide and guard.* He had to protect Jayce and if that meant telling him the truth, then… So be it. Steeling himself for what may come, he said, "You asked at breakfast if you are supposed to be a Valda-Cree mage, or skin shifter. I know you were only looking at the possibilities with what you already know, but what I couldn't say was actually how close to the truth you were." He firmed his shoulders and purposely met Jayce's furious gaze. "I was sent to find you to repair the balance in our world because you are the missing link. You are the missing Valda-Cree line, who will become king."

Jayce's jaw fell open, his entire body going slack like he'd been punched in the gut.

"The king? Like *The King*?" he croaked.

Blink.

Blink.

Rune looked down the street, and frowned. "We need to leave. We're too open here."

A hand was thrust hard into his chest and Rune snapped around. "No, wait. Hold up. King? Like really a king?"

"Yes." He stalked up to Jayce, lowering his voice. "Master Theil doesn't know that I have seen the possibility in the visions. No one else knows at all. That is why it is imperative that you get training, so you can harness the mage magic of the elements and of the Valda-Cree bloodline, and find your skin animal. The person who has the power of all three is considered sacred."

"But how…did I…here?" Jayce was trying to understand. Rune could see it in his taut expression, that he was having difficulty processing this part of his new truth. Rune could also tell he hadn't started to forgive yet.

"There was a legend that a child of King Bail's was hidden away, taken by his nurse to keep him safe. He was never found in our world, anywhere. He was feared lost, then forgotten." He dared to touch Jayce's tight chest. "I feel it with all that I am; that child is you."

"The time paradox," he choked. "I was hidden. For centuries."

Rune shook his head. "You were kept safe, in a world that wouldn't influence your inner abilities, thereby leaving you unmarked by magic. No one knew to look for you here." But even as he said it, he knew someone *had* known, because the *sabra* had been here, keeping him within their sights.

For someone. And that meant they were both in danger.

"You did," he countered, taking a step back.

"I started the search for the understanding of my visions two years ago when they began. That is why Master Theil knows some but not all of what I have seen. I began to fear what I was discovering would be used against me, or the person I sought. I'm the only one who knows who you are intended to be. If anyone else is aware of you, I can't say what they believe about you. I can't guess why the *sabra* were here, other than to stop you."

"You swear that?"

"I promise you. Now, please, we must go. We are out in the open and I don't trust this time. The *sabra* were here undetected. There might be others."

"How do I know I can trust you?"

Rune's hand tightened on his staff, determined to make Jayce understand. He did not mean him any ill will. He stood straight and met his gaze directly. "You can't. You have to decide if what I've done, what I'm doing for you, with you, creates the trust you need."

"And you're also the only person I can say I really know." He glared, then huffed a sigh, swallowing hard when his voice cracked. "Now. Everyone I knew is gone."

The loss in his voice sliced Rune deep. He knew he'd caused this to happen whether knowingly or not. "But you are alive and can do anything."

"I wish I could trust your motives, now, knowing what I do."

Rune gaped, then dipped his head. That stung, but he should have expected it. Nothing was going easily for either of them. "I can only do what I feel is right."

"I could walk away, right now."

Rune swallowed slowly. "You could. I'd do what I could to ensure you were settled here, if that is your wish. But I have to warn you. You've been to your homeland. If others are looking for you, or are tracking the *sabra* who were watching you, then they know something has changed. You are at risk here. You have to know that."

Jayce cursed under his breath. "So I'm fucked whether I do or don't." He threw out his arms. "Fine. Let's go back. I have training to begin." The accusatory sneer on his face told him to tread carefully. That his agreement was not a win.

Rune nodded and hunted for a secluded location to create the portal away from the homes and street.

Jayce was quiet, closed off on the march up the cliff returning to the temple. Night had fully fallen in Jayce's world by the time they found a safe place to portal back to the temple, and they'd lost more than two days in Windmere, where it was already early afternoon. Time was a tricky beast, and traveling between worlds was not safe, as a person could only exist in one plane at a time. When Rune took Jayce out of his time, he'd ceased to exist in the timeline, so time had moved on.

It wasn't linear, and it wasn't equal.

When they entered the temple, Master Theil was waiting for them in the main foyer. "Have you found the answers you seek?"

Jayce nodded, though his expression was no less grim. "I have. If there's a possibility to rebalance nature, man, and magic, then I will help."

Master Theil smiled. "Good. Good. Then let us begin."

Jayce followed behind Master Theil to a large courtyard through another set of doors that faced the far cliffs. Flat stepping stones created meandering lines through the manicured pebbles and crushed shell layout, with large bright green patches of green grass and flowers spread throughout. The sea was calm today, while bees and butterflies danced among the blooms lining the path. Afternoon sunlight beamed down on them. That light breeze coming off the sea had the tang of salt air, while cooling bare skin.

They stopped near a tranquility pool filled with bright red fish, that if he'd been asked, looked a lot like koi, but he wouldn't swear to anything being what he'd once known at this point.

"Please sit."

He sank down and mimicked Master Theil's cross-legged posture. "I will see if I can find your magic and enhance it to bring it forward."

"Will I feel it?" He bit his lip, wondering for the first time if any of this was going to hurt.

"You will feel the surge. Rune believes you have mage magic as well as magic of the Valda-Cree. If you also have a skin animal, you will have a lot of power and will need to learn control quickly." If Master Theil understood what that triad meant within a single person, he wasn't revealing it. Merely waiting for Jayce to proceed. He wished he knew how much he could trust the people of this world that were supposed to help him, guide him. Were they helping him for Jayce, or for themselves? Thoughts he couldn't harbor if he was going to be spending hours training with these same people.

He released a breath with his hands resting on his thighs, the same as Master Theil, then he nodded. "I'm ready."

The elder only smiled across from him on the stones. "Close your eyes. Focus on the sounds surrounding you. The water, the birds, the breeze."

Jayce did, feeling a sense of calm overtake him. It was lovely out here on the cliffs. Calming.

"Good. You're doing well." His voice was further away, or quieter. "You will feel me, but don't fear the touch. It is only my magic source seeking your energies."

He swallowed but his eyelids were heavy, and he couldn't open his eyes. Then, there was warmth, rolling through him, expanding and retreating. Almost luring him with the finesse of a dance, his body swaying gently as the waves of sensation flowed through him. Much like the pull of the tides, he realized he was responding to the natural rhythm of Master Theil's magic as a water mage. And slowly, things changed.

He hadn't known what was meant by bring his magic forward, but as the minutes passed, he could feel something inside of him unfurl and tentatively reach outward. It gradually came into focus, or maybe, into being? He wasn't sure how to describe the sensations. There was warmth and joy, almost a happiness to finally meet him, something he could sense but would never be able to put words to explain the feelings. Awe filled him as he began to actually sense things changing. To feel the changes as they enveloped him. The brush of the breeze on his skin, the scent of sun-heated grass, and the welcome of timeless earth. He could find them all, separate them, and feel them as they became a part of him. Was this what Master Theil meant by bringing it forward?

The pulses strengthened and soon he could actually see them in…color.

If magic had colors, he could see their patterns in his mind as bright purples and dazzling blues, fading to summer greens. Jewel tones, bright and proud. They glowed and shimmered as the waves of colors undulated through his soul, following Master Theil's guidance. Tendrils or waves, that formed ribbons, bowing and bending, folding almost playfully into each other. Bright and distinct.

"Jayce, I want you to concentrate." The calm of Master Theil's voice wove through the colors, in his ear, in his head, yet far away. "You need to find your elemental magic. What do you see when you feel your magic?"

"Colors. So many colors." He couldn't focus on only one. They merged, they danced. They pulsed. They were beautiful. They flowed like ribbons being pulled through the air on the end of a ballet wand. How had he never known this existed inside himself? They engulfed his vision, fading into his periphery to return brighter and bolder than ever, as though they were introducing themselves, speaking to him. The colors caressed him and calmed him while they spoke of so much power. It helped to ease him into exploring their sudden newness in his life. They were safety and protection, and honor, and peace. So many sensations tied to individual waves of color. It was as though a rainbow had become a wild creature in his mind, whirling and flowing with precision, yet all of them were separate and combined at the same time.

There was a shocked pause. "Colors? More than one?"

"Bright, bold," he whispered.

"Search your colors. What is the brightest?"

"Purple, blue, red and green," he answered. White, gold, yellow. Orange. It was like a kaleidoscope broke open in his mind. Crystal clear and brilliant.

"Find the flame in the red. Think of the way a flame stands out, a living breathing force that can be birthed or killed, yet has no true life force. This is usually one of the easiest to control because it has a beginning, a middle, and an end to its structure."

Jayce floated through the colors, searching for the red of a hot flame. "I... I think I found it," he whispered. It was *right there.* So close. How did he call it? How did he bring it to life for himself? He almost balked at the absurdity of the questions. After twenty-two years, he firmly understood the disciplines and physics of common sense rules. What he was thinking didn't *exist* in the real world. *But this isn't your real world any longer, is it?*

If what he was seeing inside of himself was any hint, the rules were about to be completely tossed, scrambled, and remade into something else entirely, and himself with them.

"Open your eyes." They obeyed this time. "Now, hold your palm up." He mimicked Master Theil. "Keep your breathing even. Find the flame and envision it in your hand. Feel the energy gather. Let the heat pull from inside you."

Jayce focused, embracing the heat of the red, seeing the flared white of the base to the red flickering tip. He gasped at the dancing plume of flame that appeared in his palm.

"Good. Excellent."

"That's beautiful."

"Now, I am going to withdraw. Do not lose the flame."

Jayce focused, searching for the vibrant colors in his mind. Gradually, the essence of Master Theil's power faded and as he did so, the flame in his hand decreased, shrank until it looked like a candle wick but it didn't die. And it didn't burn him.

"This is incredible."

"Release the flame," he stated.

Jayce closed his eyes and let the red in his mind fade to gray. When he opened his eyes, the flame that had danced in the center of his palm was completely gone.

"That is most excellent. Now again."

Jayce spent several hours into late afternoon working with the colors that swirled within him, giving them life. Fire, water, air, and earth. He was shocked that he was exhibiting strengths in any of the elements or their magics, but Master Theil's guidance gave him the patience to work through the colors, grasping the ability to touch on all the ones he could reach and what they each meant. If he was more than a little surprised that Jayce was able to see so many, or feel all the elements, he was keeping it well hidden.

"I must warn you, it will take a lot of control to learn the full scope of the magic you bear. The unity we share with the elements is exactly that, shared. We do not ever possess them for our own gain, as we are a part of each element ourselves."

That made sense to Jayce and he tucked the warning away for the wisdom it was. All of nature was one encompassing circle, birth and death, prey and predator. Or, to steal a certain song tagline: The circle of life. He bit his lip to not snort at his own silly thoughts.

The lessons ended as the sun began its descent, and they stopped to rest in the courtyard at a table with tea and a platter of cheeses, crackers, and grapes before the dinner hour.

Jayce wiped his mouth, then said in reply to Master Theil's cautions, "I understand. I'm basically a baby with a new toy."

Master Theil's eyebrow arched almost to his hairline. Jayce chuckled, knowing he'd caught the elder off guard. But hey, if the shoe fits, right?

Exhausted but exhilarated with the new discoveries, he went in search of Rune when they were done with the training for the day. The part of his brain that craved to learn was absorbing the new challenges. Now that he'd made his choices, whether they were foisted on him or not, he was going to embrace them to his fullest ability.

And he wanted to apologize to Rune for being gruff with him earlier. Not seeing his parents, to warn them, to say goodbye, cut him deeply. His heart ached and he knew, when he had a moment to himself he would have to find a way to accept that what was happening had removed him from that part of his life. However, the passage of time, and the speed of that passing was not Rune's fault. He was mad with Rune, but it wasn't lost on Jayce that he'd also forced the berserker *sabra* out of hiding, and possibly saved his life because of it. It was a lot to untangle.

He walked the halls of the temple, searching the whole main floor before realizing he wasn't there. Palming a torch, he wound down the stairs to the resting chambers, but peering down the length didn't know which one was his, or if he was okay to bother him there.

Taking a chance that he could still find him, he went down one more level to the pools and smiled at his luck.

Only now that he'd found him, he stood still and silent unable to look away from the view.

Because in repose in the steaming water, he was even more beautiful now than when Jayce had first set eyes on him in his apartment a million years ago.

Chapter 15

"Are you going to stand there, or are you going to get in?" Rune's voice was rough, distanced. Mellow.

And sexier than hell.

Jayce swallowed when Rune licked over his bottom lip. His britches suddenly felt a lot tighter. And he realized rather abruptly how that had become a reoccurring reaction around the elf. At least when they weren't yelling at each other.

Eyelids rose to half and bright blue eyes pierced him, their gleam sultry through the lazily rising steam. His stomach tightened as need bloomed through his chest, making his skin tingle.

"If you came to yell at me some more, now's your chance. I'm too tired to fight back." He sat low in the water, obscuring his body nearly up to his chin, with his head resting on the rock behind him.

Jayce located a nearby brace for the torch. "I didn't." He tugged his shirt free and hung it on a waiting hook. Sitting, he pulled off his boots and after untying the string running down his britches, he shimmied out of them as well. He blinked when he realized he hadn't thought of his underwear at all today. He didn't even know where they were. Sighing, he pushed away the changes that he couldn't help, wanting to focus on what he could affect.

Like getting into that hot water and clearing the air between him and Rune. Naked as a new babe, he strode to the pool, feeling the weight of Rune's gaze with each step. There was definitely some level of interest in that electric blue color. And he wasn't going to hide the effect this man had on him either.

He slipped into the water, sinking down to the carved rock ledge. His entire frame shuddered as soothing water enveloped him. He groaned as strain began to melt away. He hadn't realized how tight he was holding himself until the heat kicked in.

"Why are you tired?" Jayce asked, settling into a spot.

Dripping with water, a pale hand rose and wiped down his face. "I was in the training room with the novices. I'm sunk to the bottom of the roughest seas."

"Oh?"

"They're learning how to use magic in combat, both offensively and defensively."

"And they put you through your paces, huh?"

"If that's a kind way of asking if they tested me at every turn, then yes, yes they did." He groaned as he flexed, rocking his neck side to side.

Jayce moved around the pool until he was beside him. "Come here." Rune raised his head, a questioning arch to his brow. "Turn around." He motioned his request with a spinning finger.

Rune didn't blink. The air between them seemed to be holding its breath, suddenly charged. What was it about Rune that he couldn't seem to fight? Or was it that he didn't want to? Even when he was angry at him, he couldn't hate him. Oh, he'd tried. He wanted to. He'd taken him from his home, taken him from the only parents he knew. Something stopped him.

Reaching for the length of hair from behind Rune's back, he fanned it over a shoulder, covering a nipple as the strands spread out to float in the bubbling water before sinking, enjoying the shimmer of firelight against the silver highlights. This man's hair was such a weakness for him. "Now. Turn around."

Rune did, shifting around in the bubbling water to give Jayce his back. Visions of running his tongue up his smooth neck made his heart pound and kept his shaft semi-hard, hidden in the heated water. He didn't even know if Rune wanted him, if what he'd been seeing in the other man's gaze was true desire and want. What he felt around this man was more than any other he could think of, and that truth was unsettling given he was an elf, and had been utterly unknown to him a few short days before. He'd never suspected he could be attracted to anyone who wasn't human. It had never crossed his mind. His dick didn't seem to care about any of that though.

He put his fingers on Rune's shoulders, centering his thumbs to the base of his skull. "Now relax." Digging slowly, he massaged the tension from the man's muscles.

"Oh, goddess," he groaned, shuddering deliciously. "That… That is divine."

Jayce grinned, leaning close to be able to whisper right in to his ear. "I guess that means it feels good."

He panted, almost whining as he twisted, giving Jayce even more water heated skin to play with. "So good."

The purr of his voice stroked over alert nerves, pumping his shaft full of blood with a suddenness that left him lightheaded. Focusing because he was almost panting himself, he made his fingers do what he was telling them to do, instead of obeying the need to pull Rune into his chest, to feel them pressing together, skin to skin.

It didn't seem to matter. Whenever he was close to Rune like this, he had to touch him. The remembered smoothness of his cheek in the dining hall before they'd gone jaunting through time and whatever. It was like Rune was irresistible.

He loved running his hands through the long, silken length of his hair. His skin was heated from the steamy water and felt like warm satin under his fingers. With his head forward and his hair gathered against his shoulder to the front, exposing the column of his slim neck, Jayce had to remind himself to not brush his lips over the skin in front of him. Soft pants and wisped gasps were music against the burbling backdrop of the steamy water surrounding them.

The bathing cavern was empty except for them, the surrounding pools adding their own level of gurgle and swish that made it feel like the whole world was theirs in that moment.

Jayce drew a breath, remembering he actually had things he wanted to tell Rune. He found a particularly tight spot on Rune's spine and worked it until the other man was sitting limply before him.

"I wanted to apologize for earlier," he said, his voice low and private.

Rune hummed and tried to turn his head, but Jayce blocked him, keeping him still. "What for?" Rune asked.

"I don't blame you for the way things happened. It hurts that I'll never see my parents again, but it's not your fault that time happens the way it does." The ripping pang of loss was sudden. He swallowed, stuffing it down for now. He hadn't given himself time to really think about what their loss meant to him, to mourn in his own way, or what seeing the house that was no longer theirs meant to him, trying to stay focused on the here and now. He was apologizing to Rune, however the fact that he hadn't faced their loss hit him like a wrecking ball to the solar plexus. *They were really gone.* The impact was wrenching as he struggled with the reality, sidetracking his intentions.

An exhale rolled Rune's shoulders, filling the silence. "Thank you for that. I never meant to cause you that kind of pain. I don't remember my family. I was brought as a youngling to the temple for training. I didn't want to take your family away from you. That's why I didn't argue about taking you back. I didn't know how time would pass. I made a lot of assumptions when I brought you through the portal. Not taking consideration of your personal life was my worst mistake."

Jayce stopped the rub and curled an arm over Rune's shoulders to let him tuck into his chest with a shoulder. "I'm not going to lie. It hurts." He closed his eyes as Rune stroked a thumb over a cheek. "No more weekend dinners. No more phone calls. I'm alone here," he choked out.

Rune adjusted his position to cup his face, sitting sideways on the bench to be closer. "You're not alone. My visions might have brought me to you as a duty, but that's not all I feel. Not all I want."

Jayce's throat was tight as he fought down the heated swarm of emotions that threatened to erupt without warning. How did he go from giving this guy a shoulder rub to almost losing it?

The comforting brush of lips to the very corner of Jayce's mouth froze the next inhale.

"You're gay?" he blurted, his emotions derailed.

Rune didn't move away. "If you're asking if I like men, the answer is yes. I don't understand your word for that."

Jayce's entire frame shuddered with relief. "Thank god. It's been driving me crazy wanting you and not knowing." Turning Rune a little more, they settled together on the bench, closer.

"The feeling is mutual. Almost since the beginning. Everything about you pulls at me unlike anyone I've ever known."

Jayce huffed. "You know that is what makes it so hard to believe this is happening. I can't add to the Valda-Cree lines for the future. There won't be children."

A light press of fingers to his lips made him fall silent. "Shh. Let's not worry about anything outside of this moment, all right?"

With his lips so close, the puff of his breath was warm against suddenly sensitive skin but there was no pressure to rush this. Neither was moving with Rune all but facing him and practically on his lap now. Jayce's hands rested on his biceps, curled around their hardness, not letting him get away.

He circled his thumbs over the muscles beneath his hold. "There is so much I don't understand, don't know."

Rune's fingers slid to caress Jayce's jaw, their damp warmth creating sensations down his neck and chest. "I know. And you're trusting me with your life." Blue eyes lowered, and his head dipped marginally. "There is no greater trust for me." He adjusted his weight, moving closer still.

The flagging length of Jayce's cock brought on by the weightiness of their discussion appreciated the movement and quickly rose again beneath the water. Jayce sucked a breath when Rune straddled his lap in the water. No way to argue with that. Firm thighs bracketed around his own, bringing them so close.

"You frustrate me, confuse me, and make me laugh. I've never met anyone like you. Your future is only a small part of who you will become, and no, I don't know with certainty if it will come to pass, or what it means for the future of our world. Only that we both play a part in it." Strong fingers ghosted from his jaw down his throat and Jayce swallowed, reveling in the exploratory pressure.

"So what about your claim that I will be king?" he whispered.

"Only my feelings, and from what I've already witnessed of you, my belief that it will come to pass and the legends that preceded you about the Valda-Cree. About the lost child. No one of today even remembers that time, or much about King Bail. The Alendaren rulers have been in power for generations." He splayed a palm over Jayce's chest, where he could likely feel the telling thump of his heart not only caused by the conversation but from his nearness and touch. "I didn't see it at first, but the battle with the *sabra* showed me a part of you that I can't ignore. You are brave and logical at the same time. You have a level of perseverance that most couldn't compete with."

Jayce's breath left him in a slow whoosh. "All of that, huh? In only a few days?"

Rune's smile was gentle. "I've spent decades watching and learning the intricacies of a person's expression and their body's way of saying what their words don't. It comes with age," he quipped.

Jayce snickered, then he sobered. "So now what?"

Rune touched his bottom lip with a fingertip. "Now I'm going to kiss you. Because if I don't, I might expire."

"I love the way you talk," Jayce said. "So sexy."

Rune growled in his throat. Expecting a ravishing, heat by all the suns kind of kiss, Jayce melted on the spot when instead his lips were sweet, soft, sensual. Jayce was the one who almost passed out from the feathery caresses. Rune's bottom lip was a little fuller, plump to lick over with teasing flicks that seemed to be directly connected to his pelvis as he thrusted against Jayce's abdomen when he did.

They rocked slowly in the swirling water as they kissed leisurely. Jayce's hands trailed up and down his arms, learning the strength under flesh as he caressed the curvature of muscle and frame. Rune wasn't quite as wide as Jayce in the shoulders, but it was close. Not as thick, but it was the little details that kept him exploring.

The warmth of skin beneath his palms. The way his pale nipples hardened when he ran thumbs over them and the shudders that touch created told him Rune *really* liked it. The way Rune's breathing snagged and rushed when he brushed over his neck.

If anyone had told him a year ago he'd be making out with a sexy as sin elf in a hot tub in some arcane and archaic temple, he'd have died laughing.

He wasn't laughing now.

Chapter 16

After hours in the training room with the novices, Rune was worn down, depleted. He'd stretched his skills and his spells to challenge the younglings and they'd met him, made him work to keep one step ahead. There was skill and experience in creating spells and calling on inherent mage energy on the fly, without causing himself harm. The novices were still learning that fine line but they had worked hard for hours, and now he was soaking in heated water. Listening to the gentle burble of the water surrounding him was exactly what his tired mind and body needed. And then Jayce joined him. Rune's tiredness evaporated beneath Jayce's talented fingers. From his nape to his lower back, he worked magic of a different kind until he could hardly think, his body limp and utterly relaxed as water flowed around them. Then Jayce had dared to tuck Rune into his body, and his defenses against the simmering attraction for the man touching him absolutely crumbled.

Eyes that had once been brown, were now a beautiful gold amber ringed with the natural brown, stunning and remarkable with the dormant magic that lived inside him awakening. And they were so entrancing it was hard to look away from them. Whether Jayce recognized his bravery or not, Rune did. Putting the weight of their world on this one man's shoulders hadn't been fair to him. In doing so, Rune accepted his part in the loss of Jayce's family. He'd been so focused on Jayce, following him that first day, trying to decipher the type of world he lived in and concentrating on his spells to avoid detection, the thought of his life beyond the immediate hadn't occurred to him. That was Rune's failure. And because of it, Jayce's heartbreak.

He wouldn't fail him again. If Rune was supposed to be this man's guide and a guardian, then he needed to be more aware to properly protect him. The more Jayce learned, the more dangerous it would become for him. They didn't have the freedom to live in a bubble.

Except maybe for this one bubble right now. The heat of Jayce's kiss was making critical thinking so very difficult. There was calmness in his arms. A type of solitude he couldn't recall in any of his memories.

Rune's head tipped back as Jayce's lips slid oh-so-slowly across his cheek to nip gently at his jaw, teasing with kisses to skin. He looped his arms completely around Jayce's shoulders for stability. His fingers found the ends of his hair and furrowed upward, the weight heavy with moisture, thick and so soft. Their bodies melded together with perfection. There was strength in his embrace, yet the way he held Rune made him feel utterly cherished in that moment. He'd put this part of his needs away, as unnecessary, focusing on his studies and his magic, so many years since the last time he'd been with a lover. Jayce's heat and touch awakened something in him he couldn't ignore or as easily dismiss. It had been slowly reawakening almost since their meeting.

Definitely the first night when he unabashedly watched him change from the clothing he'd worn to the garments he'd procured for him. Right then, he should have put a larger wall between them, when his physical reaction had been so blatant, even if Jayce had been oblivious because of their circumstances.

Now, he didn't want to stop. He wasn't sure he could if he had to.

Jayce's lips never slowed in their explorations of reachable skin, from his chin to his water bathed throat. His tongue licked and roamed. Hot kisses and small nips of teeth that shot sparks through him, making him ache and pant in the best ways. Touches teasing across inches of sensitive neck until he was nibbling lightly on an earlobe. Rune gasped and stiffened as a current as strong as spring lightning raced down his spine and lit him up like a midnight star.

Jayce's quiet chuckle was sheer sex when he realized how sensitive Rune's ears were.

"The first time I saw you, I would have sworn your ears weren't real. But now, hearing the sounds you make when I do this—" His tongue languidly swirled from the lobe up the curve as far as he could reach. Rune stiffened with a groan, panting wildly. "Rune," he husked, his lips brushing against the sensitive skin. His fingers gripped him tight at his waist, pinning him chest to chest. "Want to lick every inch of you to see if you're as sensitive."

Rune tugged on the ends of hair in his grasp, bringing Jayce before him. Water swirled and played against them, buoying them while steam rose with lazy tendrils from the surface. Jayce's eyes glittered from the flickering firelight with a bright need, making them shimmer and sparkle like lush amber-gold flake. Slightly parted lips were rouged from their kisses, plumper, beckoning even as they promised so much more pleasure. This close, he could trace paths down his face, cradling his jaw, feeling the bit of scruff that he'd acquired in the last few days. The raw tingle in his palm sent shivers down his frame. Need pulsed through his body, for more of this, more of Jayce. Then his mouth was on Jayce's, plundering deep for his taste. Dueling and learning until there was nothing but Jayce's kiss in his world. Firm hands were encouraging his rocking, bringing their lengths together below the heated water. The weight of Jayce's shaft pressed against him, stroking him with a silken glide, driving his needs ever higher.

Jayce's broad hands drifted from around his waist to his spine, his fingers digging deep, pinning him. Rune was loving every minute of it. His strength, his kiss, even the tenderness he seemed unwilling to rush. What would Jayce's deepest passion feel like? He whimpered as his body clung, lust driving his movements as they climbed the cliffs of shared pleasure.

Fiery need raged through him, under his skin, biting at his nerves when Jayce shifted enough to grasp their lengths together in a single hand.

Rune's gasp was loud and breathy. "Goddess, yes," he moaned, biting his lip and bucking hard.

"You feel so good," Jayce growled. With a palm gripping his ass and the other on his shaft, Rune had never felt so enraptured by another's touch. Jayce's kiss stole his focus as he stroked them at the same time. Heat pooled low in his groin as his hips thrust into the tight channel created by Jayce's fist, bumping against Jayce's length as he worked them together. All the way to the root and back to the tip with a firm twist, to work their combined heat as one. The wonderful press of Jayce's cock against his own was driving him mad, pushing him ever closer to the edge. The rush of need and the want to make it last had him straining against Jayce's frame. Steamy water lapped around them as they rocked together, rolling splashes that broke against the low rock lip like timeless waves as his hips picked up speed. Jayce panted through his name, graveled and raw.

The raw sound sent a shiver of need right through Rune straight to his dick. His head rolled loosely on his neck, his focus shattered as pleasure built and raced through his system. Jayce's fingers stroked skin, gripping his ass to encourage the thrust of his hips meeting their lift and grind with his own body, then roaming his other hand's fingers toward Rune's crease. Rune moaned loudly when he brushed a fingertip over the sensitive skin of his opening. He couldn't form words, his ability stolen from him. He could imagine the stretch, the fullness and whimpered. The need for more had him clawing at Jayce's shoulders. His heart pounded with a rapid rate in answer to Jayce's questioning touches.

"Soon," Jayce breathed in warning before he bent his head to suck a spot up on his collarbone. "Want you so much. Next time, I want to see you, every inch." Hot breath on his neck made him cling tighter.

Next time?

"Jayce," he whined as he clawed into Jayce's muscles. His body wasn't his any longer. Every touch, every caress spiraled him higher, craving more of what Jayce was giving him. Nerves were crying for more of Jayce's heat, of his skin. He jerked when the fist pumping him squeezed, moving faster under the water, rubbing them against each other like kindling to start a fire, a conflagration sure to consume Rune entirely.

"Close," Jayce bit out, his body undulating against Rune's in answer, his golden gaze sharp and unblinking as he watched Rune's pleasure mount. Water sloshed, spraying them with a fine drizzle, refracting the flames surrounding them like diamonds on skin and lashes. Unable to ignore the pull of his kiss, Rune leaned forward and captured Jayce's mouth, clinging as his body came apart. Muscles tightened as the first jet filled his length, rushing through him with a grunt, another hard on the heels as Jayce stroked his shaft relentlessly.

Shudders wracked his frame when the unexpected skim of a thumb over his slit shot a shock through him, urging another pulse to be released from his balls. Then Jayce tensed beneath him, his frame bowing against Rune's chest as he ground out a growl that practically filled the enveloping silence of the chamber. Jayce's jaw clenched as his orgasm was swept away by the bubbling water in the pool.

"Fuck," he groaned, panting, moisture streaming from his temples, joined by the heat of the water to run in staggered rivulets. Gasping, he slowly relaxed, pulling Rune close, cuddling together as he milked them both until his hand simply stilled.

Haggard breaths eased as their hearts returned to a normal pace, though not a single muscle wanted to work. Rune floated and clung to the body that held him close.

"God, Rune," Jayce rasped.

Rune tenderly ran fingertips through his dark hair, playing with the bit that seemed to want to fall forward into his eyes. The single earring he wore sparkled with the torch firelight surrounding him. Goddess, he was too gorgeous for his own good. "Are you all right?"

Jayce barked a rough laugh. "That was the best. So wasn't expecting that. Been wanting to kiss you, it was driving me crazy. *That...* With you..." He sighed, but it sounded replete and content to Rune.

Rune nuzzled against his throat, kissing then licking over damp skin, tasting the mineral flavors of the water as well as the salt of his skin.

"My life has been so crazy since I met you," Jayce murmured. "Never imagined this, though."

The light drag of fingers played through the wet length of Rune's hair, pulling it out straight to let it cascade into the water in its own fall that seemed to enrapture Jayce completely. The tender sweeps relaxed him further. It was becoming obvious his hair was a weakness for Jayce.

"I didn't come down here to find you with any expectations. Not for sex."

Rune tilted upward on his neck. "You were looking for me?"

Jayce hummed. "I didn't want you to think I was holding today against you." He sighed, a quiet, pained, whimpered, broken sound that twisted Rune's heart. A deep inhale trembled his chest as he gathered his control. "But it is what it is." He adjusted himself enough to look into Rune's gaze. "I was looking for you because of how things went with Master Theil."

"Was he able to help you find your elemental magic?"

Jayce grinned like a little boy. A hand popped out of the water, dripping. "Let me show you," he mused. "Watch."

Then, with his hand down and a finger pointed at the water, he spun it in a slow circle. The concentration on his face was fierce. At first, nothing happened. He grumbled then grinned sheepishly. He sat straight, and drew a slow breath, then motioned with the same finger for patience. Rune leaned close and waited, watching expectantly.

Jayce shut his eyes and drew still, seeming to find a calm place, then exhaled and with his hand above the water again, he rotated his finger above it. Gently, the water began to swirl, a funnel in the middle of the pool.

Rune swallowed his gasp, his eyes wide as he witnessed Jayce's strengths for himself.

As the spinning water created a gurgling, sucking sound, he also kept an eye on Jayce. His expression was relaxed, focused, but not straining. Rune leaned apart to see both, his gaze going to the water then to Jayce, then back again. His eyes widened when he slowly raised his hand and the swirling funnel became a ball of water that rose upward. About the size of a lemon, it levitated above the water for a span of heartbeats before gradually dropping downward and feeding into the funnel one more time.

"Jayce," he questioned, surprised, and happily in awe. To have that much control after only a few hours... He was incredibly gifted. "You're able to control the water by thinking about it?"

Once the ball of water had disappeared, he flattened his hand above the vortex and it slowly faded, the pull of the cone vanishing completely. "Water, fire, even dirt. I wasn't as successful with the wind."

Rune blinked rapidly. "All of them?"

Jayce smiled broadly. "That's what I wanted to tell you!" He crowed quietly. "I found the colors, the magic. By the time we were done today, I was able to pull them to me without any extra boosting help from Master Theil." He gripped Rune close, hugging him. "You were right!" he whispered excitedly by his ear. "This is me!"

Rune gulped. "And Master Theil saw all of this?"

Jayce nodded not catching the note of trepidation in his question. "He helped me separate out the magic wavelengths by their colors.

Like, since your primary magic is a fire elemental, you see a lot of red when you cast, right?"

"That's exactly right." But a new fear was forming like ice in his gut. Because now, Master Theil would have figured out the secret he'd been keeping, the real reasons Jayce had been calling to Rune for the last two years. And these new discoveries only seemed to confirm what Rune had been seeing all along and trying to not reveal to anyone but Jayce. Mage magic was spell work supported by an elemental gift. The Valda-Cree family line had a much deeper ability, one that touched on all the elements and could control or call on many magics. And Master Theil had seen his ability firsthand. Because if what Jayce found in his magic proved anything, it proved he was indeed Valda-Cree.

He *was* the missing prince.

Only time would reveal if Master Theil was going to use the knowledge he had against Jayce, and against Rune, because his loyalty was now to the true King.

Chapter 17

Jayce slept like the dead that night. After hours of intense concentration and study with Master Theil and the unbelievable orgasm he'd shared with Rune, his body went horizontal and didn't move once. He couldn't even find it in him to care that it was a pallet and not a mattress any longer. The unexpectedness of Rune's kisses had swept his mind clear of most every thought in the universe, including why he'd been looking for him.

The lack of windows in the cliff's sleeping chambers made waking disconcerting. Was it too early? Was the sun even up? Had the world stopped spinning? *Again?* All valid questions to a waking mind. It didn't help that the torch right outside his door always burned out overnight, which left no way to relight his candle. Once they were cold, they were rewrapped and dipped in something that smelled a little like tar but it was thinner and wasn't as strong smelling, over and over, until the torchwood itself was useless. Then the scrap handles were used in the kitchens to fire the pits as the residual trace fuels maintained a hotter pit when they were added to the regular burning woods.

He blinked and then chuckled. The details he'd picked up in the last few days of simply living in the temple.

The very idea of electricity or cellphones was nonexistent in this world. And honestly, he wasn't really missing any of it. Oh, sure food delivery would be amazing, and maybe a good beer and a movie, but overall, there wasn't really a need for anything like that to fill his hours. It was the Jayce of the twenty-first century in his world.

Not the person he was now, not by a longshot.

Relaxing on his back, he closed his eyes and drew a steadying breath. Colors danced and wove like the ribbons he was becoming familiar with, caressing and bending as they twined through his conscious mind. He found during his explorations that they loved to move, in a way, as they spoke to him. They were so beautiful, bright, like a fine mist refracting a glowing light back at him. Or with the way they moved so sensually around each other, like ribbons curling and weaving through space and air. Their beauty represented so much to him. Peace, calm, power, energy. Master Theil's teachings and wisdom made sense. It wasn't the colors which were good or evil; it was the user's intentions. The colors and the power they represented were neutral, like the colors of the world they lived in. Nature wasn't evil or good, it simply was, existing, and co-existing with all the life forces that breathe and nourish the world in all the varied forms.

And it was an important balance that any mage-born needed to learn.

He tucked his hands under his head with his eyes still closed, watching them move and glide. Master Theil said this was a good form of meditation, to learn the colors' way of existing inside of him. Most only had one or two that they could embrace.

Jayce had realized quickly while working with Master Theil that this was no small thing that he could see so many more than was typical and be able to call on more than one, regardless of how much control he had on any individual color energy.

Rune's words echoed through his mind. That Jayce could somehow be that missing child, born Valda-Cree, hidden in his time for safety or more nefarious reasons that no one of this time would remember. Valda-Cree, with mage-born magic.

He swallowed roughly as the colors seemed to freeze in place, like they were waiting for him to come to the next conclusion.

Because if that were all true, that meant he would also have an animal spirit. The swathes of color began to move excitedly. He frowned. How did he know it was excitement and not say, agitation?

No. No, they were definitely dancing, spinning, roping together until they formed a wall of color. He swallowed and then rose to his elbows as he blinked into the absolute darkness. "Well, hell." He sat up and cupped his head as he thought. "So now what?" How did he find out if he had an animal spirit? How did he meet it? Bring it out?

And if this was expected and true, how much more was he going to have to accept and take on? He didn't believe for a minute that he was going to be king, regardless of Rune's assertion. That would be too fantastical, and he'd been raised in the world of CGI and hoverboards.

"The missing child," he murmured to the unresponsive silence. Jayce swallowed, letting it really sink it. The last few days had begun to blur. His world, his personal box, had been turned upside down and shook mercilessly. Breathing to slow his heart, to be able to think, the next truth slammed home leaving him gasping. "So that means Rune was right. Someone else does know." Raquel and Helen. They weren't his neighbors just because. And as much as he'd thought of them as friends for years, they had a purpose. Somehow, he and Rune had been a step ahead and escaped, until they'd been found. And he'd lived through their attack once he was in Trajanleh. By now, whoever had hired them, would know they'd failed. And that Jayce was alive and well. A shiver crossed his shoulders, and it wasn't because he was sitting in the dark.

Standing to his feet abruptly, the blanket at his waist fell to the floor, then he dug fingers into his hair to push the loose bits away from his eyes. He paced for a few minutes, aware of the size of his chamber in a visceral sense to not run into the walls. Then, common sense seeped in.

Why was he pacing in the dark? He grinned at his own stupidity, then slowly sank to the floor where he was, his naked ass on the not-quite-cold stone. Crossing his legs, he shut his eyes and started to play with the colors in his mind. To him, the best description was that he was stroking them, letting them stroll between his thoughts while visualizing them mentally, like wisps of colored smoke streaming between his fingers.

As his heart calmed, he could feel the growing and telltale pulse of power in the bands of color. Raising his hand, he focused and lit the baby flame in his palm. The tingle was becoming known after more than three dozen creation attempts the day before. Opening his eyes a fraction at a time, he smiled almost giddily to see what he'd created. It balanced and swayed like the end of a wick.

Turning carefully, he reached for the candle in the holder and used the heat in his palm to light the wick. And then let out a quiet whoop when it did as he needed. He fisted his hand over the flame in his palm to extinguish it, giving it a quick thank you for the assistance. For some reason, that felt right, to appreciate the power of the magic. It didn't belong to him to abuse. In truth, none of it belonged to him. He understood the importance of acknowledging that he was as much of a tool to use it, as the powers were a tool to be used, yet accepting that they were deadly and needed to be judiciously respected. A small tingle near his heart seemed to approve of his thoughts.

Which meant he had to be cautious going forward.

Man, he needed Rune. He didn't want to fuck this up.

With the candle lit, he quickly dressed. It was only a few moments later when there was a tap on his door as he tugged on his boots. "Come in."

Rune came in with a soft whoosh of his cape. He shut the door behind him.

Jayce immediately caught the tension in his frame, and that his cowl was up. His hands were folded into his cape. Very unusual for him while in the temple. "Is something wrong?"

"No, but you were sleeping late, so I wanted to make sure you were well." His gaze skittered to Jayce then away again. Then his focus fell to the already lit candle. "You are advancing quickly."

"Am I?" He had no way to know. And maybe not knowing was for the best. *Be like the bumblebee.* A phrase he remembered, if he was right, from kindergarten. That he could do anything until proven otherwise. He closed the gap between himself and Rune. And before the elf could evade, he pushed the cowl away from his face. "Don't hide," he whispered. "Do you regret last night?" Looking into his eyes, he felt the tug of something not magical at all, but so potent. Even if Rune didn't see it, or did and couldn't acknowledge it yet because of the visions Jayce knew he was trusting, they *were* being driven closer together. It was like Rune was the flame and he was but the small moth, drawn ever closer to his warmth, craving him. Jayce regretted nothing that happened the night before.

Sharp memories of last night, of their kisses, the feel of his skin in his hand with him so close, were at the forefront of his thoughts as he studied blue eyes. The rush of shared heat and then the gasped pleasure as Rune had broken apart in his arms. Even then, he craved more of the elf. Wanted to push him into the door and keep him there with his mouth, kiss on him and caress his chest like he had the night before until he was gasping and panting in pleasure

He'd loved every second of their time in the pool after the shock that Rune had wanted him as much had worn off. Even withdrawn and with worry tightening Rune's elven features, he was still one of the most beautiful men Jayce had ever met.

Rune sighed, his chin dipping to lose his gaze and Jayce wanted to tell him it would be all right, that nothing like that ever had to happen again if it was what he wanted, but what Rune said, cut his voice off completely.

"I shouldn't have, but I don't regret it."

"Why shouldn't you have? Why shouldn't we?" he breathed, inching closer until Rune had to take a step backward only to be fully blocked by the closed door. Yet Jayce didn't follow through with his most craved desires. Not yet.

"Because..." His voice faded. Wide blue eyes glistened in the candle's flickering light. Emotions and thoughts danced behind those enigmatic orbs until he blurted, "I brought you something."

Slipping away from Jayce, he put a pace between them. Jayce let him. Now that he knew Rune wanted him as much, he could be patient. It wasn't like he was going anywhere, right? "Brought me something?"

Rune quickly nodded, apparently relieved that he wasn't going to have to explain. "I did. I know yesterday was a shock, and I can't help feeling guilty that it was my choices, my impetus to follow the visions, that destroyed your prior life." He slid fingers into one of the pouches attached to his belt and pulled out a leather cord, the item on it hidden in his palm. "Do you remember the first night, your garments?"

"Yeah." Though honestly, he hadn't thought much about them as they would *definitely* make him stick out when compared to what he'd been wearing since.

He opened his palm, revealing a pale stone about a half dollar in size, oval like a large opal and full of glittering colors. Rune held the stone up. "I made this. Your past should never be forgotten and the life you led should never be treated as superficial. I apologize for making those mistakes."

Jayce curiously picked up the pendant. It was solid and a good ounce or two. "What does this have to do with what I was wearing?" He turned it between his fingers in the candlelight to see the shimmer. There was a stripe of denim blue and small speck of black, and something... He squinted as he recognized the different colors and shapes. Then shook his head in amazement, turning the stone over and over to see all the little bits. "Those are my clothes! How did you do that?"

"Spell work," he replied with a small shoulder roll. Like it was nothing, and maybe for him it was, but it meant so much to Jayce.

"This is incredible. Thank you." He slipped the leather cord over his head and dropped the stone beneath his shirt edges. "I'll never take it off."

Warmth bloomed in a lovely pink over Rune's face. "I'm glad you like it. I don't know how I could possibly make what I did to you right."

Jayce moved closer to the candle, ready to blow it out when Rune opened the door next. "Rune, I understand the hand of destiny and fates. You did what you felt you had to to save your world. Maybe that makes me naïve to what is happening and what will happen with me." He motioned for Rune to open the door. "But I trust you."

Chapter 18

"Wait."

Jayce turned and straightened at the one word.

Rune walked away from the closed door, right up to Jayce. "Do you mean that?"

"Which?" His brow twisted in with a cute furrow.

Rune's heart was beating wildly in his chest. "That you trust me?" he asked softly. He searched his golden eyes and found no deception in them. After the day before, he wasn't sure he would ever earn Jayce's trust. If he'd ever have the right after the horrible mistakes he'd made.

Jayce's smile was sweet and there was a tenderness in his eyes, smoothing the previous look of questioning concern that made Rune feel gutted and buoyant at the same time. Because he didn't deserve that trust even while he craved more. "Yes. I do."

"Even after what I did, what has happened?" He knew yesterday had been an emotional storm for Jayce. And didn't begrudge him his anger when he'd learned the truth. Pain caused by Rune's actions.

Jayce smirked. "I trust you, but I still have questions. I can't see me being any kind of shapeshifter, or skin shifter, or animal." He rolled a shoulder. "But in everything else, yes, I trust you. You haven't exactly been wrong."

Jayce exhaled sharply when Rune rushed him and pinned him by his shoulders against stone and captured his mouth. Then he groaned deeply as Rune kissed him thoroughly. Jayce's arms swept around him, yanking him close until he was feeling defined contours from top to bottom. How did this one man feel so good? How did he make Rune feel so much?

123

"Why can't I stay away from you?" he growled, nipping at Jayce's mouth before claiming him with another kiss that left them both gasping for breath. He'd spent all of his dark hours last night thinking of the numerous reasons he needed to keep away from Jayce after what they'd shared in the bathing chamber. Recriminations that he couldn't become involved with this man with what he knew, and what his visions portended. He was probably the last person Jayce should trust with the amount of influence he could have over him, not only now, but later, if the visions came to pass. He never wanted him to doubt his place in their world because of something that Rune may do or say. Like now.

"I don't want you to," Jayce rasped as he cupped Rune's ass and urged him closer, making him groan again. Thickness brushed against him, sending a wave of desire against nerves. Like the night before he felt himself succumbing too quickly, craving. There was no control once Jayce got his hands on him.

Their mouths were voracious, need pouring through him as Jayce took control of the kiss and licked over his mouth. As though he was the embodiment of *need* itself. He shivered as he went limp with desire. If Jayce hadn't been holding him as tight as he was, he would melt to the floor. He'd never felt desire like this, an all-consuming lust and hunger that drove thought from his mind. His body ached with the need for closeness and naked skin. He loved how strong Jayce was against his frame. The press of fingers against his neck as they dueled tongue to tongue until they had to breathe.

Rune's palms found and formed to his shoulders, moving downward to caress his chest. The shape, the hardness made him weak. He shouldn't be allowing this happen, but his body, his desire for this man had other ideas.

A knock on the door shocked Rune, giving him no choice but to pull away, freezing where he stood. Jayce met his gaze and purposely kept it when he reached into his trousers and adjusted his hardened length. Rune swallowed unable to look away, wanting to pull the fabric away and indulge them both.

"That is your fault," Jayce whispered. "Yes?" he answered to the repeated knock on the door.

"Master Jayce, Master Theil is requesting you join him in his library."

"I'll be right there."

Then Jayce tugged Rune close and kissed him hard, an abrupt surprise that scattered Rune's thoughts. "Time to see where today takes us. You up to the challenge?" he taunted.

"How can you be so brave?" Rune murmured as he strode for the door once more. He avoided looking at Jayce's lips. He knew where those thoughts would take him and he didn't want to have to worry about signs of his arousal in front of his mentor.

"There's a phrase from my time. Fake it until you make it. It basically means to stay optimistic and confident in the face of adversity, to keep trying, improving and life will imitate that mindset until you succeed. I was given a chance as a child to make my life better when my foster parents became my real parents." They were the only parents he knew, but there was no way to mistake that he wasn't born to them. He sent a silent prayer that they were safe and happy and could only hope they knew he was all right where he was now. He blew out the candle when Rune opened the door. "Since then I've tried to be optimistic in the face of whatever life throws at me. I know life doesn't guarantee us shit day to day." He arched an eyebrow, directing his next statement succinctly. "Especially when our lives are upended by magic wielding mages."

Rune smirked but didn't refute him because there was no argument to his part in Jayce's life's changes as he joined him at his shoulder, carrying the fresh torch from next to his door. "That explains so many of your behaviors. I knew you would have a different view from someone born and raised here, but you are so unique. Very surprising, in a good way."

"Good. Keeps my friends on their toes."

Rune chuckled as they climbed the stairs to the main halls, leaving the torch to burn in one of the stairwell scones, then traversing the sunlit hall lengths to the temple library. A light knock on heavy wood received a call to enter.

Rune allowed Jayce to enter before him, intending to close the door behind him but Master Theil's voice carried to him. "No, Rune. Please join us. I should have known you'd be together." Irritation coated his words.

Rune slid a quick wide-eyed look to Jayce. His surprise equaled Rune's. Master Theil stood in tense contemplation with his hands gripped behind his back while facing to stare flatly out a window. There was a cloudless bright blue sky with the sound of the surf crashing gently into the stone of the lower cliff face below. He'd been in this room many times over the years and had always appreciated the view to the wild seas beyond, but his master's expression and stiffness concerned him greatly.

"Master Theil?" Jayce asked, confusion marring his face at the open hostility now directed at him.

"How long did you think you could keep this secret, Rune?"

"Master?" He stepped up beside Jayce. "I don't understand the accusation."

"Oh, you don't?" He pointed at Jayce, his eyes blazing. "He can't stay here any longer."

Jayce blinked. "I can't?"

"How dare you bring the *missing prince* to my doors and not warn me!" he snarled. "How dare you play me for a fool?"

"I did not," he said evenly, hiding the tremulous shaking in his gut. He put himself marginally in front of Jayce. He knew this moment was going to arrive. Now he'd find out if Master Theil would betray them or not. "Until he finds his animal spirit, it is only a theory that he is the missing prince."

Master Theil waved a hand. "Irrelevant. He has mage magic and the Valda-Cree gifts. He will bear his animal spirit when it and he are ready. He *is* the missing prince. Did you think I wouldn't figure it out when I unraveled his magic strengths?"

"I wasn't trying to deceive you, Master Theil. I had no proof! I still don't, not really. He has been missing for centuries, believed dead. I couldn't make the leap to believe on faith alone."

Jayce whipped around, staring at Rune. He knew what was going through the man's mind. Rune was denying Master Theil's accusations even though they mirrored almost word for word the very truths Rune had been pressing on him to accept. He could only hope that Jayce understood he was protecting him by underplaying his hand to his mentor. He needed to know if Master Theil was going to protect them, or not. If he could be trusted to support them.

"I might be Valda-Cree, I never knew my birth parents, and I can accept I have magic because something in me changed coming into Caduthien and Trajanleh but I really don't know how I can do this

126

shapeshifting that you swear is inherited in the line. It's not possible. I'm human."

Master Thiel's voice filled the library with a resonating rumble.

"Cull the darkness, share the light.

"Arise, brave soul, foretold to fight.

"Upon that soul, lay the mane,

"Of lion's blood coursing in man's vein."

A chill filled the room as Master Theil finished the prophecy, all but sucking the air out of the room.

"You knew what the visions were telling me all along," Rune accused. "Why didn't you ever say so?"

Master Theil grimaced, turning to the window again. He lifted his chin as he spoke clearly, not exactly a rebuke but Rune heard what was being said. "I wasn't sure, however I was confident they were pushing you in the right direction. I did *not* think for a moment that you were seeking the lost prince. Like many, I believed his time was long past. Prophecies are not perfect and yes, they can be vague." His shoulders finally lost some of their tension. "Yet, I should have recognized the connection. King Bail was of the Valda-Cree or he wouldn't have been a crowned king of Kielbos, of the goddess's chosen line. A man of nearly unlimited mage magic who reigned peacefully. He was fair and as my memory serves, firm without fear when he ruled. I can't prove it, couldn't prove it when it happened, but that amount of power uncontrolled by the mage guild was why Carden had him murdered. The prophecy was never given much credence because in order for the prophecy to come true, the bearer of the blood would have to be able to command all the elements of nature to be able to fill the need of the crown, and…" He exhaled. "Take on the animal spirit of the rightful heir. And the prince was never found. It was believed the line had been extinguished."

"Right. The power of three. You mentioned that before. But I'm telling you, it can't be me. Yes, I'm a man so that fits, but the rest really doesn't."

Rune placed a hand on his arm. "But it does," he offered with cautious warning. "The water. You can control water and fire. The more your powers strengthen, the more likely it is for someone to notice. Word will spread, as curiosity and possibly with fear."

"And that means they are more likely to come here," Jayce said with dawning comprehension. "Will they attack the temple? Like the *sabra*? Am I putting you in danger by being here?"

"No one should. We can defend ourselves if need be," Master Theil said with begrudging acceptance. "But it's possible."

"I promised to guide and guard him when I accepted my place in the visions, Master Theil. I will not fail him on that. If we need to find a new place to prepare for his return, I will do so."

"Great. While you two are figuring out how to keep me safe and all that, what exactly am I supposed to do? I'm learning my magic ability and traits. I'll even take the leap and say I'm Valda-Cree, but what am I supposed to do with that knowledge? I can't walk into the some guy's castle and call him an interloper. Not if there's no one left alive who even remembers the name Valda-Cree or why that's important to the throne."

Master Theil spun from the window, his eyes sparking with determination now rather than anger. Rune almost exhaled with relief at Master Theil's next words. He should have believed in his mentor more, but he wasn't protecting only himself by being cautious. He was protecting the future of Kielbos, of Caduthien, and all the people who lived there.

"You must find your animal. That will confirm your bloodline. Once the word of your reappearance is known, those who know the history will support you. The Valda-Cree were the one true royal bloodline as gifted by the goddess herself. The usurpers who sit on the throne now are not blessed as such. Their weaknesses to be controlled by Carden and the others, if there are more in play, is apparent in the evil that is overcoming our lands. Villages being destroyed. People unable to protect themselves. Magics are growing twisted as more of the mages fall to this evil. Evil begets evil. There must be a balance or the incurring evil, the armies, the war we've been subjected to will only increase." He seemed to come to a decision as he folded his hands into his robe cuffs, relaxed, but resolved. "None can take your place and keep the balance necessary between man, magic, and nature. Which is why the pressure to find you is now, because the imbalance that can destroy what remains is at a tipping point. The balance the Valda-Cree kept must be returned to the throne to move Caduthien out of this ennui that is taking us to total destruction."

Jayce crossed his arms and huffed a small barked sound, glaring at the elder elf in the room. "Fine. You're saying I need to create an army. On the say-so of being *believed* to be the rightful heir. Something even I don't believe at the moment."

"There is a way to seek your Valda-Cree spirit." Master Theil tapped his chin thoughtfully, before gliding to sit behind the largest stone desk in the room. Drawing a hefty tome from the shelves to him with a wave of his hand, it came to rest on the smoothed stone before him soundlessly. The pages flipped. "If that is what you need to *convince you.*"

"What is this evil?" Jayce asked with a cautionary note in the question. "How am I going to beat or destroy something that has been breeding and growing for generations?"

Rune paced the width of the library, chewing on his lip. The gentle snap of his cloak rustled through the air as he spun on a heel, his stride carrying him through the bands of sunlight streaming through the windows. "That hasn't been shown to me. It may mean that the answer is not known yet, that our actions could have an impact on it, or that when we see it, we will know. All I know is it is destructive and voraciously consuming our lands."

"But why? And why now?"

"There is always a balance, good to bad, evil to just. With the Valda-Cree missing, the balance is teetering more and more. The structure of that evil is at least partly magical in nature." Rune gave Jayce a tight smile. "That is where the Valda-Cree, and the prophecy, come into it. We need those who are able to skin shift and mages combined to bolster your strengths."

Jayce swallowed, hard. "That makes it sound like I'll die."

He wanted to wrap Jayce up in his arms and protect him from everything hovering unseen in their future. "Nothing is promised. You said it yourself, today does not promise tomorrow."

Master Theil read over pages as they slowly flipped past him, returning them to the previous conversation. "There is a ritual that all Valda-Cree royals undertake. You haven't had the benefit of going through it. That is why your spirit animal is dormant. You haven't shared your soul or your heart with your magic to bring them together as one. The magics must merge to allow the animal presence, or it may never come to you."

Rune froze on a dime. "Ritual?" Ice coated his insides. Flashes of the vision of Jayce, strung up between torches by magic alone returned to him. A chill enveloped him. Is this where Master Theil betrays them? Will he destroy Jayce's spirit animal? Or help call it forward? Because he didn't understand why Jayce was being contained by magic, or from where or by who during the vision. He hated that he doubted anyone, but he had to know who he could trust to move forward. If his visions and Master Theil were right, and they needed an army to proceed, there would have to be more than himself loyal to Jayce. And only the blessed of the Valda-Cree could instill the confidence needed to do that.

He wanted to take Jayce far away and protect him from the coming pain but he knew it was too late for that. Their path had been set when he walked through the portal in to the other world to find him.

Chapter 19

Master Theil stated, "The ritual is usually held on the tenth winter solstice, but you didn't have that opportunity and if you want proof, then this can't be delayed."

"What kind of ritual?" Jayce queried as he minced a step backward, no more enthused than Rune appeared to be at the announcement.

"Will it work?" Rune asked next.

Jayce stumbled over to a wooden chair and sank on to it, his knees suddenly weak and rubbery. "Work? What are you guys going to do to me?" he demanded. What are they planning?

"You must be consecrated. I had forgotten about it. You obviously are of an age where it would have already taken place, to be blessed by the goddess."

Jayce was grinding his teeth in frustration now. "And who is this goddess! Please quit speaking in riddles!" He all but clawed his hands into his hair, rubbing into his eyes until he saw spots. Would someone please explain all of this to him! Little words were best.

"Ahdrer, the goddess of animals and nature who blessed the Valda-Cree in the beginning as the keeper of the races. They were the blessed family who were elevated to the throne to bring peace and stability to a young world."

Jayce hunched over his knees, his hands pressed into his face as he fought for calm and listened to Master Theil's explanation. "Okay." He breathed deeply for a moment, desperate for that calm to kick in, blinking through the shooting sparks in his vision. "Okay, so that sounds like our goddess Artemis, the Roman goddess of nature. She was made up," he derided, unamused.

"Oh, I assure you," Master Theil remarked as he continued perusing through the tome. "She is no myth. Aside from that, you would have had your family's assistance in going through the shifting change when your given animal would have come forward. With none of that occurring, you're still locked apart." He whipped up a finger and jabbed at a place on the page. "Found it! There is a rite of passage that will reveal your animal spirit when it is merged with your elemental magics. It is to be held on the winter solstice at the fade of dusk. However, you are no longer ten winters old." He leaned back in his chair, a hint at frown growing between his brows. "And we are nowhere near the winter solstice."

"And its purpose?" Jayce dropped his hands to clench his arm around his middle. Whatever the answer, he knew with a burst of clarity he wasn't going to like it.

"Like I explained, you need to be blessed." Master Theil's face was enigmatic, nearly calm with his confidence. It was everything Jayce wasn't feeling.

A firm hand cupped his shoulder and peering upward, he found Rune standing with him. He tried and failed to smile, probably getting no more than a grimace, but he was appreciative of the calm strength in his touch regardless.

He'd never been religious by any metric, but he had a feeling this wasn't going be anything like getting dunked by a priest in a cold river.

All but banished to the bathing chamber after a full day of training and instruction in preparation of the coming hours, Jayce grumbled as he sank into the volcanic thermal water.

Only this time, he and Rune weren't alone. Brin and two more were assisting.

"Seriously, I can bathe my damn self," he groused, none too quietly getting into the pool.

"This is a little more involved than simple bathing," Rune murmured into his ear when he could.

Brin and Rune followed him into the water. As much as he loved having Rune with him, the tendrils of want that the elf created in him were utterly absent with others present. He supposed it was good to know that. Exhibitionism was *not* a kink. He was absolutely fine with that.

132

After dunking in the water and being thoroughly scrubbed to within an inch of his life with soaps and salts and he didn't know what the green one was—Seaweed?—until he was a pink ball of nerves, all three climbed out and the two waiting, aided with drying him off. Rune encouraged him to sit then stretch out naked on a stone table near the wall. The stone wasn't cold, but it was unnerving as hell to be splayed like an offering at a Luau.

Jayce huffed, doing his best to hide his misgivings. Whatever he'd been feeling with Rune touching him, close to him, was utterly killed with so many in the room with them, and them...touching him. He shuddered as they moved around him. "Fine. I feel like I have no control over anything anymore. You know that, right?" he whispered for Rune alone.

Rune nodded. Then Jayce closed his eyes and breathed. The look of guilt that he'd caught flashing across Rune's lovely features was not what he'd intended. He was frustrated with not knowing what was happening, but he was not going to take that out on Rune. He raised a hand and halted Brin as he was returning with probably oil or something equally weird carried in the gray pot in his palms. "Brin, wait."

He paused and nodded, turning his back to give them a minute.

Jayce rose up on the edge and caught Rune's face in a tender palm, bringing him close for privacy. "Look, I know you're caught in this as much as I am. Right now, you're my only friend who I can trust because you *are* as caught as me."

"But—"

Jayce pressed a thumb to his lips to silence him. Out of the pool, Rune wore a simple gauze-like gown the same as the others, which did nothing to hide his beautiful body from Jayce. The backlight glow from the torches made the damp places nearly translucent, revealing the smooth shape of his hips and strong thighs before their muscled lengths vanished in the gauzy shadows. Yet it was only Rune's body that drew his eye over and over. Jayce hunted beyond Rune's shoulder, glad that the other three were focused against the opposite wall to give them a moment. "Kiss me."

Rune startled, his beautiful blue eyes going bright and wide. Then he did. A sweet kiss that helped to relax Jayce, pushing the wariness clawing at nerves away from the surface. He had no idea of what was coming, and had to trust Master Theil and Rune exclusively to not lead him wrong. Rune pulled away from the kiss licking his lips as he did. Jayce's heart thudded hard as the need for more coursed through his veins. A more he wasn't going to get to explore yet again. Those kisses packed a punch and if it weren't for the audience, he knew he'd be showing his appreciation in ways that left no doubt for Rune.

"Now, please, lie down and let us do what we need to for your preparation."

Jayce released a disgruntled sigh and stretched out on the flat rock. "Fair warning, I'm ticklish in a few places."

Rune squeezed his fingers lightly, but nodded. "Brin, we are ready."

Incenses were lit, the slow moving scented smoke curling around him as the others prepped. A woodsy scent filled his lungs with calm. It was a good thing too, as soon, there were oiled hands on Jayce and in places that he wished he could have a reason to enjoy.

"And this was done to a ten-year-old?" Jayce choked out as Rune waved Brin away from his groin. Rune's hands were methodical and thorough, but that didn't keep Jayce from responding to his touch. Brin was rubbing the scented oil over shoulders and arms, letting Rune work over the more personal and private areas. Or, if the location of Rune's fingers were any indication, Brin would likely be beaten for being too familiar. Areas that were unwillingly showing their approval of the contact whether Jayce wanted them to or not. Strong strokes and firm fingers that kneaded skin and muscle. He had to grit his teeth to fight the pleasurable sensations when he methodically worked below his balls and over his length. Then his touch was gone and Jayce released his breath with a long whoosh.

He wanted to cry because it had felt amazing, but he couldn't enjoy it, so he'd hated that it had felt that good.

"This part of the preparation would have been done by the child's mother or their nurse. Also, those who the rite is meant for were commonly assisted to bathe. There was never anything sexual implied."

Jayce swept his gaze to Rune, catching the sparkle of playfulness, though his face remained stoic. He was enjoying torturing Jayce! He growled, fighting to keep control.

"You're a brat," he muttered.

Brin snickered but otherwise his hands didn't falter. The other two thankfully didn't have their hands all over Jayce. Rather, they assisted with the oils as Rune and Brin continued to massage and if he could have enjoyed it even a little bit more, Jayce would have loved being pampered until he was relaxed and feeling quite malleable. Today was not that day.

He flipped and let them rub the fragrant oils into his back and down his ass and legs. Even the soles of his feet. He could tell by pressure and intent who was where.

Once he was done, he was assisted to stand and given a cream white robe that wrapped around him with a waist tie, sporting a high collar in the back, with a length that draped nearly to his feet. The sleeves were billowy and loose, the cuffs narrowing to points against his hands. The fabric was soft, but not lush, thinner than terrycloth, yet comfortable against his freshly oiled skin. It was all he wore as he'd left his necklace and earring in his chamber. As naked as a newborn under the robe.

"You will join Master Theil for meditation and instruction in the south courtyard," Rune informed him as the group climbed from the pool chamber to the upper floors. Firelight flickered over the walls and he tried his best to stay focused, but the tingling of anxious awareness, of the unknown, creeping toward him couldn't be completely ignored.

"Where are you going?" he asked, hoping the rush of panic hadn't been obvious.

"I need to spend some time with Iba," he replied keeping his face neutral and his attention forward. "I will be joining you later to complete the ritual."

Brin and the other two who'd helped veered off with a departing bow. "They aren't?"

"No. The ritual will only be the three of us. No one else knows of your significance at the moment," he explained privately.

Jayce stopped in his tracks. "Why are you being so secretive? I thought you wanted it known and all that stuff Master Theil said in the library."

"In time, yes. We are unprotected here. That is part of why I need to see Iba. I need her to go scouting for us. We need a secure place to plan from. I haven't had any more visions since your arrival." He pinched his lips and glanced away, searching around them before adding, "Except for the vision about the ritual. I didn't know what it was I was seeing. This is something you must go through. We had to be here long enough for this, but any longer is putting the temple and everyone here in peril. Master Theil is right in that. We can't stay."

He shook his head, gazing out into the distance, hoping for answers that simply weren't there. "I feel like I should be fighting this. This isn't my problem, and it's not my world. But then I remember Raquel swinging that damn axe through my door and I get confused. How did this all start? Why me?"

Rune's frame relaxed minutely, clearly understanding his angst while Jayce hoped he knew it wasn't directed solely at him. "I hope it will all be explained. But for now, we must go where the wind pushes us."

"And I have to get the goddess's blessing."

"You're not alone," he offered, starting to walk again. "I am not going to desert you."

Jayce knew he was trying to be supportive and encouraging, but there was one thought that still bothered him. "Tell me something."

"Always."

Jayce lowered his voice. "Do you trust Master Theil?"

"I trust him in the ways that matter. I've known him my whole life, as a mentor and as a friend."

"Then why didn't you tell him everything, and why did you still try to downplay my part in it?"

Rune came to a dragged, stuttered stop on stone, his neutral expression showing cracks. Facing an open window he moved closer to the wall. Jayce mimicked him all but speaking in whispers. "Because it never occurred to me that he could know of you being the missing prince or only my vision quest, or that he has a twin brother who is even now controlling part of the throne, if not all of it. We both kept secrets and it brought doubt." Raising a hand he stroked over Jayce's now smooth cheek. "And because I don't want to lose you and I fear the ritual."

Jayce blinked. "Fear? Am I going to be cut up and left bleeding?" He shuddered under the robe, feeling a chill regardless of the sunlight's warmth streaming around them.

Rune blanched and shook himself. "No. I fear the truth will change how you see me. Master Theil already suspects I am too close to you. And he is right."

"I meant what I said earlier. You are my friend, and I trust you."

136

Rune stiffened, grimacing before a cool detachment overtook his features once more. The elf was a master at hiding his deeper thoughts and emotions. "Let's go. There are things we both need to see done before the beginning of tonight's sunset."

Chapter 20

Rune swept from the temple as though hellhounds pursued him after leaving Jayce in Master Theil's hands. Knots tightened his stomach, and he had no way to stop the burn from consuming him.

He knew, or at least he had an idea of what Jayce would be facing this evening. And he'd been a coward to not warn him. The vision from only a few nights before felt like a lifetime had passed since. Mere days since the beginning of his journey into Jayce's world. Rune needed some meditation of his own, clarity was sorely missing, becoming convoluted with the mass of feelings becoming entrenched in the other man.

It didn't help that the memories of his kisses were taunting him. Passionate. Tender. Promising. Making him crave more than they'd already shared. Was it wrong that he felt close to Jayce after such a short time? His purpose was protection and guidance, but it was impossible to ignore what being near the man did to him. His focus had been challenged and he'd subdued his natural reactions in the bathing chamber because they hadn't been alone, and as he'd explained, there was nothing sexual in the ritual preparations.

Even deeper, he'd refused to allow himself to think about Brin's hands being all over Jayce, or the jealousy that had engulfed him when he'd been instructed by Master Theil to take the others with them to ensure proper purification for the coming ritual. It had all simmered beneath the surface until he realized how nervous Jayce was. The coming ritual wasn't about Rune, and he'd pushed his own discomforts aside as much as he was able. Jayce had tried to hide his emotions under the fiery bluntness of his sarcasm, but Rune was learning his ways. There had been no interest in anyone's attentions except his, as the lone kiss they'd shared had proven. It was hard to keep the quagmire of feelings, and the memory of the shared kisses suppressed.

Striding away from the cliffs, he walked until trees encircled him, until cooling shade and the soft murmurs of life replaced the sound of crying birds and pounding surf breaking against rocks.

Slowing his harried pace, he breathed deeply of the scents of nature, the warmth of moss and earth long unmoved. Tree trunks rose around him like sentinels, reaching for the sunlight they craved while cooling the ground beneath them with their broad arms and plentiful summer foliage. Pausing near a large elm, he rested a tender hand on the coarse bark, relaxing his shoulders, strain melting away.

"Hello, Mother," he murmured reverently as his eyes drifted shut. Life thrummed below his touch, the essence of all things living and breathing. Warmth bathed him, quenching a thirst that had been put aside for duty. Nature's connection wrapped around him, filled him until his heart beat with a resounding echo as he shared his breath and life with the force that helped sustain him and his magics and gave him internal peace.

Miles of trees, thick roots that burrowed into the earth, hummed with their imbued energy, reaching for him in answer.

"What can you show me? We need safe haven. Seek your brethren in the mountains. Protected. Undisturbed." Evening his breathing, he listened as the trees spoke, whispers and vibrations that traveled miles through roots and winds. They needed a place where they could plan, where they, and Jayce, could train. Where they could find allies and build alliances. Build an army who would be loyal to the crown, for what the royal line had once stood for.

There had to be others out there. Bloodlines and families who remembered the Valda-Cree royals. It was impossible to speculate how many remained, or who would want to have them returned to power.

The truth spread before him was daunting as he searched for a safe location. Bringing Jayce into Caduthien wasn't going to be the cure to the ails of the lands. He was going to be the bridge. Jayce was going to be the symbol of solidarity before he could ever be the symbol of peace, before he could embrace the throne as his own. At least, that was Rune's hope. There would be alliances of mages, of shifters, of breeds and packs. Covens. He sighed, knowing this was no small task with the weight of expectation being placed solely on Jayce's shoulders. Beliefs and abilities that would need to work in tandem if not perfect harmony. Their journey was only beginning and from the bottom of the mountain it looked nearly impossible to surmount, without knowing any of the pitfalls waiting for them on their journey.

He had faith in Jayce. His courage. His core strength. With the right people surrounding him, he could make a difference. Peace would be possible. It wouldn't, however, be instantaneous. That was merely wishful thinking. But it was possible. And the possibility was what they needed. Hope for the future.

A tremor interrupted his musings as the tree whispered to him. Pressing his forehead to the tree, he answered, "Thank you." He had a direction. It was a start. He needed to send Iba on reconnaissance once more.

꙳

Jayce sank down in front of Master Theil next to the koi pool in the gardens. Beaming sunlight warmed his shoulders and a light breeze tickled his hair. There was something to be said for being on the coast like this. The weather was outstanding. The views from the cliffs, the roll of the tide, and color of the water made him think of Greece or maybe southern Italy, but it was hard to say. He didn't know if this world mirrored his own, or if it had its own set of continents and seas. It might be larger or smaller. Maybe the next thing he needed to do was broaden his education of Kielbos and the surrounding lands.

He'd only been at the temple for a few days and he'd already fallen into a certain rhythm with those surrounding him. He wasn't using an alarm to wake, and he wasn't up late studying or hanging out with his friends. Aside from the one Rune apparently carried, here were no mirrors in the temple that he knew of, so he couldn't see the state of the bruises he'd collected from being thrown from his horse. He could only hope they were healing and less obvious.

If Master Theil knew he was there, he wasn't acknowledging him. Relaxing his shoulders, he rested his hands on his crossed legs and let out a breath, absorbing the sounds of the world surrounding him. A slow swell of peace overtook him, as he released his next breath, focusing on the pattern as he inhaled and exhaled. He'd never contemplated yoga or meditation, but this was something he seemed to grasp easily. And what he hadn't expected, was he enjoyed it. It seemed to leave him calmly energized, with better focus. He had a feeling as the days bore down on them, he was going to need that. A lot.

Clearing his mind, he went through the paces like the last time, when Master Theil had been directing his magic. With a clearer mind, the colors burst through him, and he couldn't help the enchanted small smile that trembled on his lips. Twenty-two years old and he'd never had an inkling of what or *who* he was.

Was he ready to be king? That was an emphatic *no*. With no idea of what he was being challenged to embrace, jumping into the fire as unprepared as he was would be guaranteeing failure.

But he could take these little steps. Find his magic. Accept those changes to the best of his ability and then move on. Training would be essential. Find out what the skin animal of his Valda-Cree ancestors was and hopefully be able to handle it. No way to avoid the deeper apprehension on the end of that thought, though. What kind of animal were they talking? A werewolf like his own myths? A giraffe? A mouse? Was he supposed to be a super-spy gerbil? And didn't that process hurt? How did you *become* something else entirely *without* it hurting?

He knew inside, they were far from little changes overall, but if he took them apart one aspect at a time, he was more confident in being able to handle what had been thrust at him.

Hell, he'd already spent two days on horseback, something he never thought he would do in his lifetime. Who rode horseback to travel in his time? Pretty much no one in a civilized, industrialized world. He was overjoyed to know they had indoor rooms with water for bathing, personal necessities, and a way to clean their teeth. He shuddered at what could happen over time. Hygiene was important.

And that made him think of kissing Rune. Because pretty much everything circled him back to the sexy elf. The feel of his skin, the strength of his body against his own. The soft moans and whined gasps he would make.

He released a breath when he realized he was starting to react to his own thoughts. Not a good thing considering the seriousness of the coming hours. He pushed the sexual musings away and focused once more on the various colors dancing against his eyelids.

He didn't know how long he'd been sitting there contemplating the cosmos when Master Theil spoke.

"Before I start with the explanation of the ritual to come, I want to give you some encouragement. And some advice."

Jayce blinked open his eyes. The sun had definitely moved. Shadows did not lie. "I'm listening."

Master Theil smiled kindly. "The challenges you face are not directed at you, to prove your unworthiness. They are challenges to ensure you are ready to accept the crown when it is time. All the previous rulers had a trial to prove their ability to rule fairly without prejudice. We are a world of many races and each has its own set of obstacles and beliefs. A true Valda-Cree will understand that and use their guidance and power to the best of their ability.

"There will come times when you will doubt and yes, you will make mistakes. But you must understand the mistakes are to learn from. You will have a lot to learn as well, but in some respects that might be to your benefit. You come to us with an unjaundiced eye. Times have changed since the Alendaren have become the ruling family. You will need to seek the truths that exist now."

"Am I really capable of all of this?" he murmured.

"Right now? No." He softened the truth with a smile when Jayce's emotions must have been all over his face. It hurt to have his own thoughts echoed back to him. "I truly feel that is why you were hidden away. Your life is not already entwined in ours; there is no pressure to appease. There is no guilt for deeds already done, mistakes already made. You are beholden to no one and that is probably what is most refreshing about your appearance. I believe you will bring a new light to our lands, as Rune has foreseen. The challenges you will meet will have purpose, to educate you, to strengthen you and much more. The advice I do give you is even when you doubt, know who you are, Valda-Cree son, as that has power of its own."

"And what about the ritual?"

"The ritual will show you many things. One of them being the beast of your ancestors. As true Valda-Cree, he will be there, waiting."

"And if he isn't?"

Master Theil silently considered the question, then said, "I have faith he will be. Rune has faith in you as well. Have faith in yourself."

Jayce chewed on his lip then quickly released it. He didn't want to become entrenched in anxiety now, not after actually calming himself specifically for the coming evening. "I'm trying."

Master Theil tipped his head in agreement. His expression smoothed over once again. "The ritual is usually witnessed by ranking family members, the high mage, and the two eldest of the court's council. Tonight, there will only be myself and Rune for your protection."

"Do you know anything about the ritual itself?"

"Only what I've found in the histories, how to perform it. I haven't witnessed one myself, so, no. I don't."

Jayce exhaled. "Rune said there was no bloodletting." He stiffened his fingers into his legs to hide their tension.

"Only a small amount, as a gift to the goddess. You're not being sacrificed, if that is your worry." Master Theil's eyes sparkled and Jayce shrugged his shoulders, attempting to hide his discomfort behind a wobbly grin. It was worth it to know ahead of time what he would be asked to do. At least in his mind, it was.

"Doesn't hurt to ask, to know at least a little about what I'm walking blindly in to."

"In that, I agree. I don't have any knowledge of it outside of the magics that we perform for you. The last time this was performed was for King Bail, and I was not privy to the rituals or training for the royal family."

He exhaled a slow breath from his lower ribs all the way through his nose. Then nodded. "Is there anything else I need to do to prepare?"

"No." He reached across the space and gripped a shoulder kindly. "You are stronger than you know. The challenges waiting for you will prove that."

"All I know is there is no going back." His voice cracked even as he tried to even out his emotions.

"That is true." He squeezed once then stood, offering a hand to assist him upward. "It is time."

Jayce swallowed and stood at his side. "Thank you for what you have already shown me."

"You are very welcome."

Chapter 21

Jayce kept pace next to Master Theil's shoulder in the opposite direction of the sleeping chambers on the lower level, down a short hallway to a cavernous room that was deeply embedded within the cliffs. Inside the entrance, Master Theil removed his sandals and motioned for Jayce to do the same. Then, one by one, the torches sparked to life around the walls, revealing mural high carvings that encircled the room and various levels of shelves along the entrance side of the walls. It looked like a pre-Arthurian era altar room, if he had to take a stab at a similar likeness. The high stone ceiling with a domed center was supported by massive carved gray stone pillars reaching to the ceiling. Directly below it was another concave circle in the floor equal to half its breadth. Opposite the side of where he was standing, there was a low profile raised flat pedestal on the other side of the concave bowl that could have been used as a flat altar for sacrifices in its past.

The room itself wasn't cold in the least but a chill found his spine nonetheless. The stories this room could tell. He didn't doubt there were hundreds. "How long has the temple been here?" he asked with a low voice. It felt wrong to be anything but respectful in his room.

"Windwise has been here since the beginning of time, or so they say. I've been in these halls almost three hundred years and I am not the first temple master."

"It's…beautiful and eerie."

"Not many are allowed in the hallowed chamber. You are intuitive in respecting this revered space naturally."

He bowed his head. He recognized the warning in the compliment.

"Follow me."

Jayce fell into step behind Master Theil, circumventing the hollow in the stone floor to the low profile pedestal.

"Disrobe and kneel in the center."

Swallowing down the sudden rush of nerves, he unknotted the tie at his waist and slid the garment from his shoulders. Master Theil folded it over an arm and waited until he was kneeling on cool stone. He knitted his fingers together on his thighs to hide their tremors.

"Practice your breathing. You will know the next stage."

Master Theil's bare feet walked away silently until Jayce heard the motion of pottery and the whisper of words next.

With his eyes closed, he focused on what he could hear while breathing evenly to keep his heart beating at a relaxed rate. The pressure on his knees kept part of his mind distracted as he tried to hear and sense what was happening around him. The whispers, while indistinct, seemed to flow further against the stone. There was Master Theil. And…he released another breath, anxiety mixed with relief rocking his chest as he realized the other voice was Rune's.

Instead of letting his imagination take control of his fears, he did as he was asked, focusing on his breathing, keeping his heart calm. The hint of lit incense curved around his head as he caught the flicker of the movement before him in his periphery. He didn't know where they'd been placed. The aroma was woodsy again with a touch of citrus and possibly eucalyptus. It was hard to say as each breath seemed to find different notes to focus on.

The slow melodious sound of a chant began to fill the air around him, but he didn't dare raise his head to watch. Something told him this part wasn't for him. The chanting continued for several minutes, a language he didn't know and didn't recognize. The flames on the walls began to flicker and sway. It wasn't long before he felt the caress of the wind against his skin, making him shiver again. Underground, enclosed under stone, there should be no sustained wind.

He knew this. But as he was learning to do, he was accepting it. Physics didn't apply with magic.

Rune approached the hollow in the ground, though he could only tell by the feet at the edge of his vision as he was wearing the same kind of robe Master Theil wore for this, rather than his trousers and boots. A slow drizzle of aromatic oil was poured into the concave ground all the way around the circumference as he patiently made a lap. It dripped and spread in a thin coating down the center to pool at the bottom, an amount no larger than the breadth of Jayce's palm.

Then Master Theil was at his shoulder. "Rise, Valda-Cree," he intoned.

Jayce did as asked, his hands lax at his sides. He pinned his gaze forward, his spine straight, refusing to allow the twitches of fear to show even has his heart skipped with the unknown nipping at his heels.

"Do you make your offering to the goddess in free will?"

"I do," he replied, knowing there could be no other answer.

Master Theil opened a wooden box lined with what appeared to be black silk and he would have gasped if Master Theil had not warned him about this. As it was, his pulse still raced unchecked against his neck. His heart was in no way calm or okay about any of this.

Waiting on that fabric rested a blade that had to be worth a fortune in workmanship alone. Long and polished steel, the blade appeared honed to a fine sharpness, sparkling reflectively in the wavering torchlight. The hilt was smoothed wood woven with designs that refracted like metals had been poured through it. There were no jewels, but its intricacies and designs were beyond anything he'd ever seen. He didn't doubt in the least that it had been blessed with magic as well.

"By the blade of Ahdrer, you offer a gift to the goddess in the name of the Valda-Cree."

He held a palm upward. Following instincts and possibly one too many fantasy novels as guidance, he repeated, "By the blade of Ahdrer, I offer a gift to the goddess in the name of the Valda-Cree."

Solemn pride emanated from Master Theil. He must have guessed right. Rune stood with them, a small blown glass cruet at the ready.

He didn't have to be told this part was going to hurt, and sadly, pain wasn't something he'd thought to question them about too deeply. Subconsciously, he knew there would be something painful in all of this. What ritual wasn't? Rites of passage? *Pffft.* He'd known. He simply hadn't wanted to know *how much* and psyche himself out even worse over it all. Because changing one's shape was supposed to be painless, right? Jayce stayed as relaxed as possible for Master Theil to press the sharp blade into his palm. Red blood began to gather as he winced with the delay of shock reaching his brain receptors telling him he'd been injured. Controlling the urge to yank his hand away, he let Master Theil finish with the knife. His free hand clenched into a fist beside his other hip as he struggled against the sharpness of the pain. Tipping his palm away from the withdrawing blade, he aimed for the vial opening until Rune nodded, signaling that part was done.

Master Theil draped a bright white cloth across the slice and he curled his arm close to his chest, guarding his hand. His chest trembled as he exhaled.

Rune held the vial aloft, saying, "With this gift, Jayce Morrow of the Valda-Cree welcomes into his being the goddess Ahdrer. Be thee the true bearer of the blessed protector in the goddess's name." He poured the red blood into the gathered oils.

They stood in silence for a few seconds alongside Jayce, waiting for what would happen next. A glance to either showed the elves were focused on the blood in the oil, so he waited with them.

And then almost swallowed his tongue, his gasp was so loud.

The oil was smoldering. Where the blood and oil mixed, it was *smoldering*.

He whipped up to look at the other two, but they seemed unconcerned, almost entranced by the building smoke rising from the oil. Until it popped into life with a burst and a spark of fire.

A flame that raced across the oil to consume it.

"The goddess accepts your offering, young Valda-Cree. We may continue."

Continue? He gaped, then shook it off. *What does that mean?* He didn't know how much more there was to all of this. And seriously? His *blood* burst into flames!

Rune leaned close. "Do not worry. You have passed the first test. You are doing well."

"Easy for you to say," he breathed in a rush. He darted a glance at the snapping flames in the oil then at his injured hand. "Naked here."

Rune smirked but quickly wiped it clear when Master Theil shot him a reprimand filled look.

"Be strong, Jayce, my friend. Be strong." Rune ducked his head and backed away from the pedestal to the other side of the blaze.

Jayce swallowed and steadied himself. With another deep breath and roll of his neck on his shoulders, he stated, "I'm ready."

Master Theil raised his hands and began to chant, the sound filling the chamber like a roll of thunder, even toned yet ominous in a strength yet unseen. The flames at his feet danced with the power of his chanting. Jayce lowered his head as the heat enveloped him, his breathing growing shallower though he was doing nothing to strain himself.

The sharp prick of unease filled his chest when a tension he couldn't see wrapped around his wrists. His eyes widened when the tension straightened out his arms, pulling them taut to his shoulders. It wasn't tight or painful, only firm and unyielding. The cloth fabric that had covered his wound floated to the ground as his arms were held high and wide. Fear chilled him even as the heat of the fire made him sweat. He flung himself from either side, but there was nowhere to go. "Rune! What's happening?"

Rune didn't look away but he didn't answer, his brow creased with worry where he stood on the other side of the fire.

The fire rose before him, grew in width and heat as though someone had added more fuel to it. He jerked at the invisible bonds, unable to move to either side. He braced his feet to keep his balance and pulled as hard as he could.

There was absolutely zero give to whatever magical force had captured him. "Rune!" His scream filled the chamber, yet Master Theil didn't stop his chanting.

He didn't understand what was happening. Heat licked at his legs, climbing his body, yet the fire was not close enough to sear. Fear became a tangible beast in his gut, clawing at him to escape. He'd lied! Jayce wasn't ready! He wasn't anywhere near ready for this.

Panic tried to overwhelm him and the only thing that stopped it from becoming unbearable was the hope that Rune wouldn't have led him to his demise like this. He trusted Rune, but right now he was scared and hated that it was showing. Hated that he had no idea of what to expect.

His eyes rolled into his head as a new wave of something foreign and magical coursed over his frame, touched on every bare inch of skin like he was a prize bull to be prodded and judged. There was a pulse, like a heartbeat, consuming his being. He tried to fight the bonds, to escape the pounding against his chest, against his ears.

In his head.

He shook, trembled, and panted. It was too much! He couldn't think with the pressure building against his head, drilling into him. Demanding more and more of him.

Arching his spine he screamed again, the sound morphing into a deeper sound he'd never made in his life.

A roar.

His hands clenched, the pain in his palm where the slice had been completely forgotten in the billowing heat engulfing him from his toes to fingernails. Straining against the invisible bonds, his eyes burned and he blinked as a fresh wave of hell crashed over him. Rocking on his feet, he felt the surging waves as they burned him to his soul, his head rising high as a fresh tsunami of agony consumed him to his bones. The chamber echoed with the sound, but it wasn't the pain filled screams of a man in agony.

His chest burned with the strain of muscles fighting against the bonds which held him and the magic trying to overwhelm him. He didn't understand what was happening, or what he needed to do. He wanted to run. He wasn't purposely trying to fight what was happening; all he felt was survival. Yet the magic holding his wrists had no give. He was standing at its mercy. Sweat beaded down his body, his skin slick with it. The fire in front of him felt like it engulfed him as heat poured through him, passed over him in blown waves as magic encircled him and engulfed him. There were no longer words coming out of his mouth. Just sounds. Whimpers and gasped pants.

Until the next scream overtook him, ripped from his body. An inhuman scream. It reverberated off walls and stone until his voice was nearly hoarse with the gasping effort. Black spots edged his vision.

All he could hear was the sonorous roar of a lion filling his ears as it rose and faded, over and over. Slowly bringing his head down, he focused through the pain and landed on the white-haired elf before him.

It is time.

The gentle yet firm voice was in his head. Even though it was too feminine to be anyone he knew, he didn't argue. Whatever was going to happen, this was it. Letting his eyes drift shut, he rested against the bonds to catch his heaving breath and sought the heartbeat, the drumming of sound in his head. Instinctually accepting instead of fighting. There was only way to go from here. Forward. Licking his lips, he focused inward.

Stilling, he let the magic fall over him, cascade around him until even his hair felt the lifting tug of energy.

What do I need to do? He panted, trying to listen, to understand. Something was changing in the waves of the heat, as the flow of magic caressed him. No longer battered at him for submission.

He ignored the strain on his shoulders as the magics moved around him, invaded him and took control. There was now a thick and bright golden ribbon that danced with the colors he recognized as his own. An undulating glow that pulsed and rolled alongside, between, and together. Merged and yet maintained its own power and individuality. He concentrated on its strength, weaving it around him like a ribbon dancer against his skin, feeding it through him, until he was the one controlling the energy flow, the same way he controlled the light of magic tied to his own strengths. Until it was the only color he could see in his mind. By his choice.

With flagging energy and staggered motions, he sank to his knees, his arms following him to the ground, as though the magic understood his intent. Only he didn't have a clue.

Again, he was following some instinct, a guess. He was supposed to be able to become, to share.

A beast.

A protector.

A king.

On his hands and knees, he raised his head and roared with all his breath, then sagged in place.

He felt the withdrawal of the restraints on his hands, flexing his sore wrists to hold his weight as it vanished.

Damn, he was exhausted.

But did it work? What had all of this proven? His limbs trembled and he stiffened them. He was not going to collapse. Not after that kind of hazing. He was not going to fail at the end. How could he tell if it had worked? Were they at the end? Was it over? Were they done? He needed them to tell him what to do next. A clue. His kingdom for a clue!

The fire burned bright before him as his vision cleared and his lungs filled, easing the strain flowing over his frame. Shivers rocked his skin. The pulse of magic lessened, faded, as Jayce gathered his strength and caught his breath. It felt like he was standing, but nothing was where it should have been if he'd been on his feet. Everything felt too low.

Raising his head, he sought through the flames before him. Confusion and shock rocked him to the core to find Master Theil and Rune on a knee, bowed in respect.

"What?" was what he was trying for.

The actual sound was nothing more than a huffed grunt.

Hunting around himself to figure out this puzzle, his searching gaze landed on paws.

Thick, yellow paws that were directly beneath him.

Oh, fuck. He raised one of the paws the same way he would control his hand and flexed the large pads without thinking, revealing sharp claws that popped out of their sheaths. Where was the knife slice? Why didn't it hurt? Was that him? Did he have claws? It was his hand, but it wasn't. Wait. He had two? He shook his head and felt a thick weight moving with him. He stopped moving completely. He was frozen as his mind took it all in, asking a whirlwind of questions.

This? This was what he was meant to become? Confusion was being overridden by the needs of the…lion? Looking forward through the flames, the desires swirling inside him already felt like the lion's wishes. He gulped as muscles bunched, then he leaped over the fire to land squarely between the two mages with a muted thud. The lion took charge, approaching the two elves before him. Neither so much as twitched as he neared.

Lowering his head, he brushed against Master Theil's shoulder.

"Blessed be, my king," he breathed.

Jayce stepped away and approached Rune. He huffed against his neck, making him gasp with surprise, then brushed against his shoulder as well.

"Blessed be, my king," he echoed.

Then Jayce used brute strength and a shoulder to push him out of his kneeled crouch, making him sprawl backwards.

With a silent chuckle that Rune wouldn't hear and ignoring the elf's squawks of surprise, he stretched out over the mage, his massive paws on his either side of his head to lick his face lightly.

"Oh, goddess!" he cried, at first frozen with shock, then he started laughing, a light, joyous peal of sound that sank deep into Jayce. "Jayce! Stop it!" Fingers dug into his mane but not cruelly. He enjoyed the firmness of them digging deep into the coat, clinging with surprise.

The lion liked the way this elf smelled, the sound of his voice, and of his laughter. This elf was a friend.

He huffed once more into his neck, knowing Rune got the message that he was safe then backed away to stand on his own feet. Once steady, he envisioned his body. Two legs, two arms, and with a suddenness that made him wobble, he was crouched beside a stunned silent Rune.

"Well, it worked," he rasped through an abused throat, feeling the pulse of the goddess's blessing in every bone, muscle, and nerve. The irrefutable evidence that he was indeed something more than human now.

He was Valda-Cree.

"Yes, yes it did," Rune replied with wide blue eyes full of awe.

Chapter 22

Rune noted Jayce squeezing his hand into a fist again, a perplexed expression on his face. The palm with the ritual slice that was no more. They were quietly clearing the epicenter of the temple to the sleeping halls below, both lost in thought.

"Did you wish to bathe, or eat?" Rune asked, breaking the surrounding quiet.

"Honestly, I just want to sleep," he replied. Perhaps unconsciously, he circled a loose hand around the opposite wrist. "Why did the skin shifter magic hold me like that?"

"So you did not run when it invaded and merged with your own magic."

Jayce seemed to consider that. "Would something have happened if I had?"

"You would have died. Instantly."

Jayce jerked to a stop. "And you didn't tell me?"

Rune faced him, apologetic but unable to change what was. "I didn't know until I studied my part of the ritual. It was the shortcomings of having no history, no true training for yourself, as well as not being completed at the correct age. I fear the hardship of your experience was brought on because the skin shifter spirit could not merge easily. You are an adult now, and less malleable to certain influences. Even as accepting as you are, as you have been about your magic. It was the goddess's will. There was no mention of it happening in the ritual tomes."

"I suppose that is possible and likely," he grudgingly agreed. "But it's not happening again, right?" A cast side-eye glare at Rune demanded the truth.

"No, only for the sake of the ritual." He felt awful enough for the way Jayce had suffered. There had been no way to warn him, because he hadn't known what the vision was trying to tell him. From the broader scope of events, it seemed the vision was guiding him to ensure Jayce faced the trial of the goddess's blessing, while the incomplete state he'd seen left the outcome unknown. Only Jayce had the ability to control that nuance, and it wasn't for Rune to see before time.

A hard exhale sounded like deep relief. "Good."

If Jayce had fears about the ritual's conclusion, or the animal he now shared with, he was more relaxed than Rune would have expected. He waited for questions, but they never materialized.

Descending the stairs to the sleeping chambers, Rune palmed a torch to light the way. Full nighttime had arrived by the time they'd ascended from the ritual chamber. Master Theil had retired to his rooms, saying they would gather the next morning for further training.

This also meant that the time for them to leave was pressing on them. He hoped Iba succeeded in her hunts.

He stopped at Jayce's door. "It has been a long day for all of us," he agreed.

Jayce pushed open the door. Walking across the space, he palmed the candle to spark from the torch flame Rune held. "I am wiped out, and honestly, with what just happened, that's a lot to process," he explained when Rune lit the wick, to return it to the table once more. "No playing with fire tonight. At least the temple is stone, and the likelihood of burning down the house is slim."

Rune's lips twitched. "I understand your sentiment. Training was not always easy for us in the early days either."

"Maybe one of these days, you'll tell me stories of the misadventures of a younger Rune," he joked.

Rune shook his head emphatically. "I'd really rather not," he quipped, happy to add lightness to the strain of the evening.

Removing the ceremonial robe to hang on a hook, Rune's breath caught at the view of Jayce's naked frame. Smooth skin remained unblemished from the torment of the merging of his gifted magic with the Valda-Cree legacy. Tone and taut from calf to shoulder, he was a specimen of beauty to Rune's gaze. The urge to run his palms down the expanse of his chest was nearly blinding. He should look away to give Jayce his privacy, but it didn't stop the want to be nearer to him.

His body's response was proof of that want. The hardening of his shaft below the robe he wore was no less than that morning when he'd been unable to repress the needs being near this man made him feel. Jayce was distracted pulling on his waiting trousers, covering the lust-inducing roundness of his hip and ass, and gratefully giving Rune a moment to gather himself while Jayce remained unaware of Rune's conflict. Jayce's naked body pulled at him to touch, to caress, and ultimately to possess and treasure. It was a depth of desire he'd never known and truly didn't know how he could have the right.

At least partially dressed once more, he palmed the necklace on the tabletop to slip over his head. He twisted the pendant between his fingers. "Does what I wear become part of the magic? Or do I have to be naked?" he wondered. The earring he added gave him a roguish charm. It was a good look for Jayce.

The question helped redirect his wayward thoughts from Jayce's nakedness and how appealing he was. He hoped he was hiding his inner turmoil better than he felt he was at the moment. "I honestly do not know." Tipping his head, he suggested, "Maybe when you are rested and want to test the theory, we should." Nodding to himself at the possibility, he added, "Yes, we definitely should. It could make a difference for your survival and how to approach the shifts." He supposed the answer was written in a text somewhere, but simply attempting the shift with clothing would be more expedient than going on a hunt for a single notation or paragraph in all the historical tomes.

"I agree," Jayce murmured, holding his hand out to study the palm where the ceremonial cut had been. "I'm still in awe of this."

Rune slotted the torch in the standing sconce in the hallway and shut the door firmly behind him. "I want to thank you. For allowing me to be a part of this with you."

Jayce's head snapped around.

"For believing in my visions even when you doubted your place in them. You said you trusted me this morning." He'd held those words close to his heart all day and even more so during the uncertainty of the ritual, when he'd been unable to help Jayce. When his pain became something almost tangible and he'd begged Master Theil to end it. He folded his hands together into the blousy sleeves of the ceremonial robe. Light played against Jayce's features, his eyes glowing with the undeniable amber hue now that he'd completed the ritual. He was mage marked. And even more enigmatic and handsome to Rune. Against his dark hair he was stunning with the splendor of the magic pulsing through him. "Now that you know the truth, and we know you are the missing prince, do you still?"

Jayce cleared the few paces between them rounding his sleeping pallet. With a cupped hand beneath Rune's chin, he held him gently, firmly. "I still do. I need someone who knows Caduthein and the Alendaren family who can teach me about them. Who can teach me about my place in all of this. You are the only one I trust with these secrets that I'm still learning. We're in this together, since the beginning." He hovered over Rune's lips. "I think I even kind of like you." Grinning, he teased a kiss over them, shocking Rune into silence. "However, I already know how others are going to judge anything I do, since the current rulers are also reliant on a mage for an advisor."

Rune blinked, trying to think. Jayce in serious thinking mode was debilitating to his mental capabilities. He'd been in a state of focused awareness over this man since Rune had been toppled by a lion, to nuzzle against him. When he should have been terrified at having a full grown lion blanketing him, after the initial surprise at being knocked around, he'd only felt wonder and happiness. Then he'd returned to his human form without any sign of hardship, taking his breath away. And Rune was still in a state of shock. His heart, his skin, everything about Jayce was causing his body to reach outward for him. "You're very astute." He swallowed, discovering his voice was rough.

Jayce dragged over his bottom lip with a thumb, melting Rune to the core. "I have my moments. The question between us is do you want to continue exploring this. You would have a better understanding if this would detract from my path, since the visions have only been happening to you."

Rune gulped, staring at the plump smoothness of Jayce's lips, wanting to feel them as much as the press of the thumb currently driving sparks through his ribs to his spine. Warmth all but poured from Jayce's bare chest, like he still stood before the ritual basin fire. "Logically, I know I shouldn't," he all but whispered. He was trying to be firm. And knew he was failing. His body was calling liar. A shout he couldn't fully silence with the way his heart pounded and the way his shaft thickened beneath the robe.

"I don't want to put words in your mouth," Jayce offered, grinning lightly, at ease. Letting him know he was giving Rune the choice. Rune could barely hold himself steady in the palm that cradled him. "I need you to be honest with me. I know that going forward, mage or not, I will only become more powerful over you, and I don't want that to come between us."

"I want you," he admitted, his voice breaking with the confession. His heart was hammering wildly in his chest with acceptance. Even if it was only once, he craved, hungered for the man in front of him.

The hand holding his chin coasted upward to burrow into his hair. Rune watched the expressions flitting over his face as he carded through the strands, the simple joy as he followed the long strands floating through the air as he released them. "My hair is a weakness for you."

"One of many," he admitted with a slight shrug, as though being seen as vulnerable by Rune, to him, was nothing to concern himself with. He encouraged Rune to step backward until he was braced by the door. "With everything that has happened, I feel like I'm being entwined with you. It's so foreign, definitely sudden, but feels so right." His tone was low, almost reverent. "Nothing like this, like you ever happened at home, before I met you. So much has changed in barely a few days. My entire life has changed. The shock has worn off and I'm starting to see and understand. And you've been the constant support for me. At first I would have sworn you had a personal agenda, a stake in what was happening, in proving who I was."

Rune's eyes widened with an immediate rebuttal on his lips, but the soft adoration in Jayce's gaze froze the words in his throat.

"But then, like I said, I realized you are as trapped as I am in this. And I think that's when I knew you could be trusted. Because I don't think I can stop from wanting you even if you were bad for me."

"Jayce," he breathed. "You're my king—"

He quickly pressed fingers to his mouth. "No, I'm not. Not yet. I'm no one's king and I like it much more that way right now. You are my friend, and someone I'm deeply attracted to. So, if you're done letting me pour my guts out for you, can I kiss you?"

"Pour your what?" He gaped. How horrible!

Jayce's laughter gleamed through his eyes as much as his voice. "A saying. Baring everything without restraint."

Relief made him chuckle. Rune's hands rose of their own volition, spanning across Jayce's chest, shocked at the warmth in his skin. The emanating heat in his skin was new, not imagined. He felt so good under his palms. There was a little hair on his chest tapering down to his belly but for his age, not much at all. He knew that would feel remarkable against his own sensitive skin. He wanted to lick over the bronze hued nipples, swirl over them, taste them. Desire swelled into a raging inferno in his chest.

"You said you would die if you didn't get to kiss me in the pools," Jayce mentioned, nuzzling against Rune's jaw where his hand had been. "I think I understand that now."

"You make me feel so much. I... I'm not sure why now, why you. I don't understand." The urgency boiling through his blood was making him tremble beneath the heated want blazing in Jayce's gaze. Succumbing as his breath staggered, he tipped his head to allow further access to Jayce's wicked mouth as it coasted over to suck lightly beneath his ear.

Jayce braced a hand next to Rune's head on the door, his other still plying teasingly through his hair. "Rune?" he breathed.

"Yes?"

"Shut up." Then his lips were on Rune's and he couldn't think of a better reason to be quiet.

Chapter 23

Jayce almost growled as he claimed Rune's mouth. He couldn't seem to control the lust surging through him. He'd experienced sex, and he'd thought then it had even been great sex. Two boyfriends but neither got to the heart of Jayce so readily, so easily as Rune. Rune's arms slid from his chest to around his shoulders, gripping his hair with tight fingers, creating shivers of electrical currents over his frame and down his spine. He'd never kissed anyone who tasted like Rune. Who kissed like he could kiss.

Soft groans filled the quiet in the room as he licked over Rune's mouth, between his lips. He liked hearing those sounds. It thrilled him knowing he was the one making the elf moan breathlessly. Those rumbles slipping from Rune's throat seemed to be directly connected to his cock, making him swell and twitch against the front of his pants. He gasped when he released Rune's mouth, succulent and rosy red, begging for more kisses. Half-lidded eyes glittered in the candlelight from across the room. Their blue bright and shimmery from the touches of silver in them. The tic of his pulse below skin called to Jayce to lick over it, to wrap him into his arms and keep him there to feast on.

The signs of Rune's arousal were brazenly obvious beneath the ceremonial robe he wore. For the first time, Jayce could agree with the lack of undergarments in this world's wardrobe, because the length of Rune's dick stood proud between them, tenting the cream colored fabric. Pitching his hips forward, he ground against the hardness between Rune's legs, loving the tremor of need that swept over his body in answer. Rune panted and whined, his fingers clutching and clawing in answer.

Withdrawing his hand from the silk of his hair, he let it drift down the front of his frame, lightly flicking over the hardened nubs of his nipples, firm and extended with arousal. When he twisted one gently, worrying it between his fingers through the material, his frame bucked in answer. He couldn't wait to suck on them. Rune's body was so responsive to his touch. He remembered the little gasps and twitches from their encounter in the subterranean pool. Rune was extremely physically responsive. And he wanted to run his tongue all over his lengths and hollows to see if he could make him do it all again and make it even better.

"Want to see you naked," Jayce breathed, licking with decadent slowness below his ear well aware how erogenous they were to Rune. "Want to see your gorgeous body in the candlelight."

"Yes," Rune whined, his reply stretched and strained.

Jayce gathered the lengthy robe in his hands at Rune's hips, bending close to nuzzle and kiss over exposed ribs as he inched it upward. He tantalized, letting his fingers brush against skin as it appeared, while keeping him pinned to the door with his broader shoulders and the seduction of his mouth adoring him. The taunting rise of the robe was driving Rune crazy, making him wait for the next touch. Breath panted between them with soft whines of impatience.

Then the robe was finally at shoulder height. Jayce shifted backward enough to slip it over Rune's head, baring him to his view, his exploring fingers, and mouth. He helpfully lifted his arms high and when Jayce could have pulled it free, he bunched it against his wrists and pressed him by his arms into the door behind him, locking him in place to simply enjoy the view. He put a half step between them and visually cherished every exposed inch before him.

"As beautiful as I'd remembered and so much more," he offered.

Rune's opened eyes dropped shut easily, his chest rising and falling with his rushed breathing. His length stood out stiff and proud in his fully exposed state, the tip smooth and slick with moisture, revealing his level of need and excitement. Lean, lightly furred legs trembled gently, arousal flushing his skin from the almost alabaster paleness to a summer rose red in several places. The kind of arousal that couldn't be faked, or hidden.

Jayce slipped the garment off his hands and respectfully hung it on the hook with his own. Then he traced the length of Rune's body with his hands, learning the way his skin felt, the warmth in it as his fingers drifted down his arms, willingly kept pinned above his head.

Adoring the lean length of his chest, purposely thumbing over his distended nipples, until he was gasping shamelessly.

Jayce leaned close and captured his lips in a kiss that swallowed his next moans as he reached around to his ass and grasped him close. Rune shuddered, his arms sinking to fall around Jayce's head and shoulders. The almost drunken desire in the kiss was making Jayce crazy with wanting more. No inhibitions. No reason to stop. No possible interruptions. He hadn't felt a need this deep, this demanding in months. Rune was driving him insane with the feel of his body, with the scent of his skin, the scent of his arousal.

He broke the kiss and started sucking on his neck below his ear, his fingers firmly clutching the skin of his thigh as he dragged him even closer, needed to feel Rune's body enveloping his own

"Need you," he rasped before licking a broad stroke up his neck.

"Yes." It was a breathed cry of passion. Where only the needs of the body mattered.

He pulled away enough to guide him to the pallet on the floor. Then he quickly undressed from his trousers, letting them drop where he stood. Rune went to bend for the bed, but Jayce halted him. "Wait. Don't move." He sank to his knees on the bedding, kissing Rune's quivering thighs. "Need to taste you. Have to know."

"Oh, goddess," Rune gasped hoarsely. "You mean…" He stuffed a knuckle between his teeth and when Jayce gazed upward with a questioning look, Rune nodded sharply.

Jayce held him in his palm, the stiff length uncut and a solid seven inches of thick deliciousness. As pale as the temple stone in the sunlight, blood pumping below skin level turned his erection a lush berry pink. He'd never been so obsessed as he was in that moment to know his taste. Closing the gap, he dipped his nose into the crease of Rune's thigh and breathed him in, captured the raw energy of pure male desire.

Rune's groan was quiet but it was enough to tell Jayce he wasn't unaffected. Muscles clenched and jumped when he dragged his tongue from the base to the tip, savoring the smooth silken texture as he took all the time in the world to reach the beads of moisture slipping from the slit.

"Oh." Rune gulped, his hands falling to grip at Jayce's shoulders. Tremors traveled up and down his frame.

"Not done," he murmured before opening wide and gliding the tip between his teeth. Nails clawed into him and Rune's toes curled where he stood as he sank slowly to the root, licking around and under, noting the sensitive points and packing them away for later for further investigation and seductive torturing. The things he wanted to do to this man to make him delirious with pleasure. Drawing back to the tip, he sucked a quick breath, glancing upward to lock with Rune's brightened gaze. A gaze looking back at him with a fiery need.

"I can't believe..." He hissed and arched, his shaft pushing deeper. "That feels." He cried out and shuddered. "Your mouth. Oh, goddess have mercy," he whimpered boldly when Jayce pulled the foreskin away to lick hungrily over the tip, sucking on the head before swallowing him as deep as he could once more. Rune's hips thrusted with abandon, driving ever deeper. Jayce framed his hips, guiding him, pacing him as he started to fuck his mouth.

Fingers gripped at his hair. "Jayce, I burn," he warned. He hummed around the mouthful he had, letting Rune know he wanted it, prompting him to take his pleasure.

It was all the permission Rune needed. Arched over Jayce, his hips pumped fiercely into the suction Jayce created. He licked at the sensitive head when he had to drag in a lungful of air, then Rune started thrusting all over again. His pale hair drifted wildly across his shoulders and around Jayce, caressing his own overheated skin as he watched Rune fall in to the sensations bombarding him.

Holding onto his hip for support, he cupped his balls with his other hand and that was all he needed find his release. Rune's cry was loud enough to make him worry for a split second that he may have been heard and that someone would come to investigate, then he had to concentrate as Rune spilled into his mouth.

His eyes widened in surprise as he gulped, lavishing his dick with long licks and strokes of his hand as he came with a sweet taste over his tongue. Not sugar sweet, but something better than the known salty bitterness of his own experiences. He sucked harder immediately needing more, craving all of it, propelling Rune through his orgasm until he was supporting himself braced over Jayce's shoulders.

He milked him through the orgasm, loving the closeness, the scent of his cum, the sheer power of his orgasm as he shot into Jayce's mouth. Wild and free, Rune jerked until he was twitching for a wholly other reason of being too sensitive. Jayce eased away with a soft sucking pop leaving Rune gasping and panting.

Leaning away, Rune slowly collapsed to his knees in front of Jayce. His eyes were dark and sultry with his orgasm singing through his blood. The kiss they shared was slow and a little sloppy as Rune wasn't moving with a lot of control. Jayce couldn't help but smile at his drunk-like looseness, happy he'd made him feel so good, and feeling a swell of pride that it had been him who had done that to him. He swept hair away from his face to deepen the kiss. Then Rune was pushing him backward, crawling over his body.

He pushed his legs out straight and Rune clambered over him, straddling his waist. The kisses that followed were less rushed, almost tender. Sweeping his palms up and down Rune's spine kept them locked together until Rune's body began to undulate against him.

Jayce moaned lightly at the fresh friction. He was ready and willing for whatever Rune wanted to give. He'd love to have some lube, to feel the heat of his channel as he slid into Rune's body.

"You feel so good," Rune panted against his throat, licking and kissing over bare skin. "Will you spend for me?"

He *loved* the way Rune spoke, so sexy. "What did you have in mind?"

Rune's eyes glittered with a new challenge, then he reached between their frames, stroking Jayce's steel hard cock in his hand. Jayce's breath caught at the sensation of being stroked by those long fingers. Rocking his slim hips massaged his nearly smooth balls over Jayce's shaft. Gliding his hands lower to grip at Rune's ass, he spread his cheeks and ran a finger over the tight ring of his pucker. Rune shivered.

Jayce froze. "Too much?"

He whipped his head in a negative. "Again." Jayce repeated the teasing pressure. Rune's kiss-bruised lips parted in a gasped moan and after reaching his release, it caught Jayce by surprise to see Rune's shaft thickening again.

Circling the fluttering opening with his fingertips, he asked, "Do you use lube?"

Rune's heavy-lidded gaze dragged open. "I don't understand."

"To ease the way, for penetration," he explained, pressing with a tip through the snug muscle to make his meaning clear.

Rune gulped but nodded. "Skin oils."

"Where?"

Rune blinked and searched the room before looking disappointed. "Not in here. I know there is some in my chamber."

"Not letting you go for that long," he warned. "Next time."

"Next time?" he asked with raw expectancy.

"There will be a next time," he confirmed. He knew it without a doubt. This was the second time they'd become intimate. There hadn't even been a true date between them, yet he felt like he knew and understood parts of Rune that no one else got to see. And that somehow Rune saw through his sarcasm to his inner fears and doubts. His faith in Jayce's future path hadn't flagged once. "Turn around."

Rune tipped his head quizzically but obeyed when Jayce tugged him to shift around until he was positioned facing Jayce's knees. "Now, let me know if you don't like this." Then he licked slow and leisurely up his crease.

Chapter 24

Rune's spine arched as he all but howled as sparks lit him up on the inside. Goddess, he hoped no one could hear them, and if they did, they ignored the noises coming from Jayce's chamber. He stuttered through a gasp, gulping to keep his wits, which only made Jayce chuckle even more over his reactions.

"Has no one pleasured you here, Rune?"

He choked when he tried to speak. Then simply gave up, moaning in a way he couldn't ever recall happening in his lifetime. And he had a *lot* of years to consider. No, no one had ever danced their tongue against him. No one had ever teased his opening with the sheer intention of torturous pleasure. No one had ever opened him in a such a manner where he couldn't think beyond his next breath.

"God, Rune." There was a nip of teeth on his ass and he flexed. "That's it. Just remember, I can always stop."

"Don't you dare," he demanded hoarsely.

Jayce's laughter turned mischievous. "My dear mage," he purred, his breath puffing against thoroughly dampened flesh, making Rune squirm with a new wash of sensation.

He needed to do something or he wasn't going to survive more. Jayce's body was lying before him in all his bared glory and he was barely holding himself upright because Jayce's oral abilities were distracting him in ways he'd never known. Even after his release had left him scattered and lacking any cognitive function leaving him feeling divine, his length was already thickening, creating a desperation to answer Jayce's seductive calls.

Then the obvious choice flexed in front of him and he bent over, cupping that delicious looking shaft and the round jewels that adorned it.

Diana DeRicci

Jayce's breath was a long exhalation when he fondled the firm rounds, full and hard with his release. Rune had lovers. He wasn't some untried novice. He *knew* sex, but had never found it overly fulfilling. It was a bodily craving that he could ignore in lieu of his more cerebral needs.

There was something about Jayce that had caught his fancy when he'd first found him. He'd followed him for a full day, learning about him. And fate was wrapping them tighter and tighter into each other, an obsession he felt powerless to resist. He'd tried staying away, leaving him with Master Theil for instruction. It hadn't been far enough. Like orbiting planets they'd come within range of each other again and again.

Even tonight, he'd had no intention of succumbing to the feral heat in his blood after witnessing Jayce's blessing by the Goddess Ahdrer. He'd speculated what the ritual would entail, but had never guessed how he would be truly affected watching the ritual and the merging of the magics that called on the Valda-Cree lion, because he hadn't been sure Jayce would actually be blessed with that Valda-Cree spirit animal. He hadn't doubted, but had been cautious in his hopefulness. It was a wonderment-filled moment forever burned into his memory that he was grateful to have been chosen to assist with the experience.

Then Jayce had neared him in his chamber, kissed him, and he was lost. Any strength he'd gathered to hold firm had instantly melted faster than ice thrown into a fire. His body was at Jayce's mercy and he had no other place he wanted to be.

He lowered his head to draw in his scent, savoring the male musk and arousal. Flesh twitched and fine pearls of fluid appeared at the tip of his cock in answer to his inquisitiveness. His tongue was licking across the head as soon as they appeared. The tip was wide and rounded, and he nuzzled down the shaft with his lips, caressing him with light nips. Jayce's reactions told him he was doing exactly what Jayce wanted.

Jayce's hips flexed and the gasps against damp skin were telling. "More?" Rune asked playfully.

"God, yes, don't stop," he replied. "Anything you want." Then Jayce's wicked tongue swirled over Rune's hanging balls and he arched like a cat, biting his lip to stifle the cries he wanted to make.

168

The single candle behind him created gray shadows but there was enough light to find and wrap his lips around the tip of Jayce's shaft. A breathy moan filled his ears like music. Then the heat of being swallowed filled his spine when Jayce copied his motions. Together they set a slow and deep pace, building the pleasure between them in a circle of need and desire that burned through them, sharing it, only to burn higher, brighter.

Jayce whined when Rune cupped his balls and sucked harder. He wanted Jayce's spend. Wanted to taste him the same way Jayce had. Wanted Jayce to feel the way his pleasure filled Rune. The glide over his tongue was driving him out of his mind, the slow pumps of Jayce's hips as he sought his own release. Stroking with a firm hand over the heft of his shaft, he took as much of Jayce's length as he could, until he felt him brush the back of his throat.

Jayce groaned, deep and loud, muffled as it was with his own mouth stuffed full. The vibrations flowed through nerves to fill Rune's body with shivers and need. The churning clench of his body was growing, reaching new heights as Jayce plied his tongue to then suck hard on his shaft, making him want to howl with each exhale. The way this man could make his body burn.

Then he did something Rune hadn't been expecting. With a wet thumb, he breached his opening gently, slowly, stroking over the sensitive nubby skin, causing only a slight burn, an extra level of feeling and Rune was lost.

Gulping for air, he shot his second spend into Jayce's voracious mouth. Twitching and writhing as each burst thickened him almost painfully until he was utterly spent. Jayce's lips encircled the tip, lapping languorously over sensitive flesh, leaving him a shivering, mindless mess. The moans of pleasure encouraged him to take Jayce hard and fast, needing him to reach his completion as well.

Soon, Jayce's hips were lifting to meet his mouth. Nips of teeth and lips against his inner thighs told him he had Jayce's full attention this time and he wasn't going to stop until Jayce had finished.

Then strong arms clutched around Rune's waist, binding him tight against his frame. He growled low and then with a sudden push, he stiffened, his cry hoarse and needful. Rune swallowed the rapid bursts as quickly as they filled his mouth, gulping down the thick fluid until there was none left.

Panting for air, the length of Jayce's shaft fell from his lips with a wet sound. All there was in the room was their heavy breathing for several, long minutes. Jayce's palms made caressing sweeps up and down his spine and over his hips, keeping them connected while he casually brushed kisses to his inner thigh. Slowly, oh so gingerly, he rose from his splayed position and jostled around to lie next to Jayce on the stuffed pallet. An arm tugging against his shoulder encouraged him to curl into him, against his chest.

"I don't know if it's allowed but if you want, you can stay," Jayce murmured, the press of his lips flitting over Rune's temple. "I'd like for you to," Jayce added. "In case that didn't sound like it."

"I'd like that," he whispered. Contentment seeped into his being and his eyes grew heavy. At some point, the blankets were tucked around him and an arm gathered him close to Jayce's chest, then the evening hours were quiet.

❧

Jayce walked with Master Theil toward the cliff's edge and copied him when he sat in the short grass. Sunlight beamed down on them and the sound of the rolling seas below them was soothing. Seagulls, as he would call them, rode the air currents bouncing off the cliff face before diving low to scavenge off the rocks below for their meals.

The temple stood some distance behind them, glistening as it did in the rising sunlight. It amazed him that the size of the temple was larger than was seen, much like an iceberg where so much was below the surface. The secrets the temple could tell would likely fill lifetimes.

Rune had left him with Master Theil after the morning meal to walk into the woods, saying Iba had information for him. They'd shared a brief kiss before leaving his chamber for the dining hall that morning but it didn't look like anyone was the wiser to their physical escapades of the night before, or that Rune had slept in his bed with him.

"We need to work on your mastery of the elements," he commented.

Jayce nodded. He'd assumed as much.

"However, there are other skills that you will need to gain that cannot be taught here."

"Like?"

"Proper horsemanship, skills with a blade, and archery. Now that you have received the goddess's blessing and your Valda-Cree lineage has been proven, you must focus on your personal betterment."

"I have a question. Well, several truthfully. How is the lineage proven?"

"There was only one lion bloodline entrusted with the abilities you are discovering."

Already sitting straight in deference to Master Theil, his head popped up a little in shock. "Only one? How is that possible?"

"Much like most royal families of history, the lineage of the family was kept close to the throne. The lion pride the Valda-Cree were blessed from was well regarded and highly respected." He peered outward, away from Jayce for several seconds as he seemed to carry on an internal debate. "This is deep in the history now, and believed nothing but myth by most, but the child of King Bail's that vanished, you, was an unwedded birth. However, a birth of love. I have to believe the rumors of the time started from your birth mother and those who helped her, possibly to encourage hope after the loss of our king, but no one dared to challenge Carden and the rumors eventually faded." His chin dipped as sadness overtook him. "The Valda-Cree family was respected across most of our world. King Bail's reign covered centuries."

Jayce stared, dumbstruck. "Centuries?" *And he'd had no wife? The plot thickens.*

Master Theil smiled gently, the sadness of what he'd witnessed fading. "I'm no youngling. I remember his youth."

"How long did he live?" The sunlight warming him couldn't dispel the chills fighting to overtake him.

"He was in his third century when he was murdered. You would have been born shortly before the tragedy of his death, and I fear was what prompted the mage council to react, to attempt to overthrow the crown. Whatever their discord was at the time, they blamed the Valda-Cree."

Jayce's frame wilted with disbelief. "Three centuries? But I'm..." *Only human.* He gulped. Yeah, needed to stop thinking like that. *Oh man.* Major mind fuck in process going on here. "Is it part of being Valda-Cree, the magic, or something else that allowed him to live so long? And will I?"

"Without mortal hardship, you could live for several centuries. As for the how…" He paused with a light shrug. "The royal historians may be able to give a more formal answer, however, I believe it is a combination of all of your abilities. The goddess blessed your family for a reason. Her intent was to have a family of her choosing present always. Beyond that?" He arched a low eyebrow in answer. "The rest is supposition to her intents."

"Unwedded," he mused. "So I'm a bastard son." Honestly, it didn't hurt as much as he would have thought it could. He had been adopted, though his raising parents were all he'd ever known. He couldn't help but want to learn more about his own personal history now that he knew it was out there.

"None will take offense in that."

Jayce wished he believed in that ideal. "If I was a bastard child, how? You were alive then. What else can you tell me?" Why wasn't the king married? Why was Jayce an only child when he'd been alive so long? If he was alive, did he have siblings that no one knew about? How was he supposed to fix all of this?

Master Theil smiled kindly. "I will. After the lessons. There are a few books in the library here where those times are recorded. Now then—"

"Wait. Just one more thing."

Master Thiel nodded for him to continue.

"Will I be expected to carry on the bloodline?"

He paused, as though to truly to consider the question. "Expected to? I can't answer that, but there will be those with the hope once your return is known."

His stomach twisted. Bile coated his throat. "But…I can't. With a woman." He shuddered at even the thought.

"Then the goddess will find a way. She always does. She found a way for King Bail to sire you and keep you safe. Now then, please focus. Even your breathing."

Jayce's mind was a whirlwind of new information as he tried to do as Master Theil asked.

Even with real effort concentrating on lessons, the whispers were now looping on repeat in his mind, taunting him with doubts and questions. And no answers for any of them.

Chapter 25

Rune sat in the shade of oaks, meditating with his hand resting on a long root as he listened to the world around him. The immediate world was calm but in the south, far beyond Trajanleh, beyond the burning village in Sucábul he'd seen that first morning, there was unrest. Screams and echoes of pain. He wasn't able to see the cause behind the pain, but he knew it didn't bode well. Vibrations trickled through the undergrowth. Marching feet. Thousands of them. Another piece of the puzzle that he was being shown.

But why? Where was this army going? Who was leading them? Directing their path? The Alendaren army would have come from the other direction, from the far north west and they wouldn't have been attacking the villages. Was this more of Carden's plan? What was the out of reach evil threatening them? Was Carden involved, or was there another player? The prophecy was in motion now. Given that, did the army tie to Jayce? And how?

He sought deeper into the growth, hunting for information, any hint of what was lying in wait. The shapes and details were shrouded, too unclear, too far out of reach.

With a slow exhale, he released the magic until there was nothing remaining. There was simply too little to learn. The sounds of the woods and inhabitants infiltrated once more. And the peace that came with it.

Deep breaths filled his lungs and energized his body with the fullness of nature, washing away the vestiges of the unrest too far away to read properly. When his mind cleared, he reached for Iba. She was soaring over treetops, seeking. He had an idea of what he needed, a fortress, impenetrable and secure. Even an army outpost would be a boon. Hidden and forgotten but serviceable. The mountains were far enough away from the city center to protect and to be out of sight of any immediate attention. They would also have enough warning of any attacks as the passes were narrow and subjected to the weather. The trees had blessed him with the possibility, now he could only hope Iba was able to find it.

The royal family had once held many stronghold locations under their widespread arms, but over the centuries, the Alendaren's had forewent or neglected them to rot, leaving their keepers and inhabitants to fend for themselves until they lay abandoned. He hoped the trees directed him toward such a place that would give them privacy without alerting anyone to their presence.

The need for preparation was irrefutable.

So much to be done. With a clearer mind, he was able to join with Iba effortlessly, soaring among the clouds and treetops as she ventured northeast. The summer breeze against feathers soothed. By the raven's eye, only the topmost peaks retained their snow. This would be the best time to travel to the mountains. The view was spectacular, rolling green tips that filled the curves and sides of the mountains, where a view of the highest crests disappeared into the clouds and beneath the summer snow.

One thing he noticed where she was flying through the airstreams was there were no smoke stacks, no chimneys or smoke trails. That boded well for their privacy.

Presenting Jayce as a mage in training, rather than as the returning Valda-Cree as of yet, would see them likely reach their destination with better expediency.

Are there any of the old loyalist families still even alive? Skin shifters and mages who had stood in support of the Valda-Cree. He wasn't the best strategist, either. They needed people they could trust. Who understood that they weren't taking a coup of the throne for personal gain but to reinstate the proper ruling family, as the goddess had blessed them so long ago. He knew after so long there would be many people who would deny a true ruling family and wouldn't appreciate or welcome Jayce's return. Those who might align themselves with the Alendarens simply because they didn't know of the Valda-Cree or know who to trust.

Rune had no answers as to why he was chosen to be a part of this. Maybe once they reach safety, more will join them, influenced as he had been, drawn together by a common cause. Or more, as he dreaded, the catalyst for full damnation and destruction. As he'd told Jayce, he truly had no way to know which cause he'd been chosen for. Aside from his belief in the way the visions were presented to him that he was fighting for the true leaders, he had no guarantees.

He sighed, leaning now against the tree for support, to restore his energy and physically to rest. So much was expected of Jayce, and in turn him, to guide him down the correct path. To teach him in the ways of not only his true people but of the people he was destined to rule. To take on the duty of the throne with dignity. To learn his magics and trust in them, and in himself. And to be able to lead. Not lead only a few either, but an entire world outward from Caduthien, all of Kielbos, really.

A gentle swoop of Iba's body pulled his attention to her and the view she was sharing. A hopeful smile began to take shape on his lips at the outlines he could distinguish through the thick foliage on the mountainside. "Goddess, you have blessed us." *Iba, investigate.*

With a caw in answer, she folded her wings close to her body and darted low, Rune sensing the drop and feeling the thrill as she homed in on the brick walls before her.

The more she revealed, the more he liked the possibilities. The buildings needed work, some repair, well-weathered and bleached from decades if not more of sun and snow. But there was a good size, two-story central building reminiscent of a keep with long wings for halls, what appeared to be two large stables, and several outer buildings that could have been a smithy or an armory. Or even barracks given their size. An abandoned, walled outpost or garrison with a large keep for the main central building was perfect for what they needed. He doubted anyone at the castle even remembered its existence for as neglected as it appeared, and it was far from any main roads, likely having used the nearby river for access more than over land. The walls were stable, though the roof needed patching on the main building. They could work on the other buildings as they needed them. The kitchen was in good shape and all the fire hearths showed to be unused. It appeared to be completely forgotten. Starting the restorations now in the early days of summer would be best.

"Yes. That will work. Make sure there are no threats and then hurry home, heart. We have much to do."

Reaching for his staff, he hefted himself to his feet. And froze. He wasn't alone. He flipped the edges of his cloak to clear it of debris as if unaware. Sending out a small emergence pulse, he uncovered the person's location deeper in the trees, standing as still as stone. It was one of the temple mages.

"You can come out. I know you're there," he mused. He wasn't threatened by whoever was lying in wait.

Hesitantly, with his head lowered, Brin approached from several yards away. "I apologize for disturbing your meditations, Master Rune. Are you going to report me to Master Theil?"

"It depends. Was it an intentional interruption or merely bad wandering?" he queried without any real concern.

"Oh." He clutched at his robe, looking away. "I was... I didn't mean to..."

Rune raised his empty hand and Brin fell silent, biting at his lip. "I see. Why did you seek me, then?"

"Take me with you," he blurted.

"Who said anything about me leaving?" he asked, concealing the shock that their movements or discussions were being eavesdropped on.

"I heard Master Theil's shouts yesterday," he answered, wincing visibly.

Rune closed the gap with Brin with sharp strides. "How much did you hear?" he demanded.

"That you must leave, and you must take the prince with you."

Rune growled. "Who have you told?" Sparks of red flicked from his fingers, and he clenched his fist.

"No one!" He sharply shook his head, his cheeks paling. "I was alone in the hall when I overheard."

"Why do you wish to join us?"

Brin let out a controlled exhale, his gaze meeting Rune's before lowering in deference. He seemed to be struggling with his confidence when his mouth moved, popped open, then closed without a sound.

"It sounds selfish to simply say because I feel it is right, doesn't it?" he said in a conciliatory tone. "That, once I realized why Master Theil was angry that your friend was with you, I realized there had to be a reason for that anger." His face blushed. "I spent yesterday in the library, seeking the history of the throne."

"And what did you learn?"

"Not enough," he freely admitted.

"But…" Rune encouraged feeling his anger dissipate easily. Brin was only a few decades younger, an early Fifth circle mage with a wind element strength. If Rune's greatest fault had been curiosity brought about by mistakenly overhearing a private conversation, he probably wouldn't be where he was today.

"Is it true? Is he the lost prince?"

"It is not my place to answer that," he hedged. Something continued to tell him to be cautious in who knew. The time was not right to allow the whispers to take root. There was clearly a purpose to the reticence, but he couldn't put his finger to it. It had to be the goddess's will. That and he readily accepted Jayce simply wasn't ready for the responsibility of being named the lost prince. Not yet.

If it were known, he would become immediately targeted by those seeking the truth and those seeking to harm him, and he wasn't prepared for either.

Brin gave him a quizzical stare but quickly let it drop. "As you see fit. I do wish to join your journey."

"Are you prepared for the work and training? There will be much to do and there will be no use for layabouts."

Brin jerked straight, his shoulders back. "I will be in your service." There was a spark of hopefulness in his gaze that Rune didn't have the heart to squash, not then.

"I will take your request under consideration."

He bowed his head deeply. "I appreciate your willingness."

"I cannot guarantee your inclusion, however, might I suggest you continue your study path." He glimpsed Brin's quiet elation before he buried it beneath an even expression. The better the knowledge, the better informed they could be of the history of events that led to this and their understanding of the prophecy, which would continue to assist their planning for the coming future. "Shall we?" He motioned with a palm. This conversation was done for now.

With Iba's expected return, they would depart the temple soon to keep Jayce safe and to protect those in the temple. They would travel north toward the mountains with her guiding them to the abandoned outpost. Repairs could be completed while stocking for the coming winter. Also, winter's camouflage would keep them well hidden while

Jayce continued his training. He would have to find others to continue the training he could not oversee. So much to do, but like Jayce had stated, they weren't going to be storming the castle...yet.

Not wanting to interrupt Jayce's time with Master Theil, Rune broke off to return to his own chamber. Sitting in the corner was the berserker's axe. Another thing he needed to do. Determine whose magic was written into the blade.

Not all magic was good, and neither were all magic practitioners. *Like Carden.* He frowned as the thought took root. Was the axe a clue to the growing unrest? Was magic aiding the marching evil he'd sensed? Standing his staff next to the wall, he crouched in front of the axe, studying the weave of sigils on the haft and on the blade. He hadn't touched it since their arrival at the temple when he'd carried it in from the stable.

Maybe it would be best for him to spend some time in the library as well to decipher the spells and maybe discover the blade's owner.

The fact that Jayce had *sabra* watching him on his plane, or that their orders were to kill if needed, could not be forgotten.

Chapter 26

"We will travel this road." Rune's finger grazed along the drawn line on the parchment. The map was unrolled and pinned in the corners with weights to avoid being tossed by the breezes entering the windows from the cliffs.

Iba had returned two days prior and Rune had been reviewing maps and working in the library almost solid since the keep's discovery. Jayce had been working with Master Theil. His magic skill was strengthening, and he would swear he could feel the force of the powers inside him now, almost like a living, breathing energy. It was weird that he could sense them, and was doing his best to accept. But he was starting to doubt he was doing it well enough, or that he would be enough when the real tests and threats began. He'd been at Windwise a week. A whole week and his entire life had been blown apart and rebuilt into something he simply would have never expected or recognized.

"As a small party, we will garner little interest. Once it is discovered we are mages, most will ignore, or abhor us. Saying we are merely traveling to another temple should appease the most wary. As a group, that is most likely to be believed."

"To stay hidden in plain sight, be what they perceive they see," Master Theil intoned, seeming to agree with the plan.

Jayce paced slowly across the library, his mind tumbling. "How am I going to gather an army?" he pondered for the room in general, not really expecting an answer from the other two in the room. "I don't have a way to broadcast the need." He sure as hell didn't know how he was going to lead an army. He'd never even held a sword, or shot an arrow. *But I have been on a horse!* He silently cheered for that one, though his ass and legs had hated him for a solid day. At least he had found he could speak to a large group during his teacher assisting hours. He snorted quietly. How much of his teacher education could he actually put to use? He supposed he was going to find out.

A light knock on the door interrupted his inner monologue of bitching.

"Come in," Master Theil called.

The study door opened lightly. "Master Theil, Master Rune, Master Jayce." Brin greeted all three with a light head nod. "I brought refreshments." He gathered the large tray from someone waiting right outside the door and then excused him. Jayce moved to the door and closed it behind him as he placed the tray on an open table. "Might I be of assistance?"

"Yes."

"Not right now."

Jayce smirked at Rune. "Which is it?"

Rune twisted to peer over his shoulder. "I've considered why you disagreed with the suggestion, but honestly, I think we need him."

"He's still in training." Master Theil pinched his lips, glowering.

"And so is Jayce, for that matter." He straightened before the table with the map. "I can't teach all the elements. I don't have the ability. Brin has asked, however, to accompany us and I think we need at least a few more to join us, as well. Or to join us later if not when we leave."

Master Theil stood to his full height, cupping his hands behind his back. "You wish to accompany them?" His gaze was stern, and Jayce was glad he wasn't the one being scrutinized.

"I have been reading the histories in the library. I believe I can be of aid."

"Why do you believe they need assistance?"

Brin gulped, his wide eyes unblinking. "I overheard the argument. About the prince. When I searched the library, I found the prophecy." He released a breath to meet Master Theil's gaze unflinchingly. "He is the Valda-Cree prince."

"You are positive?" Master Theil tapped his finger against the back of his hand where they rested cupped behind him. The only sign of his agitation. Master Theil would have been deadly in front of a classroom.

"Master Theil, do you remember Mac'korat of the Sixth circle?"

"Mac'korat?" He paused in thought, then said, "Goddess, I do. He died trying to bravely protect the king's throne when the Alendaren's dared to usurp it away from the Valda-Cree. Before the ultimatums began."

Brin straightened his shoulders, determined to not back down. "Mac'korat was my grandfather. My father still lives at Lehflande. He is nearing the Seventh circle of enlightenment, himself."

Jayce would have laughed at Rune's shocked expression. There hadn't been much to take his mage by surprise. "Your grandfather served under King Bail?"

Brin grinned, his pale brown eyes sparkling. "He did. Grandfather and Da both told many stories of King Bail's reign. I can see now why I was gifted with the strengths of the winds rather than the stability of the earth as my grandfather and da."

"Well, that certainly puts a different spin on it," Master Theil offered, not sounding entirely sold, but considering. He met Rune's gaze. "What say you?"

"I am willing to give him the chance. We do need more to aid with instructing." He rolled a shoulder. He faced Jayce. "Jayce?"

"Considering he may know something about the histories that isn't written, as well as learning control of the wind, I say yes."

"Thank you, Master Jayce! Thank you!" He was practically bouncing on his toes.

Rune raised a hand to gain his attention. "I warned you there would be hard work and difficult times to come. Have you thought on that warning?"

"I have." He scrunched his brow. "May I write my da to tell him I will be on a new duty?"

"You may, however, do not give details."

"Of course, Master Rune!"

All three chuckled at his enthusiasm. "You're dismissed."

He bowed to them. "Thank you, Masters." Then he whirled out the door, closing it gently behind him.

"The exuberance of youth."

"Isn't age merely a mindset?" Jayce offered, wondering how old an elf like Brin could be, knowing Rune's age. "I'm going to guess I'm far younger than anyone in the temple." *And I'm going to live a crazy long time.* He really didn't understand that part, but it wasn't a priority.

Rune's mouth popped open and with a shrug said, "True."

"And I have a lot to learn."

"You do," Master Theil agreed. Moving back to the window's view, he added, "Considering what has been said, and Brin's enthusiasm, I would like to offer a few more of the temple acolytes to attend your journey. I will ask them individually. If they meet your approval, they may leave with you." Jayce hoped that meant Master Theil was behind them fully.

"I appreciate your support, Master Theil." Rune turned back to the map, scrutinizing it carefully. "There is a river close to the outpost Iba found. That guards one entire side. With the mountains at our backs, we will be well protected."

"Not to interrupt a good brainstorming session," Jayce said, nearing the table. He looked at the hand scribed map. "But what are we doing?"

"We're moving our endeavor to a secure base of operations."

Jayce blinked. *Just like that?* He'd finally figured out the temple layout and they were already on the move again.

"There is much we must do, and answers we need." Rune walked around the table to stand before Jayce. "I know none of this makes sense. You've been here only a few days and so much has changed for you."

Jayce swallowed his snort. Yeah, he was feeling a little sour. Everyone was making plans around him, about him, but not really including him, or asking for much input. For all that's been done, has happened, he wasn't feeling very prophetic. Or very kingly. It made him wonder what everyone's agenda was. He wasn't used to following blindly like this.

"What should I be doing?" He crossed his arms, hating how defensive he could feel himself becoming. He was so underequipped for what they envisioned. He didn't know diddly about ruling, no idea about war strategy. Being overwhelmed had been such a constant for the last several days, it never occurred to him that he was hitting a limit. He'd been responding like a well-trained dog to all their challenges. The magic. Fulfilling the skin shifter blessing. He was beginning to lose Jayce inside of it all and it left him feeling adrift and uncertain. Who was he becoming? Did he have a choice?

He was realizing he didn't and that depressed him and angered him at the same time. Twenty-two years old and nothing had prepared him for what was being asked, *demanded*, of him now. While others in the room planned his life, he was left as a watcher on the sideline.

Rune's gaze swept over him, then he addressed Master Theil. "With your leave, I believe Jayce and I need some time outside of the temple."

Master Theil rolled up the map to slip a silk ribbon around it. "We are done with training for today." He smiled kindly at Jayce. "You're advancing quite well. Do not doubt your skill is improving."

Jayce flexed to relax some of the tension gripping his neck. "Thank you." As a class of one he had no one to judge himself by, or any other meter stick to use. He couldn't even train with the other mages as no one could know his extra abilities existed yet. Rune's voice pulled at him.

"Let's go for a walk," he offered, tipping his head gently.

"Okay, sure." Stiff arms dropped to his sides, and he turned to follow Rune, whose walking staff appeared in his grip before he'd even reached for the door. "How *do* you do that?" he asked.

Rune winked. "Mage secret."

Jayce rolled his eyes. Following Rune from the library, they wound their way through the temple, exiting through the doors that faced the cliffs. A light breeze played over them, flipping his hair over his eyes. Like it was teasing him. Together, they walked down the edge of the cliff until they reached a modified path to take them to the rocks below.

Mist from the crashing waves rose up on the breeze, creating rainbows with the streaming sunlight dancing through it. The gulls above called out with their sharp whistles at the invading forms. Watching his step on the wet path, he followed behind Rune. He wasn't sure where they were going, but being outside, able to breathe was already helping him to relax. There was no reason to worry about the prophecy, the magic he was learning to wield, containing the shock for the lion he was at his core. None of it. This peacefulness was simply from walking in the sunlight with no destination other than for their own pleasure. And he was looking forward to the surprise at the end.

Was it a rock alcove? A small beach of shells? Tide pools? He didn't really care. It wasn't training. It wasn't about the prophecy. At least, he hoped it wasn't. But he didn't interrupt Rune's descent, aware the wetness of the rock made the path treacherous.

Finally, they hopped across a few flatter boulders until they reached the lowest ground. Before them stretched a wide open beach, protected by the cliffs and rocks on one side, revealing white sand for probably a hundred yards, maybe a little more.

"This is amazing," he breathed.

"This isn't where we're stopping." Rune walked along the beach and upward away from the water.

Then Jayce saw it. An opening in the cliff face. "Is that a grotto?"

"If that is your word for a cave, then yes."

He squinted as a beam of sunlight tried to blind him with the glare off the smoother water in the cove. Then a cloud eased the brightness once more. The gentle lap of the water on the sand was considerably calmer than the water breaking further down the cliff face. "Yeah. Kind of. Usually a grotto has some kind of water involved, pools or falls. At least, if I remember correctly."

"Just follow," Rune groaned kindly.

"Sorry. It's why I wanted to teach. I love facts, love sharing knowledge." Rune motioned him forward until they stood together. Then Jayce fell silent in awe. "This is even bigger than under the temple." Stalactites hung high across the ceiling dripping as moisture rolled down them to land in the various pools. Natural alcoves and water lapped easily with the pull of the tides outside. Mineral deposits created white streaks across the stone on the water-worn smooth walls, glistening from the reflected light with bright sparkles.

"They're connected. These pools are part of the same water source as the ones maintained in the bathing chamber. However, we won't be interrupted here."

Jayce turned a puzzled look to Rune. "Are you wanting to do more training?"

Rune shook his head, his gaze secretive and playful. "Not exactly."

Chapter 27

"Rune gathered one of Jayce's hands and tugged him to follow. Walking deeper into the cave, he released Jayce when he reached a dry area and began to strip.

Jayce copied him, kicking off his boots and dropping his shirt and pants onto a nearby rock. Rune took an appreciative appraisal of Jayce's tight chest and trim stomach. He easily remembered the feel of his skin from the day of the ritual, gliding his hands over his legs and hips. As well as the cock twitching, eager to rise from his stare alone.

Rune smiled, beckoning him closer with a rolled shoulder. With cautious steps, he entered one of the closer pools, his eyes drifting shut as the warm temperature welcomed him. Because of the rolling tide and open air exposure, they didn't retain their heat as well as the ones in the temple. Which made them lovely to play in.

"Oh…ahhh." Jayce sighed, trailing Rune into the water. "This is nice." He propelled himself forward with his arms, deeper into the pool. He flipped to his back and floated with his eyes closed.

Rune dove underneath him and popped up on the other side. "Do you approve?"

"I so approve," he mumbled, paddling lightly with his hands. "I used to love to swim, but haven't been in a long time. This is great!"

Rune floated away a few feet and cupped his hands. "Good." His grin was pure evil when he popped his hands downward and splashed Jayce's chest with a high wave of water.

Jayce spluttered, sinking to tread water as he wiped his face. "Oh? So that's why we're here." There was playful retribution in his voice.

"*May*-be," Rune sang. Then he dashed underwater, hoping Jayce gave chase.

A splash that rippled through the water told him he needed to add some speed to his evasion. Jayce had taken the dare. He would have been laughing if he weren't underwater. He knew the twists and turns well, and used that to his advantage as he rose for gasps of air, then dove deep into the watery shadows to avoid capture. Water splashed against stone as they twisted and dove around each other. The clarity of the water allowed for sunbeams to slice through the water several feet deep, glistening to refract off the stone as they passed by with strong strokes.

Jayce almost had him a time or two, wisps of skin against a foot or a calf, but he managed to stay ahead of him.

Until he popped up for air, unable to pinpoint where Jayce was. He'd lost track of him and couldn't place him by sound in the cavernous space. The echo of splashing had stilled. Strong arms captured him without warning. "Gotcha."

Rune laughed freely, enjoying the feel of Jayce's frame against his spine. "You did." Wishes weren't what he was supposed to have, but have them he did. The feelings Jayce stirred within were near impossible to ignore. When Jayce released him to move away, he mourned the loss of his touch. He couldn't let himself continue to harbor the feelings he felt for Jayce. Jayce, who was his king. The man who trusted him to not betray him with visions that he'd never dreamed could exist and pertained only to him.

He buried the burst of feelings when Jayce let him go, watching him dive again to swim through the crystal clear depths. Watching the play of sunlight over his skin kept him memorized until he was swathed in the arc of shadows once more. And it didn't appear Jayce ever witnessed his lapse, revealing his longing.

He dove to trail after the other man, enjoying the exploring and time spent to simply be.

Sometime later they were laying shoulder to shoulder with their feet pointed toward the seas in the opening of the cave, soaking up sun to dry themselves. Jayce appeared much more relaxed, compared to the stress and strain he'd seen on his face earlier in the library. After hours of training and the subsequent planning, Rune didn't doubt Jayce was beginning to feel the demands of a long day. As of yet, no more visions had appeared for Rune, so he could only believe they were focusing on the correct direction to make their next steps. And Jayce was taking him at face value. His depth of trust in Rune humbled him most days.

"Feeling better?" Rune asked.

"Actually, yeah." He sighed, fingers digging idly through the loose sand at his hip as they rested.

Rune shifted to prop himself on an elbow to peer at his charge. He was determined to keep his emotions separate even as he visually drank in the view of a naked Jayce. He was a masterpiece with nearly smooth pecs and a honey trail that grew from his flat abdomen to meet with the thicker hair of his groin. Even resting, his length was an alluring, teasing treat that he wished to taste again. It was those cravings that were becoming harder to fight and ignore. He tore his gaze upward, determined to push the temptations away. What they'd already shared had been unexpected, and he couldn't presume for more. There was a reason he'd been chosen for this man's guard. He needed to only focus on that. *If I only could.*

Pushing those thoughts away, he said, "You do know, if you need to talk or take a moment, you only need to let me know. Be honest. You were feeling overwhelmed in the library earlier."

Jayce grumbled before saying, "Yes, but it's because I feel so disconnected. I don't know what I'm doing. I've never liked acting without a plan. Charging forward without a goal. Like when I was studying for myself or assisting other classes. We had a schedule, what we called a curriculum, that told us what we would be studying and what the expectations were. We had time frames." He sighed despondently. "So much of this has felt like I'm doing it by whim. Being dragged along by the nature of the cause. I really don't know what I'm doing. And I hate that."

Rune threaded their fingers together. "That is my failure." He realized now he should have taken the time to explain the visions he had received that drew him to Jayce to begin with. Again he was failing the man who would be his king. "I never explained the various meanings I derived from the visions I was given. I never explained why we are doing what we are doing other than to say it was your responsibility by birthright to help us fix it." He rolled to his stomach and reached with this other hand to play with the flop of hair over his eyes with tender fingers. "Again, my failure to take in the scope of the effects it would bear on you."

"You're not failing, Rune, just... Help me here. I've lost everything and everyone. I feel like I'm losing myself as well. I'm doing like you ask, training, the ritual. I know this is bigger than me, but I can't help feeling so very insignificant when I don't know the bigger picture. I have so many questions about how I'm an only son, how I'm going to live so long. Things that are boggling my mind and it's leaving me off kilter."

Rune continued to stroke over his hair. "When I started to receive the visions, it was one dream to begin with. I kept seeing the Valda-Cree crown. I didn't even recognize it and had to search the library archives for even a hint of its true form. It's a glorious peace of workmanship if they all are true. I didn't understand why I was seeing it in so many dreams, until I started to question why the crown only. Why not the Alendaren rulers? Then the visions began to expand. I saw war. I saw the castle, the throne, the crown, all in various ways. But the unarguable factor of these images was they were always devoid of life. There were no people. Except for the war. There, people died." His words slowed as the images came back to him thick and fast. Screams. Fire. Smoke. Blood. Nightmares that were so viciously true to life it had taken him months to realize they were part of the same visions he'd been receiving for so long. A warning that time was slipping away. "It was at that point when I went to speak to Master Theil. He said I was being given the keys to a quest and I had to see it through."

Jayce rolled to his side to face Rune, neither caring about their nudity where they lay warmed by the sunlight, at ease with the moment and the intimacy. "Then what happened?"

Rune drew a ragged breath. "Then I began to see a person in a very odd way. There were buildings like I'd never dreamed. Hard roads. And noise. So much noise." Jayce snorted at Rune's scrunched nose. "It was not anything I could have envisioned alone and knew as the visions continued I was being directed to where they wanted me to go next. The visions were nearly nightly, and I knew I had no choice but to go. Like I said when I found you, I knew you were male, dark of hair and tall like me."

"You know I'm not that extraordinary, brown hair is as common as dust on the ground. How did you figure out it was me?"

Rune smiled kindly. "Jayce, even before your magic woke to its full potential here, you were beyond extraordinary. You bore an aura glow unlike any on your plane. The only magic that was muted was the Valda-Cree blood, and that was the magic I searched for when you were otherwise unaware." He grinned impishly, knowing Jayce would recall that time in their early meeting.

Jayce waggled his fingers in front of Rune's stomach, making them both chuckle. "That magic?" he asked.

"That magic."

"I don't know anything about how to be a king."

Rune heard the unease and doubt in his voice. "Like you said to me, you are not king yet, and I believe when the time comes you will be ready. You will have forged the needs of the people, have loyal advisors and people from many clans who will believe in you and what you stand for. I also believe from what you have told me, that what you already know, your training and schooling will do more for you than either of us can honestly see now."

"You really have that much faith in me?" he whispered, searching Rune's face with bright amber eyes that seemed to glow in the reflected sunlight. A reflection of his inner beast's magic and his soul that stole Rune's breath away.

"I do. You're intelligent, brave, methodical, logical, and so much more. What I see is a man who will be honed to the best of his ability. The goddess does not make mistakes."

Jayce's cheeks flushed as his gaze lowered, hidden by thick lashes. "Goddess chosen, huh?"

"There is no doubt. You are the Valda-Cree lion that has been missing for so long. Stunning, strong, and in due time, lethal. You will bring hope to a land being torn apart by war."

Jayce heaved a slow exhale. "Thank you. I can't help feeling like I'm being led blindfolded through all of this. I don't know anything about what I am, what I'm capable of. It's disconcerting to say the least."

Rune's hand dropped from where he played in his hair to run a thumb over his cheek. "That is why we need time, you need time. That is why we are going to the mountains. There is room there. We will find you swordsmen to train with as well as the other mages who will be joining us. Brin is only the first that I believe will open the way for us."

"He was pretty excited, wasn't he?"

"A little," he agreed, smirking.

Jayce sighed and rolled to his back again, though he didn't release Rune's hand. "When do we leave?"

"In two days' time, we should have enough supplies for the journey and know who will be joining us." Rune studied Jayce's expression, knowing his next words were going to cause a reaction. "I have also been studying the axe of the *sabra* who attacked you."

Jayce flung his free arm over his eyes. "It's okay to say their name. Raquel. Her and Helen." He rotated his hand on his wrist, urging Rune to continue.

"The markings on it are old magic, so I don't know if the creator is still alive."

"Well, we've already learned that time is not parallel. I was here for a few days, and I lost years at home." He swallowed, his voice dropping a husky note. "Or rather where my parents were. I guess this is home now." He seemed to unconsciously grip the pendant he wore for a moment before patting it gently and letting it come to rest once more on his throat. Rune was glad it gave him a modicum of comfort. That mistake had been all his, and he accepted that blame.

Rune knew losing his parents left a gaping hole in Jayce's life. There wasn't a way for him to correct that, but if he could, he would. Without question. "It is possible the creator, if their employer is the same, is no longer alive if they were not aware of the way time would pass. But we still need to be cautious as we don't know who helped them return."

"I lived next to them for a few years, so it's possible. I was there for my whole life and it seems centuries passed here."

"Time is a tricky mistress," Rune agreed. Then, Jayce's stomach rumbled. "And it looks like it might be time to leave here."

Jayce sighed, then rolled close again. "Thank you." He cupped Rune's face as he squeezed lightly against the hand he still held. Then Jayce's eyes widened a little. "You know, I just realized, I've been putting all of this on me, making it about me, and yes, I'm integral, but what about you? Are you handling this okay? The traveling, the skin shifting, the *sabra*. You've all but sworn yourself to me, and you say you're my guide and guard, so I guess in a way you have, haven't you? Is this where you want to be? How you want to spend your energies, your future? I still say you're as much a part of all of this as I am, aren't you?"

Rune's heart fluttered at the genuine concern staring at him. "That is why I know you're going be an amazing leader and king. You *care*. I am handling it as well as I can. Much like you, I don't have a lot of the answers, at least not yet, but I haven't had any more visions either, so I have to assume we are traveling a path that is expected. Our plan to create a stronghold for you, to garner support and train is only logical sense. As you so kindly pointed out, you can't walk up to the man on the throne and tell him he's an imposter. No one would believe you. We have to plan, spread the rumor that the king's line has returned, and that takes time."

Jayce dipped his shoulders until his head sagged between them. "Yeah, nothing big, right?" His grin was lopsided, his gaze laden with doubts.

"Nothing big at all," Rune offered, smiling kindly. "Because when it is time, the truth of your return will only embolden those who will follow you. And you will believe in yourself, which will help those who seek the truth believe in you." He urged Jayce's face upward with a hand to his chin. "Like I believe in you and will follow you. You are stronger than you think."

Jayce swallowed thickly. His mouth opened, perfectly timed with another, louder, rumble of his stomach. Quirking his brow, he huffed a laugh. "I guess that's enough seriousness for right now, then."

Rune met his gleaming eyes and chuckled. "Let's dress and go find food."

Jayce hefted to his feet, drawing Rune with him until they stood facing each other. "Thank you," he offered. He leaned close and rested their foreheads together. Rune's heart raced at the openness before him.

"For?"

"Being as honest as you can with me, for helping me through all of this. And for being you." Light fingers swept hair away from his ear, tucking it behind. Then he leaned close and brushed a gentle kiss to Rune's lips. A soft sweep that Rune wanted to chase. "Couldn't help myself." His gaze dropped low with a playful leer at his body's reaction. "Don't think I didn't notice." He whispered into Rune's ear. "You are the sexiest elf I've ever known."

"Oh," Rune panted. Blood raced through his veins. He hadn't brought Jayce to the cave for a seduction, but his brain was suddenly swept clear of anything but the man staring at him with a bold golden gaze. A wave of hunger swept through him with a searing heat that made his heart race.

Jayce neared for another kiss. Longing, need, heat, desire all pooled inside of him. All he could see before him was Jayce, the man. A man he desperately wanted with a hunger that made thinking of anything beyond them near impossible. And by the fire heating Jayce's stare, he was feeling it too. Warmth on his skin was nothing compared to the heat surging through his veins as his heart thudded into his ribs.

Jayce's tongue flicked out and teased at his upper lip, making Rune feel weak and needy. The firm grip on his hand pulled them together.

A shout from the above cliffs out of view froze them.

Chapter 28

Jayce's eyes drifted shut as his chin sagged to his chest. "Now that is terrible timing," he growled.

Rune swallowed, gently extracting his hold from Jayce's. Both were showing signs of their need but with another shout to Rune, Jayce knew their quiet escape had been discovered.

Quickly dressing, they left the cave and walked rapidly across the sand until they could see a person at the top of the cliff's path. "Master Rune!"

"I'm here. What is it?" They both lifted a hand to block the sunlight, peering upward from the fat boulders at the bottom of the incline at whoever was calling.

"Thank the goddess!" He was waved upward. "A message! Master Theil!"

Rune met Jayce's questioning gaze and, with a shrug, both started to hurriedly climb the smooth stone path as safely as they could.

At the top, one of the young mages waited for them. He wrung his hands as he rushed through the polite greetings. "Master Rune, Master Jayce. Master Theil is requesting you urgently to his library."

"Is everything all right?" Rune demanded as they picked up the pace to the temple.

"I'm unsure. We were asked to locate you immediately and bring you to him."

"Thank you, Uria'as." They didn't speak further as they ran.

Jayce hoped everything was okay. This appeared to be an unusual request from what he knew.

Swinging through the temple doorway, they eased their pace to a rushed walk through the hallowed halls to reach the library. The door hung open as they approached, Rune only a pace ahead of Jayce.

Master Theil stood in front of the windows looking outward. Seated around the room were four people.

"Master Theil, how may we serve?" Barely inside the room, Rune bent at the waist and Jayce copied him while both kept a wary eye on the group in the room. No point in making himself seem out of the norm in front of people he didn't know, so he followed Rune's lead.

Before Master Theil could speak, one of the group stood. Easily a half foot taller than Jayce with hair as black as night pulled back to his neck. He wore a well-cared for sword strapped to his side and at least three visible daggers along his belt. Weathered in the face, he appeared older than he likely could be, like a man who had lived a not quite so safe life. "I apologize for intruding on your sacred home. My name is Terne Vorverrian." The other three maintained neutral expressions, seemingly fine to allow this man to speak for them all. Jayce pegged him as their group leader.

They were clearly all warriors, if not mercenaries, and if he didn't miss his guess, at least one of the women was *sabra*. Now that he knew what to look for. Namely the formidable axe strapped to her back. He stayed partially hidden behind Rune's shoulder, unable to hide the shiver of unease their presence gave him. After Raquel… He didn't know who outside of the temple he could trust, or who wanted to kill him. He was beginning to accept why, and for that reason among many, Rune didn't want his identity known yet. He doubted he could have fought off this guy as easily as he'd managed to avoid Raquel. The look of these four told him to err on the side of caution at the moment. Even as he wanted to pull Rune away from the threat in the room, no matter how calm they appeared to be. He kept them in his periphery as he listened.

"We are passing through, but are warning any who we might come across. The Blood Spawn army is advancing. It will not be long before they set their direction northward as they have already decimated nearly everything south of Sucábul to the Rigal Seas. I was explaining this to your master when he requested your attendance."

"How far away are they? Days? Weeks?" Master Theil held his hands behind his back, listening to the grim report.

Terne's hand gripped the hilt of his sword, his fingers tight, and he rolled his shoulders. Though he didn't directly face either Jayce or Rune, Rune shifted slightly in reaction, blocking more of Jayce's body with his own without making it seem obvious. "It is hard to say, but by their lethargic advance, likely not before winter. And then they will likely move even slower as supplies dwindle. They have stalled for weeks southward of Sucábul. The lands are blackened by their marching, by the blood they have spilled. They destroyed everything in their path. I don't know why they lingered, except that it gave us opportunities to take advantage of. We evaded capture and have managed to help some flee. Now we are warning as we can."

"It is only a matter of time before they turn to us then." Master Theil sighed with a weighted heaviness. "Evil will always hunger for more, be it power, pain, or blood."

"In this, your wisdom stands true," he offered. "I wish I had more to share."

"What of their numbers?" Rune asked.

"In the thousands. Demons, orcs, mogalls, and more." He let out a breath, his gaze raking those surrounding him, including them. "We have done what we can but we are no match and the damage we can inflict, a pinprick quickly healed. We are only a small group. The crown is useless to protect their people, so we do what we can."

"Has the throne sent any support? Any sign of an army?" Rune asked.

"None. If they care or know what is on their lands, we can't say."

Master Theil faced them with a congenial head nod. "You may stay to rest, as we are open to aid those in need. Please join us for the evening meal."

The three who had silently sat through the meeting stood and as one, they partially dipped at the waist. "We would be honored."

"Call Uria'as and Ritter. Have them given chambers and allowed to refresh themselves."

"Yes, Master Theil." Jayce took a step back, unable to not look at the four waiting patiently. The woman with the axe was giving him the shivers, her stare cold. He spun on his heel and went to find the mages Master Theil requested.

Beckoning the group away to rooms for the night with the assisted aid of the acolytes, Rune and Jayce stayed in the library and once they were out of sight, Rune closed the doors.

Iba, take a look around and make sure there are no lurkers with our guests.

A vibration of acknowledgment was his reply. "What do you think, Master Theil? Can we trust what he's telling us? Should we stay to help protect the temple?"

He shook his head. "Truthfully? It is hard to say, as for the other? No, this is not your battle. We will be safe. If we need to retreat to the tunnels, we can. Not the first time the temple has been in the path of violence." He sank into his chair behind his desk, pushing away to brace his hands on the armrests of the chair, his mouth set in a grim line. "There is also time for us to plan, and to fortify if what Terne says is accurate enough, to give us a warning."

"I would have to say it likely is. The day I went to locate Jayce, in the distance there were fires, a village under attack. But it was a lone outlier and likely not indicative of the pending direction of the army's movement." He sank down to one of the vacated couches, pushing his cloak out of the way. Jayce took a nearby chair. "There was no sign of the army that day, only the precursor warning of the prophecy that I had seen in my visions to then. From what Terne said, they have to be much further south than I was that day."

"That really doesn't put them very far from here, though, does it?" Jayce asked, bent over his knees with his hands cupped beneath his chin.

"Unfortunately, logistically, no. But an army that large cannot move quickly if they are causing that much havoc in its wake."

"And from the sounds of it, they are," Jayce murmured sadly. "So many people dead. For what? And who is a part of it? Do you think Carden has anything to do with this?"

"I wish I could say with certainty he didn't but if the throne is not protecting its people, and there is no whisper from the crown, we have to assume it is possible. We already know from the friendly communications I've been able to receive the current king is less than capable if he's even alive."

Jayce sagged backward, his gaze on the ceiling. Sadly, there were no answers there. If he was going to be the one to stop this evil, and take out the mage manipulating the crown, he had his work cut out for him. He really wished he had some idea of the cause, the motivation for a total annihilation of a world. What would that gain anyone? It definitely told him he had a long way to go to being prepared to making even a dent in any of this himself. They clearly needed more information than they currently had about what was happening and who was the mastermind leading the army. And even worse, if they were one and the same. He feared it likely was. If Carden could control the throne, whether through manipulation or usurping as an advisor, there was a chance that this was all on him. Jayce glanced up and clashed with Master Theil's gaze. There was no doubt the worry pressing in on Jayce was weighing as heavily on the elder with more proof that their world was slowly degrading into turmoil. "What do we do first?"

Master Theil pulled a hidden parchment from between other blank sheets. "I have five names to accompany you and Rune for training and support. I have spoken to them all and they are willing to continue your training. They will do you well as a foundation for your inner circle. You will need steadfast and true advisors on this journey." He handed the page to Rune who read them. Jayce tipped to lean his chin against Rune's shoulder to read over his arm.

He smiled when he recognized Brin's name at the top of the list. He was one that Jayce already knew he got along with quite well.

"Do these five, aside from Brin, know who Jayce is?" Rune asked once he'd gone over the names.

"I only told them they were being asked to continue his training because of their own abilities and that they would be leaving with you if they and you agreed. It is up to you both how and when you share the truth. That is not my information to share."

Jayce felt the way Rune's frame seemed to shudder with relief as close as they were sitting. It seemed Rune had continued to carry some caution about the amount of trust he could grant Master Theil. At least it looked like they truly had him in their corner. His reaction also reinforced the fact that Rune was going to do what he could to protect Jayce. Whether it was from an unknown in the same room or from his own mentor. Appreciation for what Rune was going through filled him. He was putting a lot on the line to keep Jayce safe.

"We will meet with them tonight, after the evening meal and discuss it with them. It is only fair that they understand that this path will be dangerous and give them the choice, even if we can't tell them why until we leave. I don't want whispers of Jayce's heritage to rile the other acolytes."

"Are you expecting to have a sign for when we should reveal it?" Jayce asked, wondering.

"I believe so. You're vulnerable right now, learning and not prepared to protect yourself. We don't know how well you communicate with your lion spirit, or if you can control him." Rune shook the page he held lightly. "It's best if we take this all cautiously until you are better prepared."

Master Theil stroked his chin. "That is probably the wisest course of action for now."

Jayce understood their caution, but it frustrated him too. Especially now that he knew the army was out there. It put the scope of what he faced in front of him, and he knew he wasn't ready. He leaned closer to Rune to ask a question but it froze in his throat with his next breath.

Being so near to him, there were the subtle scents of the minerals and salt water from their time together in the cave waters lingering in the silky length of his hair. He couldn't resist drawing the scent into his lungs. He couldn't seem to fight the elf's pull, even when they were in serious discussion, his body seemed to gravitate toward him, craving his closeness, his warmth. He'd never felt this strongly for another. He'd had sex, probably more than his parents would like to know about, since he'd been in college, but no one else had even so much as turned his eye since he'd met Rune. From their discussions he had to believe that Rune was feeling it too, this undeniable need between them, because it seemed it was only getting stronger.

What if it's more than lust?

Then Rune's words reached his brain. He snapped his focus up to Rune's face. "Wait. What do you mean control him? I thought... Aren't we one and the same?"

Both Rune and Jayce faced Master Theil. "I wish I could tell you," he answered. "I never witnessed King Bail's lion, nor at that time was I close enough to him to discuss it."

Jayce's shoulders sagged. "But that could be a good thing," Rune offered. "You are the Valda-Cree line reborn, so to say. You will have your own insights over the aspects of your skin shifter ability."

"But what if I can't control it? This is a *lion* inside me." He smacked his chest with a hard palm.

Rune squared himself on the seat to look searchingly into Jayce's gaze. What he was looking for Jayce wasn't entirely sure, but he seemed to find it. "And when the time comes, you will know what to do, your lion will know. Those who are skin shifters share the body, your being, with your animal. He will tell you what you need to know."

Master Theil seemed to agree when he said, "What you need to find, now that you have a growing protection force, is other skin shifters to balance you. Those you can learn from, learn balance and respect for your lion to be able to work together."

Jayce exhaled slowly. "Well, that's only one more thing, then, right?" He grinned lopsided, doing his best to hide the growing turmoil inside of him.

Rune lightly curved a palm to his thigh and squeezed, centering him. "You can do this."

Jayce peered at him, feeling the swarm of doubts buzzing like bees in his head. "I hope you're right."

Chapter 29

Three days later, the five mages accompanying Rune and Jayce were miles from the temple, riding in a group northward. Iba soared overhead, guiding the group while guarding them from above. Every now and then he heard the piercing cry of a hawk or maybe a falcon, he wasn't sure as it seemed to stay to their rear. Saddlebags were laden with dried foods and clothing, along with rolled sleeping wraps and blankets tied to saddles and two more horses with necessities. At least with the slower pace, Jayce was starting to feel like he was getting the hang of the horseback riding. He patted the neck in front of him, enjoying the silkiness of the coat beneath his palm.

"You're doing better," Rune offered at his side.

He rocked side to side to ease the pressure on his hips in the saddle. "It feels like it." He was a far cry from used to it, but he was getting there. He glanced at the others surrounding them. Unsurprising, they all looked so much more at ease than he did on horseback. *City boy no more.* He supposed he would have to get acclimated to this. To his left rode Grayson, leading one of the pack animals. Behind him rode Leodinn. On his right was Duran with the second pack horse, as well as Ulcieh. Brin was the only one he was aware of the accompanying mages in the group who knew of Jayce's secrets. He rode next to Duran.

The sun was high, and while it felt like summertime, it wasn't unbearably hot. The sea breezes were well behind them now. "Are we still in Windmere?" he wondered. The calls of the seabirds had faded some time ago.

"Yes, but not for much longer."

"Tell me, is the castle considered the capital of Caduthien? Or is there a name for it as a city?"

Grayson spoke up. "The ancient texts, before the Alendaren coup, called the castle and area surrounding it Rinattoah, after the goddess Ahdrer's sire. As he ruled and guided the gods and goddesses, so should Rinattoah oversee the lands blessed by her chosen hand. By the recounts of the historians, it was once a flourishing city."

"I take it by your tone, that isn't the case now."

Duran continued from there, his tone somber. "No. The city has fallen to disrepair and poverty is rampant. I come from a northern province and had to travel through Alendaren to reach the temple. It saddened me to see so much suffering." His brow furrowed with his words, memories playing behind unfocused eyes. He straightened in his saddle. "I would have liked to have seen it in its glory."

Murmurs of agreement were echoed through the group.

"I take it the Alendaren family doesn't care about the suffering of their people?"

"Not from what has been written, and the current king has been less than interested in his lands for decades. He lives behind a wall of advisors and men at arms. I can't even say if he's left the castle, as word of a sighting of the king would travel through the lands and not a single whisper has been heard in as long."

Jayce frowned. "How can a king rule without knowing his own people?"

Rune's gaze warmed with approval when he tipped his chin slightly in Jayce's direction. What could he say? It was how he felt. Leading from ignorance was guaranteed to fail.

"There have been many rulers who know nothing of their kingdom outside their own walls," Grayson spoke up.

Jayce bit his tongue to not say the first thing that almost tripped out of his mouth. *Not the way I would do it.* He would want to meet the people, the same way he made a point of knowing the students he'd worked with. Wanted to hear them, their worries. A leader, be they a king or a teacher sculpting minds, who ignored the obvious was nothing more than breathing air and taking up space.

"Tell me more." It helped to pass the time as they described the lands surrounding them, where Alendaren, once Rinattoah, stood far and out of sight in the distance. The dotted farms and villages with a few larger clans interspersed. He learned about the keeps and their chieftains. It was good to know where possible support could be found when they started branching out.

"Master Jayce?" Leodinn's voice carried to him over the quiet stamp of horse hooves on the dirt road.

"Yes?"

"Where are you from that you know nothing of our histories?"

He swept a questioning glance to Rune who only shrugged. Jayce supposed he was on his own here.

"I come from a land very far from here, and it's quite different." He didn't want to come out and say he was from a different world, a different time entirely. Not yet. "The Kielbos history and Caduthien way of life isn't known there."

"Are you here to train, then? Master Theil impressed on us each how important it was to train you and that this was going to be a long endeavor," Leodinn asked. Heads bobbed in agreement around him.

"I am. I came into my gifts late in life." He shot a smirk to Rune when he coughed quietly. Rune pretended he didn't notice the long stare. Jayce ignored his avoidance, saying, "I was raised in a non-mage household, so no one knew I had any elemental powers." That felt like a safe way of describing his adoptive parents. A pang of homesickness swiftly followed but he didn't allow it to grow. The pain of never being able to see them again, to be able to tell them why he'd vanished remained, but it was an ache only time could heal. He hoped with all that he was that they knew how much he loved them and he wouldn't forget them.

"And which is your elemental, if you don't mind my asking? With all of us here, it doesn't make much sense as Rune is fire, Brin is wind, and Grayson is earth."

"Does that mean that you are a water mage?" he asked Leodinn.

"I am. Ulcieh is also a water mage, and Duran is fire."

Jayce peered at each as they were named. "I want to thank you each for agreeing to help me get a better understanding of my own. As for which..." He didn't seem to be getting any help from Rune on this. So much for guiding him. He made an attempt at keeping a straight face. "I, uh, seem to have all of them." He focused on the reins in his hands but it was mere seconds before the outbursts started.

"What? No, that's not possible" was followed by several gasps of disbelief.

"All of them?" murmured Duran in full wide-eyed incredulity.

He flushed at their continued scrutiny. The weight of several gazes was pinned smack dab in the middle of his shoulder blades. "That's why I need help. I don't understand it."

"But you're, pardon me for being blunt, you're human," Duran stated.

Rune finally joined in. He raised a hand. "Don't be like that Duran. There are humans who have gifts as well as the magics of the fae and the witch's potions. Elven kin are not the only magic users, merely the most common."

Jayce nudged his horse closer. "We should tell them," he whispered. "If I'm supposed to learn from them, if they're supposed to protect me as Master Theil said, then they deserve the full truth. They need to be able to trust me, to trust *in* me."

Rune met his stare, then silently nodded. "Tonight. When we stop. It would be better to do it when I know we can protect ourselves from being overheard."

"We can't now?" Twisting in the saddle, there was *no one* but them on the road.

"Fine." He raised his voice to carry. "We're taking a break." Spying green fields and trees ahead to their left, he guided his mount to them and slid to land on his feet. Tying a lead rope loosely to branches allowed the animal to graze. The others joined him, doing the same with their horses. They sat with water skins, carrying bundles of bread, dried meat, and fruit under the shade. At least they'd all changed from the temple robes to britches and tunics, similar to his own. They looked like a band of travelers, unless one looked closer. Every single one of them had eyes marked by mage magic.

Iba drifted down and landed on Rune's shoulder, followed by a different bird that landed on Leodinn's outstretched arm. He was protected from the sharp claws with a leather bracer from below his elbow reaching nearly to his wrist.

"He's beautiful," Jayce remarked, gazing at the full plumage as the bird settled.

"Thank you. This is Rox. He's a peregrine falcon." He ran a finger down his side, then offered him a bit of meat, the same as Rune was doing for Iba.

"I would have assumed Rox and Iba would naturally avoid each other."

Leodinn smiled as he doted on his companion. "In any other environment, they would, but they see no threat in the other. They've also become accustomed to each other over the years."

"Does that mean you're also of the Fifth circle?" He noted the others didn't have any kind of animal companion.

"I am."

"How does that work?"

Ulcieh explained. "As we advance through our training, our magic has two parts. The gifted and natural. Rune is incredibly gifted as he can commune with nature on a level that we haven't reached yet. As we mature, depending on our natural communal ability, we sometimes are blessed with a companion animal, a soul aid."

"We all hope for one, but it's not guaranteed," Duran added with a wistful glance toward Rox.

"To add some context, Leodinn, Brin, Ulcieh, and I are all Fifth circle enlightened. Duran and Grayson are higher Fourth circle." Each bowed their head in acknowledgement as Rune went through the group. "And your companion can appear when you least expect it," he added with sympathy to Duran. "There is no timeline for them."

"I know." He plucked at the grasses before his knees. "It's part of why I agreed to this journey with you both. I was ready for something different."

"As was I," Grayson agreed, echoed by a head nod from Ulcieh. "I think several of us are ready for a challenge." He took a bite of his meat roll, wiping his lip with a thumb. "I might only be Fourth circle, but I know the trial to take me to Fifth wasn't at the temple."

"This will be a challenge, all right," Jayce muttered. Rune frowned then quickly sighed.

"Jayce's powers came to him late because he's not from Kielbos." When a couple of mouths popped open, Rune raised his hand, stilling them, asking for patience. "What he told you is true. However, it isn't simply a distant land. He comes from a place where natural and spell magic is extremely weak. It is so suppressed, it might as well not exist." Brin was watching them closely but up to then had kept his silence. Support and belief emanated from his gaze as they all waited for Rune's next words. "Have any of you studied the history of the Valda-Cree?"

"The lion bloodline of the throne?" Ulcieh's brow scrunched. "I have in my history studies."

"King Bail was the last Valda-Cree ruler," Brin offered, prompting hopefully as he leaned to take in those around him. "At least, until the Alendaren coup."

"Did you read about the king's lost son, a prince?" Jayce was glad Rune was taking over the narrative. He couldn't ask questions about what he didn't personally know.

Several heads nodded. Ulcieh said, "The history texts say he was secreted away and never found. It was believed, if he even existed, that he was dead when he never returned, and now he would be dead as his birth was hundreds of years ago. The line is sadly no more."

Jayce sipped from his skin before corking it again. "What if there was a way that he wasn't dead?" he asked evenly. "Do you still believe in the edicts of the Valda-Cree? Do you believe they would be just and fair?"

Grayson snorted softly. "It wouldn't take much to be an improvement. We're at war with an unknown army. A force we can't fight is controlling the current leader and throne. Our world is suffering even if we can't openly see the wound."

Jayce frowned. He hoped to be more than merely a marginal improvement so he let that slide. It did however show him how low the preconceived bar was. Which could be both a good and a bad thing for himself. He'd given himself heart and soul into the change Rune's visions were directing them to. He could only hope those that joined them did the same. "But would it be seen as a beacon of hope if the Valda-Cree returned?"

There was a heartbeat before Brin nodded firmly, followed by Duran and Leodinn.

Ulcieh crossed his arms against his chest. "But it's not possible. What does that have to do with your training?"

Rune growled at his rudeness, but Jayce grazed a light touch to his thigh, attempting to calm him. Jayce didn't want to come right out and tell them. If they could make the connection to his ancestry, then it would be easier for them to believe when they did see the truth. He directed his next question to Brin, simply because he knew he was already in his camp a hundred percent. "You've read, or know of the

Valda-Cree line?" Brin nodded evenly. His eyes sparkled as he kept his mouth firmly shut. *You are one smart elf.* "What do you know?"

"The original family elevated to the throne were from the Valda-Cree lion pride, eons in the past, with the goddess's gifts passed through the generations. They had a blessed magical ability that few knew the full scope of, as well as their skin shifter animal spirit. It was even said that a true ruler had an ability that went beyond the four elements, the God's Touch, it was called. It was only hinted at as it was a Valda-Cree family secret kept to protect young ones as the trait appeared."

Jayce hid his surprise. *A fifth element?* Master Theil had told him he'd be learning a lot from whoever joined their group. He wondered if that nugget of information played into the varied and multiple colors that seemed so interwoven with the tangible magics he was learning.

"The crown depicted the family strengths. Their protective nature, their strength, and the power of pride, of community. There was severe civil unrest and the Valda-Cree were honorable and fair, calming the warring factions as the king directed not only from the throne but had his brother and two sisters for advisors who could speak on his behalf around the world. The goddess's choice proved to be wise as within a generation, Caduthien was thriving." He spoke with wonder and longing when he added, "I've never seen the crown and the drawings in the library are only partials. Lions leaping adorn the sides and there were jewels for the eyes."

"Wasn't there something about the crown being blessed, as well?" Duran asked.

Jayce couldn't have asked for a better placed question. Not only to help him learn but to continue to build the expectation of the Valda-Cree. He could only hope he could meet that expectation. He understood what he was there for and why, but it was too easy to feel overwhelmed now and again.

Brin leaned into the group circle, his gaze full of wonder. "The Valda-Cree crown, when honored by the family, would glow for the goddess blessed."

Jayce blinked. "Like a light?" More fantasy illusion? He couldn't even imagine it.

Ulcieh shook his head. "More like a bright patina. It was part of the goddess's blessing, a sign of the true ruling family per her decree.

The Valda-Cree pride was large, but only a select few of the bloodline ever gained the goddess's blessing. The crown was written in the histories to help prove their successions. It kept infighting from happening as the crown's reaction was considered absolute." He sat back on his hands, stretching out his legs. "But the crown is lost. The Alendaren family had it destroyed."

Jayce's stomach plummeted. He whipped around toward Rune. How? Had Master Theil known? Why hadn't he said anything sooner? How could he prove himself to the people if the most accepted sign of his true bloodline was lost to them? How could he bring them together? It seemed every step forward they gained, they lost two in another direction.

"There will be a way," he offered to him alone.

"But you said you had all of the gifts," Leodinn pressed.

Jayce swallowed, caution tingeing his voice when he answered. "I did, I do." He didn't know what he should reveal, but when he looked to Rune, he nodded subtly. Jayce exhaled and faced the group. *Well, okay, then.* "What we've been taking the long way to explain is I am that prince. I can call on all of the elemental strengths that are natural to the mage-born."

Ulcieh was the first to roll his eyes. "Not possible. Too much time has passed. Aside from that, no one has seen a lion skin shifter in almost as long anywhere in Caduthien."

Jayce stiffened. "Are there any lion skin shifters? Anywhere?"

Grayson and Leodinn both opened their mouths as though to speak, but then shook their heads. "If there are, they are well to the north, far away. Any lion found near Rinattoah or Caduthien was executed by the Alendaren army." Grayson looked to Ulcieh for confirmation, who nodded his head.

Jayce felt his skin actually become clammy and cold. The sunlight didn't even touch the suddenness of the reaction. "Are you serious? They eradicated an entire people? A whole family?"

Brin hunched into his shoulders, pulling his legs up to circle them with his arms. "It wasn't a good time in our history. A lot of senseless death."

"But that still doesn't support your claim," Ulcieh pressed. "You are obviously mage born as your eyes are revealing. You may have one or even two elemental magics, but there is no one alive who controlled more."

"You're discounting his lion," Brin warned.

Ulcieh studied him then shook his head. "It's simply not possible."

Jayce hung his head to his chest as he absorbed what they'd shared, then straightened, letting his gaze circle the group before he stopped on Rune beside him. Stalwart at his side, to protect and support. Like always. And for once, he was glad for his presence. "I can't show you, any of you, right now. It's not safe, especially if as you said, any of the remaining lion prides were hunted and murdered. I'm still learning that as well. I've only merged once since I've arrived. This is all completely new to me. I wasn't raised with the magic, with the shapeshifter, sorry, skin shifter spirits. To me, this world is archaic, but I'm trying. After the lion claimed me, I accepted my fate was not what I had lived, what I had anticipated. I need guidance, training, and yes, I need to do more work with the lion to understand it as well."

"So you're trying to convince us you're the missing prince, come back from the dead?" Leodinn considered him with a thoughtful stare.

"Not from the dead, more…" He bit his lip, giving Rune a pleading look. He really needed these five to accept him, or they would get no further.

"More like the lost prince has been found," Rune interjected. "Someone protected him until he could be brought home."

"But the time between?" Ulcieh was clearly not even close to believing, which was okay.

"Time passed differently where I was." Jayce's sorrow was out front for everyone to see. "My parents… I was adopted where I lived. They were all I knew. How I came to be in my world, I have no idea. I remember being young and always being with them. The only reason I know I was adopted was because I do remember that part of my childhood, the meetings, and the people involved. Aside from that, I look absolutely nothing like either of my parents. It doesn't hurt to say that I never knew anything about my birth parents, but now…" He gave Rune a knowing, raised eyebrow. "Clearly my heritage is something I need to learn a lot about."

"You five were chosen to continue Jayce's training, and to become his first circle of support. Master Theil trusted you, your abilities, and valued your input to continue this journey. We couldn't share this information with you until we had left because of the visions I've received. It isn't time to reveal Jayce's nature. Not yet."

Leodinn petted Rox's tail with a light touch. A horse snorted nearby, all of them happily snout deep in the green grass. "I can see and understand that caution. You warned this would be dangerous and challenging. I understand that more as well." He met Jayce's gaze with a light head dip. "I, personally, am looking forward to it. If the Valda-Cree rise again, I will honor my master's request to be a part of this. I pledge myself to the future crown."

Jayce sputtered, quickly shaking his head. "I appreciate that, but I don't want your pledge. I'm nothing as of right now. I want people who I can learn from, who I can trust because as this grows, our lives are going to be reshaped and changed. All of them. All of us." He spoke firmly, including all of the group as he faced each. "We will learn together."

"But first, we need to get to safety," Rune stated. Iba rose with a strong flap of wings to launch into the sky. He hopped to his feet, the others copying him. "Let's gather. We'll stop for the night if there's a suitable village on the way."

Within minutes, they were astride their mounts and moving north once more.

Chapter 30

"I think the most annoying facet to this is I really don't know what I need to do next."

Rune smirked gently. "And you hate not having a plan."

He chuckled under his breath. "In the worst way. It feels so disorganized." Rune noted the distracted flip of the reins in his hands and realized he didn't even know he was doing it as he thought through the coming possibilities and challenges. There was insight to Jayce's actions. He was a thinker, a planner, and hardly impulsive. Which had its good points and its bad, but it also meant he was less likely to go haring off on some unknown idea without careful consideration. Stability. A strong trait needed in these trying times. "Master Theil seemed to believe I need an army. If my history is even close to being true to life, that's a lot of men and women fighting."

"Women?" Grayson asked with a fair note of incredulity.

"Yes, women." Jayce glared and Rune did his best to bite his lip. Jayce's progressive beliefs from his upbringing were bound to raise a few eyebrows. He'd witnessed the way women worked and mingled through Jayce's society during his observations before approaching him. "I will not withhold the ability to contribute from anyone. Considering *sabra* seem to rely on a woman's ability to not appear threatening to urge people to overlook them, imagine what a woman trained in the ways of war, strategy, and with learned fighting skills could do. Some of the best spies from my world were women because everyone underestimated them."

Brin sat straight in his saddle, his eyes wide as he looked around the group. "I never thought of it like that. *Sabra* are deadly and they are usually women."

"You can't discount someone by their outward appearance," Leodinn inputted with a sage nod.

"Exactly." Jayce smiled broadly. He gripped the pommel of his saddle to steady himself as he twisted around to consider the group. Rune noted Ulcieh's bland expression but knew his disagreement was strictly brought about by his level of belief. Only time could correct that. "But, we're not there yet."

Rune patted his mount when it sneezed. "No, sadly, we are not. Our goal is to reach the keep in the mountains and increase your training." He glanced upward and forward. "Iba says there is something ahead. They may have rooms. At least we can stop for the night and have a hot meal." He couldn't tell from Iba's view if it was a tavern or a homestead.

Brin rubbed his butt. "I'm all for stopping. I haven't ridden this much in years."

Duran nodded his head. "Me either. My legs are not happy." He braced himself in his stirrups, stretching as much as he was able.

Jayce laughed kindly. "So glad it's not just me. I'm new to the horse riding also, so I already know what I'm going to feel like come morning. Painfully aware." A couple of chuckles seemed to agree with his woeful groan.

"We're all going to be complaining," Grayson stated evenly before he broke out in a grin, getting them all to laugh.

The sun was on the western horizon when the first signs of life were visible ahead.

Rune guided them to the stable behind the buildings. "Good eve," he called, listening for movement. He waved for everyone to dismount, and he handed his reins to Duran. "Wait here." He cautiously entered the stable, seeing empty stalls and clean hay. It was dusty but not unkempt. He patted a curious nose when it rose over the gate, sniffing. Noise ahead guided him to the last stalls. There was a young man moving hay around on the floor and into a feeder. "Good eve." The young man jerked around, his pitchfork high. Rune raised his hands to show he held no weapons. At least not any that would require a blade. "I mean you no harm. I'm looking for rest for my horses and a meal."

He chuckled, the nervousness pinching his face fading. "My apologies, mage. I was trying to get this done and didn't hear you." He leaned on the handle. "How many?"

"Seven, with two pack animals. Can you board us overnight?"

He nodded briskly. "Aye, that I can, if you don't mind them doubling up." He waved him forward. "Please, bring your animals in."

"Thank you for your aid. And for a hot meal?"

He pointed beyond Rune's shoulder. "Check with Mam. She'll be happy to feed you."

Dipping his head, he half turned. "Duran, bring them in, please." One by one the horses were unloaded and set to stalls with fresh hay and water.

"I have grain for an extra coin," the young lad offered hopefully.

"That would be kind of you," Brin said with a bright smile. He opened a small pouch and offered over several coins. They clinked as he dropped them into the outstretched palm. "Plus two for the grain since we have so many horses."

The lad beamed. "Thank you! Thank you kindly." He nodded rapidly then began to help settle the horses.

Rune whispered, "You didn't have to do that. The temple gave us sufficient to see us settled."

"I'm aware, but then you're going to be known to carry the bulk of the coin. If anything happens to me, our resources are still safe."

"Can't fault his logic," Leodinn mentioned as he hung his bridle on his saddle pommel.

"Besides, aren't we all responsible for this?" Jayce asked, keeping an eye on the young lad on the other side of the barn with two of their horses. "I know I don't have any money, or coins, but we're all in this."

Grayson and Leodinn both gave him a speculative look then nodded. "I like the way he thinks." Grayson winked at Jayce.

Rune cupped Grayson on the shoulder, then said, "Lad, what is your name?"

"You can call me Brayden, sirs." He stood with his arms held close to his body by the elbows.

Rune smiled warmly. "Thank you for your aid this evening. Would you be willing to introduce us to your mam so we don't overwhelm her?" He considered their tired and slightly rumpled group. "We're a bit road weary and don't want to frighten her." He was also sincerely hoping being mages didn't go against them. They were simply too many to try to hide or disguise them all. At least they didn't dress like a band of marauders or mercenaries.

After the initial shock of meeting so many mages, Brayden's mam, Lori, was easy to talk to and very welcoming to feed them. Staying under the same roof, though, wasn't going to be possible. They only had the one common room and two bedrooms.

"It's no hardship to stay in the barn, if that is permissible?" Rune asked. She waved her hand as though it were of no concern. "It's probably better if we all stay together anyway."

"Where are you traveling to? If you don't mind my asking. It's been so many years since I've seen a group of mages." She offered to refill their mugs with apple cider. Murmurs of thanks were plentiful for her cooking and the drink.

"We're traveling to a temple in the north for further education." It was the cover story they'd devised to allow themselves reason for movement. Common folk didn't really know the education or training a mage went through so to them, it would be believable as their young often traveled to blacksmiths or even to the castle for other skills. Or at least, they had at one time. He wondered if anything other than the army still allowed for training at the castle center.

"Well, I be hoping for safe travels for ya," she offered.

"Do you know of any other villages on this road?"

She leaned against the counter while their group crowded around her kitchen table with barely a space to breathe, knee to knee. Devouring hearty beef stew and fresh, crusty bread made the hollows of their stomachs happy. They were all making appreciative noises as they scooped up the vegetables and meat in the thick crusts. "There is, at least a day's ride from here. If the owner still be Aamish, you be welcome there. He is fine with elves and has no score against mages."

Rune dipped his head. "Thank you for the information. Your son has been a help as well. Now where is the wash bin and we'll clean up the plates and bowls for you."

Grateful relief lightened her features. He didn't doubt their group was daunting for all the mouths she'd graciously fed. It wasn't going to fall to her do their cleaning as well. "That be most kind of you." She pointed to a cutout on the counter wood with a water barrel below it. "Any scraps can be set to the side. They'll go to the pigs in the morning."

"You've been most generous with your food and your hospitality," Ulcieh agreed as he finished his own clean up.

"You've been a good group of young travelers. I wish you well on your journey." Muscled arms, likely from years of farm work, crossed to rest over her bosom as she supervised the end of their meal. Rune acknowledged she wasn't going to fully let down her guard, but if none of them gave her cause to be wary, then they would be safe in the barn for the night.

Nightfall darkened the world as they settled deep in the barn not much later. "Should anyone keep watch?" Duran unfurled his roll and spread it out over the turned hay.

"A protection spell should be sufficient." Ulcieh rocked his shoulders into the hay, his hands splayed underneath his head. "I don't see anyone attempting to overtake such a large group."

"It's best to be alert, regardless," Rune said. "I'll post a spell at the doorways. Iba and Rox will tell us if something is wrong."

Ulcieh rocked his shoulder with unconcern. "Whatever you wish." He closed his eyes. Rune scowled at his tone. There wasn't much Rune could do about his ambivalence other than hope there really was no cause to worry.

Jayce leaned with his chin against Rune's shoulder to whisper close to his ear. "Let it go. Master Theil suggested him for a reason. He doesn't have to agree with everything. It'll only make it that much more difficult to get along if we force it." Tension seeped out of Rune's body as he leaned marginally into Jayce with a shoulder. "Let's get some sleep. We still have a long way to go."

Rune stood and chanted by the doorways, ensuring if anything crossed the threshold, there would be a warning. When he returned, he stretched out next to Jayce. He was glad to see Leodinn and Duran on his other side. Whether it was meant as protection or merely for the sake of comfort, it mattered little to him.

Iba, heart. Keep watch as you can. He smiled at her response. Rune knew he could rely on his friend. He closed his eyes and willed for sleep to quickly come.

❧❦

Rune studied the tree blanketed landscape before them. He couldn't see who was out there, but he knew they were being watched.

By several sets of eyes if he were to take a guess. Iba had told him there were several cats that seemed to be edging closer. He hadn't thought much of it, but now he knew why they were daring to get closer to a group of people making a lot of noise. A sweep of his surroundings in the dream revealed the back of the keep and outpost buildings, and by the signs of the repairs, they had been there for some time. Turning back toward the river, he hunted between the trees. He'd anticipated their group's arrival to stir curiosity. It appeared as though he was right. There was no way to sense magic in his dreams, but he didn't believe more mages stood in the perimeter shadows. He sincerely hoped that meant only skin shifters had come to investigate. Now that they were making strides in freshening the buildings, it was time to start looking forward, toward their goals and plans.

He partially turned away from the shadows, not giving them his back, but letting his watcher know he wasn't a threat. The pressure to let whoever was there see what they were doing was unmistakable in the dream. Currently, Grayson was in his view chopping wood for the fireplaces and the kitchen. Brin led a horse forward with a wedge sled trailing behind him, loaded with deadfall.

Rune went to assist unloading the wood. "This is a good find. Still plenty?" They gathered the ends of large logs and stacked them for Grayson to shorten and split.

"There's a fallen group of trees not too far into the woods. It looks like someone started to cut them down but never came back for the wood. It'll take a few trips to bring them all in. The winds have asked us to be judicious with our needs." He tipped his head upward and smiled as a light breeze played over them all. "The trees haven't had visitors here in a very long time."

Rune nodded. "Please let them know we will respect their wishes."

There was a skip of time in the dream and it was nighttime. The sleeping chambers on the second floor and the kitchens would be among the first to see repairs and this appeared to be Jayce's. He was undressing, pulling his shirt over his head. Rune's gaze fell automatically to his muscled chest, but he felt himself directed to the pendant he'd made for him. Pleasure that he still wore it made him smile. Then it occurred to him, Jayce was alone. He was viewing the room but wasn't in it with Jayce.

He watched and waited. *Jayce sank down to a wooden chair in the room, his shirt draped over the back. He pulled the pendant over his head and clutched it in his hand, leaning forward to rest against his balled hands.*

"Mom, Dad, I'm so sorry. I had no idea this would happen. I'm sorry I didn't get to tell you about this, or say goodbye. I don't know how long you waited before giving up, if you did. I don't blame you if you lost hope." He sighed. *His eyes remained closed as he continued baring his soul.* *"I'm not ready for this, not by a long shot. I did something today that could royally fuck up everything and I don't know if it's going to make all of this harder or not. If you were here, you could tell me what to do, help me. But you're not. I really could use you guys here with me, but I don't guess that's going to happen."* He sniffed, rubbing over his eyes with the heel of his hand. *"I'll always love you, and I'll always have your picture with me, close to me. Rune did something special to my things and he doesn't know how much it meant to me, to always have you with me even if you're not here."* He rolled the pendant in his palm to stroke the stone with a tender fingertip. *"I know it was only to appease the child in me when I was younger so I'd feel safe and always have a connection to you, but I still have the coin token Dad gave me on my adoption day. It's right next to your photo. Well, it's there even if it's much smaller now."* He grinned with a watery smile. *"I miss you so much. I wish you were here."* *His voice broke and his head sagged to his clutched fists, quiet gasps filling the dream.* Rune hated hearing how alone he felt. What did he do that made him feel so lost?

Rune wanted to leave the vision. This was obviously a very private moment for Jayce. What was he supposed to see? It didn't feel right, the way he was intruding on this time of Jayce's grief. The pendant in his clutched hands began to glow and Rune's jaw dropped. With his eyes closed, Jayce didn't notice the white aura around the stone as it pulsed lightly a half dozen times.

The token! The token was enchanted.

⁂

Rune gasped as he lurched up straight to sit, the brittle rustle of hay cutting through the cobwebs of the dreams. Sunrays were beginning to brighten the darkness to grays. A glance up revealed Iba and Rox in the rafters. Opposite them was a single owl. Rune nodded and the owl quietly fluffed out its feathers before settling. He didn't know if it was merely a curious type of bird, or a companion animal so it was best to be courteous regardless. If the owl had been watching as a spy, Iba would have chased it away. That was good enough for Rune's state of mind that the bird meant no harm.

Gathering his legs beneath him, he rose to his feet, careful of Jayce's legs, closest to him. He approached the doorway and released the protection spell. It wouldn't be respectful after being allowed to sleep in relative safety and warmth to have Brayden slam into it doing his chores.

He leaned against the frame, letting the others come awake on their own as he thought over the visions in his dream. Were the watchers allies? Or foes? There wasn't any way to discern by the dream. Would there be more people? What was their purpose? Why was he being shown their arrival? And what was the meaning of the token? Was it acting as a beacon? And if it was, for whom? What had affected Jayce to suffer so much sorrow and doubt? There were no easy answers, again. He was mulling over what he'd seen when arms wrapped around his middle, disrupting him. He straightened against the strong chest at his back, savoring the solidity and the heat.

"Is this okay? Never asked you how you wanted to behave around the others." Jayce's voice was sleep husky as he spoke. Rune leaned into his chest, soaking up the warmth.

"Are you claiming me?" he joked gently. Even as he said it, he realized it was his heart's greatest desire. He didn't understand the feelings Jayce created in him, and he knew that as king, Jayce would have responsibilities to the throne. But it didn't stop his heart from beating harder when Jayce spoke.

Jayce nipped his ear, causing shivers to tingle his nerves. "Told you I wanted to see what we have. You never actually gave me an answer now that I think about it."

Rune rubbed their heads together. "As much as I should say no and stay away from you, I can't."

The relief that eased the tension against his spine was obvious. Rune's answer mattered. "Then what happens, happens. I will say I feel less adrift with you around. You help keep me grounded. And right now, I need that. I don't know what I'm doing."

The visions of his dream played over his mind. He didn't doubt Jayce was feeling unsettled. He felt awful knowing he'd witnessed a private moment. But was confident it wasn't the pain of his loss he was supposed to see. Rune was sure of it. He would have to take some time to consider both parts of the vision to see if he could gain understanding. "Like you said, we're trapped in this together." He smiled at the flick of Jayce's gaze. "I'm getting used to that idea."

"Good. Let's get going then. We don't want to be unpleasant guests to a lady who has been as kind as Lori."

Rune agreed and with a squeeze to the hand that held him at his waist, he walked back into the barn to ensure the others were moving as well.

Chapter 31

Jayce swallowed his aching groans as they neared the buildings in the distance. Every muscle he knew of, and many more he'd never met, were screaming at him after days in a saddle. He ached and knew with certainty he wasn't the only one. They were all tired and sore and ready to be wherever they were going. He wasn't as good as a few at hiding it, and didn't care to try. They had departed from the main road some time ago and were following unkempt cart tracks into the trees. It was obvious the area they were in had been undisturbed for years by the overgrowth which stretched and rose upward surrounding them on all sides. Trees shaded them with full branches thick and heavy with leaves. The scurry and squawk of the occasional animal chastised the horses' passing as they continued deeper into the woods. As far as he could tell, they were the only people for miles.

Weather bleached stone and brick were visible between the trees in glimpses the closer they got to their final destination. Rune was in the lead with Iba riding on a shoulder. It was probably for the best because Jayce almost cried when he saw the dilapidated state of the foremost building. He didn't want to insult Rune with his less than ecstatic outlook. He'd done what he could with the time they had to move their group forward. They weren't going to find a five-star hotel on a local corner here. He had a feeling he wasn't the only one feeling the crushing disappointment at the immediate future. They all had a lot of work before them.

Rune stopped his mount and carefully dismounted next to a building, peering around him with caution. Wind rustled the leaves overhead, but there were very few signs of life anywhere else. "Grayson, take Duran in that direction and see what is here and what can be put into use quickly. I'm hoping this was the stable. See if there are any signs of pens or stalls that are still standing. Brin, Leodinn, and Ulcieh do a circle and check for traps or signs of any others who may be curious or too close. Jayce and I will check the main building." He cross-tied his mount's front legs to hobble them. "Secure your horses. They won't go far. I'm sure they're as tired as we are."

Brin stretched his hands high over his head before sagging forward and bending to reach his toes with telling groans and grunts. "I'm sure of it." He patted his horse's rump when he straightened and got a tail flick over his back for the effort. None of the horses were looking especially spry now that they were stopped. Relief was apparent on everyone's faces, even the horses'.

Brin walked into the woods and Grayson went toward the closest building to circle it.

"Let's check the main building. There may be wildlife to remove."

"Oh, goody," Jayce breathed sourly.

After taking in the scope of the repairs, they set out plans to get one of the buildings safe enough to secure themselves and the horses for the night. The first few days were spent on necessary repairs to make the buildings semi-usable and livable for humans and elves.

It surprised Jayce how quickly and efficiently that work was done, because it hadn't been his first thought to use magic. Brin and Grayson made a formidable team, with their wind and earth gifts to sweep the buildings clean. Jayce helped on that front where he could but his skills were still unpredictable and lacked confidence.

With the horses secured and safe, the work on the buildings progressed. Days bled into each other as more and more of the old keep came back to life. Ulcieh and Leodinn traveled to the next village and inquired about food stocks and supplies. They also offered people jobs. Cooks, stable hands, bakers, anyone with skills to help support the keep into the coming winter and beyond. There were a few who were wary because they were mages, but once it was confirmed that they could move their families and would be earning wages for the jobs, they returned with over a dozen workers with more to come.

The keep was soon teeming with life and repairs were being completed rapidly. It amazed him that in a few short weeks he'd gone from sleeping on a pallet on the ground in a windowless cavern to a raised stuffed bed of furs and ticking in a large room with windows. While it looked nothing like the life he'd known for the first twenty years of his life, it was comfortable and was slowly starting to feel more like home, more natural. There was a continuous hum and bustle of life now through the keep that blew him away after being the first to arrive to a deserted landscape. The scents of baking and wood smoke permeated the air, invigorating everyone and proving life goes on. How things had changed for him since that Saturday night Rune crashed into his life.

Waking up on one of those mornings, he sat on the edge of the bed, running his hands through his shaggy hair. Then he realized he had no idea what day it was at all. At some point it had ceased to matter. No one on Kielbos would even know what a Gregorian calendar was, much less if it would even apply to their own world. Days were days and seasons were seasons.

Sunlight streamed through the windows, telling him it was past time for him to get up. The room was still pretty bare and plain, however none of that really mattered. The view that caught his eye was outside. He pulled on his pants as his gaze followed the people below. One elf in particular was easy to find and hard to ignore. Pale hair was gathered to swing down his back as Rune worked in the morning sunshine. He was helping move wood that Grayson was chopping down to size for others to store throughout the keep. He wasn't wearing his cloak, which made it easier for Jayce to admire the view of his shoulders and muscles as he moved wood logs from the sled behind the horse with Brin's help. The elf made his mouth salivate with wanting. They hadn't so much as kissed since they'd left the temple and he was starting to feel the withdrawal. He wanted to spend time with Rune but the repairs to the outpost had been lengthy and time consuming. He needed the connection they'd been building. The lack of it in his life was becoming noticeable.

Rune had insisted he sleep in a shared room with Brin, as all the mages had paired up, and it only made sense to continue the portrayal of what others looking in would be expecting. He understood it, but Jayce hated it. Once others began to appear to work at the keep, appearances were important. He didn't feel like he was anything special, but their course meant he had to make the effort. The mages were already treating him differently, and he hated that too. They weren't neglecting his training in lieu of getting the keep running, and those long hours of practice were paying off. They'd come a long way since their first days on the road and right now, they were his closest friends. He frowned as he thought over the disparities. He had the largest suite in the private wing of the keep, with the only washroom *en suite*. He wasn't the lord of the manor, or whatever they called them here. He wasn't anything, but by some silent agreement that they'd never confided in him, all of them were acting subservient to him when he was the least qualified from the word go. Even Ulcieh was attempting to act respectful, though he was definitely doing so under duress. As of yet, Ulcieh still regarded him with suspicion and doubt. Jayce couldn't demand his respect when he harbored the same misgivings.

Jayce looked around and found a warmed spot in the room lit by a sunbeam. Without rugs yet, the stone was still quite cool in the mornings. In time, the rooms would appear more settled, more lived in but it wasn't a priority as much as making their new keep safe and secure for now. New keep gates were currently being built and would be up and operational in a day or two. There were steps to the process. He understood the undertaking of his destiny wasn't going to happen in a season, and probably not within a year, depending on the advance of the army. Before he could be distracted by rising panic on how to handle *that*, he pushed the worry of the future far away. For now. It couldn't be changed and he wasn't ready. He had other priorities to focus on.

Sinking down to sit cross-legged in the sun's warmth, he relaxed his mind and with his eyes closed, sought the colors the way Master Theil had taught him. He'd been practicing this part of his meditations when possible, even if it was only to connect with the powers he held, to recognize them. There hadn't been opportunity since their arrival to investigate his lion since the ritual and he wanted to know more about him. The ever-present colors were rolling and swaying as he moved mentally between them. Gently, like a light breeze brushed through them, they undulated as though saying hello. Their touch was kind, welcoming, and he paid attention to each one, being respectful and thankful for their presence. Master Theil's teachings were helpful, but it felt like it was a part of him to respect them this way.

When he reached the purple band, there was a sense of power in the color. Imagining his fingers flowing over it, he felt the tingle, the spark, and sensed a throb of power. He'd been curious about it more than once. A beat that felt like a pulse, a current. And he realized what the color represented.

Lightning.

"Are you the God's Touch Brin mentioned?" he wondered aloud, feeling the wonder and surge as it danced for him. He wanted to test it, to see if he could call it, but knew better than to try indoors. "You want to play, don't you?" The purple spun bright against his closed eyelids, making Jayce chuckle. "We will. Where it's safe. We need to meet properly." The color calmed and gradually faded into the background, seemingly appeased with his words. Then the one he wanted moved forward. "Hello friend. You and I have started quite the journey, haven't we?" A rumble only he could hear filled his ears. He smiled in answer. He supposed if a lion purred, it would sound like that. "What do you want to do?"

Jayce opened his eyes and raised his hands. He felt the pulse of power under his skin. Heat from the gold ribbon gathered, spreading through his body. There was a surge of power, one he recognized, and this time didn't fear it. He knew the lion was pushing forward more than he was actually taking the wheel to make the change happen. But he needed this. There were too many unanswered questions and too many things he didn't know about the lion. With hardly more than a thought, he was resting on a haunch, braced over his front paws. And promptly yawned.

Now why'd you go and do that? he chided. Seriously, they'd barely woken up half an hour ago. He shook his head, feeling the weight of his mane as it floated around him. Then he looked around himself. Where were his pants? They weren't shredded on the ground.

Oh! That's what you wanted to show me. The magic protects us both. A sense of satisfaction was hard to miss as the lion slunk downward and rolled in the sunbeam, thick paws in the air as it batted at dust motes in the air. *Can you talk? Can you feel me?*

An image of the lion and Jayce walking side by side filled his mind. Both were glowing in the golden aura of the lion's spirit. *Ah. I think I understand. We are separate, but sharing the same magic, right?*

A rumbled purr filled the bedroom. Jayce became quieter, letting the lion come more to the front. The power and strength of the animal was heady. He also sensed a stubborn streak. He was a cat after all.

That thought made him smile even more. Did all of that mean the lion was a fully separate entity and he was only along for the ride? How much did he control? He understood now why Rune believed he needed other skin shifters in his support circles. These were questions the mages simply couldn't answer.

The hushed brush of his tail flicked against the stones as the cat enjoyed the sunbath. *I wish you could talk.* He hated to admit it, but with Rune staying in another room, he was feeling the weighed loneliness of his expectations. He helped with the keep repairs. The setup was large and everyone was needed to see their keep running smoothly. When he wasn't outside, he worked with Brin and Ulcieh learning the history of Rinattoah and of the Caduthien Empire, about all the parts of Kielbos. Learned Valda-Cree history. The meaning behind the Goddess Adhrer's teachings. Including as much history as they could provide about King Bail and his father before him, King Luca. All things he had to know to cope and deduce his own answers to questions he would have to face. Daunting didn't even begin to cover it.

He learned the ways and etiquettes of court. That was a mind warp. The level of confident arrogance that previous kings had ruled with was mind-blowing to him when all he could see was their own stupidity in their actions, but he could see why the style of rule was effective. If the current king was anything like the kings of his history, he could easily see how simpler minds could be manipulated. Charisma and confidence had carried a lot of kingdoms from crown to crown, and when that didn't work, like here, brute strength of numbers and fear rarely failed.

It was information he loved to absorb. How to speak in public, how to address others of the nobility, or even how to maintain a certain demeanor. He'd been working hard on all of that. Now he was ready to really dig into his training. Self-meditation and practice behind closed doors to hone his magical talents wasn't exactly what he would call challenging. There was only so much he could do under those conditions. There had to be more he could do. But what? He'd been learning as fast as he could under the mages' guidance and tutelage.

An image of a large pride filled his head, distracting his internal monologue. More lions, tigers, panthers, snow leopards, lounging, playing tag and chasing tails, or letting the younger cubs play over them in a large room. There were people, mages, children, and more noise than he could possibly separate, but in the middle of all of it was Jayce, or rather, Jayce as a lion. At least everyone seemed happy in the image.

Is that what you see? Or what you hope for?

The lion huffed.

We need to work on your communication here. I need you to be able to talk.

A growl was clear. Well, that was him told. He didn't even know when the image or thought was reflecting to, was it here at the keep, or later, or even much later in the future? There was no way to know. He wondered if there was anything else the lion could show him, but the pondering thought got him a grumble of relaxation as he stretched out to bathe in the sunlight. Spending time with his lion had been good, but now he only had more questions for Rune.

He had to find his elf.

Jayce closed his eyes and willed his body back. It was less shocking this time when the magic retreated and he found himself stretched out on the stone floor. The shock of cold rushed a shiver over his heated back because of the way the lion had been laying on the stone. He supposed learning to communicate and how to react as a unified team was why he needed other shifters surrounding him. That did make sense, but he didn't know any. "You might be king of the jungle, but I still rule us," he muttered. He only wished he knew if what the lion had shared had been prophetic or wishful thinking. Hopefully their communication would improve over time. He and his lion were very new at this. And he honestly had no idea what the lion was trying to tell him. The images meant nothing to him in their current state. He'd missed out on more than a dozen years of shared training and was now rushing to make up some of that ground. And feeling so inadequate for it.

One day at a time. By the time he felt settled, his lion had fully retreated, leaving him to start his day.

Reaching his feet, he finished dressing and sauntered downstairs to grab a bite to eat.

There were new faces all over the outpost's main keep now. Reaching the lower level he headed for the kitchens. He smiled at a few, getting confused raised eyebrows in return before they respectfully dipped their heads in answer. Were they not used to people being sociable, or was it him? He knew he wasn't around as much as the others because of his training, but still, what was so different about him? He really needed to talk to Rune. With what he'd been shown, he needed a second opinion. And he missed Rune. He needed that damn elf to quit avoiding him.

Holding a hot sausage roll and a mug of coffee, he ambled to the rear of the keep to find Rune. And thank goodness for coffee, he happily thought, taking a hearty sip. He would never make it out of bed if it weren't for the existence of the one drink that he needed to function. Fortified again, his elf wasn't going to get to avoid Jayce any longer.

It seemed to him more people were moving to the keep proper every day as he greeted more new faces. Locals had been arriving over several weeks, helping set up stocks and supplies, while continuing repairs. Jayce and the others had been there a little more than two months, if he were to take a guess. The keep and the buildings surrounding it were running smoothly and jointly with the rest of the outpost now that they'd received some TLC. There were pens for goats, sheep, and pigs. Chickens ran rampantly underfoot. All he could do was shake his head. This was so out of his experience. He'd never so much as stepped foot on a farm, and here he was suddenly in the middle of more livestock than people in some places.

He finished his breakfast in two bites then gulped his coffee, admiring the view as pale hair appeared. He could watch Rune endlessly. He was stunningly beautiful, and he loved his smile. He knew by now his favorite elf was a true morning person and he couldn't fault him that love. The morning sunlight loved Rune right back. He chuckled to himself, remembering those first few days when he'd been more inclined to strangle him than kiss him. Now his very absence was like a sore toothache. One he was about to cure.

He nodded to Grayson who noticed him approaching first. He got a head dip and a wink in answer.

"Morning." He stepped over a log and was at Rune's shoulder.

"My lord." Rune dipped his head graciously.

"So that's how it's going to be?" A single eyebrow rose high. Well, that explained a shit ton that he hadn't noticed until this morning in people's faces and behaviors. Too many new people to be cognizant of the little changes. He'd had a lot on his mind as well.

"It's how it needs to be," Rune offered quietly. "We hired your keep steward this morning. I'll introduce you."

"Nope. Right now, you and I are going for a walk." He leaned close to make his next words private. "I know you're avoiding me, and given your greeting, I understand why, but it stops now." He met wide blue eyes with a mild glare. "I can't do this without you. You need to quit avoiding me."

Rune bit his lip, but slowly nodded. A flash of longing was bright in his gaze before he turned away to bury it.

"Gray, we'll be back. We're going down toward the river."

Grayson blinked at the shorter version of his name, then smiled. "I like that nickname, my lord."

He snorted quietly. "Consider it yours. Don't know why it hasn't come up before now." He tapped Rune's bicep. "Let's go." There was no escape for the elf and a single look told him as much.

Rune silently joined him, his stride even as they wound their way through the woods. Jayce noted he would periodically peer into the trees, as though he were searching.

"Something wrong?"

"No, at least, I don't think so. Iba is keeping watch, as is Rox."

"Good." He smiled knowingly when he noticed Rune drifting his palm over the trees as they walked past. "Any good gossip?"

Rune shook his head as his shoulders relaxed the deeper they walked. "Thankfully, no. We're probably as alone as we can be." He sought Jayce's gaze then looked away.

"So why is everyone suddenly being so... I don't know? Weird? Bowing and crap? I get why *you're* giving me a title, even if I don't feel like I truly earned it."

"We needed a way to bring you into the public's awareness without revealing your true presence. Calling you your highness would cause too much curiosity and questions we can't answer. It was actually Ulcieh's idea. Brin and I seconded it."

A single eyebrow rose as shock trickled into his voice. "Ulcieh? The one mage who thinks I'm a loaf short of a basket right now?" *Will miracles never cease?* He hoped not.

Rune snorted, dropping into a chuckle as his steps slowed. "We've been referring to you in that way for several weeks now."

"Ah, so that also explains why you've been avoiding me." And all the oddball looks he'd been getting.

Rune's face reflected his pain even as he said, "I had to. I'm too close to you." He paused and leaned with his back to a tree a good distance from the back of the keep, where privacy was guaranteed. Squirrels chittered in reprimand overhead, jumping from the branches above to grow quiet as they settled a tree over. Blue eyes were imploring, but Jayce also saw the longing, the denied wanting in them.

"Why do you keep fighting it? Did you ever think I'm feeling this too? I told you that morning in the barn what I wanted and you agreed, and the minute we get here, you go cold shoulder on me. I need you Rune. I need your input, your support. I need at least one friend who is really my friend, who I can trust because this is only going to get more convoluted and stressful as we move forward. Please don't cut me out again."

Rune bit his lip, his chin lowering and Jayce caught him with a palm, stopping his evasion. "It felt like I had to," he whispered.

"Are you getting more visions?"

He shook his head then lifted a shoulder.

"Well that made absolute sense."

Rune dared a half smile, his hand waving half-heartedly through the air. "I know. It doesn't make much sense to me either. The only thing I know is you need to concentrate on your future, not on me."

"But don't you understand? If I don't have you in my corner, I can't think at all." Reaching behind him, he pulled Rune's hair forward, running his fingers through the pale strands. "I met my lion again this morning, and he showed me some things."

Rune's shoulders tensed. "What? Where?"

He gently pressed a finger to Rune's lips. "In my room. I was alone. But he was showing me things, and I don't know if they were wishes or like you, visions. I need you, and I don't think I'll ever stop having that need. I don't know what all of this means, why I feel so strongly about you, but I do know it's a *need*." He swallowed when Rune's gaze dropped to his lips. A hungry groan was all the warning he had before Rune jumped forward and claimed his mouth in a kiss charged with need and longing.

Chapter 32

Jayce leaned in and blanketed his body, pinning him to the tree. Damn, Jayce had missed this. Rune gripped at his biceps and jerked him even closer, and Jayce was happy to oblige. He pushed a knee between his thighs and Rune submitted to him readily, hungrily moaning as their frames brushed and pushed into each other, demanding as much contact as possible. An indrawn breath was all he needed to deepen the kiss, plunging his tongue into the heated welcome of Rune's mouth. Fingers gripped, their strength and Rune's needy hunger clear as he held Jayce close for the kiss. His heart pounded as he sank into the heat.

He could get lost in Rune's kisses. Tender or passionate, he loved them all. He sighed when he broke from the kiss, gasping for breath. It had been too long since he'd tasted his elf, since he'd felt his weight, his touch. Craving more, he bowed his body, dragging his hips in a slow rocking motion against the telltale sign of Rune's arousal. Groin to groin, he ached, the hunger for bare skin, for connection was a needful scream inside his head.

Then he jerked apart, panting.

That scream wasn't in his head. The scream repeated, loud and shrill. And utterly terrified.

"Where?" He stilled to listen and then was running his ass at full speed with Rune at his side. He ignored the whip of low branches as the sounds of a scuffle could be heard ahead. He hardly felt the uneven ground as he charged in the direction the screams had come from. Dogs barked and dangerous snarls reached them as they closed in.

"Damn it; shut her up!" The crack of skin being hit hard ricocheted through the tense silence. A whimpered sob following that hit broke his heart and fueled his anger.

Jayce spotted them between thick tree trunks. Two bulky men circled by two large dogs were dragging a young girl of maybe ten years through the woods by her arms. He had to believe she was from the keep even if he didn't know everyone by face. Where else would she have come from if she wasn't?

The next moments happened with barely a thought to what he was going to do. The gold glow he knew to be his lion coated his vision with a thick distortion. He wouldn't have fought him even if he had known the lion's wish beforehand. They were of the same mind in unanimous agreement. His next running step pushed him into a leap as the heat of the lion swarmed over him with the rush of a waterfall. He landed on four paws and roared.

He bounded into one of the startled, frozen attackers, taking him down with a heavy swipe of his paw. He didn't get back up. The other man pulled a sword and whistled for the two cowering dogs as he whirled on rear paws to face them. Dust and leaves stirred around the group, settling quickly. It was as though the winds were frozen, not moving anything.

"I wouldn't if I was you," Rune snarled. Flames hovered over his hands, ready to be freed.

The lion stopped a pace in front of the kidnapper, baring his teeth with a menacing snarl at the dogs. His tail swished with agitated strokes, only needing a sign to end them. They instantly tucked tail and ran away, no match for the king of beasts.

"Let her go."

The girl flinched when the man clutched her arm, jerking her closer. It was clear he was using her as a shield to protect himself from the lion. Tear tracks stained her face. Stupid ass didn't realize she wasn't the one in jeopardy.

"I said let her go. You're alone and help is coming."

Jayce looked over his shoulder, seeing Rune give him a small nod. He pushed the lion to the back of his thoughts with a grateful brush of thanks for his quick thinking, then stood on his own two feet. "You heard him. Release her. Now!"

"So you filthy lot of mages and animals can use her?" He spat on the ground.

Suddenly at least half a dozen large cats prowled out of the woods. Panthers and tigers, a snow leopard. Growls vibrated the air.

Jayce smiled in surprise, that smile only growing as he realized what he was seeing. He immediately recognized these cats from the lion's imagery of that morning. They were friendly. He had a feeling these were the shifters he'd been waiting for, that Rune knew he needed to strengthen their alliances and to train. But there were bigger issues facing him at the moment. His snarl deepened when the kidnapper refused to release the terrified child. "I believe you just insulted everyone here." His voice dropped to glacial. "Release her and you might be allowed to leave."

Yowls of disagreement filled the quiet.

"Or maybe not. They seem to have a difference of opinion."

Wild eyes took in the tightening circle of cats and growing gathering of people who were closing in on him, regular people and mages alike. The kidnapper's partner was flipped over and once confirmed alive, had his hands bound and was dragged away. Jayce clenched his fists, the colors on the edge of his visual awareness agitated, on edge. They all wanted to have a part of this man's hide for harming a young girl, for harming an innocent.

"You're outnumbered. You're not going to get out of this."

The girl suddenly yanked herself free and scrambled forward, leaping into Jayce's chest. He caught her easily, wrapping her limbs snugly around his frame. "Shh. You're safe now." He turned to Rune with a glare, giving a succinct order. "Secure him. We need to know why they wanted her."

Then he stiffly stalked back toward the keep with the sobbing girl clinging in his arms, complete faith in those behind him.

⁊⊷⊰

Utterly overpowered and without the child to use as a shield, the man was easily subdued.

Unarmed and on his knees, with his hands tied behind his back, the tension surrounding Rune because of the girl's attack began to fade. "Take him to whatever holding cell you put his partner. I'm going to check on the girl then we'll question them." The prisoner was marched away, encircled by angry workers, pitchforks angled for business if he should try anything. Waiting for the group to leave with the male attacker, he then dipped his head to the felines waiting at the edges now. "Thank you for your assistance. You are welcome to join us at your convenience. I believe you've been expected." Tails flicked as heads bobbed and one by one they slunk back into the woods.

"Master Rune?"

"Yes?" He turned to the speaker, a woman in her twenties with her hair severely pulled tight from her face.

"Was he... Did Lord Morrow, did he..." Her eyes were wide over very pale cheeks. She twisted her hands into her apron. Her lips trembled as tears slowly trekked down to drip onto her blouse. It was useless to suppress her emotional sobs. "A lion."

He gave as soothing a smile as he could. "You are safe, Silvie. Everyone asked to come to the keep were told there would be mages and skin shifters. You must know you're safe. We promised that for every person coming to give us support, whether they work here or support in other means."

She gulped hard. "I—I know, but the lions. There hasn't been a lion skin shifter in Caduthien in hundreds of years." Sucking air hard to calm herself, she said even as the trembles in her voice eased, "I never thought we'd see them again. Not in my lifetime."

"What part of the keep do you work in?"

"I'm one of the laundresses." A quick curtsey had him smiling kinder. He knew she was calming from the shock from witnessing Jayce in full roar if she was remembering to actually genuflect before him. He was in awe himself. Jayce had more strength and bravery than he was aware to jump into the middle of whatever had been happening without hesitation.

"And you value the history of the Valda-Cree." It wasn't exactly a question but she answered it as though it was.

"My mam was very prolific in stories. One of my great granddas and a great uncle on her side was in King Bail's army."

"Good. We need to build on those memories. Can I count on you?"

"Oh! Yes, of course, Master Rune! I'd be honored!"

"It's early days, but we need those with memories and stories of those days to pave the way." The hustle and noise of the keep was growing louder the nearer they came to the back of the main keep. The trees were thinning as the pathways were getting used once more around the buildings giving him a better view of the walls and people working. "If you'll excuse me, I need to check on the child."

"Of course." She smiled broadly, wiping the corner of her apron over her face. "I'll be gettin' back to my own business. I feel blessed to have seen today happen."

As he walked away, Rune hoped there were more who felt that way, and not cursed. Whether it was predetermined or not, the truth of who Jayce was would be running rampantly very soon over the land.

The hallways were alive with chatter as he walked through the keep, solidifying his thoughts that the gossip about Jayce's lion reveal had started to spread unfettered. "Have you seen my lord and the girl?" he asked one of the passing men.

"He took the lass to the kitchens and hasn't left her yet."

Rune nodded his thanks and strode across the keep to the kitchens. He found Jayce with the young girl sitting on his lap as they ate cookies.

"How are you, young miss?"

Her eyes sparkled and she blushed, sadly bringing out the red mark of where she'd been slapped. He hoped the memory of her attack and near abduction was already being pushed far out of reach. "Much better, Master Rune."

"This is Sophie. Her mother is Lois, one of the cooks." Jayce hunted across the area when a woman turned curiously with the mention of her name. "It looks like she was stalked in the trees while hunting for wild mushrooms." He ran a hand over her back, offering comfort when she shuddered.

A brief squeeze to Jayce's shoulder before quickly releasing him said he got the picture when Sophie's gaze dimmed and she huddled close to Jayce again.

Jayce nuzzled the top of her head with his chin, fine strawberry blonde hair snagging in the bit of scruff he'd neglected to shave that morning. "But you're safe now. The bad men are gone, and we're going to start guards to watch." He looked up at Rune. "Isn't that right?"

"Immediately." He absolutely agreed. It was his failure that he hadn't thought of it before now, before something like this could occur. As soon as he figured how to schedule it and with whom to make the rotations happen, they would have a constant watch.

"Come give your mam a hand, love." Lois, a tall blonde woman neared. Sophie hugged around Jayce's neck fiercely before sliding from his lap. "Thank you, my lord. For saving her," she added once

Sophie was out of hearing range in the hubbub of the kitchen. "I didn't even know anything had happened until someone ran in goin' on about her screamin'."

Jayce stood and reached for a hand, holding her kindly for a moment, stopping her from trying to bow. "You're all protected, Lois. I promise you that."

Relief filled her features when she said, "A few of us had concerns. Not many had worked with the mages before, but I'm glad you have people watching out for everyone."

"We all do, Lois." Rune stepped up next to Jayce's shoulder.

"My lord?" Jayce spun. "Sorry to interrupt, but there be people at the gates."

"I'll be right there." He pinched Rune's hip and tugged before walking out of the kitchen. He aimed for an empty side room and quickly yanked Rune in behind him, stifling his surprise with a kiss when he planted him against the door, blocking him with his body.

Rune's head spun as the kiss went on for what felt like forever. It was fierce and demanding in a way that Jayce rarely showed. He loved everything about it.

Jayce panted when he released him. "I'm sorry. Oh, fuck, I'm so sorry. I don't know what happened. I was running and suddenly everything went gold and he was there before I knew what was happening." He clutched at Rune, trembling with the crash of adrenaline and guilt. Finally being able to let it out made it happen with a rush.

Rune's hands rose to cup his face, sweeping from side to side seeing his torment. "It's done. Whether it's good or bad, we won't know, but it is done."

"Fuck, Rune." He swept his arms around him and held him close. "I was so mad, it didn't even hit me to be scared. They were taking her," he choked out. Rune curled one hand behind his neck, holding him close while he swept his other up and down his back, much the same way Jayce had calmed Sophie in the kitchens. Strong arms cinched around his middle as though afraid to let him go.

"But they didn't. You stopped them. You. You were magnificent."

Jayce blinked, his eyes pinning Rune in their golden heat. Goddess, when did he fall for those eyes? His heart pounded as his body longed for his touch. There wasn't time, not right then. He didn't know how Jayce felt either. When did he fall in love with his future king? He knew it as unarguably as he was breathing right then. The thought of anything happening to Jayce during the confrontation had him silently quaking with his own feelings. What was he going to do? He didn't know and it didn't matter. They couldn't do a thing about it right then. Turmoil over his feelings wasn't something he could worry about right then.

"Too many saw my lion to pretend it wasn't me," he rasped, wary.

He swallowed as he gently pushed Jayce upright, his voice low and husky when he said, "What's done is done. You're needed. Those at the gates could be our allies waiting."

Jayce shuddered and exhaled without moving. A moment later he stood straight. "Right. But you're officially my right hand. I don't care what kind of eyebrows it raises, or whispers it causes. We know what happened to the throne and how Carden has influenced it over the years. I'm not King Bail and you're not going to jeopardize what we're attempting to do. I don't know what that makes you, but going forward, you have an official capacity to keep me from wigging out, got it?"

Rune stared askance then slowly nodded. "I believe I understand."

"Good." He kissed him hard one more time, his eyelids at half, hiding the deeper emotions locked in his eyes. "Let's go meet our neighbors."

Rune stood there stupefied as Jayce pulled open the door and marched out toward the front room of the main keep. His will to challenge the very fates of their world left Rune scrambling, in awe of their future king. It made Jayce seem like an unstoppable force. A force that would be tested over and over before he could take the throne. Rune knew it without a doubt that he *would*, one day.

On the alert, he trailed Jayce to find him in the front hall, speaking to their guests.

"Welcome!" he called with a wide arm sweep. He twisted and whispered quickly at his shoulder, "Rune? What do we do?"

Rune responded in kind, too quiet to be overheard. "Let me have refreshments brought in. Take your seat, my lord." He pushed gently on his back, out of sight.

Jayce whipped in the other direction and noticed the chair on a low-profile dais. Rune had it placed there weeks ago, knowing the time would come when Jayce would be expected to greet people at their hideaway keep. Jayce groaned, but did as was told, stalking over to it and plunking down. Rune called out for their steward, Javi, as he settled. They hadn't discussed this part of his expectations. They'd been caught up in repairs, gathering workers, teaching history and training him for days to come. Now one of those days was upon them. He hoped Jayce was able to bluff his way through their first meeting with curious strangers.

Rune sent a runner to the kitchens for refreshments and food. He stepped forward to stand behind his right shoulder, his hands at his sides. Outwardly calm when he was as scattered as the winds, he greeted the group of over two dozen visitors. "I am Master Rune, Lord Jayce Morrow's assistant and advisor." His voice carried easily across the greeting hall. High ceilings allowed for the sound to travel. The double doors at the other end of the hall to the outside stood open, allowing in plentiful sunlight.

"Lord Jayce? That's an unusual name," the blond haired man out front mentioned suspiciously. Sharp glances took in everything surrounding him before coming to settle once more on Jayce.

"It's from a different land," Jayce offered unconcerned. "I want to thank you…" He waited expectantly.

"Cedri Arin, of Tanglewood clan."

"Thank you, Cedri Arin, for your assistance regarding the issue with Sophie. You didn't have to step up and expose yourselves."

Rune silently applauded Jayce's conversational flip of attention. He didn't know if Jayce was aware of what he was doing, but it was perfect for redirecting the interest away from himself. At least for the moment.

"We were aware mages had taken over the old keep. However, we were unaware that one of the lion shifters was sharing residency with them. We needed to ensure you and yours were not going to be a threat to me and mine. Or that the men in question were not affiliated with you."

Jayce twisted to peer toward Rune with a questioning stare, slightly hunched over his knees, unsure. He leaned close to keep his words private, and whispered in his ear. "It's your choice now. Your lion has been seen."

Jayce rolled a shoulder and fell into silence, his face unreadable as he thought over what had happened, but didn't take long before coming to a decision. He stiffened his spine and curled his fingers over the ends of the chair rests, his head held high, no longer looking divided. The assurance in his posture was echoed in his tone and all but emanated from his pores, a hard to misinterpret cloak of authority. "That's a fair concern. We are not here to cause distress for you and your families. As you can see, we have many here we need to protect. What happened with Sophie was unexpected and steps will be taken to ensure we're all safe going forward. That has been addressed already. What I would like to know is do you know of the Valda-Cree lions?" He spoke calmly, as though the question was merely discussion reflecting on the weather, his gaze lighting on every person before him, studying the room as much as Rune, if not even more. Rune was proud of his calm, the resonating strength rolling in his voice nearly vibrating with his inner power. The cloak of imperviousness might be temporary to get them through this meeting, but the authority rolling from Jayce wasn't faked. It was the first glimpse of who he would grow to be.

Several gasps were clear in the front room, surprise circling through their audience as whispers grew.

"The Valda-Cree?" Incredulity from several of their group echoed the shocked voices surrounding them. Rune was able to see expressions, some questioning, others confused, all while able to see who spoke to their closest neighbor in hushed voices. Jayce was keeping a calm façade from his place before them.

Cedri's shock was clear as his voice rose. "Their family was wiped out, legend. No lion skin shifter has been sighted inside Caduthien for centuries. If King Bucol hears even a whisper, there will be hunting parties and bounties on your head for crossing into Alendaren territory. All lions have been shunned to the north country because of the eradication against them. It was the only way they could protect their families."

Jayce searched over their group and pointed. "You? What's your name?"

A man likely in his twenties was shoved forward when he flinched and hesitated. Pale hair like Rune's but with a hint of gold or flax rather than the telling silver of his own elven ancestry glistened in the streaming sunlight from the high archer windows. Bright blue eyes were wary with apprehension and caution when he whipped around to his side, berating whoever pushed him with a sharp snap of words. Facing Jayce, he dipped his head. "Uh, Royce, my lord."

"You were part of the group in the woods earlier, were you not?" There was command in his tone. A gentle demand to be truthful. A shiver danced over Rune's spine. Goddess, hearing him like this was doing incredible things to his heart rate.

"I was."

"And what did you see?"

His hands fisted at his sides to hide fidgeting. Rune studied him as he gave his answer. "I saw you charging for the two men who held the young girl. We were watching to see if it was safe to be of aid."

"And then?" he prompted calmly, encouraging.

Royce swallowed heavily. "You skin shifted into a lion on the run."

More gasps filled the tense silence. As if it was only of mild consideration that he was asking, he inquired, "Is that not possible for skin shifters?"

Royce rapidly shook his head. "No, my lord, we have to undress. Only the...the royal family had the magic to shift like you did," he ended with a rasp of realization, his chin dropping low. As if he was revealing a heinous secret.

When the volume rose to an unruly level, Jayce lifted a palm and Rune saw him control the people present without even raising his voice until silence permeated the air once more. He slowly stood, and with a small nod to Royce, thanked him for his input. Rune saw him slip back into his group, hiding, trying to appear smaller. He wasn't a large man, but that hair stuck out like a beacon. He sympathized. Jayce moved to address the room, calming many of the whispered mutters and chatter.

"The times we are facing are dangerous. There is danger lying in wait in Rinattoah. To me, the heart of this land will never be Alendaren. I will never grace this land, your land, by a monster's name. Their blood was never spilled for the goddess nor granted the goddess's blessing as rulers and the erosion of these lands and its peoples only proves that. There is an invading army being pushed northward from lands far south of Caduthien by a hand we can't see, yet the Alendaren crown does nothing to stop it. I am making no promises. I am only saying I am here to do what must be done. I am here today because of things I had no control over, however, now I have a chance to change Caduthien for the better." He paced a few steps across the dais.

"But the Valda-Cree are dead!" someone shouted. "They were executed by the crown. It's been centuries since their reign."

Jayce paused his steps, his mouth quirking up at the corner. "I've heard that so many times since I arrived here." He wiped a hand over his mouth, using time to gather his thoughts without seeming to be hesitant before he spoke. "Time is a cruel mistress." Rune caught the fleeting glance filled with pain. He knew what Jayce meant, what he referred to. His return expression was full of compassion. The golden eyes he loved so much warmed once more, became steadfast with determination before he returned to the crowd, which seemed to have grown in the last ten or fifteen minutes. Many from the keep had joined the crowd to hear Jayce speak. "Time. We need time to prepare. To train. I am not going to force anyone into a position they are not fully prepared to take, regardless if you believe in me or not. That none of this is possible because the Valda-Cree are dead." He shrugged a shoulder. "I'm looking over those here, and I know you're saying it's not possible. I know you're thinking I'm young, that at the very least I'm probably lying. All I can tell you is I am not. But I do know this. What once made Rinattoah formidable and powerful and beautiful can be again and that can be said of all of Caduthien, for all of Kielbos." He fully faced the group of feline shifters. "I appreciate your bravery earlier for the young girl's sake. You are welcome to stay. We mean you no harm whether you stay or return to your own."

Walking from the dais, he said to Rune, "Make sure they are fed and comfortable. Whatever their choice, it is not to be coerced."

Rune bowed in acknowledgement. "Of course."

"You're the best," Jayce whispered for him alone as he walked away.

Rune believed he was witnessing the beginning of Jayce's confidence to rule starting to flourish.

Chapter 33

Rune and Duran followed the men assigned to guard the two who'd attempted Sophie's abduction to their temporary jail.

Duran leaned close. "I truly didn't expect to need holding cells so soon. Any idea why they were trying to take her?"

Rune looked around, then simply shook his head. "Bankor, have they given you any trouble?"

"No, Master Rune. They've been silent, only asking for water."

"They can have water and food. We will not torture anyone. Do I make myself clear?" He frowned at the anger coming from the two before him. The attempt to take Sophie had hit them where they weren't expecting it. While nothing was ever completely safe, it was past time to put a watch in place. This attack was proof enough. The differences between all their peoples were only going to come closer to the surface as time passed.

"Yes, Master Rune!" Both Bankor and Gegli called out. Bankor opened the sliding doorway to one of the unused storage buildings. It was suited for winter storage. Or at the moment, a holding cell. Leaving the door wide, he allowed Rune to enter first. "They be in here."

He held a metal key that looked newly pressed to suit the lock on the door, unlatching the doorway on the inside.

There was a single window, high and too narrow to crawl through, with two pallets and a small table with two chairs. So not the worst type of cell they could be confined in.

"Stand at the door, be ready," he ordered. He didn't know what these two were capable of, even though he'd seen how cowardly they both behaved, to dare to take a child. The two who'd accompanied them stood to either side of the entrance and settled into a watching stance. They weren't armed, but honestly, there was no way the prisoners who'd tried to take Sophie could overpower Rune and Duran together.

"Gentlemen," Rune started calmly. They never looked toward him from where they lay on their pallets staring at the roof as though they didn't have a care in the world. And except for needing a bath, they likely didn't. "I need to know what you were doing in the woods and why you are stalking the children." He strode to the far wall while Duran took up a spot closer to the ajar door, crossing his ankles. Neither captive so much as twitched at his question.

Iba, heart, could you give me a hand, please?

"I'd really appreciate your cooperation as we now have very frightened children in the keep, and we can't have that. They will not be stalked and taken." He crossed the space and smacked the table. "Tell me why you are here!"

They jumped but otherwise refused to speak. Sweat was building on one's brow. He seemed younger, maybe not as hardened as the other. The one Jayce managed to sideswipe and take out. *Iba, aim for the one on the right, a little flyby, heart. Let him see your beautiful talons.*

"If you do not wish to answer I'm sure we can find ways to *claw* the truth from you," he drawled, timing it perfectly for Iba to sweep into the room and circle it with a low dive over the man with the frightened eyes. He screamed and covered his face when she spread her wings right above his head, crying out loudly, stretching as though to land right on his face, the sharp points glistening in the sunlight.

"I'll talk! Call off yer demon bird!"

"Jimmy, shut up!"

Duran wiggled a finger and zapped the belligerent man's knee with a touch of heat. He cried out, cursing a streak, leaping backward to crash into the wall, his wary gaze locked on both mages.

Thank you, Iba, heart. I promise to give you a treat later. She swept back out through the window like she'd never been.

"Now then, Jimmy, what were you doing in the woods this morning?"

"Don't hurt me," he whimpered, his hands still over his eyes. He'd curled up on his side into a ball to protect his face.

"She's gone, but I can always call her back. Keep that in mind if you think lying will do you any good."

He peeked through his fingers as though unsure Rune was telling the truth. Jerking to sit up, he shoved himself against the back wall, then hugged his tucked legs close. "We needed the girl to find out why the mages wanted people from the villages for the keep."

Rune refrained from rolling his eyes, barely. "Is that all? You could have asked without scaring a young child." Disgust turned his mouth down. "There's more to this. We approached the villages openly for what we needed. Are you planning to attack?" He wasn't going to reveal the number of mages living at the keep. That would put them at a disadvantage. "What else are you looking for?" Cold silence met his demands.

"I don't believe them. We've hidden nothing." Duran scowled. He straightened and walked outside. Rune could hear him speaking, if not the exact words, to one of the village watchers at the door then he returned. "If they won't tell us, maybe one of the skin shifters who watched them take Sophie will have some insight."

It took a few moments before the young blond Jayce had addressed at the keep gathering, Royce, appeared in the doorway. "Yes, sirs? How can I help?" He quickly took in the two outside, the two mages, and the two prisoners. His expression was grim, with flat eyes. Good to know he wasn't keen on children being taken either.

"These two aren't being very forthcoming about why they wanted Sophie. Did you or yours see them at all?"

"We've been watching for a couple of days. I'll freely admit that, but only Cedri knows why. These two came up early this morning from the other side of the river. There's a low place to cross right now because of the season. Them and their dogs. They must have thought they were alone, because they weren't being quiet."

Rune liked how earnest and honest Royce was being. He couldn't sense any subterfuge coming from him, or from his words. "Go on. Were they loud enough to hear their plans?"

"They were going to take one of the mages and make an example of them. They didn't like the mages taking over the keep and taking their working folk from the village. I'm guessing they got the girl for more information on numbers." He glowered at the cowards on the floor. He didn't have to say what the future held for the girl after, if they'd managed to take her off keep lands. "Even I know better than to think I could take a mage captive with only two people."

"Bankor, do you recognize either of these men?" Rune demanded.

He leaned through the doorway and with a swift perusal quickly shook his head. "No, Master Rune. They're not from our village."

"I want to know which village they're from. I'll check with Ulcieh to see how many he approached and where the one on the other side of the river lies." He left the room, the others following to lock the doors once more. Once they were a distance away and out of earshot, he said, "Thank you Royce, for your assistance. I want a group put together to escort them home. I have an idea that should put a stop to these plans of theirs."

"You're not going to execute them?"

Rune swung around to Gegli, glaring. He immediately dipped his head in apology. He accepted mages could be seen as cold-blooded because they had powers humans simply couldn't understand because they didn't experience them, but they weren't killers. At least not the ones he personally knew. "They deserve to be punished, but we don't know if their entire village supports this or if it's two men who feel they're entitled to something because we offered a better life to some of their families and they didn't like who was doing the offering." He waved a hand dismissing the misunderstanding. "Bankor, Gegli, you both can ride, yes?"

They nodded.

"I want you both to find me two more to act as guard for when we take care of the filth in that building. I will accompany them in a day or so to return them home. I want them to stew. To wonder if we are going to do something worse or not. Sophie wasn't harmed only because Lord Morrow acted as swiftly as he did. Food and water, but no discussion with or around them. Is that clear?" Nods of agreement were sharp. "Good. Thank you for your input Royce. You do Cedri and your clan proud."

He bowed his head and scurried away, a single look behind, but it wasn't at Rune. He was looking, almost longingly, at Duran.

"Bankor, can I rely on you to watch the prisoners?"

He straightened to answer. "Yes, Master Rune. I will ensure there is at least one person on shift with the key and one watcher."

"Good. I'll check with the shift at nightfall."

He and Duran walked together on the pathways to the main keep. "How are Jayce's lessons going?" he asked, now that they were alone.

"Incredible. If I didn't know better, I'd say he's at least higher Second circle. His grasp and control are truly remarkable for someone whose training is so new." Waving to several nearby as they walked, Duran lowered his voice to speak between them. "He told us about his prior life, his goals. I'm almost sorry he had to leave that all behind, but the way he's driven to succeed, to learn who he is says a lot. He loves the history with Brin. I believe what we saw today is true to what he believes. He's the one we've needed." He neared to whisper, "Even Ulcieh is impressed. But he'll never admit it."

Rune snorted. "He's taken on a lot since this began for him, for us." He, more than any of them, knew the cost that had been levied against Jayce to begin the journey to take the king's mantle.

Duran put a hand on his arm, slowing them both. "You have feelings for him, don't you?" Wide brown eyes expressed his shock.

Rune froze on the spot. "Why would you say that?" He almost hissed. Whipping around, he grasped one of Duran's arms and pulled him into a shadow, and away from ears.

He lowered his voice, rushing to say, "You do, though, don't you?"

Rune scrubbed a hand down his face, agitation making it hard to breathe. "I can't. He's going to be our king. I'm his advisor, his guide to ensure the prophecy comes to pass."

"But he trusts you," Duran insisted.

"And look at the current throne." He tossed a hand, like that explained everything. To him, it did. "The throne's advisor has been this world's downfall."

Duran shook his head. "Do you really think you would do that to us? To him? You wouldn't have been entrusted by the goddess to see this through if your heart wasn't pure. Remember that. He needs people he can trust."

"That's why you were chosen, all of you. Master Theil put all of you, along with me, as a chosen inner circle of advisors and more. He needs strength and stability."

"If we were chosen, then why are you doubting your feelings?"

Rune's heart thudded into his ribs painfully. "I'm not doubting them, and that's the problem." He wasn't going to admit to Duran what he hadn't said to Jayce first. When it was abundantly clear that his heart needed and craved the sarcastic, brave man he'd come to love even as he knew it was the worst thing he could want. "I'm an elf, a mage; he's Valda-Cree, the born ruler."

"The only part of that which matters is you're an elf." He plucked his own earlobes. "Hard to miss."

Rune chuckled, then grew somber. "And the rest?" He knew the answer but what Duran said took him by surprise.

"He's Valda-Cree who was born to rule, but he's a man who has made it stridently clear he does not like women sexually. Who may have feelings for the one elf who's been by his side through everything."

"He told you all of that?" Rune blinked. That didn't sound like Jayce. He wouldn't share all of that, would he?

"Not about his personal feelings, but it wasn't hard to draw conclusions with the way he praised you and his expressions when he spoke about you during our sessions. He knows you've made sacrifices the same as he. It made sense to be honest with him when I am the same way when he said being with a woman was beyond impossible. The closer we all are, the stronger our bonds of trust and friendship will be. You have to see that."

Rune grimaced. "Oh, I do." But he didn't like Jayce getting that close to anyone else. He didn't think he'd ever tasted the bile sourness of jealousy, but there it was. Jayce was his, or at least, he desperately wanted him to be. Knowing he was sharing personal truths with the others made him feel cranky, and he wasn't used to that. He couldn't think of one person bringing that emotion to the fore in his lifetime.

"Then why can't you see it for yourself?" Duran looked around, ensuring they were still alone. "I've seen the way he looks at you. You're not alone in feeling something more. You have to remember, he has a lot to concentrate on. He has to become a whole new person, and none of us know how much time he has to do that. If he has feelings for you, and I know there's something in the way he looks at you, then he has to weigh those feelings and his own happiness against the world he's fighting for. You have to be as strong if not stronger for the both of you in this *exactly* because of who he's going to be."

"How do you know so much about feelings, and love?"

Duran's smile was soft and knowing. "Because I watched a master at work. I learned how to discern the smallest detail from someone's facial expressions and what they mean. I learned from you."

Rune groaned, tipping his head back to stare upward through tree limbs. "I'm doomed, aren't I?"

"Love is never a bad thing," he offered, giving a saucy wink before walking away to leave him in the shadows.

A rustle overhead had him peering into overhanging branches when all else was quiet. Soulful bronze eyes peered at him unblinking. "Hello there. You must be looking for one of us, aren't you?" A slow blink was his answer. Rich earthen brown feathers covered a roundish head, the compact beak opening slowly to release a quiet *whuhu-whuhu* of sound. Rune turned and pointed. "He went that way."

When the owl nodded and then thrust skyward to fly in the direction Duran had gone, Rune smiled. "Your journey is just beginning, my friend."

It was dinnertime before he came across Jayce or any of his friends again. There was loud banging and laughter coming from the dining hall. He supposed that was a good sign.

Jayce was already in his seat at the head of the table, talking to Cedri on his left. There was an open chair on his right side. Rune sat down and rinsed his fingers to wipe them on the towel before the food was brought in. Like it was normal and expected.

It wasn't usual for them to take a common meal so he knew this was Jayce's doing. An olive branch of welcome for their visitors. Not only were the skin shifters present, but so were a few of the village elders who were at the keep with their working family members. Usually the mages ate as they wanted, when they could, with duties being seen to as well as the keep running smoothly. When they'd opened the gates for inclusion, they assured anyone working with them that any family was also welcome. He looked down his side and spied Leodinn and Brin in conversation, with Ulcieh on the other side. He wondered where Duran and Grayson were or if they'd begged off after the day they'd already shared.

It took him a moment to realize Royce wasn't present either. *Interesting.* It wasn't long before the courses began to be brought in. Meat platters and steaming bread with bowls of vegetables and gravy. He purposely saved a strip of the beef and set it aside for Iba. He wouldn't forget his promise.

"How long are you planning on staying, Cedri?" he asked the man across from him.

"I've sent a runner back to the clan to let them know we are well and welcome. Not many are as open as Lord Morrow has been for hospitality when it comes to the skin shifters."

"It takes time to open people's minds to acceptance," Jayce mentioned. He tipped his head toward the table. "This in and of itself took weeks in the making. I know every person at this table by name, now though, don't I Callum?"

A gentleman with a white beard and thinning hair raised his tankard. "Aye, you do, my lord. It be a pleasure to feel like you really listen to the troubles of your people when we talk to you."

"I try. I know this hasn't been the easiest transition, for any of us." He sipped at the drink in his mug. Rune would bet his best cloak it was simply spiced cider, and that he meant every single word he was saying. "I truly believe the only way a person can make a difference is to know firsthand what ails their people and their land."

"You're very unlike King Bucol," Cedri remarked.

"I hope so. I want to prove that I will do what I say, and hopefully not make too many promises I can't keep. Very few are going to believe in what I'm fighting for on faith alone. That's what I need people like you for."

Rune bit into his roll, hiding his own smile. Jayce surprised him yet again. He hoped those surprises never stopped coming.

"Like me?" Cedri sat straight. "I'm not sure I'm following."

Jayce grasped at a bit of carrot and popped it into his mouth. "Damn that's good." He chewed and swallowed. "Sorry, that was tasty, roasted. Just, good stuff." He wiped his fingers and mouth clean then twisted to stare right in to Cedri's face. "I need allies. I need people of all families who can help reinvigorate the once and now forgotten legend of the Valda-Cree to become the reality that I'm here now. I'm not quitting until peace and balance is restored. Or I'm dead, but if that happens, there's going to be a whole lot more wrong than what I'm trying to influence. Like global annihilation. But that's for another discussion. Right now, I only need to know, are you with us to try to right what is so badly wrong or are you going to go home and let life go on? Either is an acceptable answer. You have your own lives. This is my journey. I'm asking for strong people, mages, skin shifters, everyone who feels this is the right path to take, to join us. It won't be long before the figure on the throne knows I exist and I'll need to be ready for that when it happens."

Cedri looked down the table. Rune watched as Jayce gave him time to commune with his clan and family, sipping his cider without a single sign of worry about the coming answer. He wanted to pull him out of his chair and kiss him until neither of them could think. The moves Jayce was making were profound for their direction, for their future.

He almost spit his drink though when Jayce dared to wink at him.

Damn, Jayce was wiped out. It was exhausting needing to be self-aware now that he knew without a doubt every motion, every word, was being scrutinized for a hidden lie, a weakness. He'd never played poker but it was clear he was going to have to learn how to be made of stone and fast. Dinner had been an interesting affair with the mages and the few shifters in the room along with those from the village who'd chosen to stay to listen. The mistrust was clear, the subdued layer of tension that had floated between the different faces. At least no one drew a weapon at the dinner table. It would take time for them to realize they were all working toward the same goal. That working together was the only way their future could be salvaged at all.

Because even he could see the omens in the distance. It was going to take everything Caduthien had to defeat the black cloud of the encroaching army. Which meant he needed to start taking charge and making plans. The cat was out of the bag now, whether they were ready for it or not. He didn't know if this was the right time, barely months after he'd learned of who and what he was, or not. There had to be a sign, right? Rune was guided by visions.

Jayce was running on fumes for instincts. It was exhausting and exhilarating all at the same time. He'd been charging from one change to the next since the day Rune had appeared in his life.

Gazing outward of the bedroom window after dark was like watching a whole different world. Torches were lit alongside buildings and between walkways. It was a far cry from campus and classrooms. A hand rested on the stone cornice, his body wrung out from the day he'd had as he let his mind wander. It was quieter below, and felt so wrong. There was so much life in the keep now. It hadn't taken long to bring the keep back to life once they'd started this chapter of their journey. Now if felt so wrong for it to be so quiet. He sighed and withdrew from the window, pulling his shirt free to drape over the back of the chair next to his bed. He sank down to toe off his boots but instead palmed the pendant Rune had given him when it swung freely. His one tie to his past life, before everything changed. All he owned in memory of his parents. Slipping it over his head, he felt the pang of their loss acutely. Their absence was likely dredged up by the suddenness of today's changes, feeling so alone even when he was surrounded by people he was supposed to know and trust. Exposure that the Valda-Cree line did indeed still exist, new allies, new plans. In a single day. How quickly their lives and directions could change. He sighed and held the stone between his palms. Exhaling, he rested against his clutched hands, unable to hold back the swell of loss.

"Mom, Dad, I'm so sorry. I had no idea this would happen. I'm sorry I didn't get to tell you about this, or say goodbye. I don't know how long you waited before giving up, if you did. I don't blame you if you lost hope." He sighed, releasing more anguish. This had been a long time coming and after today's upheavals, he needed to feel like they were still there for him, guiding him. "I'm not ready for this, not by a long shot. I did something today that could royally fuck up everything and I don't know if it's going to make all of this harder or not. If you were here, you could tell me what to do, help me. But you're not. I really could use you guys here with me, but I don't guess that's going to happen." Hot pressure built behind his eyes. He screwed them tight, pushing back against the pressure while fighting for breath between the ache in his chest and sadness of his heart. "I'll always love you, and I'll always have your picture with me, close to me. Rune did something special to my things and he doesn't know how much it meant to me, to always have you with me even if you're not here." He rolled the pendant in his palm to stroke the stone with a tender fingertip. "I know it was only to appease the child in me when I was younger so I'd feel safe and always have a connection to you, but I still have the coin token Dad gave me on my adoption day. It's right next to your photo. Well, it's there even if it's much smaller now." He grinned with a wobbly smile as the memories swirled. "I miss you so much. I wish you were here." His voice cracked and his forehead sagged to his clutched fists, quiet gasps and sobs breaking from his chest while he clutched the rock and its contents, its memories, like it was a lifeline as pain and grief swelled and escaped unhindered.

A knock on his door broke the heavy silence and startled him, jerking him out of the chair to his feet. He dropped the necklace over his head and then yanked his shirt on, swiping abruptly over his eyes and cheeks. "Yes?" He swallowed twice, clearing his throat when he sounded hoarse.

"My lord, may we enter?"

He faced the window, rubbing over his face again before turning around. "Come in."

One by one, the mages filed into the room, forming a half circle around him. Duran shut the door. And then, almost in sync, they sank to a bent knee, bowing their heads. Like the day of the ritual, all six bowed low. Jayce gawped, unable to do more than squawk before Rune started to speak.

"We come to pledge our faithful support to the future king," Rune stated with conviction. "Your servants were chosen with the prophecy in mind and today, you have proven yourself worthy of the prophecy's call. To have not only the courage of the Valda-Cree lion but your wisdom and bravery shined for all to see in the day's discourse. We have witnessed and encouraged your known blessed gifts that you are steadfastly learning and embracing to see you fulfill your destiny as foresworn by the goddess herself. In this, we give our undying vow."

"Guys!" Exasperation colored his tone. "Stand up. Please." Slowly, their heads lifted and he motioned for them to rise. With his hands braced at his hips, he huffed out a breath as he paced stiffly before them, waiting for them to grudgingly stand. Wow. He took in the expressions, the resolve standing before him and knew they would not back down. Their minds were made up. He had to take the bull by the horns and make this count. "I'm only saying this once, so listen well. We were put together for a reason, whether it was Master Theil's idea or an impulse from a higher power that he was only following, a compulsion that we do this together, it doesn't matter the how when you get to the bare bones. We simply are, for better or for worse, doing this together. You six were chosen for your skills, your wisdom, and your personal beliefs so I had ears and eyes to help me fix what is broken. I will never accept an oath of fealty if any of you feel it is coerced in any way." He stared into each elf mage's eyes. "Tell me now that you freely support the ideals of the Valda-Cree and the future we can restore."

As one they called "Aye!"

Tension seeped from his frame and his arms fell to his sides. "Then I accept. With some rules."

Rune's lips twitched but he otherwise stayed silent. He liked being organized and having a plan. Yeah, so sue him.

"First, we need a couple of benches and seats in the next chamber over. That empty room is now our meeting room. I'm not letting you crawl all over my bed and we're not fighting over the one chair." He caught the glimmer of laughter from almost all of them. Brin was blinking in surprise and Ulcieh was staring at him like he had a screw loose. Basically another day. Rune seemed the least stunned by his demands, but then he knew Jayce best. "Walking into that room, I am nothing more than Jayce. We all need a place where we can simply be because even I know the strain this journey is going to put on us is something none of us have ever known. All of us. Do you agree?"

"Aye!" was loud and strong.

"Good. Ulcieh, I'm entrusting you the duty of beginning the search and testing for military leadership. From today, you will be my Engagement Advisor. After today's problems, it's past time to get a military started, as well as the local watch. You have the calculated sharpness that is needed to weed out the weak and indecisive. I know going forward we will have to make adjustments. Please know I trust you to make those decisions, but come to me if you have any questions."

Ulcieh's jaw had loosened, clearly gobsmacked by Jayce's succinct dictates. "Yes, my lord."

"Duran and Grayson. I want you both to be the liaisons between the mages, the workers, and the skin shifters. You are to choose one other from each and work as a team to keep things running smoothly. As people begin to find us, altercations due to differences are going to occur. We need to be aware of them and be able to address them without causing distress or worse, doubt. We can't be strong if the core is weak."

"Yes, my lord," they stated clearly in unison.

"Brin, I want you to work with the keep's steward. We have a lot of needs that I don't know, not only how to run such a large holding, but how to ensure we have what we will need to see us through the coming winter. I believe your personality will help soothe ruffled feathers when people think they are not being treated fairly."

"Yes, my lord."

"Lastly, Rune is my First Counsel for reasons that are between us. Leodinn, you will be Rune's right hand man, er...elf as needed." He winked when they laughed. "Do any of you have questions?"

None spoke up.

"Good." He rolled his shoulders, feeling some of the strain of the day evaporate now as plans he felt confident in were becoming concrete in his own mind. "I know it took some time to get to this point, but I think after today, seeing there is support for us, we must take advantage of it, try to build on it. We need to track the army and its movements, as well as try to get information about the throne. We need to prepare, to not go into that viper nest blind. There will be a lot more going against us at that point than for us when it comes time to face those battles." Nods all around showed they agreed. "Then the only other thing I'd like to add is going forward, I want to meet with regularity, together. We have our footing here now, and the people who are here seem to be content, as much as we can make life for them. That leaves the rest of the discussions up to us to plan, and we will need to be honest with each other going forward. We will need to know each other, how we think, how we might react when under pressure. We need to become a team, and that can only happen with dedicating ourselves to our next goal. So, going forward, we will start meeting frequently." Up to now, there'd been a barrier of sorts between them, whether it was because of the prophecy, elves versus Valda-Cree, or whatever could be seen, he needed to eradicate that barrier completely. If he was supposed to rely and trust in these men, then it needed to be done wholeheartedly and absolutely.

"Next door?" Brin queried, pointing questioningly to his side at the conjoining door that connected the two rooms into part of his suite.

"Yes." Waving to encompass his bedroom, Jayce took in the sparseness. "Kinda not the place for group discussions or planning. But I appreciate the fact that you all came to me as one tonight. It's good to know where we stand." He ran a hand over the back of his neck. "It's definitely been a day."

"You've given this some thought," Ulcieh remarked, maybe with a hint more respect in his voice than he'd shown previously.

And you thought I wasn't listening to your lessons. Maybe he was finally winning over the recalcitrant mage. They'd butted heads more than once over lessons and learning magic control. He hoped this was a sign their friendship was improving. "Some, but really it's how I see each of you. You're unique and have skills that I really don't. But I have to make it look like I know what I'm doing to make this happen. That's why each of you was chosen. You support me while I support you. If I were to try this alone, I would fail. So, bluntly, I need you way more than you need me. And maybe by the time I'm faced with the reality of having to claim what appears to be my birthright, I'll be a little more ready." He wasn't so sure, but the course had been set when the lion revealed himself rescuing Sophie. As was commonly said on his world, watch that first step, it's a doozy. And there was no way to know where it would take him. He carded stiff fingers through his hair.

"Anything else?" He waited but when no one added anything, he told them good night. All of them except... "Rune? Can you stay a minute?"

Jayce waited for the door to be solidly closed then cleared the gap between himself and Rune. He flicked a wary glance to the door making Rune smile, his lips soft and beckoning.

"Expecting the door to talk?"

"Not exactly. Just seems every time I get my hands on you, we get interrupted." Rune's laugh was warm when Jayce playfully scowled over Rune's shoulder. "Now, come here." He tenderly grasped a hand and pulled him into his body. Seeking hands settled on Rune's waist, bringing them nearly chest to chest. "Wasn't expecting that."

"We talked after dinner. We all agreed it was time. Things are happening and we had a choice to make. You know I support you, as does Brin and Leodinn without reservation."

"I know the only truly hesitant one was Ulcieh. I'm glad that may be behind us now."

"As am I. Tonight helped a lot. Sharing the responsibility while acknowledging weakness shows a humble and wise man who will grow into a humble and wise leader." Jayce slid a hand upward and tugged on Rune's hair until the leather tie came loose. Rune's eyelids fluttered at the sensations when the heavy strands slipped like silk between his fingers.

"I'm not so humble as to not go for what I want," he said. "I don't know what is going to happen to me, or to us as a group as time marches on, but I do know I want you with me, every step of the way." He released that fall of lush hair and cupped his cheek, caressing the curve of his face as his feelings swelled. He locked gazes and felt his heart somersault. "I'm pretty sure I'm in love with you, Rune. I've never felt like this, with anyone. You make me so angry, but then all I want to do is kiss you until we're both naked and sweaty and too blissed out to be angry any longer."

Rune's eyes widened, unblinking as he twice tried to form words. Jayce took pity and touched his lips with a finger, calming the rise of anxiety he found in his beautiful eyes. "If you can't or don't feel the same, I understand. I wanted you to know. There is a lot about my history that I simply will never know, but I can do what I need to, what I feel is right, for the future of Kielbos, for all of us." Dropping a hand to dovetail fingers with Rune, he added, "You will be part of my future. I know that irrefutably, without question. And I want you to be, if you feel the same. Unless this isn't something you want…" He waited, for any sign that Rune was with him, or at least moving the same direction, but when he didn't make so much as a peep, he began to pull away while Rune's silence lengthened.

"No!"

Jayce's heart staggered as a pain unlike anything he'd ever felt stabbed his chest. "I understand. I didn't mean to make you feel—"

"No, that's not what I meant." Rune cupped his face. "I never thought… I can't lose you." He gulped, audibly. "I love you, too."

Jayce kissed him without preamble. One second he was staring into clear blue lightning, then he was drowning in Rune's kiss. Shivers traveled along every nerve ending, making the air, his skin, his hair crackle with the need coursing through his veins. Holding his face, he tilted to deepen the kiss, moaning as longing and need burst through him. The press of Rune's tongue was heaven and he opened willingly, needing the connection, the bonding. The firm pressure of Rune's fingers dug into his back, massaging as he pulled him that much closer. Tighter. It felt like heaven.

Mate.

Jayce blinked and jerked away from Rune.

Considering him with concern, Rune asked, "What's wrong?"

"I don't know," he croaked. "But I think my lion just spoke to me."

"What?" Rune's jaw swung open to snap shut. "Spoke to you?"

Jayce nodded hard. "Why? How?"

"I don't know. Is this a first time?"

Jayce nodded once. "When he came out this morning, I told him it would help a lot if he could talk. I'm not good at interpreting growls and pictures. I didn't know they *could* speak. Iba doesn't." But she was a familiar, not a soul spirit in the form of a cat that could take over his body with magic. He truly didn't know what to think.

"What did he say?" Rune took a step back and Jayce bit his lip.

"He said, 'mate'."

Rune gasped and paled. "No, he can't. You're my prince." He shook himself hard and hopped several steps away. He muttered and shook his head, then rubbed his hand over his face before staring at Jayce like he'd never seen him before then to pace again with stiff steps.

Jayce narrowed his eyes. It was obvious he was conflicted. "Why are you so scared? You just said you loved me. I love you, Rune. You have to know that."

"But the royal line," he sputtered.

"Yeah. And your point is? Or did you forget that I'm gay? That means I'd rather slit my wrists than be with a woman. You know as well as I do that it's more than not being able to function for sex. Unless you can lay with a woman." He crossed his arms in challenge. He'd never felt so much as a whisper of interest when it came to being sexually attracted to a woman, much less actually go through with it. The idea of it physically left him cold. Being drunk wouldn't have mattered, or any other way that might be cooked up. It simply wasn't going to happen.

Rune shook his head, his cheeks sucking in as his lips puckered in distaste.

"Then forget about it for now. We have this, us, between us, now. I'm nowhere near the throne and we still have to win the battles ahead. Every time we get close to each other, you run." He waited what felt like an eternity before the truth hit him square. And it made so much more sense. His stomach soured as he finally figured it out. "You really don't want this, do you?"

Rune pleaded. "I do. But I'm your guide—"

"And my guard." It took several seconds but when Rune didn't move closer, he did what was needed. He backed up, and felt bitter pain slice through his frame when Rune didn't follow him, making no effort to stop the chasm deepening between them. Rune's expression was pale with agony. "Go to bed, Rune." When Rune went to speak, he glared. "No, until you're ready to accept I am just me, the man you see, regardless of how this came to be, this can't happen. I love you, but you can't keep pushing me away like this. We're going to have bigger battles than this before it's all said and done." Jayce refused to force this, but damn it hurt to reject his heart like this. He turned away, wishing he had something to do with his hands. "Go to bed." He heard the door open and managed one last barb before he could stop himself. "I expect you at my side in the morning. If you're going to be my First Counsel, start acting like it. You will be with me to meet our visitors at the table in the morning."

Rune's voice was quiet but clear. "Yes, my lord."

He waited for the door to close before letting the pain envelop him, his shoulders sagging as his heart burned to a cinder.

Exhausted all over again, he fell into bed without bothering to undress this time.

Chapter 35

Steeling himself the next morning to face Jayce, Rune approached Jayce's wooden door. There was no answer to his first knock. He frowned. It was barely sunrise. He knew Jayce didn't like to wake early. Yet a solid round of knocking didn't seem to rouse him. Cautiously, especially after the previous night, he opened the door and found himself startled to be staring straight into his bedroom.

Where the bed lay rumpled and very empty.

Glowering, he turned away to head to the kitchens. If he wasn't there, he was going to at least get his meditations done. He didn't sleep well after their argument. Which was solely his own fault. He'd thought over what Jayce had said, as well as Duran. He needed to make the choice. Jayce was not a duty. He was so much more than that.

But...he is my prince! Gah! What was he supposed to do? None of this was easy. Follow his heart, or ignore everything for the greater good? He truly didn't know. He'd never felt like this for another person, mage, man, or otherwise. Was it Jayce specifically? After over a hundred and forty years, he sincerely didn't know. He wanted to beat his head against the closest wall to settle the confusion, but there were people watching. And he was supposed to look like the sane one.

Those in the halls moved out of the way as he stalked past. His cloak fluttered with his stride. He had a long day ahead, already planned. This was not an optimistic beginning.

Ulcieh met up with him in the halls, a parchment roll in his hand. "I have completed a weapons inventory."

"Do we even have any?" Rune asked with an arched eyebrow.

"To answer, truthfully, no."

Rune grimaced.

"I spoke with Maxon first thing. He has already started blade pressing. We need at least enough to train with and arm the watch."

"Agreed."

"I've also collected a few respected names. I understand you've worked with a few of them over the last months. Your insight would be valuable."

"I'll be happy to give you what information I have."

"We also need to discuss a guard for Jayce, Lord Morrow," he promptly corrected. There were always ears and eyes in the hallway. It wouldn't do to be so familiar. "It's expected. As well as a master at arms."

Rune rubbed fingers over his eyes. "As soon as I find him," he grumbled. At this rate he wasn't going to get to meditate at all.

Right then a loud roar froze everyone in their tracks. "Goddess, what is he doing?" he barked. Rune sprinted through the halls and out the keep doors. People were frozen, looking around as much as he, but his quarry wasn't visible. "Where is he?" Rune demanded. No one answered. Not that he was expecting it.

With Ulcieh right beside him, he followed the sounds of hard throws and impacts to the side of the keep where there was open ground, likely once used for training as the barracks buildings weren't far in the distance. They burst through the line of the watchers and Rune almost raced to intercept the next charge, but was grabbed by his arm and wrenched backward.

"Don't!" It was Bankor who'd caught him, stopping him. "That's Cedri."

"What are they doing?" Unable to take his eyes off the two large cats, he watched them charge and tangle, jaws open in bold snarls, pushing off their back legs trying to get control. The lion and tiger were very evenly matched.

"Fighting," he answered, dry as dust.

"I can see that!" he snapped. "Why?"

"I don't really know. I would say for practice. I don't see either of them drawing blood and neither has used claws."

Rune whipped around to take a real look at both cats, and what Bankor said was true. Neither animal had their claws extended and while they were huffing and hissing, there wasn't true anger behind it.

He grumbled a sigh of relief. "I swear he's going to be the death of me," he muttered.

"Isn't this the next stage?" Ulcieh whispered close to him. "Training with the skin shifters to understand his lion, so they work together?"

Rune bowed his head, attempting to calm his heart. He knew what this meant, if they were seeing the beginning of the alliance with the cat clan. By this time, with all the noise they were creating, quite a crowd had gathered to watch. Knowing this was expected and needed didn't make it any easier to watch Jayce take a hit that had him rolling to his back, panting hard. His coat was dark with sweat and dirt. They'd clearly been at this for a while.

Jayce resolutely stood and placed a paw firmly forward, watching for the next opening.

Cedri's tiger prowled in front of him, pacing from side to side, head low, fangs exposed as he snarled through panted breathing. Jayce's lion let him do all the work, exhibiting a far calmer patience with only the tip of his tail twitching, until the tiger dared to glance into the crowd, a split second of distraction, and the lion attacked. Launching from mid-crouch through the air, he wrapped his front legs around the tiger's neck and threw them both sideways, rolling with their momentum until he very deliberately braced large paws on either side of his neck, then stared down.

He chuffed in the tiger's shocked face.

There was a shimmer of body, fur and shape, then there was a naked man beneath the lion. He was laughing. "Good play!" The lion shook his head and mane then raised his head and roared, declaring his victory far and wide. "All right, you've made your point," Cedri groused without any real heat, patting the furred chest over him. Cheering surged through the crowd.

Respectfully, the lion eased backward, careful to not step on the man beneath his paws. Then as quickly as the tiger, Jayce crouched as the lion receded and he retook his form, however he was fully clothed and grinning as he stood, offering a hand to assist Cedri to his feet. Pants were offered and Cedri stepped into them.

As the crowd dispersed, Rune and Ulcieh neared

Jayce slapped him on the shoulder. "Thank you for that."

"Is he more settled now?" Rune heard as he approached.

Jayce's head came up and almost instantly, his gaze locked on Rune. The flatness in his gaze spoke volumes. "Yeah. He's feeling better." The silence continued until Jayce whipped around to Cedri. "Thank you for letting me bring him out for a bit."

"The more you do, the better you'll understand each other. Most shifter children encounter their first shift between their third and fourth year so by the time they're young and playing around, they already have a working relationship with their skin animal."

Jayce's face fell. "I didn't have that opportunity."

"Don't worry. You'll get there. He's very strong."

"I'd like to talk more, later," Jayce said as Cedri brushed himself down and finished dressing.

"Sure. With your approval, I'd like our group to stay for a while."

Jayce offered a hand and Cedri met him, arm to arm with a clasp. "You and yours are welcome. The offer stands from yesterday." A huge grin overtook his face, playful teasing apparent in his tone. "You didn't beat me, so yeah, you get to stay."

Several guffaws and teasing barks of laughter surrounded them.

The light faded from Jayce's eyes when he faced Rune, even if little else was revealed on his face. "First Counsel," he said in greeting, then, "Ulcieh." Both dipped their heads in answer, Rune feeling the sting of being addressed by title. He understood Jayce was far from ready to forgive him.

"I'll leave you to your day, then, my lord. It was an invigorating pleasure."

Jayce nodded as Cedri turned and joined some of his friends, other shifters that Rune recognized, including the pale blond, Royce.

"How are things this morning?"

Rune listened halfheartedly while Ulcieh repeated his news to Jayce. "Good. Good." His hands rested braced on his hips as he listened with a cocked head, the single loop in his ear glinting in the warm morning sunlight. "Do what needs to be done. If we need to find a way to garner more materials, see if there are people who have goods for trade with other villages yet. We need to assign someone to the treasury." He looked at both. "I want a serious, unanimous, trustworthy individual."

"Yes, my lord," Rune offered. "Have you eaten this morning?"

"No. I couldn't sleep."

Rune's lips thinned. The pain was hidden but he knew what Jayce wasn't saying. This couldn't go on. Chatter faded as they walked into the keep. Jayce spoke. "Ulcieh, could you find Brin for me? I have a suggestion from Cedri that I want to run by him."

"Of course." He bowed and reversed his steps, leaving the two alone.

"How was your morning with Cedri?" Rune asked.

He brushed a hand over his arm, knocking off dirt, then said, "I got to ask him about the relationship between me and my lion. It was good information."

"Did he... Did you ask about the lion speaking to you?" The memory of the night before still left him feeling shaken. *Mate.* What if he *was* Jayce's mate? What did it mean? Could he answer the call to submit to him, and his lion? Rune truly didn't know.

Jayce kept his voice low, imbuing respect for the information. "I did. While it's not discussed outside of the skin shifter clans, it appears to be a common trait, but not universal. It's considered a blessing of higher strength and unity."

"That makes sense. No, I wasn't aware of it at all."

"There are also other skin shifter breeds. Bear, fox, wolf. Rarely are they found within human circles. They tend to live together as clans."

Rune opened the door to the side of the keep. "Which would also make sense as I rarely came into contact with skin shifters during my travels. Some but not often."

"Don't think I'm ignoring the fact that you aren't talking about what my lion said about you, about us," he said flatly while they were still alone, his tone and gaze firm. "We will be discussing it, but not here."

Rune swallowed slowly. "Yes, my lord."

He reached the head chair at the table to situate himself comfortably. "Kirn! I'm here!" he warbled cheerfully. "I almost wish I had Master Theil's ability to levitate items. That would be fun."

"You didn't mind his pranks?"

Jayce shook his head, leaning over his cupped hands on the table. There was almost a wistfulness in his words. Jayce had grown close to Master Theil in the days he was at the temple under this tutelage.

"It was different and not meant to harm. I hope we get to see him again."

"I'm sure we will."

A grinning woman swept into the room from the kitchen with a steaming mug in each hand. "My lord, Master Rune. Ready to eat?"

"Always," Jayce offered with a warmth that Rune missed for himself. Goddess, he was really being an idiot. The broad smile. The warm laughter. Jayce always had a kind word or a few minutes for anyone in the keep. What he'd said the day before about knowing who was working around him was true. He was out daily, walking through the various buildings, talking to those who were overseeing improvements or supplies, or any other duty being completed. Jayce knew everyone. It was the kind of person he was. It wasn't taking twenty-four hours to see for himself what he was fighting. And the pain it was causing both of them to deny it. There was no mistaking the coolness between them.

The wall between them was as felt as the heat of the morning sun on his skin outside.

"What has been decided about the two prisoners?" Jayce asked as he finished his food.

"They will be escorted to their village by guard. I was hoping to question their village elder, if they have one, about their intentions."

Frown lines drew Jayce's eyebrows together. "We need to know if there is a larger attack planned."

"I agree." Rune sipped at his coffee.

Jayce methodically settled his own mug. "When you take them, I will be joining you."

Rune's eyebrows rose high. "My lord?"

"That wasn't a request."

Rune breathed slowly through his nose before bowing his head. "Yes, my lord." He didn't dare argue in the dining hall.

Brin and Ulcieh appeared and were quietly seated and served. Rune felt the heat of Jayce's censure surrounding him. Side looks from Brin received a short head shake. Tension seemed to live like a cloud over the table. When Jayce stood a little later, they all stood.

"There are a lot of things I'm going to have to get used to," he remarked, meeting the gaze of everyone standing individually to include them. Speaking quieter, he offered, "I don't want any of you to feel that what is happening is going to diminish the friendship I already share with you. I'm going to do my best to keep my word on that. With that, enjoy your meal. I'm going to see if I can find somewhere to think for a little while."

"My lord?"

Jayce shook his head at Rune. His face was pinched. "Stay. Find me later."

Rune nodded, watching Jayce vanish into the keep.

"What happened?" Ulcieh demanded as soon as he was out of range and they were all sitting. "He's been acting very cross all morning. Today has not been normal for him. Unable to sleep, looking for Cedri for training first thing in the morning." Ulcieh's perplexed state mirrored them all. Except for Rune.

"I'm aware of that," Rune bit out. He pushed his plate away, his appetite gone.

"Did something happen, Rune?" Brin studied him with an acuteness that made him want to slide under the table.

He rested his chin against his gathered hands instead. He shook his head, not wanting to expound on his own problems so openly.

"Is this because of the attempt to take Sophie?" Brin wondered.

"No." He raised his gaze. He was greatly at fault, but he wasn't about to share that with anyone else. "Continue as we have. We're making progress. He's got a good head on his shoulders. If he's been overwhelmed, it isn't showing."

Brin lifted a held biscuit layered with eggs to take a bite while Rune spoke, taking his time to add, "I'm beginning to understand more. He's finding his footing. To be thrust into this situation the way he has been, he's handling it far better than could have been expected. If he has a bad morning or seems out of sorts after the kind of day yesterday was, it doesn't reflect on us or on him negatively. This hasn't been easy and yet he's taken every challenge and met it with resilience, an unflappable demeanor, and courage." He pointedly looked at Ulcieh. "Keep in mind, he has no history in Kielbos. If he's cross and needs to let his lion out to express his rage, or to rest and think, or even to practice skills, then I don't think we need to be worried. This is his way of working through his challenges. We need to respect that."

"That only works until word of his return reaches the Alendaren throne. Then there will be no second chances."

Their faces grew pensive with that reminder.

"He knows that." Duran stood right behind Rune's shoulder, surprising him with the interjection. He hadn't realized he'd been there, but he'd obviously heard everything Brin had said. "He also knows that if he fails, there is no second chance. That's a lot of expectation for someone who wasn't raised here. Who knew nothing of this world. Born here I'll give you, but he knows nothing beyond the months he's been with us. What we've each taught him." He shrugged a shoulder. "Truthfully, he's handling it with a bearing that implies his heritage. He's trying to shoulder the mantel. He only needs us to support him to do that. Like last night. He knows what we're going to be up against even if it's undefined. He has vision. We have to be strong enough to embrace his vision. I can guarantee we are not going to like every suggestion."

Brin puffed up. "I like being Master Brin, Keep Master."

Duran chuckled. "You would. That's why he chose you for the task." He ran a finger over his chin. He leaned with a hip against a close chair. "He chose for each of us with surprising foresight and wisdom."

Ulcieh's eyes widened. "Why did we not see this sooner?"

"What?" Rune asked, copied by the other two.

"He's trying to find ways to prove himself. Like you said, he was literally plucked from his world and dropped into ours, thrust into this chaotic prophecy."

Rune immediately shot a hand between them all to cast a privacy silencing bubble to envelop the table and all four of them. "We need to be careful of our discussions going forward, before anything more forward is said. We can't be lax in our duties or discussions. There are ears and eyes everywhere."

All three nodded. "My apologies," Ulcieh stated, repentant. "It simply hadn't occurred to me before now. He is so driven to learn not only the mage magic, but his lion, and also the Valda-Cree history. It's easy to see when you take a step back from the view."

"If you'd seen him those first days, you wouldn't recognize him as the same man today." Because he wasn't. Jayce had changed considerably already in such a short amount of time. He crossed his arms and leaned into his chair as he thought over that first meeting, his first hours with Jayce. Shame filled his stomach. He had completely missed the transformation of Jayce's fear from the sarcastic young man who was swift to berate Rune for his actions, to hiding his fear, hiding his indecisions. Hiding his feelings. Not wanting to reveal where he was scared or feeling overwhelmed. Not with so many already holding expectations for him.

Except for when he told you he loved you. That had definitely been a risk of his heart. And the pain he was suffering for it.

He realized he was to blame for that, causing a large portion of Jayce's doubts and fears. By acknowledging the feelings between them but refusing to accept them *and* him, he'd pushed back on Jayce, possibly making him second guess anything he's done and everything going forward. He tilted his head upward to stare at the ceiling.

"Goddess, I'm an idiot."

Quiet snorts followed his words. He gave everyone a firm stare but couldn't help the small twitch of his lips when he was met with equally bold expressions in answer.

"How long have you known?"

Duran pulled a chair out to finally sit. "That he's in love with you? For a while now."

Ulcieh nodded. "I've had suspicions, but he's always been very tight-lipped around me."

"He knew you didn't believe."

"He never tried to force me to," Ulcieh pointed out.

Brin braced his chin on a hand. "Really? You thought he could? Or would? That's not like him. He's methodical, logical. Not brute strength. Even his lion is calculating."

"But if he's in love with me," Rune said barely above a whisper, which he knew Jayce was, "what about the succession of the crown?"

"Look," Brin said firmly. "You're focusing on the wrong thing. King Bail lived for centuries and would have lived longer if he'd been allowed. I had found in the temple archives he had one other son besides Jayce but he died along with his mate. That was why he didn't have more children. It almost destroyed him. I didn't remember until we started his training." Brin leaned over the table, firm in his opinion. "Jayce is young, and as long as we keep his ass alive, he's going to be king for a very long time. So what if he prefers men? If he has his heart set on a stubborn mage, then the only thing stopping him is you."

Rune glowered hard.

"Well, it's true." Duran faced him with an elbow on the table the other bracketed on the chair rest, his hands clasped before his chest. "King Bail was only the fourth of the Valda-Cree pride to take over the throne. His father, King Luca, ruled for close to seven hundred years and lived for much longer." Duran stared him straight in the eye. "You wouldn't be this conflicted if you didn't care."

"He cares, but he's trying to be noble." Brin grinned broadly and winked when Rune scowled at him.

"*He* is right here in front of you."

Ulcieh picked at a thread on his shirt sleeve. "Well, maybe *he* needs to get *his* head out of his ass and see what *he's* doing to him, as a man. Because right now, I've never seen him more shutdown and surly."

That said a lot coming from Ulcieh. Rune cleared his throat. With the silencing bubble he could be more forthcoming with his fellow mages and friends. "Did you know his lion can speak to him?" All three sets of eyes widened. "Thought that might be your reaction. It's common enough but not universal, or as Cedri explained to him."

"And why is this important to this discussion?" Brin's eyes narrowed at him sharply.

Rune's gaze swept away to one of the walls, avoiding looking directly at any of them. "He told Jayce I'm his mate."

The immediate eruption from the other three at the table made him extremely glad he had the foresight to put up the spell.

"But don't you see!" he cut in sharply when they paused to build steam for another round. "Carden has had full control of the throne for centuries."

"And you're an idiot."

He blinked owlishly at Ulcieh. "Excuse me?"

He flapped a hand. "Repeating what you already said. Yes, you're an idiot. Do you trust yourself so little that you fear you'll do harm to Jayce?"

"Goddess, no! Never!"

"Then what is stopping you? Look, I'll admit I was the last to believe in the prophecy or Jayce's ability to be the one, but his integrity hasn't been in question. Why are you questioning yours?"

Brin all but beamed with righteous approval. Rune cocked his head and stared into his gloating face, refusing to back down. This was too big of a step to be wrong.

He swung around as Duran added, "Did you ever think that the goddess chose you because he needs what you represent to help him get to the throne? Did you ever think caring for each other could only strengthen the Valda-Cree while he's on the throne? So there won't be natural children. Right now, that is the very least of our concerns. Very least. We're in hiding, without an army, with very vulnerable people who don't know how to lift a blade, with only six mages charged to protect the one person that could save our world from destruction and you're worried about things that are not in your nature. Rune, I second Ulcieh." He scoffed. "You're an idiot."

Rune groaned and dropped his head forward. "Okay. Okay. I see what you're saying. All of you. I need to get out of my own way."

"Yes" was chorused definitively.

Chapter 36

Jayce stayed out of the keep most of the day, avoiding numerous people inside while he strolled through the working grounds talking to the people outside. He knew the days to simply be alone, to walk without worry for his safety were counting down. When he'd not only require a personal guard, but far more protection everywhere. He didn't know when it was going to happen, but the pressure to make the next move was hanging over his head like the sword of Damocles. He wasn't crazy about any of the possibilities for his future, but he understood that protocols and behaviors are expected. There was no way to deny them indefinitely.

The sounds of life surrounding him made him smile, distracting him from his tumbling thoughts when he saw several of the visiting shifters playing tag with the children. Back and forth, tumbling with laughter. That freedom was what he wanted for everyone. Skin shifter, man, and mage. Happiness. A chance to grow up, to grow old, in peace. On Earth, he would be one of many who could help, but his place on Kielbos could change an entire world. His directions may have changed, but this happiness was who he was in his soul. Sharing it was his goal if he was to be who everyone thought he should be. He drew a breath to ease the wave of apprehension. That was a lot of pressure, even if it was early days yet.

Days and weeks of history with both Brin and Ulcieh had been stuffed into his head. It was like his history of Lincoln and Roosevelt, of world wars and dictators was fiction. He was the only one who knew of those events. Instead of North and South America, there was the Grand Continent, the throned center of Kielbos. None of it looked the same either, not by the maps he'd been shown. His Earth truly was no more.

Somehow, he'd managed to fit in with that world when he clearly shouldn't have. There had been no hints of his magic, not a whisper of his lion. He'd played T-ball and had four sets of D&D dice. None of that was his life here. He missed it, but not enough to want to go back, knowing his life, his family and friends, were likely gone or dead. There wasn't any way to reverse Raquel's and Helen's dying, and knowing what he did about them now, he wouldn't want to. They'd been close enough for him to feel betrayed, but that was all. The bitter loss was his parents. He was trying to cope with losing them. The emptiness in his heart where their love had been. Too many moments where it wasn't easy, but he was getting there.

It helped there were friends here now, and a growing circle of people he could turn to, aside from the people who were looking to him to make changes in this world. What he really needed was someone to tell him what to do, or at least give him options.

Somehow, he, Jayce Morrow, was going to be the unifying force to bring peace to a land slowly being devoured by the will of a dark siege and remove a malevolent ruler and his henchmen, or the henchmen who controlled the crown's will. *Yeah, just another Tuesday*, he mocked himself silently. He huffed.

Why me?

He didn't have the answers. He'd accepted he was the hidden child prince. He even accepted he was magically imbued with a shared skin spirit, gifted with extra mojo from the Goddess Adhrer. It was hard to argue with what he'd experienced. It was also hard to accept that so much was being placed at his feet because of a prophecy. Clawed fingers pushed hair up and away from his face as frustration continued to fester. Getting out of the keep and away from everyone had seemed like a good idea at the time. Truthfully, he didn't know what he needed with the way his thoughts scattered and bounced around.

He raised a hand and called for a small surge of wind, determined to give himself focus, letting the magic shoot downward and outward to stir the leaves on the ground into a funnel. This was new to him, but he was feeling more confident every day. A little at a time. The mages were committed with improving his skills, improving his control. It seemed to him something was sticking. Master Theil's words were never very far from his thoughts about respecting the abilities he carried, though.

Small twigs and summer acorns mixed with the swirling leaves, a tiny tornado that he controlled between trunks in a figure eight, in and out, making it shrink and build at will. This ability was so unfathomable, yet he enjoyed the thrill it gave him to play.

He flicked his fingers and the wind funnel died away easily, everything settling to the ground with a faint rasp like it had never moved.

"Jayce?"

His feet froze to the ground. Playing with the leaves had distracted him from the approach of footsteps.

"May I join you?"

He closed his eyes and nodded. Swallowing down the pain of last night's rejection, he slipped on a neutral expression. Sunlight dappled the ground and then Rune was beside him. The calm beauty of the day seemed to mock the pain his voice alone could cause. They walked in silence for a few minutes, Rune's staff a soft staccato scuff to their pace. Iba was flying somewhere overhead, he could hear the soft swish of her wings. *Huh. Was that new?* He wondered if his lion affected his human counterpart abilities. He almost laughed at his own fantasy. He was obviously thinking of all the shapeshifter books he'd read. It did make him wonder if it were possible though. More questions for Cedri.

"Do you remember when we first met and I demanded your name?"

Jayce tilted his chin upward, his thoughts roaming over those days. "I think so. When you appeared in my apartment and scared the crap out of me."

Rune's high cheekbones warmed to a light pink. "Yes, well. There is power in a name given freely, without coercion. It can be used in spells and the caster can force the person to do certain things."

"Really? You would have done that to me?" He gaped at the elf beside him. Was this another sign of how far he could be betrayed by those he trusted?

"If it was needed to protect you? Then? Yes. You were a little stubborn that first day. I didn't know you, didn't know what we needed to do, other than bring you here. I've never gone against someone's wishes by forcing their will by the power of their name, but at the time, it was the only way I could think of to get you to come with me."

Jayce scoffed, at least understanding the reasoning behind the thinking of Rune's confession. Didn't mean he liked it, but he understood. They strolled without direction, the silence of the surrounding trees calm, letting them meander without interruption.

"Then the *sabra* appeared and they spoke your name."

"I guess secondhand it doesn't hold power."

"No. It doesn't, but you are a wise man and understood what you saw even if you didn't want to believe it then." He touched Jayce's bicep lightly. "I am sorry for taking you from not only your home, but your family."

"Water under the bridge now." He rolled a shoulder. They'd cleared the air on that several times. What was done, was done.

Rune drew a breath, and said, "Runybathaczar."

"I'm sorry. Did you sneeze?" Jayce halted at his side.

Rune chuckled. His confusion must have been all over his face when they faced each other as Rune laughed a solid belly laugh. "No. It's my full name."

"Runybathaczar? I can't even spell that."

"Rune is easiest on everyone, plus I'm protected with the anonymity. Only a few people know my name. You are among them."

"Huh. Because of the spell stuff?"

Rune grunted with a side eye stare when they started walking again. "Because of the spell stuff."

"And everyone here? All of the mages are using some form of their name?"

"Everyone. It protects us."

Jayce froze and bent over his knees, suddenly feeling extremely ill. "Oh crap. Oh crap. Shitshitshit."

"What's wrong?" Rune demanded.

"Everyone knows my name!"

"You are not at risk, not any longer."

Jayce straightened, gasping as the sudden wave of panic receded. "Are you sure?"

"Positive. Not only because your name is as public as the evening winds, your power protects you. I'm not convinced even then, when I first found you, if I would have been successful had I tried to coerce you. You are growing to be far more powerful than I. As you said, it is inevitable."

"So why are you giving me your name?" Jayce strode over to a large boulder to sit with the river several yards. "This spot is beautiful," he said offhand, trying to keep from reaching for Rune even as his hands itched to feel him, to cradle his weight and warmth. Thick trees swayed in the breeze and the roll and rumble of the river was soothing. The slope of the land melded into a smooth meeting with this part of the river. It looked like an easy place to walk into the water and splash around. With the cloudless sky, it was simply a warm summer day with the natural sounds all around them. Once settled on the rock, he bent a leg upward and rested an arm across it. "I'm assuming you did tell me for a reason. You seem to have a reason for everything you do."

"Several reasons. First, because I trust you with my life. It is no small gift to know a mage's name. I need you to know that I do trust you. I may not agree with everything, but I trust your judgment. Second, because I love you. If I love you, I must also trust you with who I am, all of me, because it is the only way to give you that which is most vulnerable to me: myself." He neared the boulder and standing close to Jayce, looked into his eyes, and Jayce shivered with the brightness of the blue pinned on him. The silver reflected the sunlight and looked exactly like the lightning strikes he'd originally compared them to. There was absolutely nothing subversive in that stare. It was as he'd heard–the eyes were the windows to the soul, and right then, there was so much life and emotion in them that his heart tripped with him caught in their stare. "Third, but likely not last, because it's been pointed out to me that I'm being an ass."

Jayce's brow rose high, listening to Rune's words while taking in the determined stance as he stood before him with the river backdrop. He meant every word.

Rune reached for Jayce's loose hand. He threaded their fingers together, and Jayce felt the pulse of their skin when he stroked his thumb over Jayce's closest knuckle. The tingle of power, be it physical or magical, was something he'd never known before meeting Rune, and he didn't want to let it go.

"You didn't have to fall in love with me, and I didn't have to fall in with you, but somehow, it happened. You could love any person, mage, shifter you desired, be it now, or decades in the future."

Jayce immediately shook his head, not letting the hand he held go, or lose the gaze before him. "But that's why I think I did fall for you. You saw me as Jayce first. It was just us. Moving forward, I would always be suspicious about the motives of any interest, whether emotional or merely physical." He glared mildly. "It wasn't until you got it into your head about me being prince whoever, that you freaked out. I'm still only me. And the me I am loves you."

"This will complicate things going forward," Rune warned with a light scowl.

"For who? You and I are the only two who are truly trapped on this path. Everyone else volunteered and is equally free to leave. They aren't beholden to me, or to this cause. You and I, though? We have a mission, a goal if you will." He shook his head, a warm smile ghosting over his lips as Rune listened to him, and he hoped, listened well. "To me, it's almost fate that I fell for you. You and I started this together. You and I are meant to see it through the end. Together. Loving you is actually the easy part."

Rune blinked, breaking the spell he held over Jayce with those bottomless eyes. "How?"

"The prophecy. It's going to change us no matter what we do. It feels right that I know we're in this together knowing the future is still uncertain. And because I felt something for you even when I was freaking out in my apartment. This stunning elf appeared out of nowhere. I thought you were beautiful then. I think that now. I hated that I was so attracted to you. You ripped my world apart and changed it. And that changed me, but I don't hate you for it. Not now," he admitted. He dipped his head, and heat filled his face, watching Rune through his lashes. He was sure he was blushing up a storm. "I don't know when I fell for you. It's always been this feeling, this heat, and you're the cause."

Rune swallowed slowly. "I feel that, too. I've never been drawn to another like I am to you."

Jayce threaded the fingers of his hand into Rune's loosely swaying hair. "See, fate. And no one argues with Sister Fate."

Rune's eyes fluttered with the tug of his hair. "No one would dare," he murmured. Jayce loved how the simplest of touches could melt his elf, because he loved his hair. He wanted to see it wrapped around himself, wanted to be blanketed by the length and feel the sweep of it over his skin. Damn, Rune turned him on so easily. Being this close, exposing themselves emotionally was no small feat for either of them. It had taken them a long time to get to this point in their journey. Respect anchored his love, and he knew that now. Pain in the ass that his elf could be, he loved him nonetheless.

"I'm not going to make a big deal out of this, but going forward, you are mine. The lion agrees with me." *And someday, I'll be able to make that claim official.* But he knew better than trying then. There was simply too much to do, to work through, not only for himself and his future, but for the futures of those around them. He could wait for his full happiness so long as he had the opportunity to see it on the horizon. If he lived that long.

Rune blinked, his eyes soft and unfocused. "Your lion? He's still talking?"

"He's become more vocal since this morning's calisthenics. There haven't been many opportunities to bring him out without exposure since he was first brought forward. It's not all that surprising that I'm the one having difficulty adjusting to this part of my life. He's along for the ride and has been very calm about it. And I believe it's a good thing that it appears we have a very tight bond. We need to work out the kinks between us." He sighed, feeling the press of the world on him again. "In time. I only wish we knew how much time we have, hell, that *I* have to get my shit together."

"What happened to your fake it until you make it?" He nudged into Jayce's knee, teasing him.

Jayce huffed a laugh. "It's a front. I'm scared shitless." And he couldn't dream of admitting something that raw and personal to anyone else.

Compassion filled Rune's eyes. "Let's go to the river and do some water work. Take your mind off your worries over the future."

"Sure, but…"

He stopped Rune from trying to step away, pulling him close instead. Dropping his legs to either side of his, he drew Rune between them. Expecting him to put up resistance, Jayce was happily surprised when he didn't. Welcoming the chance before wrapping his legs behind his thighs and boxing him in with his hands at his waist, feeling the heat of skin through his clothing.

"Now that we've had our first official fight, you know what the best part about having a fight is?"

Rune tipped his head, his expression disbelieving. "No. There's a good thing to arguing?"

Jayce laughed silently before tugging him closer. "Yeah, the makeup sex."

Rune blinked hard at him before slowly grinning. "I don't believe I've ever experienced that."

Jayce tsked. "Then it is up to me to show you." The way Rune's eyes glowed with heat and longing made him feel warm all over. Tucking Rune's lean length against his own, he brought them together, sealing their lips in a slow, sensuous kiss. Firm fingers dug into his back, holding him as close as was possible as the kiss deepened leisurely. Teasing tongue play and soft teeth nips. He could only hope he was driving Rune as crazy.

Beneath the cloak Rune wore, he slid a hand downward to grasp a side and heft him firmly into the grind of his hips. A low, needy groan rippled between them in answer. Pleasure throbbed through his veins with their combined heat, stoking the fire higher as the kiss went on.

Iba's piercing call overhead was clear.

Jayce sighed forlornly when they broke the kiss. "See? I get you alone, and we're interrupted."

Rune snickered, running his thumb against Jayce's lower lip. "I'll be thinking of this into the evening," Rune promised.

"Thank you, Iba," Jayce said. Iba flew near to land on Rune's shoulder and leaned close to nuzzle Jayce's cheek. Jayce let his hands fall free when Rune took a step away. And it was none too soon as voices filtered through the trees to reach them. While they might not be hiding, per se, there was no need or reason to flaunt what they shared until they were able to make it a secure announcement. The last thing Jayce wanted to do was put Rune in jeopardy over their relationship.

Chapter 37

Jayce sat at his place at the dinner table, smiling fondly at the mix of faces, friends, new and even newer. Chatter was lively, which to him was a good sign. Elves, humans, and shifters were beginning to loosen up as they spent more time together. It gave him hope that this was possible. There were disagreements, they were unavoidable between different beliefs, different ways of life. But so far, everyone had been willing to keep a cool head and compromise. For now.

While he was appearing to be attentive and listening to various discussions, what he was hiding beneath the table was the way his foot wrapped around Rune's ankle, keeping him close. The gentle reminder with his teasing made Rune's face occasionally warm with a delicious pink color that Jayce sincerely wanted to tempt into a full-blown blush. Thoughts of caressing and kissing his elegant neck, to nibbling on his ears, which he knew would drive Rune absolutely insane, and all the things he wanted to do and experience were still ever-present in his mind. Sitting hidden at the table, he'd been half hard since the dining hour had begun.

There were a lot of questions facing them in the future but right now, this was almost perfect, which in of itself told him it wouldn't last. But he was okay with the moment as it was. Cedri and Ulcieh were having a lively discussion with Rune and one of the villagers, Thernball, who assisted Maxon at the forge. It almost reminded him of the times he'd spent playing Dungeons and Dragons with his friends, strategizing and considering options for their next move.

Only here, now, there was a real risk at stake if they got it wrong. Lives could be, *would be* lost, and it would be because of him. That weighed heavily on him. There was no chance to pack it up and resume the campaign if it all went to shit. No do-overs. It made the outlook of their future sobering. And there was no guarantee of being right one hundred percent of the time. It simply wasn't possible.

They'd already come so far, as a group, with a single-minded goal. The keep was up and running. He was continuously making strides with his lion and with his mage skills. The skin shifters were befriending them. He was finding his support and those he could trust as they worked together. All the signs of the prophecy were being ticked off one by one.

There were still so many questions, though. Was the creator of Raquel's axe still alive? Rune didn't believe so, but who would truly know? Who had hired Raquel and Helen? Had they kept in contact with their employer through the years they'd been in Jayce's life? How were they going to form an army? How long did they have before the Blood Spawn army would be pressing at their doors? When would they need to face the Alendaren forces? How was he going to take back the throne? How long could they stay secreted away? He didn't really feel worthy, and the lack of confidence left a hard to eradicate ball of doubt in his stomach.

There really wasn't much working in their favor when he ran through the long list of questions plaguing him.

And there were those who were already suspicious and unsure of their intentions, thus the two men who'd attempted to take Sophie with the purpose of a more insidious plot.

"My lord?" Rune's murmured voice close to his ear pulled him blinking from his thoughts. "If you are done, may you release the table?"

"I'm sorry." Bashful heat warmed his cheeks. "I checked out, didn't I?" Amused blue eyes told him he'd hit the nail on the head. Not that Rune would ever make such an accusation with so many present. Clearing his throat as though his delay was intentioned, he stood calmly and everyone else followed, the scrape of chairs rather loud in the ensuing silence. "Thank you everyone for joining us this evening. I will continue to do the evening meals as often as possible. Going forward, there will be a sign that the keep table is open to all for the evening meal. As our keep grows, please know that I welcome any and all. This will be a time for conversation and sharing of ideas. Also know I and my advisors are here for your questions if any can't share this time. Please let your friends and family know they are welcome.

I greatly appreciate your willingness to share this time in friendship." His gaze roamed around the group, happy to see so many listening and relaxed. At least this much was working. "With that, the table is released."

"Thank you, my lord," was chorused several times.

"Rune? Join me?"

Rune's smile was telling, however brief it was, when it flashed across his lips, proof his mind hadn't been far from their evening together, either. Jayce walked away from those standing at the table, Rune at his side. The gradual sound of chatter and feet walking in the other direction to leave the keep faded as he neared the stairs to the second floor landing.

He opened the bedroom suite door and waited for Rune to follow through. The door closed with a muted *thunk*, silencing any sounds from below reaching the upper rooms. They were finally alone. And they were finally on the same page.

Jayce brought Rune closer, unhooking the waist strap he wore and draping it along with his short sword over the stand to the side of the bed. Tonight would not be derailed due to not having any oils. A pot of corked oil waited for him. He was going to spend hours loving on and learning Rune's body. "Spent most of dinner thinking of this evening."

"I keep thinking about the evening at the temple, after your lion was awakened." Rune's voice was soft, nearly breathless, his cheeks that lovely pink going to red that Jayce loved to see on his pale skin.

"It's been too long since I've held you like that." Jayce urged Rune to turn, sliding his hands beneath his loose shirt to caress his sides. Rune's eyes sparked with arousal at the contact. He dipped close and inhaled against his neck. Extending his tongue, he languorously licked upward, tasting, tickling, until he reached the shell of his ear. "I haven't forgotten what this does to you, either."

Rune moaned when he drifted against him, a shudder rocking his body as Jayce controlled him with the barest touch, waiting. Rune's hands had risen and gripped at his sides as he nuzzled and caressed. When he licked over the curve, nipping gently, Rune quaked against his hold. Jayce murmured in appreciation, glad he could make Rune feel so good.

But he needed more, wanted to touch, to see, to kiss everywhere. With his hands underneath Rune's tunic, he lifted it upward and drew it up over his head with slow motions, exposing him like a gift.

"So damn beautiful." The shirt went the same direction as the sword belt. A flash of gold pulsed through his vision, and he knew his lion was showing his approval. Rune's happiness meant his lion was happy. Then a different impulse gave him pause.

Are you sure? Right now?

Soon.

I will. Tonight. We need this first. He was not about to be cockblocked by his lion.

"What's wrong?" Rune was studying him with concern. "Your eyes are bright."

Looking into brilliant blue eyes he could fall into, he said, "My lion has made a request. He would like to meet you, himself."

Rune's jaw slowly dropped open. "He wants to meet me?"

"Well, he met you at the temple, officially, but that was before he realized who you were. Then he called you friend. Now he is calling you mate. He also wants to bond with you."

"I—I'd be honored."

"Good." He grinned. "Now, where was I? Oh, right. I was about to instigate all types of pleasure then revel in the debauchery of that pleasure with you."

Rune snickered, his frame losing some of the tension he'd formed from learning Jayce's lion had demands as well. "And there's the Jayce I love," he said gently. "I humbly accept your petition. Please, debauch away."

Jayce laughed at the sensually playful smirk. "Goddess, how I love you." He covered Rune's lips and thoughts of his lion, of concerns over their future, over anything other than the feel and taste of his kiss vanished. Warmth seared him, quickly bubbling to a heat that had him pushing for more. Fingers dug into his neck, keeping him right where Rune wanted him, where Jayce wanted to be.

With an arm circling his chest, he tugged Rune into his frame and felt the puff of his gasp as their frames collided. There was no hiding their arousals so close. It felt like heaven, and an addiction. Rune's bare skin was smooth and silken beneath his palm. Gliding his other hand to Rune's ass, he pressed them together. No one he'd ever seen, spent time with, could compare with the elf he embraced. The quake that rocked Rune when they pressed shaft to shaft drew a moan from Jayce. No one had affected him the way this elf could, either. This man, elf, owned him heart and soul and he was going to make sure he understood he'd accept nothing less in return.

Spinning them a few steps, he brought them to a halt near the bed's edge. Separating to breathe, he licked from Rune's jaw downward. When he tipped in answer, giving free rein, Jayce smiled even more. Coasting from clean shaven lower jaw to collarbone, he licked and kissed a meandering pathway, slowing as he enjoyed the journey.

Rune's skin was flushed with arousal, his kiss-rouged lips lightly parted as he panted. "Jayce," he whined gently.

"Patience, love." He sat on the edge of the bed and undid the buttons and draw tie to his trousers. Rune's stomach fluttered with the brief brushes from his knuckles and caresses, fingertips that flitted over skin. Then he leaned close and kissed around his belly, nipping lightly at his bellybutton until Rune giggled through his gasps. A glance upward revealed a small glare. "Ticklish?"

"I refuse to confirm that."

"We'll see if I can confirm it, later."

"I'm still waiting for the debauching to begin."

Jayce shook his head. "Okay, call me out, why don't you."

Rune merely smiled, his fingers lovingly slipping through his hair. When the front length fell forward, he helped by pushing it back. "Every time I've seen that, I wanted to sweep it out of your face. It's hard to keep my hands to myself when we're not alone."

Compassion and understanding had him kissing flesh. "I know that feeling so very well. When we're alone, anything. I will never deny you."

Rune peered into his gaze for several seconds before nodding in answer. Then the time for further words was gone as he finished opening the placard to Rune's trousers and revealing his stiffening length. Jayce inhaled, loving the scent of this male's skin, of male arousal, and knowing it was all his.

The hefty shaft before him was thickening, a pale berry red as blood stiffened the length. With closed eyes absorbed in his discoveries, he neared and nuzzled at the base. The fingers that had so tenderly caressed his scalp mere seconds ago were suddenly clutching firmly into his hair.

Opening his mouth, he played with the swollen tip, swiping his tongue across the slit with slow strokes. Shivers and shudders rocked Rune's frame. A quick glance upward revealed closed eyes, a man utterly enthralled by his mouth and touch. A powerful rush of sensation calmed him. He'd known for some time that he and Rune were meant to be together, but the opportunity to physically share each other and share their feelings had been difficult to reach. Now he knew his feelings without a doubt.

Tonight, his every intention was to love and please his elven lover.

With deliberate attention, he glided down the length of his shaft until he filled Jayce's mouth. Swirling and licking, he sucked to the tip, swallowing the fluid that escaped. It was as sweet as he remembered. So very addicting. And somehow, better, richer. Quiet, rumbled pants and moans drove him. He lost track of time as he loved on Rune, his own hands framed around his hips to squeeze and caress, feeling the trembles of his pleasure as they rode up and down his frame, until Rune's fingers gripped hard, tugging him away.

"You...must stop," he panted, shuddering in stages, a hard staggered whole body twitch when Jayce released him, licking his lips to catch his flavor.

"I love the way you taste. It's sweet somehow." Rune blushed, his lashes lowered. It only took a few minutes to divest the rest of Rune's clothing and jerk off his own, leaving it all on the floor.

Settled together on the bed, Jayce's mouth was everywhere, caressing and kissing over Rune's frame. Rune's arms wrapped around him like cables, unrelenting and holding him tighter and tighter. "Tonight I am going to take you," he warned the elf. "Tell me now if you don't want that."

Rune quickly shook his head. "Please. Need you." He swallowed and took a slow breath. Clear eyes were sparking with the lightning he loved so much, revealing the swirl of his emotions and the true conviction behind the words. "If you still want to bond, I gratefully accept your heart as mine."

"Rune." Like he would have it any other way. He dipped close and claimed his mouth with a searing kiss that left no doubt that before the end of the night he was going to be claimed, marked, bonded, and forever Jaycc's.

He reached for the pot on the table, a few sudden concerns making themselves apparent when he realized they *only* had the oils. "I know we don't have anything like condoms." When Rune's brow twisted in query, he waved it off. "Not relevant, but I need to know, is there a risk for disease? It's not sanitary and the other plane was riddled with health problems."

Rune chewed on his lower lips as he put thought into it. "I don't recall any for concerns. There is also the factor that you are a skin shifter at heart. Your ability to heal and stay healthy is tied to your beast."

"So I can't get or share anything?" That seemed like a stroke of luck. One he wasn't going to argue against.

"Cedri or others may have more information, but from what I know, no."

Jayce's grin grew. He'd definitely be picking over Cedri's brain for more. "Good to know. This will be a night neither of us will forget." With the pot settled on the bed near Rune's shoulder, he drifted fingers down Rune's chest, teasing and petting until any coolness of their brief discussion had been replaced by a needy heat, until the miles of pale skin revealed his wanton hunger. Goosebumps trailed his slow travels downward. Rune's legs shifted restlessly, widening, silently pleading for more touch, for more of Jayce. But he was enjoying his exploring. The times they'd shared before had been rushed, driven by adrenaline and events. Tonight they had hours and hours.

It was a sublime pleasure to raise love marks on his chest, to see those and know that he was marked for and by Jayce. The gentle purrs and rumbles in his head told him his lion absolutely approved of them. Rune's breathing was deep, then ragged and gasping, his fingers stiff and pulling, urging, but he was taking his time and there was little that would change his course.

He licked through the join of his hip, tracing the opposite side with his fingers, feeling the flex and jump of firm muscles when he teased the length of his inner thigh. The way his body reacted told him how deeply Rune was affected by his touch. He licked over the flesh of his balls and Rune's reaction was instant.

"Jayce," he whined.

He rose up and kissed his lips, languorously, letting his palm coast over his shaft before gripping firmly. "Yes, love?"

"Oh, uhn…" He shook on the bed, grasping for Jayce. "You make me burn."

Hungry eyes glistened brightly in the last of the fading light when he stroked the cock in his grip. He pumped him a few times until he had no choice but to let him go to use both hands.

Jayce pulled the cork free from the top of the bottle then tossed it over a shoulder, out of their way. Focusing to create a gentle heat, he warmed the oil in the pot before drizzling a little over his fingers. Rune's eyes rolled into his head at the first stroke over tender skin. He whimpered, a raspy sound that made all the nerves under Jayce's touch stand to attention. Knowing it had been a long time for Rune since he'd been with anyone he took his time easing into his body, gliding through his opening to the first knuckle.

He winced then gasped at the intrusion, pushing into the pressure almost immediately. Even though Jayce took his time, it seemed like every minute was a minute too long for Rune. Gliding in and out, stroking velvet skin and pushing against nerves had Rune arching off the bed. He couldn't wait to feel him surrounding his own cock. Rocking his hand and twisting gently, he split Rune's focus by licking over the tip of his shaft, purposely sipping at the slit to smile at the grunts slipping from Rune.

"Are you ready?" he asked.

"Goddess, yes," he ranted, breathless. "I need to feel you. Now!"

Jayce moved around on the bed until he slotted between his thighs. Slicking his hardened length, he nestled between his cheeks then gazed upward. Braced over Rune, he slowly pressed forward until he popped through the ring of muscle, both gasping at the suddenness of the pressure.

"Mercy," Rune gasped.

"Do you want me to stop?" Rune had to only say so and he would stop everything. He'd probably die, but he would stop.

He rocked his head on the bed, his hair scattered until it surrounded him like a glistening halo on the pillows. Raising a hand, he tugged on Jayce's arm, bringing him down and closer. "Need this, need you."

Jayce didn't fight those sentiments, he was swimming in his own feelings and needs and emotions and they were all tied neatly around the elf he was gazing at. Raw and wild, this moment was theirs. Slow thrusts brought them closer together until he was resting flush to skin. Both were breathing a little heavier, neither able to look away.

Encased in the heat of Rune's channel, the urge to move was overwhelming and nature took over, forcing his worries and concerns that were clearly not going to appear to the background. There was only this, and he'd never felt anything so enlightening or in the same breath, erotic, in his life. The heat of Rune's body was unlike anything he'd ever known, and he felt himself gliding deeper into him with each thrust.

Rune's legs rose, gathering around Jayce's waist and they both groaned as he sank even more with his next thrust. Grasping hands clutched as Jayce's hips rocked them into the bedding. Rune shuddered with a breathy moan. He wanted to spend the rest of his days urging those sounds from his elf. With that, Jayce's need multiplied, pinning his gaze on glassy blue eyes as Rune swam in the pleasure of being taken.

"Getting close," he warned, sensing the tension to orgasm growing in Rune as well. Rune nodded, reaching upward and finding his mouth for a passionate meeting of lips before he crashed back to the bed, panting. The telling surge from his groin gave him little warning, like currents woven around his spine the urge to come rushed to a peak. Growls slipped from between his teeth as his lion surged forward, a roar rolling up his throat and filling the room as the pressure of his release eclipsed his vision with a golden light. Following an edict that he couldn't fight, his lion urged him to lean close to Rune's shoulder. A rumble filled the room as his mage's intoxicating scent filled his nostrils. A scent now married to Jayce's own, and his lion. Opening his mouth, incisors grew as the lion's will pressed forward and at the height of his pleasure, he bowed close, biting down hard, holding his mate to rut against. Pleasure filled his limbs as the sweetest taste filled his mouth. He'd never known anything like it. With the confirmation of his bond, his lion calmed, proudly huffing with his claim made and clear to the world. Jayce licked over the bite, the pierced marks evident even as they closed and healed nearly instantly. Arms and legs clenched. Rune cried out with the twitch and thickening of his cock, while pulse after pulse filled his channel, prompting jets of white high onto his body in answer. Jayce shuddered at the sight.

As though every muscle in his body suddenly hit reset, he sank forward, blanketing a panting Rune. Long arms cinched around his middle, letting him know his lover was perfectly content with that position. They both moaned pitifully when his shaft eventually slipped free from the cage of Rune's heat. Burrowed into his neck, he kissed and nuzzled over the sign of his claiming, eliciting shivers and moans of delight from between Rune's lips.

"I hope that was okay," Jayce offered, a wave of worried unease in his tone. Cedri had explained the animal's baser needs and that it would likely happen during intercourse. Jayce wasn't going to tell Cedri he could have been a little more informative now that the deed was done. The lion had certainly made himself known, though all he felt now was pleasure and pride in the fact that Rune now wore his mark. His lion was a bossy, possessive bastard.

Rune's smile pressed into his temple. "It was perfect."

It wasn't long though before the thought of moving reared its head. He flopped to the side, feeling the stickiness of their releases as they moved apart. He grimaced as he flicked his fingers against his chest. But he was still resting in the afterglow. There was nowhere to rush off to.

"Would you care to share the bath with me tonight?" he offered, strumming lazy fingers over Rune's ribs sometime later.

"I would love that," Rune replied, his voice rougher, raw from the experience. "I've never felt like that before. You are truly one of a kind."

Jayce grinned, inordinately tickled at his words. "Thank you. I don't have a lot of experience but that means we get to learn things together, right?"

Rune's grin had a bit more challenge in it when he replied, "I assure you, we will be doing that a lot together."

Jayce snugged an arm under him and pulled him into his shoulder. "I like the sounds of that."

Rune nuzzled into his throat where he'd flipped closer. "Me too," he breathed. "Me too."

Chapter 38

Rune blinked his eyes open, noting the delicious heat and aches that were new across his frame, the way his skin felt alive. Gingerly, he skated fingers over the mating mark on his neck. The once free-ranging mage had officially been claimed, and he'd never felt more settled by that fact, or more proud to feel the slight tightness where the healed bite's bruise colored his skin. The bruise would fade over time, but the marks, the scars of the teeth that had claimed his very heartbeat and soul would remain forever. A shiver of wonder and happiness danced over his frame as he replayed memories from the night before. It was a future he'd never dreamed. Now he couldn't live without the man beside him.

Jayce lay on his stomach, facing away, giving ample parts of his bare back to curl up against and enjoy the body heat shared between them as the gray of predawn began to force back the inky darkness of full night.

This time of day was when he would usually be up and driven to be outside to meditate, to commune with the Mother and feel the warmth of her embrace as he re-centered his magic. Jayce's nakedness was too alluring to leave after a night like last night. He wasn't ready to call this night done with his mate. He sighed, never feeling more relaxed than at that moment, keeping the man he loved in his arms. Snuggled into a shoulder with an arm over his strapping back, he sighed and allowed his mind to quiet.

He realized he must have drifted back to sleep as a steady knocking on the bedroom door roused them both.

"My lord? Are you in there?"

Jayce groaned as he flipped over to stare at the ceiling through closed eyes. "I think so. Do you have coffee?" He palmed Rune's hand to kiss the knuckles, his lips soft and warm. Rune almost sighed at the tender feeling.

Brin's chuckle was clear even through the door. "I do."

"Goddess, this is why I love you guys," he muttered. Rune smiled at his grumbling. His lover was *not* a morning riser. He dropped a quick kiss to Rune's lips and flopped around until he was sitting against the top of the bed. "I'm going to let him in unless you have an objection." Golden eyes sparkled playfully as he waited patiently with an arched eyebrow.

Rune shook his head. "If anything, they'll say it took me long enough." He snickered. He was careful enough to ensure he was fully covered where it counted, with his hair draped over his shoulder to hide his mating mark. That was private between them for now. Too new. He wanted to cherish it before it became common gossip knowledge around the keep.

With a shrug toward Jayce that he was ready, Jayce called out. "Come in, Brin."

Brin eased open the door and quickly slipped inside to close it briskly. "I apologize for waking you so early." Rune chuckled as they shared a knowledge-filled look. A look that lacked any signs of surprise at finding him in Jayce's bed. "However, there is a group downstairs that is asking for an audience."

"An audience?" He grasped the mug with a rumbled thank you. He sipped deeply then licked his lips. "Perfect." Then his brow furrowed. "I thought we were secluded here. How do so many keep finding us? First the two assholes who went after Sophie, the cats from Tanglewood, now a group of visitors. I don't get it."

Rune slipped from under the covers and quickly dressed on the other side. "We *are* secluded. I'm sure we'll get to the bottom of this."

Brin wrung his hands then stiffly dropped them to his sides. "There is a couple in the group who claim to know you personally. Volpes. That isn't truly unusual as the skin shifters have been welcome here, but what is unusual is their persistence that they are your parents."

Rune froze the same as Jayce.

Jayce choked hard, caught mid sip. Rune patted his back until he waved him off. "Did you just say *my parents*?" He searched upward expectantly toward Brin through his lashes.

Brin nodded, nibbling on his lip as his gaze whipped between Rune and Jayce.

"What? How!" He leaped from the bed, forgetting he was naked.

Brin quickly whirled, speaking over his shoulder. His hands flared wide, helpless. "I don't know. They arrived less than an hour ago with quite a large contingent. Ulcieh wasn't sure to even let them in, there are so many."

Rune's eyes widened. "How many?"

"It's hard to say, as not all of them followed through the gate. Cedri left to find their encampment when I came up here to inform you."

Jayce hurriedly jumped into his pants. "You called them something, *volpes*? What is that?"

Brin continued to face the opposite wall until Jayce tapped his shoulder that it was safe to turn around. "Volpes are fox skin shifters."

Jayce sank back to the bed's edge. "Fox." Shock made his voice tremble. He pushed the rowdy fall of hair from his forehead with an unsteady hand. "I'd say impossible but if these months have shown me anything, it is that everything is possible. Tell me what you know."

While he and Rune finished dressing, Brin filled him in. "They arrived under a banner of a northern pride. A small armed group of twenty entered the keep grounds with the two who say they are your parents included. Your mother?" Rune could tell by his tone Brin didn't know if he should be wary or hopeful. "She implied you activated a token and called to them."

Confusion clouded Jayce's features. "A token? But I don't have anything from before."

Rune's gasp and the memory of the last visions he'd experienced during their travels north stopped him in his tracks from circling the bed.

"Rune!" Jayce growled, his brow tight. "What do you know?"

"A token," he whispered, replaying the memory, then his eyes widened. "Of course! Do you still wear the pendant of your prior life's possessions?" He whipped his cloak up and over his shoulders, locking the clasp.

Jayce pulled the cord from beneath his shirt, exposing the oblong stone. "I don't take it off. But what could I have that would be...a...token." His face went slack as he gasped. "The coin!"

Rune smiled widely, pleased to have at least discovered the secret of one of his visions. The token was meant to reunite Jayce with his family. "The coin your father gave you is enchanted."

Jayce's eyes glistened with unbridled hopefulness as he processed through the possibilities. "My parents are really here? They're really not dead?"

"I don't want to say for sure, but you do have people who have asked for a meeting." Rune put a hand to his shoulder and squeezed. "Part of me hopes they are who they say they are, but you also need to remember who you are now."

Jayce heaved a huge growl. "Right. Everything is being watched, everyone is judging me. Damn it!" He shook out his hands and said, "Okay Brin. Go downstairs and treat our visitors as proper guests. I would like to meet this couple separately. *Only* them. In a side room somewhere. I will address the group after. Do that now and let us know where you have them. I need to get my head on straight after this news."

"As you wish." He dipped his head. "If it helps, I hope they aren't lying. They seemed like a lovely couple."

"They were the best," he replied, choked up.

When the door closed behind Brin, Jayce started pacing the floor. "How Rune?"

"I truly don't know, but can hope they will be able to explain. I forgot about the vision with the token. It was weeks ago."

Jayce waved it off. "It wouldn't have mattered. You didn't know what the coin meant. I've had it for twenty years. *I* didn't know."

"But if this is all true, then you have more support for your return than we'd first suspected."

Worry and doubt filled his golden eyes. "Do you really believe that?"

Rune walked close enough to stand in front of him. The warmth of skin filled his palm when he cupped Jayce's cheek. "I do. This won't be easy. We've known that, but any good that comes your way, that aids us, should be welcome. Think about it. They came here under a northern banner. You are not alone."

Jayce wrapped his arms around Rune. "I'm not alone. Never have been since you found me." He neared to breathe against Rune's neck, right against the claiming mark, making both of them shiver with awareness. "You don't know how much you mean to me if you think

296

for even a second they're going to take your place in my life." He growled and Rune calmed. His lion was warning him and he smiled, the beast could be downright pushy when he felt he wasn't being given due respect. His voice was raspy after the snarl. "See? Even he knows. I love you, *we* need you. Never doubt that."

"I promise," he breathed, letting his fingers card into the length of hair at Jayce's neck. "I love you too." He pressed tender kisses into Jayce's jaw until he reached his lips. In spite of the rawness of the moment, the anticipation at the start of their morning, he was feeling himself respond to Jayce's kisses.

He laughed because of course, Jayce noticed. His hand slid down Rune's spine to cup his butt and pull him close. Shared smiles full of want and adoration grew. Jayce neared for another kiss when Brin's return knock sounded on his door.

"My lord? They are ready for you."

He pressed his forehead to Rune's. There was so much wary hope in his gaze it made Rune want to wrap him into his arms and hold him, protect him in case they were all wrong. But that wasn't something he could do. He regretfully straightened and pulled himself together. "Let's go."

Jayce opened the door to walk out, and was immediately boxed in by Rune and Brin with two others behind them all. A side look at Rune revealed little, but he wouldn't argue the protocol, or the reasons for the show of strength to protect him. There were unknowns in the keep. Armed unknowns. If he lived as long as everyone seemed to believe, then eventually the bodies surrounding him would feel natural. Rune knew this would all take time and adjustment, for all of them. Like he'd said, their lives were going to change, all of them. What he was seeing in Jayce's acceptance of the guard was only a small glimpse of that change.

They followed Brin down the stairs and then down a hallway away from the front meeting hall until they reached a closed set of doors. Rune knew this particular room had likely once served as a den or library with the shelves on one wall, but they had no such tomes to store, so it stood empty aside from serviceable furniture.

Rune tapped Jayce's elbow, an agreed upon tell to let him enter first after their surprise visitors from Tanglewood. Jayce waited to the side and allowed Rune to open the door.

When he walked in, the waiting couple seemed as anxious as Jayce, holding hands and sitting close to each other. They stood when he said, "Sir, ma'am, may I present Lord Jayce Morrow." The woman clasped a hand around her throat, hope and fear clear in her gaze as well as a lower trembling lip.

Jayce walked into the room and it was as though for a split second all the air got sucked out of it.

"Jayce!"

"Mom!" He was across the room and hugging her tight as he swung her around, her petite stature so tiny compared to his broader height. Her auburn hair was twisted and gathered in braids around her shoulders, her face flushed with happiness as tears trekked down her cheeks. He hugged her hard before setting her down on her feet. "Dad." They embraced heartily, struck silent by the shock.

Rune faced Brin. "It's safe to say they're telling the truth." They were all grinning. "Please have Javi or Kirn bring in some coffee and rolls for everyone."

Brin dipped his head and exited the room. Rune motioned the other two closer. "Stay guard by the door."

"By your will," one answered.

"Thank you. Let Brin in when he returns but please let them have a few moments for this reunion." Then he shut the door quietly.

Jayce stepped back and reached for Rune. "Mom, Dad. This is Rune. He's the one who found me."

Rune wasn't surprised by the displeased censure from both. He was aware Jayce was being kind by not saying he was the one behind Jayce's abduction and vanishing from their lives.

"This is Nolen and Harmony Morrow, my parents."

Rune came forward and bowed deeply. "It is my honor and pleasure to meet you both."

"So you're the one who took our boy from our world, huh?" Faced with his fists on his hips, Nolen gave him a sharp-eyed up and down. Rune did his best to keep the other man's stare. Disapproval sparked like lights in his green eyes.

"I would say if I could make wishes, but the fact that you're both here clearly means you knew of the possibility. You're volpes, correct?"

Harmony limply sat. "It's best if we both tell the tales to get us current. There is a lot to share."

Brin returned while Jayce described their adventures. Cups of steaming coffee and fresh meat rolls and butter were offered, then Brin left them. Gratefully, his parents didn't interrupt but once or twice for clarification during the whole monologue. It was with a sigh of relief when they were caught up. And he was eternally grateful that he hadn't made Rune sound like a villain out to do dastardly things to Jayce. Even if Nolen occasionally peered doubtfully in his direction. He didn't begrudge them any animosity. He'd never once suspected Jayce's adoptive parents could be a part of the picture.

Harmony sank back on the cushion, a swell of relief obvious in her smiles now. "Well, given that we knew it was possible, we're extremely glad that you have such strong friends now to support you."

"When we were notified of the break in at your apartment," Nolen continued, "we feared the prophecy had come for you. But we had to abide by the rules of the plane we were living in. There was an investigation, and your disappearance along with the damage to your place could never be explained. We were questioned for months, not only about you, but about the two girls in the hall who also went missing."

Jayce slumped. "Raquel and Helen. They were *sabra*."

Nolen jerked straight in outrage. "Are you kidding me? We had *sabra* right outside your doors? How did we never know that?" What was left unsaid was how long they'd been there, and if they had been keeping tabs on Jayce, who else knew. It was impossible to answer.

"Do you know of a mage named Natugenus?" Rune asked them before they became too enraged over the *sabra*.

Harmony shook her head, a questioning glance to Nolen received the same results. "Who were they?"

"She was the one who scrolled Raquel's axe. I have it with us but it is under a spell in the keep armory. They attacked us not long after we managed to reach Trajanleh. They are both dead. We managed to escape their attack."

"Well, that's good!" Rising fear tightening her features quickly eased once she heard the *sabra* were no longer about. "Where did we leave off? Oh, right. So it took us about two years before we could leave without causing suspicion, follow through with closing our lives there. We didn't want to be slowed down once we made the decision to return."

"Two years." Jayce's dropped into his hands. "I am so sorry."

His dad reached outward and rubbed his shoulder. "It is what it is. By then we were certain you'd come home. We had a means to return but we had to wait for a full moon on our plane to activate the spell because there isn't much magical energy there. It was partly why that world was chosen to keep you hidden and protect you. Your own magic and lion wouldn't feel repressed, they simply wouldn't emerge as there was no magic to tether them to, or call them."

"How long have you been here?" Jayce asked.

Nolen replied, "A little more than three weeks now. We have safe harbor with one of the northern prides. They have parchments from their elders that they've kept secured that explained who we are. They were rightfully scared stupid to expose those same papers to anyone outside of the pride. They didn't believe us immediately when we appeared but I know what is on those parchments like my own name. I helped King Bail write them to explain you and us, if it should come to pass that you returned. When we first wrote them, we had no idea if you would be the cause for the prophecy or if you could return for any other reason."

Jayce snorted a soggy chuckle. "You would remember. There wasn't a single fact that slipped your mind. It's why I wanted to teach like you did. You could answer anything."

Nolen's gaze lit with mirth. "Well yes, but it was also because we loved you, kiddo." He turned to Harmony.

"We accepted our duty with pride and honor. There is no family alive for us. We never had children, and we realized once we did what was asked, we couldn't until if–or when–we could return. You are our son in every way there is that counts."

"So, that means I really am King Bail's son." Tension lowered his voice with a fractured rawness.

Harmony nodded, her gaze softening with gentleness. "You are. And I'm sorry we never prepared you for this. We were told not to. King Bail's last command to save you was to let you live freely. If you never returned, then life would go on. We were all aging on that plane, so there wasn't much we had to hide. And very little of the magic we know was usable. Enough to see us hidden in plain sight and to secure your safety. We were simply what everyone saw. A family with an adopted son."

Jayce ran his hands over his knees then settled. "I know King Bail died tragically. How old was I when I was taken away?"

"You were about two weeks old when we began to suspect there was a plot against Bail. His first worry was keeping you safe. The night he was murdered, we'd barely managed to get the pieces in place for the eventuality. We had to do what we could right then." Harmony reached to clasp one of his hands. "Your father loved you like his next breath, but you hadn't been introduced to the court yet. No one outside of a very select number knew you even existed. He lost his first son and wife to childbirth. You were a miracle because of a woman from his pride who offered to be a surrogate. You were his miracle."

Jayce lurched to his feet and snorted. "Master Theil said I was a child of love. So I guess now we know even he isn't always right, huh?" He tried for a humorous tone, but Rune heard the bitter hurt.

"But your father did love you," Rune offered gently.

Nolen actually nodded in agreement, surprising Rune. "Bail fought the council to continue his bloodline. They were bent on denying him without taking the traditional steps. It's why no one knew about you. The council told him he had to take another wife if he wanted an heir, but his wife was his mate and he couldn't do it."

"Was Carden part of the council then?" Rune questioned with a grim sense of foreboding.

"He was. He was one of the council elders."

"Now we know, or can make a solid guess, as to why you were hidden." Rune spoke to Jayce's parents. "It's in the history books that Carden killed King Bail and with the help of the council placed the current lineage on the throne. Carden has singularly been in control of the throne and its leadership since King Bail's passing."

Harmony covered her gasp with a shaky hand. "No!"

"Brin said you arrived under another pride's banner. Who is supporting you? Or protecting you to travel?" Jayce stood across the room with his hands behind his back. He gazed unfocused toward a window. "Do we have more allies in the northern prides? Or am I slowly walking right into my own death?"

Nolen answered. "There are several elders who accompanied us, the Kinsi are among them, the pride who honored your father's requests. Once they realize we are telling the truth, they will alert their prides and clans. Right now, I'm sure they feel like they're humoring us. Who is going to believe the validity of an aged parchment written and signed centuries ago and sealed with a now deceased royal crest?"

"Did King Bail leave any of the royal insignia or the crowns with you, or where they could be found?" Rune asked.

Nolen turned and grasped a satchel that had been hidden behind him on the seat cushion. "I have a ring. It was Bail's, he gave it to us to hold onto when we fled. It is the closest vestige of the Valda-Cree without it being the crown. I've had it all these years."

He rummaged then pulled his fist free and opened his palm. Rune swallowed and bent closer. "May I?" he asked before reaching for it.

"If Jayce trusts you, then we do too," Harmony offered kindly.

"Thank you," he replied respectfully. He palmed the ring and walked over to the lone window to hold it up to the light streaming in. Gems and gold glistened. Ruby red eyes on the hand carved lion head and streaks of mane lined with brilliant diamonds. It reminded him of Jayce's mane with the darkness and lightness woven through the design. He felt Jayce would have been the exact image of his father by man and by lion. The head had a side tilt to it, like he was raising his head to roar, his mouth agape in mid sound. "And you saw King Bail wearing this ring?" Lifting his gaze, he asked the pair on the couch.

"He only wore a few pieces daily. That ring, and when he could be seen by anyone from outside the castle, a circlet of woven fine golden wires that emulated his mane in form. The other piece was a necklace that was his wife's. The Valda-Cree crown was only worn on special occasions."

"The crown has been destroyed, or so the books say now." Rune ran a finger over the ring, feeling the warmth of the gold. There was an enchantment on the ring. "Jayce, please put this on. It feels like it's calling for you."

Jayce quirked a brow, but did as asked. The ring fit best on his right ring finger. "It's heavy."

"Do you feel the heat in the band?"

"I can, yeah. Is it supposed to do that?" He lifted it to study the ring, as well, tilting his hand to watch the glimmer and sparkle, much the same way Rune had.

Rune clasped over his hand, covering the ring and closing his eyes. A shudder of power rocked his shoulders. "When we have more time, I need to delve into the ring. It carries a spell, a protection." He peered at the detail closely before squeezing Jayce's fingers and releasing his hand. "Your father wanted you to have this. I don't doubt it."

Jayce straightened. "We can spend more time getting caught up later. If we want to move forward with any direction, then the next step for me, for the Valda-Cree, is waiting in the front hall. Waiting for me." The heaviness in his sigh was understandable. It had been a busy morning already. He directed to Rune. "Please find the others and station them around the hall to watch, then meet me in the west foyer. We'll greet our visitors properly."

"As you wish." He bowed and with a guiding hand, took Jayce's parents to the front hall to rejoin their group, leaving Jayce with his current guards.

Once his parents were rejoined with their entourage, Rune headed for the foyer and found Jayce standing with Bankor and another. Jayce's expression was nearly unreadable. But the relieved glint in his eye was enough to tell Rune he was grateful for his presence.

"First Counsel," he greeted. "Are you ready?"

Rune called his staff to his palm, pushing his cloak behind his shoulders to reveal his sword. He doubted it would alarm anyone, but any illusion of supposed strength they held, the better, until they could physically install arms across their guards. "Yes, my lord."

"Bankor, open the doors please."

The guards moved together as one and split the doors wide to allow him to walk confidently through into the greeting hall with Rune a pace behind at his right shoulder.

The coming hours and days would reveal even more hidden secrets, Rune was sure. Even though shadows lingered in their future of untold and unknown challenges, the arrival of Jayce's parents surrounded by allies was a joyous occasion. One he was sure Jayce would embrace for the sign it was. With a side glance to his lover, his future king, pride swelled within his chest. Their adventure had started out with its fair share of road blocks and tempestuous moments, yet he was seeing the evolution of the king right before his eyes. The man he loved.

About the Author

Diana DeRicci is the sexy, flirty pen name of Diana Castilleja. A romance author at heart, DeRicci's writing takes you into a saucier spectrum of sensuality and sexual adventure, where a happily-ever-after is still the key to any story. Diana lives in Central Texas with her husband, one son and a feisty little Chihuahua named Rascal. You can catch the latest news on all of Diana DeRicci's writing and books on her website Listed above. Feel free to drop Diana an email. She'd love to hear from you.

www.dianadericci.com

Purple Sword Publications
www.purplesword.com

Made in United States
North Haven, CT
02 April 2022

17787082R00189